Brayden Rider
Tales of a Medieval Boy

C.L. Barnett

To Andrew,
Continue your love
of reading!
Chris Barnett

ISBN: 1478297778
ISBN-13: 9781478297772
CreateSpace, North Charleston, SC

For Sierra and Ava. Their imaginations are my inspiration.

Table of Contents

Chapter One

The Templar

Bernard burst through the main gate of the manor courtyard, pushing open the heavy wood doors, which creaked irritably at being disturbed. The clouds obscured the moonlight; the darkness made his passage treacherous. Bernard rushed on, carefully minding the roots and flagstones that covered the ground. No torches were lit this night, and only rarely had he walked the length of the courtyard without the benefit of light. The wind swirled leaves around his feet as he approached the manor home. The October night air was cool and crisp, a reminder the cold of winter was not far off. Bernard squeezed the parchment he held tightly in his right hand and continued on—the message had to get to the lord without delay.

He crossed the main courtyard quickly and came upon the manor house. As he looked up at the thick stone building he thought fondly of the many days he and the lord's family had walked the grounds, enjoying conversation with guests, the smell of the spring trees, and the stories and music of travelling minstrels. It had been a peaceful home to retire to after so many far-away adventures. He shook his head, struggling to bury the thought that those happy times were over.

Pale candlelight flickered in the home's fogged glass windows. He bounded up the hard stone steps and strained to lift the thick iron door ring once, then twice. It crashed down upon the massive wooden door. Moments later he heard a thud as the heavy wooden crossbar that bolted the door shut fell to the floor. He squinted as Alice Rider opened the door, filling his eyes with warm light.

"Welcome home, Bernard," she said softly. The lord's wife wore sadness and concern on her face, as if she had already received the bad news from afar.

"It is good to be back, Alice, very good indeed. Is he in?"

She nodded slowly. "Please, come in. And please," Alice's voice dropped to a whisper, "talk him out of what he plans to do."

They entered the main hall of the manor house. Torches illuminated walls busy with colorful tapestries and hung cloth. The site of so many dinners and visiting guests, tonight the room had a quiet, somber feel. A massive wooden table dominated the center of the hall. It was ringed with sturdy, elaborately carved wooden chairs and covered in thick round burning candles. At the table's head sat a large man, his head held low. As Alice shut and relocked the front door, the man raised his head, stood, and faced Bernard.

Bernard bowed slightly as Sir Ban Rider du Bayonne stepped forward. Though he had been gone only a few short months, Bernard found himself stunned at the lord's appearance. Sir Ban was donned in full chain armor hauberk over which draped a snow-white surcoat emblazoned with a bright red cross. A small patch in the shape of a shield was stitched across his heart, a flying golden griffin woven within. The griffin was the lord's symbol, Bernard knew, signifying valor, perseverance, and the guardian of treasure.

Sir Ban's sword dangled from a black leather belt, and in his right hand he clenched a pair of heavy padded gloves. Sir Ban had been growing his hair long, and it flowed down around his shoulders, as it had in his youth. His beard was full, if now a bit grayed. He stood almost a full head over Bernard, tall for a man of his age and no less imposing than the warrior of ten years past.

"Hello, my friend," Sir Ban placed the gloves on the table and waved him over. Bernard thought again how the lord looked every bit the knight he remembered at Acre so many years ago. "Welcome back to Bayonne."

"My lord, your armor…"

"Still fits?" Sir Ban smiled, looking down at himself. "Aye, but the belt is a tad tighter than I recall."

"I'm just surprised, my lord," Bernard said.

A small pair of hands appeared from behind the lord, grasping Sir Ban's surcoat. The great man turned and placed a hand on the small, scruffy head of a young boy.

"Come, Brayden, you know Bernard." The little boy, no older than six, stepped forward and smiled shyly.

"The monk!" he called, pointing. Bernard could see another boy, taller and older, peering around a corner at the far end of the room. Long locks of blonde hair fell to the older boy's eyes and shoulders.

"And you of course remember my nephew, Siegfried." Bernard nodded at the boys and the two children smiled back.

"Yes, it is the monk, or really, the priest." Sir Ban looked down proudly at his son. "Brayden never shies away from speaking his mind. They remember you."

"Or were warned of me," Bernard replied.

The lord shot Bernard a stern look.

"Alice, please take Brayden and my nephew into the bedchamber," Sir Ban said.

Alice stepped forward gracefully. She kissed the lord on the cheek, glanced hopefully at Bernard, and shooed the boys into an adjoining room.

"If you don't mind I'm going to sit once again. This armor pulls on the shoulders, and I am not a young man anymore." The lord returned to the large chair at the end of the table. He let out a sigh, disturbing the numerous candles that circled the table edge. "Your time in Paris and Rome was fruitful I trust, and your trip home was a safe one?"

"Safe, yes, my lord. Fruitful, no," Bernard replied, shaking his head.

"So the conspirators remain unaccounted for. A pity."

Bernard nodded. "Perhaps, my lord, with more time, we could…"

Sir Ban shook his head impatiently and Bernard silenced himself. "You have something for me then?" The lord gestured toward Bernard's hand.

Bernard looked at his hand. He had completely forgotten the parchment. He loosened his grip and looked down. The parchment was badly crinkled.

"Judging by your appearance, my lord, you already know the contents."

The lord nodded slowly. "That I do. King Philip has made it clear that no one shall be spared. I will not wait here to be arrested while our brothers suffer injustice and unfounded accusations."

Bernard handed Sir Ban the parchment. The lord glanced at it, and then held it over a candle. The paper burned quickly, flames licking upward as the document disappeared into smoke.

"Sir, there is still time to…"

"Escape into the night?" Sir Ban interrupted. "Someone should instruct the king never to tell a man you are coming to arrest him. I'll not run."

"But your lands, my lord. Would you not be better suited managing them elsewhere for a time, without the harassment of the French Crown?"

Sir Ban sighed, shaking his head. "These lands were without me, without us, for almost twenty years. What is a few weeks or months? And if you mean take to England or elsewhere, Alice has argued this point and my answer is the same. No. I will not flee while innocents plead and suffer these unfounded charges. I ride for Paris tonight. I will stand by the defense of the others the best I can."

Bernard knew many of the men of whom the lord spoke. Rumors of the fate of the brothers had been spreading for weeks. Of those still free, it was said some had disappeared, while others had fled. Bernard could tell Sir Ban had no intention of doing either.

"But your family…" Bernard stepped closer, his hands outstretched, unwilling to give up trying to change Sir Ban's mind. "If they are found they will be held and ransomed against you. It is the treasure of the Temple King Philip and his minions want, nothing more."

"If true, then I'll be spared, to our advantage." Sir Ban smiled. "Philip the Fair. Indeed. The King of France is consumed by ambition and impoverished by avarice. We both know he could not carry out the destruction of the Order alone. Facing him is the only way in which I'll uncover the traitors among us."

Bernard took a deep breath. Despite his best effort and the long months away from home, he had failed in his mission, and now his lord, this brave man and friend, was to suffer because of it.

Apparently seeing the pain on Bernard's face, Sir Ban stood again and walked over to him. Bernard realized that despite his strength he moved slowly against the tug of the heavy armor, not quickly and powerfully as he had in his youth.

Sir Ban put a large hand on Bernard's shoulder. "Old friend, we've known each other for many years and you have never failed me, and you do not fail me now. Your efforts, your wish to save us, will not go to waste."

He looked back at the room into which Alice had taken the boys. "No harm must come to Alice, Brayden, or my nephew. They must be delivered from this dark time, and stay in hiding until I return. I know of no one I trust more. See them across the channel to Strandshire safely. I have prepared a cart packed with provisions and money for the journey. You will find protection under the eminent Lord Marshal and his knights in Wales."

"And Siegfried?" Bernard asked. "He will be a man soon, a man without land or property of any kind."

"To the protection of my half-brother, Sir Allard. Siegfried is old enough now to be taken in as a page. He is fast and strong, and will soon be fit to be a squire. It is as my sister would have wished, bless her soul. I plead to you to protect them and raise them well until my return."

Bernard tried to smile, his expression betraying sadness and concern. "You'll be along soon enough, my lord, I'm sure," he said, his voice quaking.

"I pray you are right, old friend. I pray you are right."

There was a heavy thud at the door. Sir Ban nodded at Bernard, who walked over, removed the crossbar, and opened the door. Ralph the manorhand stood at the entryway, panting. Sir Ban had hand on sword but drew away quickly, smiling as Ralph collected himself. Ralph was old enough to be a squire and responsible for the manor's upkeep. Bernard knew him to be a clumsy lad, but a lad with a strong heart nonetheless. In many ways, Sir Ban treated Ralph as if he were an elder son.

"Bernard, welcome home." Ralph nodded to Bernard and then took a long, deep breath before continuing. "My lord. Word comes from afar. The Templars are arrested this Friday the thirteenth!"

Bernard and Sir Ban glanced at each other. Sir Ban raised a hand. "Thank you, young Ralph. Your timeliness rivals the dawn."

"I've locked the gates, the mill and the barn my lord. No one will be getting into the manor," Ralph added.

"Ralph," Sir Ban said, "I ride for Paris tonight, perhaps for a long time. Until I return I bequeath you these French lands and the manor home. I trust you to care for them as steward in my absence or until Brayden is ready to claim them. You'll find these rights written, signed by my hand, and stowed away in my chest."

Until Brayden is ready? No, not that long, my lord, please, Bernard thought. Not that long.

Ralph bowed deep, momentarily speechless. "I will do as you bid, my lord. Thank you."

"And, Ralph," Sir Ban continued, "you will accompany me to Paris. Not one of the king's accomplices will keep my horse or armor, if it comes to that. Go now and prepare the saddles."

Ralph stood staring into space, as if in shock at his lord's words.

"Well? You heard the lord. Hurry on," Bernard scolded gently, waving his arms to dismiss him.

"Yes, yes, my lord. Thank you." Ralph bowed once more and exited the manor. Bernard was sure he heard him fall down the stairs on his way out.

"Papa?" The two men turned to the very serious face of the boy. "Is it true? Do you go to Paris?"

They both looked down at Brayden, admiring him with pride.

"How will he be raised?" Bernard asked quietly.

"You mean, shall he be a knight? He will be strong, and Lord Marshal will have him for that purpose, I'm sure, but no. His fate shall be different. This family has seen enough of the sword, though I want his mind trained sharp as a blade. That will carry him further than any suit of armor."

Sir Ban kneeled in front of his son.

"Brayden, I do go to Paris this night. Bernard and your mother will take you and Siegfried to the isle, across the water. A fine adventure for my brave boy. Protect your mother and listen to Bernard, my son."

"Why can't you come, Papa?" Brayden asked, his eyes welling with tears.

Sir Ban wiped them away with his large hand. He grabbed the boy's arms and pulled him close. "Be brave, my boy. No evil will keep you from my heart. Through strength and goodness we shall be together again. Beau Séant, my son."

"I will be brave, Father. I will."

Alice stood at the bedchamber entrance, her eyes deeply sad. Outside, the sound of the wind gave way to the whinnying of horses.

Chapter Two

The Young Knight

Distant thunder rumbled as the great horse trotted uneasily along the muddy trail. With nightfall had come the storm, and Sullivan shook his mane, forcefully trying to ward off the merciless wind and chilling cold. He let out an angry snort, and Caelan reached down to comfort his mount. He straightened out quickly, forgetting for a moment the wound in his side. Pain throbbed through his body, and he covered the area with his hand, wincing with every sway of the horse.

The cold rain had actually been a distraction from the pain, keeping his mind off of it, but now with every step the horse took, it shot from his back and across his torso. A sudden shiver ran up his spine. No, not the fever, Caelan thought. He pulled his cloak tight around his neck, though not an inch of the cloth was dry.

His armor felt heavy, constricting. Despite the wound, he had left it on, but now, instead of protecting him it was sapping his strength. Caelan peered through the rain into the gloom, knowing another attack could come without warning, from any direction, and he'd be in no condition to run or fight. In the first attack he'd counted four men. He had felled one and, despite being struck from behind, had fought the others off.

Those three others were still out there somewhere, he thought, waiting to finish him.

Sullivan snorted again.

"Shh, my faithful friend. We're not done in yet."

He shivered again, and wondered where they were. Since the attack and their descent into the storm, they had lost their bearings. Now, he could see nothing. He shook his head, trying to keep his mind clear, anxiously looking for a road. He knew that with the onset of fever, the pain, and the cold eating into him from the wind and rain, he might not last the night if he didn't find shelter.

A howl came from somewhere beyond, deep in the forest. Man or beast, he did not know. Though hunted everywhere, wolves were still common in the wilder parts of the country. He urged Sullivan on, trying not to think of it. The horse protested at first, and then responded as the sense of danger sank in. Caelan struggled to stay upright as Sullivan sped forward.

The horse slowed as they began to climb a hill. Caelan's shivering was becoming uncontrollable. There was a bright flash, then a loud rumble. Sullivan whinnied fearfully as the thunder made the ground shudder. The horse's pace quickened again, as if he knew that if shelter were to be found he would have to find it, the rider, his friend, too distracted by pain and fever to be of any use.

A faint glow became visible through the murk.

"Light I see, Sullivan," Caelan muttered. "Ahead there. Perhaps Heaven itself is opening its gates to us."

But he could not focus. As he looked up, the trees above seemed to merge into an impenetrable canopy, a swirling whirlpool of darkness and motion. He felt dizzy and tried to steady himself.

There was another burst of lightning, and thunder filled the air. Sullivan snorted and reared back in panic.

Caelan jerked backwards as well, and then fell for what seemed an eternity before he collapsed in the mud. He heard himself cry out in agony, but it sounded distant, unfamiliar. He could see Sullivan standing several paces away, swaying nervously, as if waiting for him to get up. Caelan tried to stand, but lost his footing and collapsed again. The pain in his side now enveloped his body. His mind focused on the trivial—his saddle packs lying on the ground, their contents spilled everywhere.

Near-constant lightning painted his surroundings in dark greens and gray. The thunder seemed to shake the forest to its floor. He squinted as rain pelted him from every direction. He focused on the shapes in the dark. Were those faces he saw out there against the trees? The villains back to finish me off, he thought absently. Barely able to lift his head, he looked around. Sullivan had trotted into the woods, disappearing from sight. The light, so distant, seemed nearer now, and getting closer.

* * *

The abbey had not looked cleaner, Bernard thought. In the four years since he'd escaped France, he had rebuilt much of the old church, inside and out, finally giving the residents of the surrounding villages a respectable place of worship.

Bernard inspected his surroundings with satisfaction. Pride might be the devil's work, but if ever it was warranted, it was now. The pigeons had been evicted and the pigs had relearned their proper place, agreeably wallowing outside and now getting a well deserved bath in the storm. The dogs still milled about inside the abbey, as did the cats, but necessary evils came with benefits too: he hadn't seen a rat in weeks, and the animals themselves were fine company. His work done, the candles lit and the kettle warm, the friar of Honeydown prepared for a restful evening in the midst of the storm.

Crack! Bernard jumped. The sound came from just outside the door. He rubbed his eyes in tired frustration. The pigs were up to no good once more, no doubt. While it could be a wandering fool looking for shelter in the storm, the hardy pigs would more likely scare off a stranger than be frightened of one. He rubbed his sleeve against the window, clearing the frame of fog but still unable to see anything in the dark.

"Deserving of a look, I suppose," Bernard muttered to himself as he grabbed his staff, and a lantern. He shoved open the front door. It was very dark. Soaking rain was falling hard on the abbey, the fence, and the pigs. The pigs! Not a single one remained in the pen. They had scattered into the woods, their snorts faint against the sound of the pounding rain and the howling wind. He examined the fence, and noticed that a nearby section lay broken. Even in the storm the sows had made the most of their latest opportunity to escape.

"Oh come now. What a night for a break," he groaned.

Get the pigs first, Bernard thought, fix the fence next. He covered his head with his hood and stepped into the muck. The rain and wind almost knocked him over as he navigated the muddy ground, watching his footing.

"Oh, forget the pigs," he grumbled, deciding instead to return to the safety of the abbey. When he next looked up he gasped. There, standing just at the tree line not ten feet away, was one of the largest horses he had ever seen. Its white coat cast an eerie glow against the dark wood, but there it was, snorting loudly, nodding its head, and digging into the dirt with its hooves.

Bernard stumbled over the break in the fence to get closer. The horse trotted off as he closed in, and then stopped, looking back at him and swaying his head. Bernard moved again towards the horse, which once again trotted deeper into the woods and then stopped, as if waiting for him. This continued several times, until Bernard himself stopped, suddenly concerned about how far they'd gone and how much farther they might go.

"Now where do you take me, friend? I fear if we go much deeper into the woods, neither of us will be heard from again!" He wiped the rain from his face.

The horse circled and snorted loudly. Bernard stepped closer and heard a muffled groan. Near his feet lay a man sprawled facedown in the mud.

Without hesitation Bernard dropped his staff and lantern. Grasping the man under his arms, he dragged him headfirst through the mud toward the light of the abbey. The man was not big, but he was heavy, and Bernard strained with every step. The horse whinnied approvingly, trotted past, stopped beside him and lowered itself to the ground. Bernard paused in amazement, and then struggling, began to lift the stranger onto the horse. After much exertion, he was finally able to hoist him on top of the powerful steed. Bernard grabbed his staff and the lantern, took the horse's bridle, and led them through the woods toward the light of the abbey windows. After several slow, difficult minutes Bernard had managed to drag the man inside the abbey, pull him across the main hall of the church, and lay him on a bed of straw in a small antechamber.

Bernard quickly lit more candles, fetched warm broth from the kettle, and held a spoon to the man's lips. The stranger slurped gently. Returning the spoon to the pot, Bernard hurried out of the room and moments later returned with several heavy wool blankets and a damp rag he used to wipe the man's face clean. The man's eyes were closed tight, and he was hot to the touch. Bernard looked him over. The stranger was young and handsome, certainly not much past his twentieth year. Bernard could see bright blood against his silver tunic.

"Firstly, let's get these ragged threads off of you," Bernard said, shaking his head in disgust. "Those bandits again, I suppose. They'll attack any defenseless soul they find."

Bernard tugged the soaking wet cloak and tunic away. Every inch of them was covered in thistles and filth. He felt metal. Bernard paused and stared curiously. The man wore a light chainmail coat under this linen garment. He hadn't noticed it before now, hidden as it was under the wet cloak and the beating rain. The linen shirt was red with blood, and Bernard worked swiftly to remove the man's remaining wet clothes and the armor to get to the wound. Around the man's waist was a thick black belt to which was attached a broadsword wrapped in his cloak. Its handle was adorned with crosses and a dragon. Bernard sat back, rubbing his chin.

"Perhaps not so defenseless after all," he said to himself.

As if hearing Bernard's voice, the stranger's head rose suddenly. His eyes were wide open, and he looked in every direction, as if trying to focus. Bernard leaned back quickly in surprise, keeping an eye on the sword still strapped to the man's waist.

"Rider. Bring me the Rider boy!" the stranger moaned, his head turning from side to side. His eyes blinked momentarily, then fluttered closed. He lay back, unmoving.

"Shh, rest now, friend," Bernard said calmly after a few moments. "You're safe here in the abbey."

As he was preparing dressing for the man's wound, the abbey door flew open and two of the pigs entered, eagerly seeking shelter from the storm in the warmth of the building. The weather had been too much even for them, Bernard thought. He got up and shooed the animals inside, anxious to shut the door. Holding the door handle, he peered into the stormy darkness once more. Outside, not twenty feet away, was the enormous white horse standing absolutely still. It seemed to be staring hopefully back at him. Bernard nodded in the horse's direction.

"I'll do my best by your friend," Bernard said. He shut the door and turned to the pigs. "Well, make yourselves at home for one last night, my putrid friends. Old Bernard has a visitor, and we'll need all your prayers to keep him with us through the night."

Chapter Three

Brayden

The morning sun beamed in through the yellow horn windows, bathing the interior of the barn in a golden glow. Built just three years before, the sturdy structure was shared by the villagers, who kept their tools, oxen, and cows inside, safe from predators and the wandering thief. Bales of hay lined the walls, making the air stale but sweet to the nose.

Brayden opened his eyes and stretched, yawning widely. The loft overlooked the stalls, and while cramped, provided the best place to count the sleeping oxen, or cows, or sheep. He peered below, casually inspecting the animals. They were where he had left them earlier in the morning, waiting patiently to be released. He yawned again and rolled over, looking up at the timbers that supported the thatched roof. It must be getting time to move them out, he thought. He started to get up and then stopped. Just above where he lay, a colorful spider hung from invisible thread. He forgot all about the animals once more, and watched the spider as it dangled, diligently constructing its web.

"Brayden!" John Fields called.

Brayden jerked upright as the deep voice of the village reeve filled the barn. The barn animals responded in kind, stirring in their stalls, anxious for attention. Brayden also stood quickly, too quickly. He bumped his head on a low rafter and fell back on the soft bed of hay. John Fields stood below, hands on hips, looking up at him, his face filled with disgust.

"Boy! Sleeping late again I see. Serves you right, banging your head. Precious daylight is being wasted. Get down here now or I'll have you milking them all night until tomorrow!"

Brayden wasted no more time, grabbed a nearby rope, and swung down to the ground. He immediately rubbed his head, the bump already prominent and sore.

"Sir," Brayden said, brushing the hay off his clothes, "I was here early morning doing count. Honest I was. I'm sorry. I'll have them up early until the Sabbath."

John Fields grunted, his hard gaze softening slightly. As the reeve, he was the man responsible for management of the village's chores and accounts. Brayden understood the job to have some stature in many villages, but under the bailiff in Honeydown it was considered a thankless position that no one else wanted. Despite this, the man worked with pride, and had bestowed nothing but friendship upon Brayden's family since their arrival in the village. His mother and Bernard thought highly of the reeve, and because of this, Brayden hated to disappoint him.

"I'm sure you will, Brayden. But the cows can't be late like this. They need to be on the pasture. Winter will be here soon enough, and others are taking notice." He paused, as if afraid of being overheard. "Like the bailiff. He will have your hide, and mine too. It's bad enough as it is."

"What, sir? What is?" Brayden bristled at the mention of the bailiff, certainly the village's least favorite resident.

"Brayden, your mother is a fine woman and while you're a tad lazy for my tastes, I've no doubt of your good intentions. But there are men here in Honeydown who only see a widowed woman whose lands will fall to the next man she marries. You'd just get in the way of that. Do you understand?"

"My mother is no widow. My father is alive," Brayden said sternly.

"Not afraid to speak up either are you? Good. Listen, I know nothing of your father, and I know you believe he's alive, but you're in small company around here." As he spoke, John Fields helped Brayden get the last of the hay out of his hair and off his clothes. "You can't give them any excuses. Do you understand? These are difficult times, and many predict they will get harder. Land is all one has, and everyone wants it, no matter the size, no matter the cost." John Fields looked him over. "Not in great shape, but not bad either. How is the head? Nothing vinegar and parchment can't mend, I suppose."

Brayden shrugged. The pain was gone, replaced by the memory of his father and the feeling of loneliness those thoughts evoked.

"Now forget all of that," the man urged, as if seeing the boy's mind wander. "A good day's work is what you need. Get those beasts moving!" He turned and hollered at a pig that had poked its head in through the main door of the barn. "Outside!" he yelled, scurrying after it and swatting away with his tally stick.

"Yes, sir!" Brayden called.

"And don't forget your cattle stick and horn like last time!"

"Yes, sir!"

"And stop calling me sir!" John Fields shouted.

"Yes, I will, sir," Brayden responded, realizing he was uncertain what else to call him.

Brayden picked up his cattle stick and horn and took to work opening the stalls, swatting and shouting at the animals. The cows grunted their disapproval, but quickly made for the main door, anxious to finally get outside. Brayden followed John Fields into the yard and squinted in the sunlight. Honeydown was already alive with activity.

Vast green and brown fields stretched out before him as far as he could see. The dampness of last night's rain still hung in the air, giving the breeze a fresh, clean scent. Horses, sheep, and donkeys dotted the landscape, tended by villagers who looked small and insignificant in the distance. Muddy, rutted paths crisscrossed the fields where villagers led oxen dragging plows or carts, some empty, others brimming with hay or wheat. Thick, dark, forest ringed the flowing pastures in every direction, and fluffy white clouds hung low against the deep blue sky.

Small brown cottages lined the muddy roads that stretched away from the barn. From where Brayden stood, the thatched-roof homes seemed all the same size. Birds of every kind flew in and out of the roofs, tending to nests, taking straw, or feasting on insects.

Though occupied, many of the homes were in disrepair. The recent rains had flooded at least two of them, and nearby, Brayden could see a man busy at work patching holes in one of the cottages, while another man pushed muddy water out the door with a broom. As he walked up the road away from the barn, all sizes and colors of dogs and cats milled about, darting in and out of the homes and wandering up and down the road, always on the lookout for the rats and mice that infested the area.

Brayden looked about and sighed. While the memories of the manor in France were still there, this village was home, and had been for the past four years. At least they were always busy. Like all the residents in Honeydown, and those of all the other villages in Strandshire manor, and no different than all the people of all the manors that dotted so much of Wales and the rest of Britain, theirs was a life of constant work and repetition. There was little or no surplus food from year to year, so what the villagers grew, they ate. John Fields knew this and spent his entire day ensuring that everyone was kept busy. Brayden felt guilty for having fallen asleep. As he watched the activity in the streets of the village and the fields beyond, he promised himself he'd do better. It was not an exciting place, but he had grown comfortable here with his mother, and with Bernard in the abbey nearby.

John was walking in the distance. He turned and waved at Brayden. While most of the animals were well on their way to pasture, one of the cows had stopped nearby. Brayden was raising his stick to give it a swat when a thin, pale hand grabbed his wrist and turned him around with a jerk. Corbat Handhafte, the bailiff of Honeydown, sneered down at him.

"W-whats this, b-boy, another mid-morning s-s-snooze? You b-best drop that s-s-switch or I'll be b-beating you with it," Corbat said, stuttering as he tightened his grip on Brayden's wrist.

Brayden winced, and the stick fell to the ground. As the bailiff glared down at him, Brayden noticed that Corbat's few remaining teeth stuck out at hideous angles and were the same sickening yellow as his eyes. The man's hair was thin and filthy, his flesh ghastly white, though sickly blotches of pink tattooed his cheeks and forehead.

"I, I'm sorry Sir Handhafte. I was out early this morning to check on the bessies and must have fallen asleep. I won't do it again."

Corbat's grip tightened again, making Brayden's hand turn purple.

"You're a u-useless l-little one. B-but never mind. I'll make you my whelp y-yet." He pulled Brayden close, inspecting him. The man's foul breath made Brayden turn his head away. The bailiff snorted, then suddenly released Brayden's wrist and threw him to the ground, where he landed in the mud with a splat. Out of the corner of his eye Brayden could see the reeve approaching.

"S-s-say hello to your mother for me, b-b-boy. My offer s-s-still s-s-stands and will until she s-s-says yes, and d-don't get in my way. I'll h-have your h-hide hung on my wall and f-feed your b-bones to the d-dogs. I can always-s-s find another horn boy." The offer, Brayden knew, was his mother's hand in marriage, an outcome too hideous to consider. It was too much for him to take.

"You'll never take my mother, you filthy wild boar!" Brayden blurted reflexively.Corbat's eyes turned dark, and his face flushed red. He stepped closer, his hand cocked back. To Brayden, he seemed huge, terrifying.

The strike never came.

"Corbat!"

The reeve stood between them. Corbat stared angrily at the man but made no move to strike. John Fields was the same size as Corbat, but a good five years younger. He had held the office of village reeve since before Corbat's arrival, despite the bailiff's attempts to remove him at every election. Brayden's family was not the only one in Honeydown who respected the reeve, and his integrity and fairness were traits the bailiff did not possess. Brayden watched the men as they stared at one another. He compared the reeve's and his own clothes to those of the bailiff. Despite his hideous features, the bailiff dressed well; Corbat's well-made clothing was a stark contrast to the ragged garments worn by the villagers. Crime across the countryside had exploded, but for whatever reason, the bailiff had not suffered as the others had.

"Mind your b-business, Fields," Corbat hissed, finally stepping away from Brayden. "You are r-reeve only at my p-pleasure. I'll hold you r-responsible t-too when we go to market with n-nothing, or s-s-suffer the w-winter hungry."

"I'm afraid the local banditry will determine what gets to market, not the boy's laziness and certainly not any effort of yours."

Corbat looked as though he was going to lunge at the reeve. The bailiff's yellow eyes were frightful, and his grotesque nostrils twitched repulsively. John Fields stood firm, however, holding his white tally stick back as if ready to swing.

Corbat finally backed down, seeming to think better of it. "Get those b-beasts t-to pasture b-before I have you both s-s-strung up," he spat. He gave them each one last long stare, and then shuffled up the street, berating any villager unlucky enough to pass him.

John Fields reached down and helped Brayden up. He was again covered in hay and mud. His head still stung, and his wrist was purple from where the bailiff had squeezed it.

"You're a right filthy mess again," John Fields smiled, as he brushed off bits of debris. "He's a cruel man, and for now we're cursed with him. We'll all starve here before he musters the courage or the money to stop the banditry from stealing our crops and raiding Honeydown and the other villages of the manor. I fear our strong harvest will be for nothing without protection. Oh, if only Lord Marshal and Sir Allard were here!"

Brayden recognized the names. Lord Henry Marshal and his champion had been gone since soon after Brayden, his mother, and Bernard had arrived in Honeydown. Rumor had it they had died fighting the Scots, or perhaps been kidnapped. Some said they were never coming back at all. Whatever the circumstances, life had gotten progressively worse for the people of the surrounding villages since their disappearance.

"Now, to the well." John Fields pointed to the center of the village. "Get cleaned up. And my guess is you've not eaten."

Brayden looked at the ground, anxious to avoid the reeve's gaze.

"Up early, with no breakfast I might add, just to do count and fall asleep until late up in the loft. I'm going to have to have a word with Alice about this."

Brayden felt the blood drain from his face. What would his mother say?

John Fields winked at him. "But not today. I'll take the cows to pasture," he volunteered. "Old Robert is wandering around out there somewhere. I'll enlist his help, for what it's worth. Run and check on your mother. Get some food in you. Then I expect you back here later in the day to gather the sheep and bessies. They wander in the woods something fierce this time of year. You can also get the barn organized. We'll be loading it with grain, God willing, soon enough." He paused. "Do you hear!?" he said loudly, as if to ensure he had the boy's attention.

"Yes, sir!" Brayden called, already splashing through mud puddles on his way to the well.

Chapter Four

Honeydown

The shortest route home from the well led Brayden straight through the center of the village. His clothes were still filthy, but after visiting the well, at least his face and hands were clean.

"Mother's not going to be happy about my clothes," he muttered to himself, still thinking about the bailiff and what the man had said.

He walked on, trying to clear his thoughts of the awful man, and finally found himself smiling at the thought of Old Robert trying to catch sheep. He was the village's eldest member, and in his younger days had served variously as beadle, hayward, and even reeve. He was now almost completely blind and not much of a pinder, but no one ever stopped working, and when he wasn't wandering the fields keeping the animals in check, he enjoyed a more satisfying role: that of ale taster. As Brayden walked, his stomach growled loudly, reminding him of how late in the morning it was. He hurried along.

He could see the Hill manor house in the distance. The house sat on a high perch on the outskirts of the village, and even from where he stood it looked large and impressive. It was a squat, square two-story stone tower jutting up from two smaller wings. The only house for miles around with a stone roof, it lay secure behind a rugged stonewall, though even from here he could tell the wall had collapsed in some places. The manor house had belonged to James Hill, long the bailiff of Honeydown. Hill had the reputation of having been a fair man, from what Brayden had heard the older villagers say. When Hill disappeared, Corbat assumed the privileges of bailiff without the absent Lord Marshal's approval.

The bailiff. Brayden shuddered at the thought of the man's threat to marry his mother. He and his mother had been victims of rumor since arriving in Honeydown, particularly about Brayden's father and the timing of their arrival soon after the arrest of the Templars. He did not understand it all, and for their own good his mother insisted nothing be spoken of his father or their true origin around the other villagers. Still, even the rumor that she owned or stood to inherit substantial property was a possibility many people, and particularly the bailiff, found enticing.

The intensity of activity in the village had picked up with the advent of midday. Numerous skilled craftsmen had come to town, and cottars, too, had arrived to find whatever work they could. The increase in lawlessness had hurt travel and trade, so it was pleasant to see visitors again. Not only did the travelling men bring services the villagers desperately needed, they brought with them news from nearby villages and beyond.

Outside one cottage an unfamiliar tanner was lecturing on his trade over a piece of prepared leather. He stood over a small pile of brown and beige scraps left from shoes he had already made and sold. Brayden looked down at his bare feet and wished he could take the scraps home to try his skill at building new shoes. The rain, the hard work in the fields for the harvest, and the coming onset of cold meant business was brisk. Everyone wanted new shoes, Brayden overheard the man bragging.

A loud clang erupted nearby, followed by several cats scurrying away. Mills Tinker, the travelling fixer and maker of brass and metal pots, had tripped over the threshold of a nearby cottage, and all manner of tools, pots and pans were rolling down the muddy road. As the man struggled to get up, Cecilia Gibson and two of her sisters rushed over to help the clumsy man.

"Morning, Brayden!" Cecilia called, catching Brayden out of the corner of her eye. She waved before turning her attention to Tinker. She was a pretty girl, with dark red hair and a fair complexion.

"Ah now up with ya," she demanded. "Can ya fill pots as well as ya fix them? Food has been a bit scarce, but what else is new?"

He walked on as people rushed past him carrying a variety of goods. The arrival of the craftsmen seemed to lighten everyone's spirits. People were gathering around the new arrivals, asking questions. The craftsmen were having trouble replying to one question before another one was asked.

"Have the bandits taken the castle?" someone asked.

"No," one of the travelling men answered.

"I heard the King is dead," said another.

"Don't be daft," a villager retorted.

"And what of Lord Marshal? Is it true he was cast into irons and shipped for France?"

Brayden listened, returning the smiles of passersby. Another of Cecilia's many sisters was carrying several large jugs of ale on her way to the pasture, and she giggled at his muddy appearance as she passed. No doubt, he thought, destined for Old Robert and the other men working the fields. Brayden did not remember her name, but she would do this all day, every day, providing relief to the laboring villagers working in the pasture with a smile and a wink. Savaric Straw, the local thresher, walked past Brayden next, pulling a large cot of hay.

"Hello Boden!" he called. He never got Brayden's name right in at least a dozen tries. Brayden waved as Straw stopped at the nearest cottage.

"Ah yes, you're definitely in need of a new floor!" Savaric shouted jovially, as he began to spread hay over the floor of the house, to the satisfying laughter of the occupants.

Many of the cottages were in utter disrepair. The craftsmen had stayed away from Honeydown for weeks. For some the rain made travel treacherous. For others, the very real fear of bandit raiding parties had scared them off. Attacks on villages and travelers had only grown in occurrence and ferocity since Lord Marshal's disappearance.

The discontent of the villagers had finally forced the bailiff to take action, and he had agreed to reimburse them any losses if they were robbed, though if anyone had actually been reimbursed, Brayden did not know. And while the reeve would not admit it, Brayden and others suspected that a less-than-friendly encounter with John Fields had helped motivate Corbat into bidding the craftsmen to pay a visit.

Brayden recognized the smoky smell of Dunstan Smith's smithy. Covered in soot from his beard to his shoes, the blacksmith was busy placing pokers in the oven. Several others rested in a nearby bucket of water. Dunstan's talents were always in demand, he liked to brag, and the blacksmith travelled frequently from village to village, selling his wares and services. Plows, blades, hammers, chisels and numerous unrecognizable tools littered the little shop and covered the walls. Black dust was everywhere. Today, Brayden was happy to see him back safely, and he waved to his friend as he approached.

"Morning, boy!" Dunstan shouted, motioning him over.

As Brayden came up to the short stocky man, Dunstan leaned over and put a cupped hand to Brayden's ear.

"I'm back in town for a bit, but not too long. Come by later," he said quietly. "I'll have your blade ready for you."

"Thanks, sir," Brayden said, again promising Dunstan to secrecy. While his mother would not approve of him wielding a knife, rumors of the recent bandit raids convinced him they needed protection, no matter how small. Brayden had expressed his fears one afternoon to Cecilia, who had mentioned them in passing to the blacksmith. Brayden knew Cecilia and the blacksmith were close, but whether she was aware that Dunstan had actually made the blade, he did not know. Brayden just hoped his mother wouldn't find out.

He walked on, moving quickly as his stomach complained again. Animals of every kind milled about the village streets, disregarding each other and the people going about their daily tasks. Cats, dogs, pigs, and geese poked the ground for scraps, casually entering and exiting the cottages with no fear of reprisal. The geese were still slim, but would be rounded up and kept in fenced gardens for fattening in the coming days.

Suddenly, a rabbit bounded out from between two of the cottages. Villagers and animals alike paused momentarily, all staring at it with great interest.

"I saw it first!" someone shouted.

"A worthy breakfast on four legs!" another called.

"Hop into me pot!" cried another of Cecilia's sisters, brushing past Tinker, brass pot in hand, almost knocking him over once more.

A wild cacophony of barks, snorts, and shouts erupted as animals and humans gave pursuit, chasing the scruffy rabbit down a side road and out of sight. Brayden couldn't help but laugh at the sight, though he understood the seriousness of the situation. Food had indeed been scarce, he thought, and soon would be even more so. He hurried his pace home.

* * *

Like the other houses of Honeydown, the Riders' was a simple cottage of gray wattle and daub, with a thatched roof and an attached herb garden. While their means provided for a larger home than most, with what could have been spare rooms and elaborate shelters for the chickens and geese, Bernard and his mother had decided discretion was warranted, and elected to live as the common folk did. Brayden didn't mind. His time in their manor home across the channel with his father seemed almost like a dream. This was the home he knew now.

He opened the wood door of the cottage and went in, leaving his shoes by the entrance. Immediately the welcome smell of his mother's pottage filled his nose. His stomach growled loudly.

"You're back late," his mother called from the center of their home. Alice was standing by the hearth, over which hung a large black pot filled with steaming stew. A variety of vegetables poked out of the top of the pot, and she was breaking apart herbs and adding them to the mix. Brayden coughed. The hearth in the center of the main room meant chimney smoke was ever present, though he got used to it soon enough.

"What happened to your clothes?"

He looked down innocently. She noticed everything, he thought.

"I slipped leaving the barn. With the rains, the mud is fierce."

She looked at him curiously, and he could tell she knew better. "Rumor around Honeydown is you had a run-in with the bailiff. What happened?"

"I fell asleep in the loft, doing count."

"I'm sure. And?" she asked.

"The cows left the barn late."

"Brayden, really. And?" she pressed on.

"The bailiff caught me, and John Fields came to my aid."

"John Fields is a fine man."

Brayden nodded. His mouth watered as she began ladling the pottage into a deep bowl for him.

"Sit down," she directed. "I want you to mind your sleep next time. We all have to work, tired or not."

He reached for the bowl.

"Off." she swatted his hand down. "First, tell me what else happened, the whole of it."

Brayden sat on a low bench next to a small table and set down his horn and stick. Their furniture was sparse, but they had more than many, his mother frequently reminded him.

"The bailiff spoke of marrying you. He says he'll have my hide if I get in the way."

"Oh really? And?"

"Then I called him a filthy wild boar."

She smiled and shook her head. "Which is not nice to say, no matter how true it may be," she said. "And your clothes? Truly now."

Brayden shrugged. "I fell."

"Or were pushed?" she asked.

He nodded silently.

She looked at him sternly as she handed him the bowl. He dug into the pottage with both hands. The stew was a wild mix of herbs, meat, barley, onions, turnips, and cabbage. It was thick and gooey, but filling.

"Now, now. We're not wild boars ourselves," she said, handing him a thick wooden spoon from a hook on the wall, one of the few spoons in the village.

Brayden looked up, taking the spoon. Everything, it seemed, was attached to that wall, from iron cooking instruments to heavy wool blankets and various tools.

"You're welcome. And who, pray tell, is with the animals in the fields now?"

"Old Robert," Brayden responded, stirring his stew with the spoon.

"Old Robert! Oh, Brayden. The poor man can't see beyond his nose!"

"But he says since the blurred vision took he can hear much better now, and especially at night."

Shaking her head, she went to the hearth and took a bowl for herself. He looked up at her. Long dark hair draped her shoulders and fell down over her brown smock. She was tall in comparison to many of the villagers, and her face was pretty, but strong. Her eyes were bright, but often heavy and sad. She pulled another bench close and joined him at the table, bringing out their other spoon from beneath her smock. Her face remained serious.

"Brayden, listen. I know it is never easy, but mind the bailiff and his directions. He is a reality of the village, and will be for the foreseeable future. Do not draw attention to yourself by being late. Next time, come to me and I will engage him. Do you understand?"

"If I was older, like Siegfried, I bet he'd leave us alone."

"True, Siegfried is older, but no braver than you. Now do as I ask."

"Yes, mother," he answered.

As he ate he thought about Siegfried, who soon after arriving in the village had been sent to the castle to live with the older boys. They had not heard from him in months, and there had been resentment at his leaving amongst the other villagers, who hated losing another able body. He was likely a squire by now, or soon to be, Brayden thought.

"I bet if we told Corbat more about father he'd mind himself!"

Alice smiled a sad smile. "Yes, I'm sure. But remember, we are not to talk about those things."

"But you said we must be proud of those things!" he insisted.

"Being proud does not mean you brag or talk when you should listen," she answered. "Be very proud of your father, and pray for his safe return every night. But that business is ours and ours alone."

"And Bernard's," he added.

"Yes, and Bernard's."

They ate quietly for a few moments, the sound of the village and the activity outside constant. Brayden recalled little of their trip to

Honeydown from France, only that it had been long, hard, and at times, frightening. He had remained in the stern of the ship and in the rear of various carts with Siegfried for much of the journey. Throughout it all Bernard had been their constant protector and companion, guiding them safely to the island and overland to Strandshire. Brayden could not believe that in all the time they had been here they had heard nothing from the continent about the Templars or his father.

"Have we ever heard from father?" he asked, regretting the question as soon as he'd said it.

The answer was on his mother's face. She didn't need to reply, and was silent for a moment before shaking her head. She reached over and took his hand, squeezing tight. He knew she thought of his father every day.

"Speaking of Bernard," she said, changing the subject, "why don't you take some of the stew down to him? I'm sure he's forgotten all about eating today and would love to see you. He's been so busy working on the abbey. I hear it is finished. Take a bowl to him when you're done."

"Yes, mother!" Brayden replied excitedly. His mother knew he'd take any opportunity to visit Bernard and pester the old monk for a story or two about knights and adventure.

He gulped down the pottage, prepared a bowl for Bernard, and bolted for the door.

"And Brayden," his mother called behind him.

He turned. She handed him his horn. Her face was serious. "Stay on the marked paths and don't wander. Mind John Fields and be back as he said well before nightfall to bring the pasture animals in."

"Are you as worried as the others are about the bandits?" he asked, pausing at the door.

She smiled at him and patted his head. "No, not while I have you to protect me. What I don't want is a visit from John Fields saying you never returned. Now go before Bernard's meal goes cold!"

Her remark about having him to protect her filled him with pride. "And I'll soon have a blade from Dunstan Smith!" he blurted, and then cringed instantly, cursing himself for letting the secret slip.

"No blades, Brayden," she said sternly. "I mean it. We're not warriors. Not anymore."

"But it is a small one," he stammered.

Her stare silenced him. He knew there was no point in continuing. She came toward him, but instead of scolding him, she pulled him close, hugged him tightly, and kissed his head.

"Now go along, say hello to Bernard for me, and get back to the fields. Remember, Old Robert is nearly blind, and with all the ale he drinks he has a tendency to nod off, as does someone else I know."

"Yes, mum," he called, heading back out the door.

"And Brayden," his mother said.

Halfway toward the road, he turned once more.

She held up a pair of worn leather shoes in one hand. "Your shoes."

"Yes, mum!" he said, coming back to grab the shoes. Then he ran down the road.

Chapter Five

The Abbey

Brayden ran quickly through the center of town, once again past the cottages and across the fields, towards the woods of Honeydown. The muddy road gave way to a muddier path, and Brayden had to balance the hot bowl, carefully avoiding rocks, ruts, and puddles as he ran. Directly ahead of him was a seemingly impenetrable green wall of trees and foliage.

The path led up to a well-hidden hole carved into the forest's perimeter. He dove in quickly, and the bright midday sunlight disappeared, filtered by the vast canopy of oak, birch, and rowan trees that towered above. Sunrays shot down everywhere, their streaks of light visible in the misty air, their beams illuminating the dim ground like sunlit pools. The fingers of God, Bernard had once told him.

The noise of the village was long gone, replaced by quiet, natural solitude. The wind rustled the branches and their leaves, birds chirped happily above, and somewhere in the distance he could hear the comforting sound of a trickling brook. The woods were alive. It seemed every few paces there was motion. Though he could not always see them, Brayden knew the forest hid red deer, polecats, red squirrels, and hares of every color. Animal tracks covered the ground. The deer especially would sneak into the fields to eat when they could, only to dart back into the protection of the forest when spotted. The bailiff had ordered nightly patrols, in which he himself did not participate, to shoo the deer away.

Brayden followed the remnants of the path, carefully holding the pot as he went. There was an old road that led to the abbey, but Brayden knew this path was the best shortcut, and he enjoyed being alone deep in the forest.

He did not want to arrive with cold stew, either, but the rough terrain slowed his progress. He almost tripped over a thick root when he was surprised by several fallow deer that shot out from behind a thicket and ran down a hill and out of sight. Brayden paused, and wondered if it was him they feared or something else. It reminded him again that danger lurked here, especially at night. While predatory animals were rarely seen, Brayden knew the real monsters were not animals, but people; the bandits and robbers who had been attacking the caravans and villages hid in these same woods. After one recent attack on a caravan, his mother and the reeve had urged Bernard to seek safety in the village and abandon his work in the abbey. The old monk would hear none of it, though with the exception of Sunday's Mass, few now came to visit him. Bernard argued that this was due to the work needed for the harvest and that the abbey remained the safest place for miles around. Brayden wondered how true that was.

He slowed, making sure to stay on the path, and came upon the brook. He followed the clear shallow water until he found the best place to cross. The channel of water was narrow here, with smooth brown stones poking through the surface. He knew that to make it across he had to balance just right. He took one step, then another.

"Ah!" he yelled reflexively, as he slipped on the first stone, then another. Both of his feet were instantly submerged in the cold water. He adjusted himself to avoid falling over, and then ran to the far side of the brook, splashing all the way.

His shoes were soaked, though he had at least managed to save the contents of the bowl. As he trudged up the bank he suddenly noticed that his horn was missing. He looked anxiously around the stream, but could see nothing except rocks and rushing water. He must have dropped it some yards back.

"Mother will not be pleased," he mumbled aloud. "My horn missing and I've near ruined another pair of shoes!" He put a hand to his face in disgust and walked on, water squishing between his toes. A thin wall of bright green lay ahead. He was coming to the edge of the woods. Without hesitation, he bounded through the break in the forest and entered a lush green meadow.

Cuckoo flower, rosemary, and other flowers of every color covered the ground, and their sweet perfume filled the air. He ran into the sunlight with delight, the tall grass whipping his legs and hands and drying his feet. He could see it clearly now. The abbey of Honeydown stood alone at the far side of the meadow.

The abbey itself towered over the smaller trees at the meadow's edge. The sturdy building was made of dark gray stone and roughly shaped like a cross. At the end of the longest section, or nave, as he had been told to call it, was a tall V-shaped entrance with a high oak door. At each end of the other sections of the building were tall spires growing up from the walls. Glass windows, many of them stained, lined the sides. The roof was now intact, and in the bright sunlight, Brayden could see a thin trail of smoke emerging from the abbey's lone chimney.

"Bernard!" he shouted, climbing the steps to the door. The squeals of the pigs and clucks of the hens answered him first as they registered their collective interest in the bowl of stew. Stone and wood enclosures surrounded the property, keeping the animals secure. Inside the pens, the animals were free to wander about. One portion of the fence looked newer than the rest, as if recently repaired. Brayden minded the ground, and then something out of place caught his eye. Large hoof prints were carved into the dirt. He put his foot inside one, and was stunned by the size. "That must have been an enormous horse," he said out loud. He knew Bernard did not own a horse of his own, let alone one that big.

"Ah, my favorite visitor has arrived," said a soft, friendly voice. Brayden turned. Bernard stood before him in his ragged brown cloak holding a gnarled wooden staff. He reached out, pulled Brayden close, and hugged him tight. Bald of hair and square of jaw, and by many years the eldest member of the village, Bernard was still strong and sturdy, Brayden thought. His friend possessed a robustness many of the other men of the village envied, if John Fields was to be believed.

"Mmm. And what have we here? Alice's pottage? Your mother is too thoughtful. I could smell it from afar, and I haven't even tasted it yet."

"I'm afraid it's taken cold," Brayden said. "I couldn't get here in time."

"Nonsense. Nothing a little time over the hearth can't mend." Bernard led Brayden toward the door.

"Were you fixing your fence? Was it the pigs that escaped again?"

"Ah yes. The pigs again, indeed."

"Bernard, there are hoof prints outside the pens. Really big ones all over."

"Really? I'll have to look later. Come, let's heat this up."

Brayden glanced once more at the prints, still curious as to their origin.

He followed the old cleric through the thick abbey door. They stepped inside the nave, and Brayden paused. Even though he had been in the building before, he was awestruck every time he visited. Bernard had been hard at work the past few weeks, and it showed. Multi-colored sunrays penetrated the grand hall, lighting the floor and walls. The ceiling, towering above, was a complex layering of stone lines and curves. His eyes tried to take it in as he slowly traced up one wall and down another, finally settling at the far side of the abbey and onto the high altar, itself elevated above the floor and decorated with bright tapestries and more glass.

"Impressed, young man?" Bernard beamed, trying to conceal his pride.

"Oh yes," Brayden responded. "How did you fix it so fast?"

"I was not always a priest, you know. I've had some experience as a builder, and every now and then I get some help from the village or a roaming cottar or two. Come, this way."

They walked past the wood benches that lined the nave, and rounded the corner. At the far end of the transept was a door that led into the rectory where Bernard lived. The rectory was a simple room with a table and chairs, shelves and a small stone fireplace at one end. The room had one door that led outside and two more connecting to small antechambers. One of the antechamber doors was closed.

Brayden stopped in front of the closed door. "What is in there?" he asked.

"Always curious, hmm? Good. Just piles of old tools and blankets, mostly. Excuse the mess; the work on the abbey has left very little space for things. Come."

Bernard directed Brayden to the fireplace. As he walked, Brayden's still wet shoes left tracks across the stone floor.

"What's this?" Bernard asked. "Wet feet too? You truly risked life and limb to bring this delicious meal to me. Here, hand me your shoes. I'll put them on the spit."

"But your pottage," Brayden said, noticing there wasn't room for both the stew and his shoes.

"The pottage will keep. You need dry feet for your day at work. An old man can eat later. Let's get those dry first."

The shoes went on the spit. Bernard poked the fire and sparks flew.

"Now, let's let them sit. Come, I want to show you something."

They left the rectory and stepped back into the nave. Bernard led Brayden up the altar steps. Tall metal candlesticks lined the walls at intermittent locations, and on a heavy wooden table at the end of the high altar was an open, illuminated Bible. The thick book's gold lettering shimmered brightly. They turned around and paused, looking down the length of the structure.

"Old Hobin would have been pleased, I hope," Bernard said proudly, his hands on his hips.

According to Bernard, the abbey had been built by Friar Hobin many years before. Hobin's skill as a mason and architect had serviced lords and ladies in the building of manor homes, cathedrals, towns, and even castles across Wales, France, and Southern England. He had been particularly prolific in his later years, and there was likely not a structure of substance within one hundred miles that Friar Hobin had not designed or helped to build.

The abbey was his last, and built in his old age when he desired only quiet. With the friar's passing it had fallen into disrepair, left to the woods. Knowing the residents of Honeydown needed a proper house of worship nearby, Bernard had spent the better part of the last two years rebuilding it, and making it his home in the process.

Brayden looked up over the high altar. There, a man's height of stained glass window sat embedded in the wall, the sunlight shining through, bathing the chapel in a rainbow of colors.

Bernard seemed to notice him staring. "Marvelous, isn't it," he stated.

"Who made this?" Brayden asked. "I never noticed it before."

"I don't know. Friar Hobin knew many artists across England and France. I have not yet been able to find a signature or initials, but Heaven saw fit to keep it intact. It had been covered in dust and leaves for so long, it took a long time to clean it, but I'm certainly glad I finally did."

Brayden inspected the people represented in the window. "They're knights."

"Sure enough they are," Bernard answered, messing Brayden's hair. "But what are they doing?"

Brayden looked closely. He could identify assorted biblical scenes lining the perimeter of the window. The topmost pane, a large semicircle, was obviously the Savior with what he guessed were Saints Peter and Paul beside Him. Armor-clad people, knights, approached the Savior empty-handed, but carried what looked to be reliquaries as they walked away from Him. Brayden guessed that each reliquary held a relic or holy treasure inside.

The large rectangular bottom pane was of two men in combat. A knight in a white tunic emblazed with a red cross was crossing swords with a much larger man. The knight's right hand held aloft the larger man's left. The larger man was missing an eye, while the knight's expression was not one of anger or fear, but of peace. Under their feet was a city surrounded by water. Directly behind the knight stood a lady.

"King Richard the Lionheart?" Brayden suggested at length.

"Braver."

"St. George?" Brayden replied.

"Hmm, stronger. And do you see any dragons?"

"No. He is a Templar, isn't he?" Brayden asked.

"That he is, and a mighty fine one. This tells the story of this knight's battle with a Saracen giant, and how his victory saved many of the citizens of Acre. Do you see the lady holding the dagger at the knight's side?"

"I do."

"With her aid he slew the giant."

"How could a lady help a knight?" Brayden asked incredulously. "Siegfried says ladies can't fight and have no place near warriors except to cheer at jousts."

"Your cousin spends too much time listening to fiddlers and fools at the tournaments. Tell me, would your mother fight for you?"

He nodded silently. Of course she would, Brayden thought.

"I know this story well," Bernard said. "Let me share it with you."

* * *

"Many years past, the Templars and their armies still held onto the Holy Land, as they had for two hundred years. That grip was growing weak, and year after year the brothers grew weaker and weaker while the enemies that surrounded them grew in strength and spirit.

The fortress city of Acre stood alone. Immense walls protected it by land, and the sea was the city's moat. A great Saracen sultan ruled, and sent his most powerful warrior, Alcouz, to besiege and starve the city.

Many of the Saracens were brave and strong, but Alcouz was different. He was a giant of a man, missing an eye yet powerful, and cruel. He was a man of his word, though, and made an offer to the inhabitants: if any one Christian knight could best him in single combat, he would let the city go free. The winner would also take Alcouz's family prisoner to do with as they chose. There were few knights left to defend Acre, and Alcouz dispatched those who dared answer his challenge, one after another."

"But one young knight was not afraid," Brayden suggested.

"All men fear something, but this knight could summon the courage of a lion." Bernard smiled and continued. "Some said his heart was made of iron, others that youth makes us all fools. I think it was the love of a lady that made him strong. He knew his only chance to save her was to defeat Alcouz. He told her of his intent to challenge the Saracen and save the city. She knew she could not dissuade him, but bade him carry her dagger upon his belt. This dagger was shiny and delicate, encrusted with jewels and engraved with poems. Not a blade meant for combat. Our knight balked, but seeing the sincerity of his ladylove and having pledged himself to the task, he agreed.

The other knights chided him for planning to carry such a feminine blade into battle. His pride hurt, he pleaded with her to let him remove it, saying his sword and shield would be enough. She said no, and bade him not only to carry the dagger, but also upon victory to spare the Saracen's family from enslavement. He balked once more, but finally agreed.

The other citizens laughed at this promise, and called upon the knight to break it. He thought his ladylove mad. He took her to the city walls and showed her the bodies of the knights who had gone before. She implored him to trust her, and despite all arguments, she would not compromise. For a final time he relented.

On the day of the battle he strode out with sword and shield, and the dagger hidden in his tunic, out of sight. His ladylove and the city's citizens watched from the walls. The great warrior Alcouz stood across the dusty plain. The man's one-eyed gaze never left the knight. He held a Damascus sword in one hand and a spear in the other. His red robes flowed like blood in the desert winds. When he saw the knight, Alcouz gave a powerful yell, shaking the walls of Acre. Our knight stood firm. Alcouz charged.

With a hurl of his spear Alcouz pierced our knight through the leg. Our knight fell to his knees. Within minutes Alcouz was upon him, his blows relentless. The blue steel of his blade shattered our knight's shield and sword into fragments."

"Without armor a knight is defenseless," Brayden said.

"Don't be so sure," Bernard replied. "Alcouz approached, ready to finish him. At that moment, our knight remembered the dagger. He pulled it out. The small shiny weapon caught the sun, blinding the Saracen's one good eye. It was only for a moment, but it was enough. With all his strength he struck at Alcouz, taking out his remaining eye. The terrible man stumbled back in agony, and then fell to the ground, dead. The knight picked up the Saracen's blade and held it aloft. Acre had been spared, at least for a time."

"Was the dagger magical?"

"Magic is a thing for alchemists and mages. Things don't have to be magic to do magical things. Much is up to you."

"Did our knight take Alcouz's family prisoner?"

"Remember the tenets of knighthood as I've told you. The greatest of which, though practiced rarely in this age, is mercy. Our knight spared Alcouz's family, letting them go despite the insistence of his betters to bring them to the sword. The sultan was thankful and, out of respect for the knight, he called off the siege.

"So the knight's ladylove, by asking him to carry her dagger and spare Alcouz's family, saved the city," Brayden stated.

"A woman's wisdom and talent should never be underestimated, and neither should mercy."

"But what happened to them afterward? How did Acre fall? Where are they now?"

Bernard smiled, raising his hands to stop the barrage of questions. "That is all the window tells us, and that is all we'll say on this subject for now. Another time perhaps. I have to give you a reason to visit me again. I will tell you that, in time, the sultan would bestow upon our knight the honorable name, Haidar. Do you want to guess what that means?"

Brayden thought for a minute, his eyes searching for the answer on that glorious glass window.

"Lion," Bernard said, giving him the answer. "Indeed. A good name for a knight."

Brayden's nose twitched. A strange, stale burning smell had filled the air.

"The shoes!" Bernard hurriedly gathered his robes and darted into the rectory, Brayden in tow. "We'll be having them for midday supper!"

* * *

The shoes were smoking, but not burned. Bernard removed them, then took the bowl and placed it on the fire to heat up the contents. Brayden waited for his shoes to cool and then placed them on his feet.

As Bernard was stirring the pot, Brayden thought he heard a cough in the room with the closed door.

"Did you hear that?" he asked.

"Oh, probably the cats again," Bernard responded quickly. "You'd better start for home. Alice and the reeve will be looking for you. Stay on the paths from now on, and no visits after dark. Listen to your mother and stay close to the village," Bernard insisted.

"But what about you? Are you safe here?" Brayden thought again of the stories he had heard other villagers tell about what lurked in the forest.

"I know you would do a fine job of protecting me, but I'll manage. God's house will keep me safe for now."

"Sometimes I wish I were bigger. If I was I would never let anyone harm our village."

Bernard smiled. "Brayden, don't yearn for what you will one day be. Stay a boy as long as you can. Your time will come."

The sweet smell from the bowl was beginning to fill the room.

"Now, get going," Bernard continued. "People are going to ask what became of their blue boy. I'm sure the sheep and the cows are in the forest again by now!"

"Thank you, Bernard," Brayden said, getting up and heading for the rectory's exit.

"No, thank *you*, Sir Brayden, for keeping me company," Bernard said, bowing his head. He pulled the boy close and hugged him firmly. Brayden broke free and ran out the door, waving good-bye.

"And thank your mother for the pottage!" Bernard shouted after him.

Chapter Six

A Little Blade

Brayden ran back through the forest and came upon the fields. The sheep and cows were wandering about everywhere, and at length he found Old Robert sleeping peacefully on a bed of clover, bees buzzing around his nose. With some prodding Old Robert awoke, tipped his cap, and slowly rose, smelling strongly of ale.

"Good morning, Brayden," he said as he turned and stumbled down the slope. "It is a fine dawn, a fine dawn."

Brayden said nothing but let himself smile, hoping the old man would find his way back to the village in one piece.

The animals made no attempt to hide their preference for the open meadow, but there was simply too much risk in letting them wander the fields at night. At least when they were in the barn the villagers could rest easy knowing they were safe.

John Fields had warned Brayden about being late, and Brayden knew he'd be scolded for losing his horn. Brayden whooped and hollered, trying to keep the scattered animals from wandering off further. Without his horn, he couldn't call for help even if he needed it. Several of the animals had strayed past the hedges and were nuzzling the long grass on the fringe of the forest. The animals protested as he shouted and swatted, but slowly, one by one, he turned them away and down the hill towards the village.

Evening was approaching quickly, and the sun hung low in the sky, its bright yellow light replaced by orange and amber hues. Brayden scanned the forest line once more, and then stopped, staring in disbelief. One of the younger sheep had strayed far off, and he could just see its fluffy white coat half hidden in foliage.

"Please come," he muttered. A second later, the sheep was gone, disappearing into the wood. "Oh come on now, you silly thing," he said, wiping the sweat from his forehead and the hair from his eyes.

With the rest of the animals well on their way toward home, Brayden ran after the stray sheep. It poked its head out, and then darted back into the brush, disappearing from sight once more. He dove in after it and caught up to it quickly. The animal was busy nibbling on the forest brush, braying in pleasure at the sweetness of the forbidden foliage. Brayden grabbed tufts of its wool and pulled it back towards the meadow, the young sheep struggling against him.

It was then Brayden realized he was not alone. He stopped tugging at the sheep and looked around. He could hear voices nearby, and quickly hid behind the brushes. Not thirty paces away he could see Frank Mills and Matthew Baker approaching slowly from the same path he had taken earlier.

He knew neither of the men well, only occasionally seeing them at town gatherings and during Mass. They were middle in age, both in their mid-twenties. Covered by the brush, Brayden knelt quietly and listened. He was relieved they weren't outlaws.

"We'd be fools not to be afraid," Frank said. "There is no protection here. None at all."

"Surely the bailiff has summoned help," Matthew responded. "What of the knights of the castle?"

"Have you seen any of them? Have you seen any lawmen in a year?" Frank bent close, looking around as he spoke as if he didn't want to be overheard. "Rumor is, Lord Marshal and his company will never return. Rumor is they are dead. Every month we are more cut off from the other villages. The roads are not safe. Outlaws are everywhere, even this forest."

Frank looked around, waving mysteriously with his hand. "Even this forest grows haunted."

A chill went up Brayden's spine. He had completely forgotten about the sheep.

"We cannot leave the village, that much is certain," Matthew suggested.

"Maybe you cannot," Frank said, pointing at Matthew square in the chest. "But I intend to leave, tonight. You're a landholder, and encumbered by little ones and a fine lass. Besides, they'd never let a cook like you go, not this close to Michealmas. No one in the manor will miss a villain like me."

Brayden couldn't hear Matthew's response, but the man looked upset, and he walked away.

Frank's voice grew louder. "Fine, they'll find your head on a pole just as they found James Hill's!"

Brayden stumbled back at the mention of the missing bailiff. He knew James Hill had disappeared carrying grain to town for sale. His oxcart had been found, but he had not. From what Brayden had been told, it was then that, with Lord Marshal gone and with the blessing of the lord's steward, Corbat had quietly taken the man's home and position. Brayden stood up slowly, anxious to get out of the forest and back home.

"Brrraaaahhhh!" Brayden jumped, realizing he had stepped back and onto the foot of the little sheep. He looked in the direction of the men. They had both stopped where they were and were looking around, fear in their faces.

"What was that?" Brayden heard one of them ask.

They couldn't see him in the dark of the wood, and Brayden had no interest in being discovered. He pushed the sheep forward, driving it out of the forest. This caused him to trip. He landed on the ground with a thud.

"Shh, someone is out there," the other replied. "Shall we try to catch him?"

Brayden had no interest in being caught either. He crawled forward slowly, then jumped up and ran, leaving the two men behind as he darted out of the forest and into the field.

* * *

After much prodding and coaxing, the sheep and cows were finally secure in the barn. John had kept him late, fulfilling his promise to hold Brayden so they could get the barn organized. The reeve didn't ask about where Brayden had been, and Brayden didn't volunteer to tell John Fields what he had overheard.

At long last he was let go. Brayden waved goodnight and made his way through the town with haste, several times almost tripping on the ruts of the roads, hoping not to miss Dunstan Smith before he retired for the night. The air felt heavy, and nightfall would be upon the village soon. It smells like rain again, he thought. It had been an unusually wet summer, and while the roads were always a mess, the harvest would be strong, God willing.

He came up to the blacksmith's shop and found, to his relief, that Dunstan was still there, putting his tools away. The fire in the pit was out, the remaining orange embers dying slowly.

"Brayden! Good to see you this evening," Dunstan said, grinning happily.

Brayden smiled back. Dunstan's long dark hair was tied back in a knot, and despite his short stature, he was still one of the strongest looking men Brayden had ever seen. The blacksmith grabbed a wet cloth and started wiping his forehead and hands clean.

"Best I clean up, you know. Cecilia should be by soon. We're going for a walk tonight," he said, not concealing his excitement one bit.

Brayden had heard much talk around the village of the blacksmith and Cecilia in recent weeks. His mother had hinted they might one day be married. Whatever the reason, his friend was in good spirits.

"Do you still have that blade, the one we spoke of earlier?" Brayden asked, glancing around for any sign of onlookers.

"Why, yes, yes, I think indeed I do," Dunstan said, looking around and keeping his voice low as if to preserve the secrecy, even though not a soul was near.

"May I see it?" Brayden insisted.

"Oh course! But remember, no word to your mother. She'll not be happy with me, and she's a customer, you know."

"I promise," Brayden replied. He wasn't about to reveal the discussion he had had with his mother earlier in the day on the exact same subject.

Dunstan reached down under a table and after a short search retrieved from a shelf an item wrapped in cloth. He placed the item on the counter and carefully unwrapped it.

His blade lay before him. Brayden stared, somewhat disappointed. It was short, not even half the length of a man's forearm, and it was dull gray, not shiny like a sword. The edges were bumpy, not smooth, though the blade came to a sharp point at its end. The hilt was metal wrapped tightly in leather, and the pommel was nothing more than a plain round metal knob no bigger than a knuckle.

"It's so, little," Brayden said.

Dunstan seemed to sense Brayden's reaction, and put his hands on his hips. "You're a young boy, brave, but a boy nonetheless. A broadsword would do you no good."

Brayden smiled to conceal his disappointment. He appreciated Dunstan's help and didn't want to hurt the man's feelings.

"It's fine, sir," he said. "It's perfect."

"Good. You'll need your hands to use it. Your eyes can't help much. Pick it up and let's see how she wields," Dunstan insisted.

Brayden reach for the weapon, and at that moment Cecilia came upon them. She waved at Brayden and winked at Dunstan, her bright smile distracting them both. Brayden noticed instantly all the blacksmith's attention was suddenly diverted to her.

"Hello Dunstan. I see we have company tonight," she said, giggling.

Brayden hastily covered the blade with the cloth.

"Now come on, I wasn't born yesterday," Cecilia said, looking at Brayden. "Who do you think commissioned the knife?" She crossed her arms, feigning disgust. "Try it out!"

Brayden let out a sigh of relief and unwrapped the blade once more. He picked it up at the hilt and turned it over. He ran his fingers over the edges. Though bumpy, they were sharper than they looked.

"Ow!" Brayden yelled as red blood dripped from his thumb. The knife dropped to the ground.

"Boy!" Dunstan scolded. He rushed to the back of his shop and emerged with a clean cloth. Cecilia grabbed it, dabbed the cloth in a nearby bucket of water and grasped Brayden's thumb, holding it tight.

"Never touch the blade!" Dunstan said. He reached down, picked up the weapon and wiped it on another cloth. "At best, you rust the steel. At worst, you cut off your own hand! Ah well, we know now it is sharp enough. I've not made one yet that couldn't cut through wood, or flesh."

Brayden nodded silently in agreement as Cecilia wiped his thumb. She smiled down at him, relaxing her grip. He looked away, embarrassed. She was young and pretty, her eyes soft and caring. He understood why Dunstan liked her.

"Hmm. Looks like the bleeding has stopped. Hold it tight for some time longer," Cecilia cautioned. She kissed him on the head, and then turned to Dunstan. "Now, maybe this isn't such a good idea. I hate to be a bad influence. I assume Alice doesn't yet know?"

Brayden spoke before Dunstan could defend himself. "I asked for it, to protect my mother and our house, and that is exactly what I'm going to do."

"And whether your mother knows it or not, I'll wager," Cecilia said.

"We've little, but each other," he replied as he lowered his head to look at his ragged shoes and filthy pants.

Delicately, she pulled up his chin and looked at him straight in the eyes, her face full of understanding. Dunstan held the blade, as if awaiting her approval. "Well then, your mother is a lucky lady. I'm stuck with this one here."

Cecilia turned and winked at Dunstan once more. The man blushed, and took the signal. The blacksmith wrapped up the blade and handed it back to Brayden, hilt first. Brayden took it without hesitation, pulling it out of the cloth and inspecting the sharpness of the blade once more.

"Now," Dunstan began, "I don't work for free, but you don't look like you're ready to settle on payment tonight."

"No, no, sir, I'm afraid I'm not."

Dunstan crossed his arms and shot a glance at Cecilia. "Very well then." He smiled. "A blade like that could catch two or three hens, but I suppose two or three eggs will have to do."

"Oh thank you, sir," Brayden cried. "I'll have them for you tomorrow, and they'll be golden." He slid the blade up his sleeve and ran off towards home, excitedly waving goodbye.

He was anxious to get home, and knew what to expect when he arrived: a small dinner, a short reading, perhaps a story or two, and then off to an early bedtime–and he didn't mind one bit.

Chapter Seven

The Attack

Brayden awoke to the chickens squawking loudly outside. Something was disturbing them, he thought, but what? Perhaps it was a fox. He absently thought of the chicken pen, but it was secure, he was sure of it. He sensed something else, as if something terrible was happening outside.

A small candle flickered on the window ledge above his bed, its soft glow harassed by the near constant draft from the window. Brayden rubbed his eyes and sat upright. The candle's dim light barely illuminated even their small home. He looked across the cottage and his blood ran cold. His mother's bed was empty, though the door to the cottage was closed tight. Fear coursed through him.

"Mother?" he called out quietly. There was no response. Then a wild scream filled his ears. The shrill, almost inhuman sound penetrated his spine, and he sank deep under his rough woolen blanket, covering his ears with his hands. He began to shiver uncontrollably. Suddenly, men and women seemed to be yelling and shouting from every direction. He realized the truth: the village was under attack.

The door swung open with a loud bang, and Brayden braced himself. He wanted to cry, to be taken far away. A strong gust of air from outside mercifully extinguished the struggling candle. He stayed still, praying silently not to be found.

"Brayden?" His body went limp when he heard his mother's familiar voice. "Come here quickly, help me with the door."

He dove out of bed as she placed a lit lantern on the table. He helped her brace the door shut with a chair. She then picked up a large wooden board and placed it on the cross bolts. He stood back, staring at the door, unable to move.

"Brayden, here!" she ordered loudly, snapping him out of his stupor and urging him over to her with her hand. "We must move my cot and the table as well to block the door."

"Mother, where were you? What is happening outside?" A single tear formed in his eye and fell down his cheek. He wiped it quickly away.

"Oh, I'm sorry, my son, come here." She embraced him tightly, and then knelt down. Her face was serious.

"Listen very carefully to me. Men are attacking Honeydown. I don't know why, or who they are. They set fire to the barn and let out the livestock. John Fields is gathering the men, but I don't know what will happen. We need to be strong. Come, help me."

He followed her instructions without asking. They lifted one end of her heavy wooden cot over and shoved it against the door. They ignored the straw mattress, which fell to the floor in a clump. The table was next. It was awkward, but they had it against the door in moments.

Finished, they stood back, silently watching the door from the middle of the cottage. The shouting continued from all around, and they could hear the noise of a struggle outside.

"Mother, what is happening?" he asked, his shoulders shaking, his voice cracking.

She looked down at him reassuringly, rubbing his shoulder. She opened her mouth to speak but was interrupted by a sudden pounding at the door. Alice screamed, and they both jumped. Then they heard it, a voice so cruel and chilling it caused them to shake where they stood. The noise outside seemed to subside so the voice could be heard.

"Let me in, maiden. Let me in or I'll blow this door in," it rasped. Brayden looked around. The voice seemed to be coming from every direction at once.

Alice grabbed the lantern hastily and blew out the candle. Their home was bathed in pure darkness, save for a faint yellowish light that shone through the ram's-horn window. There was silence, then the demon outside spoke again.

"Let me in, maiden. I *will* blow this door in. Let me in, and I'll *only* take the boy." Brayden froze, the fear so enveloping he almost fell down. He put his hand to his mouth as his stomach lurched, as if he were upside down.

"Leave us be!" Alice shouted. The door began to shudder violently. The unrelenting pounding grew stronger.

"Leave us be!" his mother screamed again, almost pleading this time. Brayden clapped his hands over his ears. The pounding seemed to be coming from the windows and the walls, as if the monster outside had swallowed their cottage whole.

Alice pushed Brayden to the rear of the cottage and grabbed an iron poker from the hearth. She held it up near the door, ready to swing, one arm outstretched to keep Brayden behind her.

With a crash, one of the boards of the door flew in, splintering against the floor. A dark, long muscular arm struck at the cot, knocking it backward with inhuman ferocity. Alice fell back, stunned, the cot trapping her momentarily against the wall. The horrid arm moved wildly, almost unnaturally, desperately reaching and grabbing for anything it could find. When it could not lay its hands on a victim, it slid over the board on the cross bolts, attempting to lift it. The intruder would be inside their home in seconds.

With his mother still struggling with the cot, without thinking Brayden ran to his bed and reached under the mattress. He pulled out the blade Dunstan had given him, rushed to the door, and with closed eyes slashed at the arm again and again. Hot blood covered Brayden's hands as the man outside screamed in agony, his arm twitching furiously as if possessed. The man howled, cursed him, and the arm finally retreated.

They waited, breathing heavily.

A horrid scream broke the silence and echoed through the cottage. Alice ran over and pulled Brayden close, covering his ears.

"Alice!"

Brayden jumped and dropped the blade. It was the voice of John Fields.

Brayden's mother bound to the door, shoved the remaining furniture aside, and ran outside with the poker, ready to strike at anyone she saw. John Fields and two other village men were there, each armed with a pitchfork and a torch.

Brayden followed her through the doorway and looked around the village before them. Several of the cottages were on fire, illuminating the main road. He could hear yelling and crying, and people were everywhere. Some were tending to the fires, while others milled about, blank looks on their faces. Chunks of cottage wall, fencing, and roof lay scattered all about. Carts were overturned. Animals were loose from their pens, and many were running about the village, as panicked as the people themselves.

"It happened so fast," John Fields panted. "It happened so fast. Thanks to the Lord we were able to save the barn from the blaze. He froze, staring down the road in the direction of Dunstan's shop. "Oh no," he said quietly. Brayden looked in the direction the reeve was gaping, and his own heart fell to the pit of his stomach.

Not fifty paces from them sat Dunstan Smith, in the middle of the road outside his shop. He was rocking back and forth, sobbing. On his lap lay the lifeless body of his lovely Cecilia. Dark blood covered them both.

Alice pushed Brayden into their home and pulled him close to her. She squeezed his head gently as he cried.

Chapter Eight

The Messenger

Cecilia was buried under a large oak at the north end of the churchyard. Bernard said the old tree's branches were like outstretched arms, holding and comforting the dead. She lay in the sunniest spot, as Dunstan and her sisters had requested. A small bouquet of heather sat upon her resting place.

The days that followed the attack were hard on the villagers. Most kept to themselves, and few ventured far from the village for anything other than firewood. The fear of banditry and of another attack kept travelers and tradesmen from Honeydown. Without the visiting tradesmen, many of the villagers' homes remained unrepaired.

During his visits to the village, Bernard heard little laughter and felt no happiness in the air. Even with a strong harvest and the coming holiday celebrations, the people were dour. While they still did their work during the day, they no longer shared ale at night. Everywhere he went the homes were locked, and other than for Sunday Mass, few visited the abbey.

John Fields had spoken of going to the castle in search of help, but the bailiff refused to let anyone leave, stating that everyone was needed for the harvest. If there was a glimmer of a silver lining, thought Bernard, it was the harvest. The weather had been good to the countryside this year, and the harvest would be abundant enough to keep the village through the winter and even perhaps to give them surplus enough to trade.

Of all the villagers, Bernard missed Brayden most. Gone were the days and nights spent telling stories. Children were not to leave home after late afternoon, and John Fields, wisely, Bernard thought, kept Brayden and the other children out of the fields and woods during the day.

Bernard checked in on his patient, and satisfied with the man's progress, decided to pick wildflowers and take them into the village. They would cheer up Alice, and it was a good excuse to visit Brayden and the other children, if only for a short time.

* * *

Caelan awoke to sunlight, squinting and rubbing his eyes. He was in a small, dull room filled with tools and blankets. He sat up, and while his side still ached, the pain had noticeably diminished. He looked down at his wound. The dressings were clean. He could not recall the face of his healer, but he owed him a debt of gratitude.

The small room was lit by a large clear window in the wall behind him opposite a large wood door directly in front of him. He pulled back the heavy woolen blankets. I'm not a prisoner, he thought, glancing with relief at his armor and sword, which lay nearby next to his tunic and satchel. A large wooden bucket and a neatly stacked pile of clean linens lay on a bench at the end of the cot. Caelan stood, running his fingers along the wall for balance. The whitened stone was thick, cool, and solid. The building he was in was of substance.

While he put his tunic on, he tried to recall his arrival. The pain in his side as he walked brought back memories of the journey, the attack, and the rain. Somehow, he had survived, but he had no further memory of this place. No matter. Whoever had taken him in had cared for him well.

Caelan cupped an ear and stood listening at the door. Hearing nothing, he pushed the door open slowly and looked out into a large well-lit room. Unlike his small bedchamber, ample light filtered in through several windows, giving the room a warm, comfortable feeling. A sturdy wood table and chairs sat at one end, and a modest fireplace filled the far side of the chamber upon which hung a small pot over a smoldering fire. Shelves lined the walls and held all size and manner of plates, utensils, and books. The place looked well taken care of, he observed. The floors were clean, as if they had been swept just moments before. The room had three other doors, all closed.

As he walked into the room, he groaned. With each step the pain in his side grew stronger, reminding him to move slowly. Using the wall for support, he pulled on the handle of one of the doors. The door swung open quickly, almost knocking him over. He froze. Before him was a sturdy old man in a brown robe. Before Caelan could speak, the man stepped forward, smiling, one hand outstretched, his other full of wildflowers.

"Welcome, friend," the old man said, bowing slightly. "Welcome to the abbey of Honeydown."

* * *

"Please, sit," the old man said as he motioned in the direction of the table and chairs. "I was going to the village, but forgot my walking staff. My apologies for the surprise. Though seeing you awake and about, I must say I'm pleased."

The pain in his side still fierce, Caelan sat down with a sigh of relief as the man walked over to the hearth and began ladling the contents of the pot into a small wooden bowl.

"Here, let's try some of this." He handed Caelan the bowl and turned back to the fire.

For a moment Caelan forgot the pain as he inhaled the smell of the rich broth. He cupped the bowl and sipped deeply. It was a tangy, complex medley of flavors, tart, but relaxing.

"What manor house is this? You aren't a lord," Caelan said. "So who then do you serve, old man? Is your master about?"

"Bernard is the name," the man responded without turning, "and the only master of this house is God. I expect He'd keep you as a welcome guest, though I may not." Bernard walked over and set a cloth covered-plate before Caelan.

"I'm sorry, friend. I meant no offense."

Bernard waved his hand. "You've been through an ordeal, young man. I don't know how polite I'd be myself." He pointed at the bowl. "The broth is savories, skullcap, and thyme, among other things, if you are interested in learning. Stay silent for a moment, and let it go to your head."

Caelan drank again, nodding silently in appreciation.

"Now, for the real test," Bernard said as he pulled the cloth from the plate, revealing a small assortment of breads and fruits. Caelan's stomach growled enthusiastically. He had no recollection of his last meal and was surprised at his own sudden hunger. He reached for the tray with vigor and finished the food quickly, washing it down with the remaining broth.

Bernard looked him over. "A strong appetite is a good sign. You've been here for almost two weeks. Prayers and my own remedies seem to have worked. Either way, your fever is broken and you should be fully healed soon."

"Two weeks? I must be on my way," Caelan said. He started to push himself up, then fell back without resisting as Bernard pushed him gently down into the chair.

"You're not a prisoner here, and are free to go under your own will. But, I said you *should* be fully healed, not that you *are*. I doubt your blood is poisoned, though I've administered more last rites in my time than effective cures. Another week or two of rest is what you need."

"You're a man of medicine?" Caelan asked.

"Far from it. You've reached our abbey quite by accident, I suspect. Where were you headed?"

"I am going to the village of Honeydown. Is it far?" Whatever was in Bernard's potion had worked. With it and the food, Caelan felt his strength returning slowly, and the pain from his wound had subsided.

"Far?" Bernard chuckled. "Dear lad, you're in it."

Surprise, then relief, flooded Caelan. Despite the attack and the storm, I was on the right path all along, he thought.

"I am Sir Caelan de Spero," he said, pushing the bowl and plate away and leaning back in the chair. "I am in the service of Lord Marshal, wherever he may be."

"A fine man to serve. It must be an errand of some urgency. The banditry in these parts makes the roads dangerous, the forest even more so, as you yourself have noticed."

Caelan shrugged, not hiding his lack of concern. "I've my own means."

"So I've noticed." Bernard glanced quickly at the sword and armor resting in the other room.

Caelan shrugged again and smiled slightly.

"You're a knight then," Bernard said, more a statement than a question.

"Since my twentieth year," Caelan replied.

"And that was no hackney you rode in on."

"Sullivan?" Caelan said, his eyes widening as he sat straight upright. "You've seen my Sullivan?"

"Ah, so that is his name. The horse is tied to you to be sure. He has not strayed far since you arrived. He's an impressive creature, with an even more impressive appetite. The other animals grow nervous of his being a long visitor," Bernard said, sharing a smile with the knight.

Caelan sat back in his chair and relaxed. "Thank you, old Bernard. Without your kindness these past days I'd likely be finished. And if I offended you earlier, my sincerest apologies."

Bernard waved his hand once more. "No worries, dear lad. My thanks is seeing your strength return and fever gone. I must admit, I am curious. Why Honeydown?"

"If you would be kind enough to hand me my satchel bag, I'll explain."

"I gathered your bag and its contents the morning after the storm. I hope it's all here." Bernard walked into the smaller room and in moments returned with the leather bag, and placed it on the table.

"I am living now at the Castle Strand," Caelan began, "returning from Ávila in Castile some months ago after fulfilling an errand for my liege-lord. I have found, though, that much has changed since Lord Marshal disappeared. First, nothing has been heard from the lord or his champion, Sir Allard. No word on where they are or even if they live. Rumors abound of their kidnapping, or worse."

"The rumors abound here as well, Sir Caelan," Bernard replied.

"Second, with support from some of the vassals, Sir Bellator has taken stewardship of the lord's lands. Nothing is being done to protect them, and the villages suffer regular banditry and deprivation. At the least Lord Marshal would have appealed to the king or the other barons for aid, or dispatched his own forces to protect the people. All of this, and Bellator does nothing."

"Aye. Our little village here has suffered mightily indeed. There was an attack just a few days past." Bernard bowed his head, as if thinking of the event brought him pain.

"I'm sorry Bernard, but bless his royal blood King Edward is a weakling at best, letting his people suffer so," Caelan continued, "and the barons' power grows stronger every year."

"Has anyone confronted the steward?"

"Of the other knights and vassals I know of only two."

"And what of them?" Bernard pressed.

Caelan lowered his voice and glanced about the room. "Strange happenings seem to haunt the castle. Both disappeared with no sign. Some of the guards say the castle took them."

Both men sat in silence as the statement sank in. Bernard rubbed his chin.

"I am not one for ghosts or mysticism," Bernard said, "but all the same I've overheard some of the stranger stories about the castle upon arriving in Wales. Only rumors, I'm sure."

"That may be, but I have other suspicions about Bellator," Caelan finally continued. "Lord Marshal's only surviving heir is his young daughter, whom, with the lord's demise Bellator could marry in order to increase his lands and power substantially. It is only rumor, as you say, but in my short life I've learned to expect the worst."

"Not an unwise consideration, my friend. I understand now there are machinations afoot that we can only guess at," Bernard agreed.

"You asked, though, why I am here. I deliver a message," Caelan said, as if anxious to move on. "When on duty I take chambers in the castle, taking care to sleep with my sword by my side. One morning I awoke and found this slipped under my chamber door."

With a grunt of pain, Caelan pulled the satchel bag toward himself and inspected its contents. He produced a small piece of parchment and handed it to Bernard. Bernard held it gently up against the light. The top of the parchment was singed as if it had barely survived a fire, and only the bottom half of message remained. Bernard read the elegant script aloud, handling the fragile document with great care.

Make haste. I know not of him, only of rumor he makes refuge in your manors. Bring Brayden Rider before me by the 31st of October, and bring him alive. You are a loyal servant, my friend. Your tithing does not go without note. But do not fail in this quest. Only with success will I bless your plans. Only when I have what I want.

T

"A message, and a mystery," Bernard said at last. He inspected the wax signature closely. It was the single letter "T."

"Do you know who left you this note, or who it was originally for?"

With a grunt of pain, Caelan shook his head. "I do not, though I suspect the intentions of whoever delivered it to me were noble. I came here because I had been told a Rider family settled in this area some years ago, though I don't know them by their faces."

"So you've come to help?" Bernard asked.

"If you mean to suggest I am in league with the author of that letter, I am not. I am a knight. What higher duty do I have than to protect those who need it? Do you know of this Brayden fellow?"

Bernard looked deep into Caelan's eyes, as if measuring the younger man's sincerity. Caelan stared back, unwavering, wanting this man to believe him.

"I meant no harm, and I do indeed know him," Bernard said at last, crossing his arms slowly. "You are correct. He lives in Honeydown village."

"You must take me to him," Caelan started to get up, but fell back, groaning loudly as the pain in his side returned. Bernard motioned him to stay seated. "Perhaps he can lend light on this mystery. Perhaps he knows of Lord Marshal's whereabouts. And I fear he is in danger."

"That he is in danger seems abundantly clear. That he can assist us in any way with Lord Marshal's whereabouts, less so."

"What is his method of employment? Miller, farmer, carpenter?"

Bernard chuckled and shook his head. "None of those. Brayden Rider is a ten-year-old boy, who likes to dream and has a penchant for sleeping in, nothing more."

"Ten?" Caelan asked. He couldn't believe it.

Bernard nodded. The knight lay back once more, staring at the ceiling.

"Why would someone be interested in a ten-year-old peasant boy?" Caelan wondered aloud.

"I mentioned some days ago that our village was attacked, by outlaws, we thought, at first. However, they singled out the boy's home. He fought bravely, saving himself and his mother. I suspect the letter you hold and the incident at his home are related."

"So it would seem," Caelan said. "It sounds as if the boy has the heart of a lion."

Bernard smiled. "He is strong."

"The wax letter there at the bottom," Caelan continued. "Does it hold any significance to you?"

Bernard examined the simple signature, considering it carefully. "None that I can name," he finally replied, shaking his head.

"This Brayden Rider," Caelan pressed, "does he share kinship with a Sir Ban Rider, the Templar?"

Bernard stood and silently walked over to the fire. He picked up a spoon and stirred the pot. "He does indeed," he responded at length. "Brayden is his only son."

"You know of him then? Sir Ban himself?"

Bernard nodded, continuing to stir. "I do," he paused. "His humble servant I was for many years."

Caelan sat upright once more, his face ashen.

"Bernard of Acre," he spoke at last. "Saint Bernard the unsainted. Friend and healer of commoner and king alike. Of course. There had been rumors of your arrival upon this island years ago. You've lived here in this abbey all this time. Surely it is I who should bow to you."

Bernard raised his arms and waved his hands. "I'm a humble friar now, and I will not have bowing in my presence, Sir Caelan. Whatever I did I did long ago. My interest now is in rebuilding the abbey and ensuring the safety of the people here. I am hopeful, upon your strength returning, that you will help me with the latter."

Bernard took Caelan's bowl and refilled it from the pot. Then he produced another piece of bread and placed both next to Caelan.

"Brayden, his mother, and I came from France together four years ago. Of our lord, Sir Ban, we know not. Brayden's mother's name is Alice, and I will speak with her. I urge you to consider that you are not yet ready to move. But do not fear Sir Caelan, your services are desperately needed here, and you will uncover the truth." Bernard raised a finger. "But, not until you are better healed."

Bernard intoned several blessings, after which Caelan ate the broth and the bread. They sat in silence for a few minutes.

"How do you feel?" Bernard asked after the knight had finished eating.

"Better. Much better than when I awoke," Caelan responded.

"Good. Now, I am happy to help the occasional pilgrim who graces this old rectory, but the abbey is what you must see. Before you return to rest, let me take you through. Some time at the altar will heal you well."

Caelan agreed without resistance, noting the pride in the friar's voice. He stood slowly with Bernard's help, and walked with him into the magnificent abbey of Honeydown.

Chapter Nine

A New Friend

Brayden poked a stick in the dirt and watched as the ants scurried around his feet, searching in vain for whatever was responsible for disturbing their mound. He kicked his leg out as one crawled onto his foot, quickly knocking it away.

How much longer he'd have to wait he did not know. He had been sitting outside his own home for what had seemed like hours. Although occasional passersby tipped their caps or waved at him, he had spent the entire time alone.

At least the rain had stopped and the mud was gone, he thought. So far the harvest had been going well, cheering everyone's spirits. While fear still hung in the air, with luck the weather would hold out and the winter stores would be secured. The fruit trees were being picked as well, and he and the other villagers were happy about delicious apples and blackberries being back in their diets.

He had been excited to see Bernard after so many days, but felt left out when the old friar asked for some time to speak with Brayden's mother and the other adults in private. If not for me, he thought, that horrid man with the evil voice would have broken down our door, surely hurt my mother, and taken me away. Brayden sighed, poking the stick back into the mound and watching curiously as the number of ants underfoot swelled.

The door opened suddenly and Dunstan Smith exited the cottage. Since Cecilia's death, he had taken to wearing a dark, wool robe. It fell to his feet, covered his arms and was far too long for the short man. Brayden could see its tail dragging at least a foot behind as Dunstan walked.

"Boy," Dunstan said, his voice gruff and dry. "I'm off for a time. Leaving Honeydown. You'll be well taken care of. Bernard will see to it. Take care, boy."

He hurried on silently as Brayden started to get up to go after him. Before Brayden could call after his friend, his mother was at the door.

"Brayden, come in please," Alice called.

He followed his mother into their home. Inside, Bernard and John Fields stood in the middle of the main room in front of the hearth. They smiled as Brayden entered, and he immediately grew suspicious, anxious to know what had taken so long and why he had been excused. It is my house too, he thought. He wondered if they had been talking about the attack, or if something was wrong with him, or his mother. He stood silently, waiting for them to speak, unwilling to start the conversation until they explained themselves.

"Brayden," his mother finally began, "I'd like you to stay at the abbey for a time."

"With Bernard?" he blurted excitedly before catching himself. He forced himself to calm down, telling himself to remain suspicious.

"Yes, with Bernard. I'd like you to stay with him for a time, perhaps until Michealmas. He needs help stocking the abbey and preparing for the celebration."

Michaelmas wasn't for at least two weeks, if Brayden correctly remembered the calendar and the frequent lectures Bernard had given on the days, weeks, months, and holidays. Brayden did not have to force himself to remain suspicious. Bernard had almost singlehandedly rebuilt the abbey. That he needed help now preparing for a holiday seemed odd. Bernard watched him, as if reading his face and mind.

"We'll have a grand time," Bernard said. "I should have asked for your help in rebuilding the abbey. It took a lot out of me, and I'm behind in preparations. We'll stay up and tell stories until late, and chase the pigs in the morning. You know, it's the time of year to start fattening up the surplus."

"It is the safest place, Brayden," John Fields said. "Strong and sturdy stone walls and thick, heavy doors."

He could hold his tongue no longer and turned to his mother. "What of you, mother? Why now? Who will protect you while I am gone?" he asked earnestly.

She smiled. Her face was reassuring, caring, and without a trace of fear. "That is just what we were talking about. John is organizing lookouts and guards. When we're ready, and certainly by Michaelmas, you'll come home again. Until then, I want you to stay at the abbey, do as Bernard bids, eat lots and listen lots and keep up with your French and Latin. Come." She spread her arms and beckoned him to her. He walked forward and she hugged him tightly. "I'll call on you," she whispered in his ear. She kissed his cheek, and John Fields winked at him. Bernard was already at the door, his hand outstretched.

* * *

The weeks leading to Michaelmas were busy ones. Aside from the necessity of stocking food for the winter, rents had to be paid and other debts were due. Brayden was thankful to be spending so much time at the abbey and away from the commotion. While he was as excited as anyone about the flurry of activity around the holidays, with the curfew the reeve had imposed, children could not stay out late anyhow. Not only that, but the bailiff would be everywhere at once, demanding money, owed or not. The bailiff didn't visit the glebe, however, and Brayden was happy to be away from him. While Bernard joked that if the bailiff came within fifty paces of the church, every angel in Heaven would swoop down and cast the man away, Brayden suspected his friend had warned the bailiff that except for Mass, he was not welcome at the abbey for any reason.

They kept busy tending to the animals. Soon those that would survive the winter, and those that would be feasted upon, would be selected. Though he longed for the autumn feasting, he found himself distancing himself from several of the pigs, sheep, and goats he had known and helped Bernard care for since the spring, realizing that now they would not likely live much longer. Bernard did his part to distract him, and reminded him that many of the plants would also die and, like the animals, would be reborn in the warmth of spring.

Brayden knew the holidays marked the changing of the seasons. Winter in Honeydown would come before too long, and the novelty of snow would wear off quickly, replaced by long weeks of cold drudgery and boredom. He was lucky, or least had been told he was, that his mother and Bernard took such an interest in his studies. His days inside by the warmth of the fire would be filled with language study, reading, and writing. They would speak Latin at breakfast and French in the evening.

Bernard set few rules at the abbey. When done with his daily tasks, Brayden was free to wander the fields around the abbey, though he was instructed to stay within shouting distance. The only part of the abbey forbidden to him was the small room off the rectory; the only door in the abbey Bernard appeared to keep permanently closed. The room was filled with winter clothes and blankets, which Bernard wanted sealed off to keep out rats and other pests.

Though Brayden enjoyed his freedom, his thoughts drifted frequently to his mother, her delicious cooking and the warm hearth in the middle of their little home. While he worried about her being alone near the bailiff, Bernard assured him she could take care of herself, besides which, John Fields and many other villagers were always nearby.

* * *

Today they were out by the edge of the meadow. Brayden knew all too well Bernard's love of and outright fascination with root vegetables. Bernard believed, and accurately, from everything Brayden could observe, that they lasted almost forever and gave the body robustness bread could not. Bernard hated searching for them though, so Brayden did most of the digging.

"Hmm, this will not do. Not at all. Brayden?"

"Yes, Bernard?" His hand was six inches deep in the dirt, the worms within wiggling wildly around his fingers.

"I think that while we are blessed in finding so much gingerroot, we've nothing to place them in, not even a pocket. Would you be kind enough to run in and bring back a bowl? Best to keep them together until we're ready."

Brayden nodded, wiped his hands on his pants, and darted off in the direction of the abbey. He walked up through the nave, past the high altar, and into the rectory. He looked up at the shelves and quickly realized he could not reach a single bowl. He looked around for a chair to stand on, and then remembered Bernard had taken the chairs outside so they had a place to sit when they weren't working. He tried pulling at the wooden table, and then pushing it, but it wouldn't budge.

There was nothing else to stand on. It was then he noticed that the door to the small room off the rectory was slightly ajar. Bernard had said the room was filled with blankets. They could simply wrap the roots in one of the blankets and carry them back that way. He walked over to the door and pushed hard against it. It opened, and then jammed. Brayden pushed harder.

"Ow!" someone shouted. "My foot! Old priest do you seek to reinjure me?" the voice boomed.

The door swung open, and Brayden fell forward into the room and onto the floor. He looked up in surprise. A young man in a white tunic and brown pants stood before him.

"What's this?" the man asked, fists on his hips. "A boy paying me a visit?"

"I'm not a boy," he blurted, too stunned to move. "My name is Brayden."

The man paused, staring at him strangely. "Brayden Rider?" he asked after several moments.

"That is what I said. Who are you and what is your business here?" he demanded. It was then that Brayden saw the broadsword leaning against the wall of the small room. His mouth opened wide and fear entered his mind. He suddenly regretted giving up his name so quickly to this total, potentially very dangerous, stranger.

The man ignored him. "While I've heard fresh voices about, I didn't know we shared this fine abbey permanently. Come on, lad, let me help you up."

His grip was strong. He lifted Brayden off the ground effortlessly and looked him up and down. Brayden did the same. The man was taller than most, and well built. His blond hair fell to his shoulders. His blue eyes were bright and calm.

"My name is Caelan. I take it you too are a guest of the parish priest?"

"Bernard is my friend, and I live here with him by invitation," Brayden answered curtly, straightening his clothes. "How long have you been here?"

Caelan shrugged. "Too long. I had opened the door to get some fresh air. Bernard had asked that I stay out of sight, but I just cannot stand this little room any longer."

"Ah, I see you two have met one another," Bernard said, as he entered the rectory from the nave. "How fortuitous. Brayden Rider, meet Caelan de Spero. Oh, pardon me. *Sir* Caelan de Spero."

"You're a knight."

"That I am, my boy."

* * *

"So that is the Rider boy, the one with the stout heart," Caelan said.

The knight sat at the table across from Bernard, who with Brayden had brought the chairs back inside. Bernard had broken bread and pulled out a stash of thick, creamy butter. Having sent Brayden to the abbey well for fresh water, the men ate heartily, awaiting the boy's return. "Why bring him here?"

"Alice alone knows you're here. I assured her Brayden is safer here in the abbey from another bandit raid than anywhere else, what with you being here and her trusting my opinion of you."

"Or safer from the author of that letter," Caelan interrupted. "So you protect the boy?"

Bernard nodded. "I gave an oath to Sir Ban, my friend, that I would help raise and protect his son until his return."

"I'm feeling better, Bernard. I'd like to go into the village myself. I'd like to meet this Alice Rider woman and assure her my intentions are just."

Bernard shook his head, at the same time thinking how much he had grown to like this earnest young knight. "Not all the villagers can be trusted, particularly not Corbat Handhafte, the bailiff. You abandoned your post, Sir Caelan. Whatever I may think of it or how noble the cause, I suspect Corbat will not think twice about arresting you in order to court favor with the steward."

Caelan sat back, a look of recognition on this face. "I know of this bailiff and his reputation. The other villages have complained about him, and I've seen him, and heard his name in the castle halls."

"Is he an acquaintance of the steward's?" Bernard asked, suddenly intrigued.

"Perhaps, though I cannot say directly. He was present at the castle the same day Sir Martin was killed."

"Oh?"

"Sir Martin was on horseback," Caelan continued, "during a tournament last year. Though second only to Sir Allard in fighting prowess, he was killed, stabbed through his armor as if it wasn't there. A quite unbelievable accident, as I recall."

"Killed by whom?" Bernard asked slowly.

"His friend, the steward, a much weaker man."

Bernard sat back in the chair, rubbing his chin in thought.

The door swung open. Brayden walked in, struggling to balance a full bucket of water. His pant legs were wet, and a trail of water followed him inside. Bernard rushed over, took the bucket, and beckoned Brayden to the table. He sat and let out a sigh of relief.

"Thank you for the water," Caelan said. He leaned close to Brayden and with one eye on Bernard, he whispered, "As one who has had nothing but pungent herbal stews for several weeks, fresh water is a welcome change."

"I heard that!" Bernard said in fake irritation. Brayden smiled at the joke.

"We left the man's portion for you," Caelan said, motioning to the bread and butter.

"Thank you." Brayden took his knife from his belt and cut himself several large slabs of butter, which he spread carefully on a piece of bread.

"So, Bernard tells me you're handy with that knife."

Brayden shot Bernard a glance.

"It's all right. I mentioned what happened the night of the attack. It was the talk of the town," Bernard said.

Brayden blushed, suddenly embarrassed.

Caelan smiled. "So, young Brayden, I hear you've yet to visit our castle."

"With the banditry, Mother says it's unthinkable to leave the village this year. It seems I've been promised a visit every year since we arrived, but there is always something," Brayden said, shaking his head.

"So you've heard stories?"

"Oh, yes, I make sure he hears stories," Bernard said, smiling.

Brayden did his best to ignore the priest and went on. "I hear that its walls are white as bone, and the mists of the mountains descend upon it and hide its towers in the dawn. I hear that armies have been broken at its gates. I hear of the great hall and its colors and the feasts that take place and the dancing. Is it all true?"

"Yes, it is true," Caelan said, leaning closer. "And more. Much more."

"Now, Brayden, listen," Bernard interrupted, quickly getting their attention. "Sir Caelan is on an important errand, but the nature of his visit is known only to him. It is important that no one, not even Siegfried, knows he is here or who he is. Can we entrust you with this?"

Brayden looked at Caelan, excited at the prospect of a secret. "Yes, yes, of course you can!"

"Siegfried?" Caelan asked, looking at each of them.

"He is my aunt's son, and a squire at the castle," Brayden answered proudly.

"Ah. I know of him then. Close with Sir Bellator, he is," Caelan said. He looked at Bernard, who raised an eyebrow in response.

"May I see your armor?" Brayden asked.

"Ah yes, your armor," Bernard said, as if shaking off a trance. He suddenly moved with great energy, speaking before Caelan could answer.

"Brayden, finish your food, and then accompany Sir Caelan outside. Meet me in the field in one quarter of an hour."

Brayden and Caelan shared a quizzical glance as Bernard disappeared into the small room. He walked past them moments later, awkwardly carrying the armor.

"Where are you going with that?" Caelan asked.

"One quarter of an hour, and bring your sword!" Bernard was already out the door.

* * *

They walked into the late afternoon light. Caelan had strapped his sword and belt around his waist. Brayden kept stealing glances at it, wondering how it must feel to carry such a weapon, wielding it as a way of life. He had heard stories from Bernard and others about the adventures of knighthood, the travels and tournaments. He remembered images of his own father, but since then he had not seen a knight, let alone spoken with one. Brayden admitted to himself that he was a little disappointed. This man had not appeared in shiny armor or carrying a lance. He did not look like a warrior. He was, Brayden observed, just a normal man.

"How did you come to be here?" Brayden asked as they walked.

"I am searching for someone, but was attacked en route. Your friend, the old priest, saved me."

"Attacked by whom?"

"Likely the same scum who raided your village. I was wounded, and Bernard healed me."

Brayden looked at the ground, considering what Caelan had just told him. This knight, this man, was far from invincible. He wondered if Caelan had encountered the fiend who had almost broken into their home.

Bernard was nowhere to be seen. They walked the perimeter of the abbey once, then twice. Brayden was the first to finally spot him.

"There!" he shouted, pointing.

Bernard was in one of the glebe's furthest meadows. It looked as if he was talking to a tall person on a hill. As they approached they realized the figure was not a person, but a scarecrow. Rags and straw hung from it, and across its torso was Caelan's armor. The knight's eyes grew wide with disbelief.

"Priest, what is the meaning of this!? I admit your humor surpasses mine, but I insist you take down my armor at once."

"I think after this you'll prefer to leave it out here with the birds. Your sword." Bernard stretched out his right hand as they neared.

"Pardon me, Father?"

"Your sword. You mentioned that Sir Martin was killed while at tourney by a much weaker man. Was he a novice?"

"Absolutely not. Sir Martin was my senior by several years in experience and strength."

"Was he in armor?"

"Of course. Chain and plate, of the same design as mine."

Caelan looked at Bernard's outstretched hand. He pulled the sword out of its scabbard slowly, turned the blade toward himself, and handed it, hilt end, to Bernard. The priest held it aloft, its steel catching the rays of sunshine full on. Brayden was surprised by how steady the blade seemed in the old man's hands. Bernard could wield it without the slightest shake or wobble.

"You see, I don't think Sir Martin's death was an accident," Bernard said evenly.

With no warning and with the speed of a man half his age, Bernard sliced at the scarecrow several times. He cut to both sides with fantastic agility, and then lunged twice into the straw-filled chest. When finished, he stood in silence, the sword held upright in his hands. After a moment, he swung it in an arc and handed the blade back to Caelan. Impressed by this display of swordsmanship, it took several moments for Brayden and the knight to refocus on the scarecrow. What they saw made them stare in amazement.

The armor was in shreds. Long gashes covered each side. Deep holes were torn where Bernard had stabbed at the scarecrow's chest. Caelan approached, standing next to the straw man and ran his fingers through and around the cuts.

"I don't believe it," Caelan said, shaking his head slowly. "I'm lucky to be alive at all."

"Indeed. Your armor offers you no protection whatsoever, and offered none to your associate on tourney day. Another lucky strike from your attackers, and you would have suffered the same fate as him."

"But surely the workmanship—" Caelan cut himself off. "The castle blacksmiths are the most talented in Wales. Their fault here is an impossibility."

"This is more than poor workmanship or a simple mistake," Bernard responded. "In battle I've seen chain and scale rip in some places, though hold together fast in all others. But, I've never seen metal ripped and shorn across the whole body like this. I took to inspecting it while you recovered, and it is as if another, weaker alloy was used in the making. No, this was no simple accident of smithing. It was made to fail. I fear there is greater mischief at play than we supposed, mischief that may have felled Sir Martin."

Brayden looked at Bernard, not recognizing the name.

"How did you come upon it?" Bernard asked.

"Supposedly a gift left me by Lord Marshal before he disappeared, a reward for my trip to Castile." Caelan glanced at the armor once more. "The mark then. What of it?" Caelan asked.

"There is none," Bernard replied curtly. "Whoever the armor maker is, he leaves us no clue. Let us speak of this with no one, for now."

A strong wind blew through, making the trees shudder. The sky was turning dark quickly.

"So, we have bandits freely terrorizing the countryside, a mysterious letter, Lord Marshal's disappearance, and now this," Caelan said.

"What letter?" Brayden asked. He felt as if he was being talked around.

"Come," Bernard said, momentarily ignoring the boy and waving them both to follow. "A storm comes in from the east."

They turned back toward the abbey, leaving the remains of the armor for the crows.

Chapter Ten

Ride on a Warhorse

Brayden and Caelan spent the next several days together, chatting and wandering the fields and meadows of the abbey when Bernard did not have them both hard at work. Caelan's side had healed enough to enable him to spend some time each day tending to various chores around the abbey. Brayden found that the knight liked digging up root vegetables about as well as he did.

Everything Brayden had read and heard told him knights were well travelled, but to his surprise Caelan had travelled far less than he would have thought. Apart from his trip to Castile that he would not discuss in detail, Caelan had in fact never left Britain. He had, however, fought briefly in Scotland and in numerous skirmishes against the Welsh. His real passion, it turned out, was something else entirely.

"Do you not have a horse?" Brayden asked one warm afternoon. They were sitting in the meadow by the abbey, enjoying the midday sun. Insects buzzed about their heads, and the air was fresh and clean. He had often wondered how Caelan had arrived at the abbey across the meadows and through the woods, and he remembered the tracks he had seen in the ground by the abbey the day of the attack on Honeydown.

Caelan was playing with a flower, twirling it in his fingers. He smiled. "I do, and I miss him dearly."

"Where is he now?" Brayden asked.

"I know not. Old Bernard says he carried me here and waited in the churchyard for me while I healed. Bernard claims he saw him walking about the abbey one day, and after that he disappeared entirely." Caelan shrugged. "I suppose he is enjoying his freedom while he can."

Caelan lay back and looked at the sky. It was a clear day, with only a few fluffy clouds drifting silently across the blue.

"Aren't you worried?"

"He can defend himself against any predator still in this wilderness, but one."

Brayden didn't need to ask about the people who lurked in the wood, bandits and otherwise, who would just as soon eat the horse as ride him.

"His name is Sullivan," Caelan continued, smiling and happy to talk about his friend. "I won him at a tournament two years ago, and he has been my loyal companion since. He's big, and pale in color, with a long, thick mane. If you spot him, let me know."

Behind Caelan, Brayden could see Bernard emerging from the abbey's main entrance.

"Ah, gentlemen. Relaxing, I see. Time for pannage, and the pigs are ready. The fee has been paid and the nuts are already dropping, ready to eat. Brayden, if you would, please fetch another bucket of water. I want to start on the stew as soon as I return. Sir Caelan, please enjoy doing whatever it is you do when not defending us from villainy."

Caelan smiled and waved the old man off.

Brayden looked at the knight. He found he had so many questions for his new friend, he didn't know where to begin.

"Tell me," Brayden began, "what is the tournament like?"

Caelan sat up. "It is a magnificent spectacle. The entire kingdom, indeed, many kingdoms, come out to see it. The ladies and gentlemen are dressed in their finery, and pennants flutter from every pole and lance. Food seems to be everywhere, and ale is poured from every cask. And the combat. Brutal, yes, but in no other way can a knight earn more riches and respect than doing well at a tournament. No way, save one."

"Have you ever lost a match?"

Caelan laughed. "You are always so full of questions. Yes, indeed I've lost, and in fact I've lost more times than I've won. But I've made my victories count, be they in jousting or melee. Take Sullivan, for example. The man I challenged had won him from an older, inferior opponent, someone who no longer had any business donning the armor. This man was a prideful fool, though, and I challenged him to one-on-one combat, careful to incite his pride at just the right time. His distraction gave me just enough of an edge, and I defeated him."

"You killed him," Brayden asked, leaning forward completely engrossed.

"No! While some meet their ends through accident, knights are needed to defend the lord, his lands, and this country. Killing is bad form. No, Sir Osbert de Claire is still very much alive, and still very resentful. Sometimes I wish…well, never mind."

"You said there was another way knights can earn riches. How?"

"Have you ever heard of treasure hunting?"

Brayden thought back, trying to remember tales he had heard from Bernard and other men in the village. The fact was he knew little on the subject, and leaned closer, hoping the knight would go on.

Instead, Caelan simply scruffed Brayden's hair. "Then that is a story for a different time. Now, go on and fetch the water Bernard asked for. Get that chore over with before we forget. We'll speak more when you return. I'm going to take the roots we picked earlier into the rectory. I don't suspect Bernard takes kindly to laziness, and I'm not about to corrupt you."

When he wasn't digging, he was fetching water, Brayden thought as he grabbed the bucket and headed for the well. The sky was still light and the trees green, but a cool breeze reminded him that summer was well over and every nice day was precious. The harvest was completed with the threshing of the wheat, and rye and winter wheat would soon be sowed. Assuming the danger was past, Brayden would be called back to help defend the newly planted seeds by fending off birds with a sling and stones. This he did not mind so much, as it passed the time faster than watching the cows and lambs eat all day on the meadows.

Brayden attached the bucket to the rope and dropped it into the well. Moments later, he pulled it up, untied it, and began carrying it to the abbey. The water sloshed and dripped all over his pants and feet as he walked. This happens every time I fetch water, he thought. He put the bucket down to think. Perhaps if he carried it in the front instead of to his side, he'd remain dry. He tried this, only to thoroughly soak the front of his tunic. He shook off the water, exasperated. As he did, he heard a loud snort behind him. Brayden turned, and, not five paces from him was the largest horse he had ever seen.

* * *

Brayden jumped back in surprise. The horse stepped forward confidently, bobbing its gigantic head as it walked. It stopped above the water bucket, paused, and then began to drink from the bucket eagerly. Brayden watched in stunned silence as the horse finished the water.

Brayden stepped closer slowly, and stretched out a hand. The horse seemed to evaluate him cautiously, and then straightened his head. Brayden patted the huge animal on the snout, and it let out another muffled snort in approval.

"Brayden!" Caelan shouted from behind him. "You've found my Sullivan!"

Sullivan broke away from Brayden and quickly trotted over to his master. Caelan reached out and wrapped his arms around the horse's thick neck. "Welcome back, friend," he said repeatedly, stroking Sullivan's mane.

"He must have been wandering about the woods," Brayden suggested, "perhaps afraid of Bernard and me."

"Perhaps, though he doesn't look it now."

The horse backed up, turned, and began walking in the direction of the meadow. At twenty paces he paused and turned his head. Brayden and Caelan stood, dumbfounded.

"Perhaps he wants us to follow him," Brayden said.

"You may well be right," Caelan agreed. "He's done this before, though usually in the direction of food. That's not the case now. He's in the middle of a field full of grass!"

Caelan walked forward and followed Sullivan several more yards before finally catching up with him. Sullivan stopped as Caelan stood beside him. Brayden walked up to them.

"Well, friend, it has been a while for me, but I think I'm up to it now." He turned to Brayden. "Would you care for a ride? Let's see where Sullivan takes us."

Brayden smiled broadly. A ride on a warhorse—he couldn't believe it.

Caelan took his hand and, with a heave, lifted him atop the powerful horse. Sullivan was hot to the touch, and Brayden's legs were stretched wide as they straddled the animal's girth. Atop Sullivan, he felt as if he towered over the meadows and churchyard. Each motion of the horse made him sway, and he pulled tightly on the mane for balance.

Caelan heaved himself up. His arms surrounded Brayden.

"Okay, friend, let's go!" Caelan spurred Sullivan on, and the great horse leapt forward. Brayden jerked back against Caelan's chest, and then steadied himself between Caelan's arms as the horse picked up speed. The knight's grip on the horse's mane was loose; the young knight was really letting Sullivan take them where he wanted them to go.

Sullivan leaned to the right and then to the left as he galloped. Brayden's ears filled with the loud thuds of the horse's hooves hitting the ground and with the animal's deep gasps for air. The green of the meadow rushed past them. Sullivan dove into the forest edge at the end of the long meadow and thundered through the woods, jumping over logs and splashing through gentle streams. He twisted around trees, galloping without fear of imbalance. The fresh forest air filled Brayden's lungs and blew through his hair like a strong wind. It was as if he was living in a dream, and he closed his eyes, imagining how far they might go. It was the most thrilling experience he had ever had.

At length the horse slowed to a trot. Caelan was still letting the horse take them where it wanted. Brayden opened his eyes, entirely unsure of how far they had traveled.

"Sir Caelan?" Brayden asked. "May I ask you a question?"

"Anything you like," Caelan responded, as he ducked to avoid a low hanging branch.

"The other day you mentioned a letter. Who was it from? What did it contain?" Brayden had been anxious to be alone with Caelan to ask him about it. Bernard missed nothing, and he thought he'd have better luck prying the information out of the young knight without the friar around.

"Oh, that. It was something I came upon."

"Something? Was it about my father?"

Caelan looked up at the sky through the trees, and then took a deep breath. "I don't think so, friend. It was about something else. Ah, here we are, it seems."

Brayden couldn't help but notice the relief in Caelan's voice as he changed the subject.

At last Sullivan had come to a stop in a rocky area. A high hill of stone climbed at least twenty feet before them, making it impossible to see what was on the other side. Sullivan stood at the base of the hill, repeatedly lifting his head as if signaling.

"I suppose this is the end," Caelan said. He dismounted first, and then helped Brayden down.

Brayden momentarily forgot about the letter. "Is it always like that?" he asked, thinking of the ride and looking up at the horse with awe.

"Not always, sometimes I get to steer. Come, I get the feeling whatever Sullivan wants us to see is over that rocky hilltop."

They began to climb. Brayden noted that both of them were in their bare feet, making the climb slow and hard. Brayden watched Caelan as he climbed, realizing for the first time that the knight did not have his sword.

They reached the top and stared down. Below them was a small clearing in the woods. A creek ran just north of the clearing, its gentle trickle a constant, pleasant sound. Rocks had been purposely stacked in a rough semicircle in the middle of the clearing, surrounding a small mound of logs. It looked, Brayden thought, like a camp.

Brayden was a bit surprised that he had never encountered this area before. Then again, he admitted, he had never ridden a horse before and had lost track of how far from the abbey they actually were.

They waited for a time and were about to leave when suddenly they heard voices. Brayden ducked down, and while he couldn't see any people, he could hear movement below. On the very edge of the clearing were two horses tied to a tree. Even from where he lay he could see they were much shorter and thinner than Sullivan.

He began to point, but Caelan motioned him to stay still. The knight turned his head in the direction of the voices. Two of the mangiest, meanest-looking men Brayden had ever seen were walking into the clearing.

One was wearing what looked like animal fur all the way down to his knees. A hard metal cap covered his head, and his dark beard ended midway down his chest. At his side he had an axe, at his other, a long dagger. The other man was no more inviting. While his beard was shorter, he wore nothing but rags kept close to his body by a series of leather and rope belts. Attached to these belts were small bags, of what, Brayden could only guess. The second man's only weapon was a short sword. The men's voices became clearer as they approached the center of the clearing.

"As we've sent Sker and his party north to wait for us, we finish our business here first," the man with the long beard said.

"So, we attack without them, Samain?"

"Indeed, fool. While I'd prefer Sker at our side as well, the little man said to do this now, while they drink and feast."

Brayden suspected Samain was the leader of whatever band of thugs these men belonged to.

"What of the Bailiff Handhafte?"

The bailiff? Brayden felt himself go white. He looked at Caelan, who nodded, indicating he had heard it too. Brayden's head was spinning at the realization the bailiff was somehow involved with these men. He stayed absolutely still, trying to hear more.

Samain waved a hand. "The little man said no more waiting on the treacherous bailiff. We take the boy ourselves, and then the rest of the village is ours."

The man in rags chuckled. The two men continued talking, but had turned their heads and Brayden could no longer hear them.

Caelan leaned over to Brayden and whispered, "It was dark, but that man opposite the one called Samain, it is he who stabbed me in the forest on my way here. I'm sure of it." Caelan made a fist and hit a nearby rock. "I have no weapon, or I'd slay them both here and now. Come, there is nothing we can do at the moment. Let's go and tell Bernard."

They snuck back down the rocks and to the forest's edge, where Sullivan was waiting for them.

"The boy," Brayden began, forgetting for now the mention of the bailiff's involvement. "They said they were going to take a boy. Who could that be? What could they want of him?" He looked up at Caelan pleadingly. He thought he might be beginning to understand the truth about what was in the letter, and why the knight was really here.

Caelan winked at him and lifted him atop the horse without answering. He led Sullivan out quietly, looking around in all directions for signs of the men in the clearing. Seeing nothing, he joined Brayden atop Sullivan, and they made for the abbey as fast as they could ride.

Chapter Eleven

Visitors

With Michealmas only two days away, Brayden returned to his home in the village to aid his mother in preparing for the holiday. A grand feast would soon take place, with music and dancing celebrating St. Michael the Archangel, whom the children knew as protector against the darkness and marker of the seasons. The village would also be celebrating a successful harvest. Despite the late rain and the threat of banditry, grain would be plentiful for the winter. Spirits were as high as they had been in months.

Brayden had brought home root vegetables and herbs from the abbey, his favorite being ginger. His mother promised that the ginger goose would be the best they would ever eat. Though happy to be home, his thoughts kept drifting to what he had heard in the forest with Caelan. Someone, somewhere, was after him. He did not know why, but it scared him. Their village was small, and he stayed in almost constant sight of his mother, the reeve, or one of the other villagers. He knew they'd protect him, but he secretly wished Sir Caelan and his broadsword would've returned to the village with him.

Brayden and his mother sat and talked for a long time, enjoying a plate of fresh fruit between them. Brayden knew Bernard had spoken with her of what he and Caelan had discovered in the forest, and up until now they had avoided the topic altogether. That suited him fine, as he was more than happy to talk of the warhorse, Sullivan, and the stories Caelan had told him of the castle, the tournaments, and the young knight's dreams of seeking treasure.

"Has he found any?" his mother asked.

"Treasure? I don't think so, but he won't say for sure. He did promise that when I grow older I can help him look."

Alice smiled. "I'm sure he'd like your help, and that is very kind of him. Remember, though, Brayden," she warned him, "Caelan's business here is his alone. Don't speak of him to others."

Brayden nodded without answering. Bernard and Caelan had also sworn him to secrecy, though he still didn't completely understand why so much was being kept from the other villagers. Brayden had also promised his friends he would avoid the bailiff, though upon his return home he found out that the bailiff had disappeared. Not a soul had heard from him in days.

"Mother, what do you think they are up to?" He could not stop thinking of what the man named Samain had said in the forest.

"The bailiff and the outlaws? I don't know, Brayden."

"Could it have something to do with father?"

Alice bowed her head then rose, and cleared the table. She stood by the hearth for a few moments, her back to him.

"I don't know, Brayden. And we'll not talk of it again."

Brayden watched her, wishing he hadn't asked the question. Wishing he could say or do something to comfort her.

"Why don't you run down to Dunstan's shop?" she finally suggested.

"He's back?"

Alice nodded. "Just returned, for Michaelmas. You've both been away, and haven't seen each other in some time. I suspect you'll lighten his mood like you always do, like you do mine. Stay on the roads and in plain sight at all times. I'll join you down there shortly."

He gave her a hug and stepped outside, looking around for any sign of danger. He took off down the road, but looked back toward their home. His mother was standing at the doorway watching him. He reached Dunstan's shop in minutes. The smith was busy working as he always was, with a steady stream of people coming to and from the shop.

The last time he had seen Dunstan the two had barely spoken. Brayden walked over nervously, not sure what to expect.

"Brayden!" Dunstan yelled. The smith waved him over with a hand covered by a long, thick glove. While Dunstan still wore his dark robes, to Brayden's relief his friend's face was covered in a welcoming smile. Brayden grinned back and entered the shop.

"Oh, I thought you were busy and might not want to be disturbed," Brayden said.

"Nonsense. I'm always happy to see you, and I can always use another hand around the shop."

The shop was smoky and ash-strewn, as usual. Now, though, in addition to bits of metal and various tools scattered about there were two piles of sharp iron rods, each no longer than Brayden's leg, neatly stacked in two corners of the shop.

"What have you been working on?" Brayden asked, looking at one of the piles.

"Oh, those? John Fields asked for them. He didn't say why, but I'm here to serve. How are things?"

"I'm fine," Brayden said. He was curious about the rods but held back from asking any questions. "I missed the village when I was away, and my mother."

Dunstan nodded. "I know what it is like to miss someone very much, boy. But the time away from Honeydown was good for me. Sometimes it is worth getting away for a bit."

Brayden shrugged. He knew his friend was talking about Cecilia. For Brayden, sadness at her loss had been replaced by anger; anger at the men who, in attacking their village to get to him, had also taken her life. His fists formed into balls as he thought of the men Caelan and he had seen in the woods.

"But yes," Dunstan continued, getting Brayden's attention. "Keeping busy is what is best for the soul. I'm the only blacksmith around still willing to travel to the other villages, so I get a lot of business."

"Mother lets me carry my knife now. We don't talk about it, but she doesn't ask." Brayden paused, looking the smith in the eye. "I wanted to thank you. It saved us."

Dunstan shook his head. "Nonsense. You and your mother saved each other. All I gave you was a tool. You had the strength to use it."

Brayden remembered that night and how frightened he was. "That voice, I'll never forget it."

Dunstan patted him on the shoulder. "You're a brave boy."

John Fields came running up to them. "Dunstan, Brayden. Good day to you both. Let me show you something." The reeve reached under his tunic and pulled out a short dagger. He placed it on the dark wood counter. Brayden pushed against the pommel, and the dagger rolled back and forth gently against the wood. The hilt was wrapped in dark brown leather; the blade was straight and clean.

"Where did you get it?" Brayden asked.

"Some of the other boys found it near the barn. They gave it to me and while I've asked around, no one has claimed it as their own. Notice the engraving?"

Brayden looked carefully. Faint etchings of serpents covered the blade. On the pommel, just barely visible, was the letter "T" embossed in a circle.

"Hmm. You can find all sorts of things if you look hard enough," Dunstan suggested. He stepped back into his shop and tended to the fire. As he poked at it, several large pieces of ash flew out of the shop and into the road.

"Have you ever built a suit of armor?" Brayden asked, staring at the dagger as Dunstan walked back over to where he stood.

"What?" Dunstan said, obviously surprised at the question.

"If I commissioned you, could you build me a shirt of mail?"

"I…I don't know. It is not easy, boy. Few know the technique, even fewer can master it. I know it takes a fair amount of time."

Their conversation was interrupted by Bernard, who was approaching slowly as if being careful to avoid the ruts in the road.

"Ah, welcome, old friend," Dunstan called.

"I was lonely at the abbey and thought I'd pay a visit. Dunstan, welcome home. Always good to see you. And Brayden, how did I know I'd find you here? Are you two caught up on all matters metal?" Bernard stepped into the shop and shook John Fields' hand.

"We are indeed," replied the blacksmith. He patted Brayden on the head.

"Ah, something blew out of your shop and onto the road. Here you are."

Brayden watched as Bernard held up several scraps of burned parchment, one of which looked like a map.

"A map of the coast?" Bernard asked, inspecting the fragment before handing it over. Brayden knew Dunstan travelled more than any of the other villagers and was Honeydown's chief source of news outside of the cottars and visiting tradesmen.

Dunstan dipped his head. "I had planned to take Cecilia there before the winter. She had never seen the ocean, near the castle, on the other side of the mountain."

An understanding smile crept across Bernard's face. He put a hand on Dunstan's shoulder, as if to give the man strength.

"Bernard, here," John Fields said. "I was just showing this dagger to Dunstan and Brayden. No one in the village has claimed ownership. There is a single letter carved on the end."

Bernard leaned over and picked up the dagger. He inspected it from every angle and finally put it down. He looked up, and Brayden saw his friend's complexion had changed. Bernard's cheeks suddenly looked hollow and ashen.

"You okay, old friend?" Dunstan inquired. "Are you having a spell?"

Bernard quickly waved his hands in the air. "No, no, I am quite fine. Perhaps the walk has taken a toll on me. Every trip from the abbey seems to get longer."

John Fields grabbed the dagger and tucked it away under his belt. "Bernard, you don't think it was dropped by someone on the night of the attack, do you?"

Dunstan shot Bernard a glance, but Bernard did not return it. He was staring into the distance. The rest of them turned and looked in the same direction, toward the meadows, down the main road leading into the village.

Riders on horseback were emerging from the dark green wall of forest. They were fast approaching Honeydown.

* * *

The bright midday sun illuminated the distant figures. Metal upon metal reflected its rays, casting a glow around the approaching party. Not artisans or craftsmen or merchants. No, Brayden thought, those people would not dare make the journey through the forest to Honeydown in these dark days. A group of villagers had gathered around the shop. Even at this distance those assembled could tell these were warriors.

"Knights, friends. Men-at-arms from the castle," Dunstan said, as if reading everyone's thoughts.

Already villagers were running through the fields and meadows toward the riders. The tight column of horsemen now rode slowly, purposefully, filling the narrow road with colorful flags and elaborate surcoats covering steel hauberks. Brayden counted six riders in front, one of them leading the way. Behind the men on horseback was a wooden cart pulled by two dark horses. As the group rounded a corner, Brayden could see the cart carried two heavy casks. The cart was followed by another column of armed men walking side-by-side, two deep and three long.

Before Bernard could stop him, Brayden said goodbye to Dunstan and the others and ran to join several villagers who were running to the caravan. He was soon close enough to see the surcoats clearly. Against the ragged plainness of the villagers' clothing, they were a sight of stunning color and beauty. The leader's surcoat displayed a fearsome blackbird on a red field. Another rider wore a golden cross across a chest of sable. A third was draped in a tunic of red and black checkerboards. Next came men wearing chevrons in deep azure, another man wearing dancing wild boars across a dark gray field, and finally a man wearing a green clover on silver.

Two of the riders carried their lances high, large shields fastened across their backs, each matching in glorious color the coats of arms on their clothing. The metal on their feet, legs, and arms sparkled as if electrified with lightning. To Brayden, they seemed almost majestic.

He ran across the field and stopped with the other villagers to line up on either side of the road. Everyone seemed to be chattering at once.

"They've come to save us," said one.

"They bring good news," said another. "They must, after all this time."

"Perhaps Lord Marshal himself has returned," called another. "Maybe there is fresh ale in those very casks for the celebration!" cried someone else, jumping excitedly.

Brayden struggled to find room along the road, and joined the others in pushing and jostling for a view.

"Brayden, here!" He heard a familiar voice. It was John Fields, waving him over to where the reeve stood in the center of the road. "Come hither."

Brayden pushed his way past two older villagers and joined John Fields before the caravan. The reeve winked at him and put his hand on Brayden's shoulder. With the other he waved to the approaching men with his tally stick. Bernard joined them moments later, taking a place next to the reeve.

The horsemen were before them now. The soldiers on foot and the cart stopped abruptly behind. In contrast to the knights, the men-at-arms wore ragged, brown leather armor, or none at all. Around their waists were thick belts from which dangled one or more bladed weapons. Some wore simple leather hats or metal caps on their heads. They looked grimy, and all appeared ill tempered from the march. The difference between their clothing and manner and that of the incredible men on horseback was striking.

Like great painted statues, the horses towered over the townspeople. Even the adults seemed to have shrunk into the shadows cast by these noble animals. Each the size of Sullivan, they were draped in cloaks and cloth, in colors and symbols matching that of their riders.

The leader wheeled his horse around, the blackbird clear and almost ominous. His stare was cold, his eyes unfriendly and questioning, as different from Caelan's warm eyes as they could be. He had a long dark mustache, and his beard was short and exquisitely trimmed into a small triangle at the tip of his chin. Like Caelan, his hair came to his shoulders. He examined the villagers, and then stared at John Fields for several moments before speaking.

"I am Sir Osbert de Claire," he began at last, "captain of the lord's guard and servant of our noble steward. I bring you greetings from the steward of Honeydown, Spero, and our lands along the Welsh coast: our gracious Lord Bellator."

Brayden stared in disbelief. Before him was the very same knight Caelan had mentioned, and exactly as Brayden had imagined him to be in appearance and personality. His voice was smooth, but touched with a determined arrogance. In concert with his eyes, the man reminded Brayden less of a dragon and more of a serpent. Sir Osbert looked around once more, his expression blank, as if he was aware of his rank and was utterly disinterested in the humble villagers around him.

"Where is the bailiff, Corbat Handhafte?" Sir Osbert continued, addressing no one in particular.

John Fields stepped forward. "Sir Osbert, welcome to the village of Honeydown." He bowed slightly. "I am John Fields, reeve and servant of Lord Marshal and his steward. The bailiff disappeared just days ago, we know not where. He occupies Hill Manor, up there." John Fields pointed in the direction of the big house.

Sir Osbert looked to where the reeve was pointing and grunted. "Our business is with him, not with this rabble. We bring him wine, food, and gifts, which will be bestowed upon you as he sees fit, or sold instead, as he wishes it." He turned to the other horsemen. "Have the cart brought up to the manor house. We'll wait there and rest for the night." He looked down at the reeve accusingly. "And watch for thieves. These cottars have eager eyes and quick hands." He snorted disapprovingly, and then motioned the horsemen in the direction of the manor house. The knights broke up and trotted forward quickly. Sir Osbert faced the crowd.

"We seek a knight who has gone astray," Sir Osbert said. "He has abandoned his duty at the castle and will be arrested on sight. Have you witnessed his presence? He would be riding a golden brown steed."

John Fields looked at Bernard, who simply shrugged. "We have not," he replied.

"Very well. We will continue our search for him." Sir Osbert looked suspiciously at the large group of villagers that had gathered around. "You lot, if you see a young, fair-haired knight, be warned. He is wanted by the steward, and is a very dangerous, deadly man. Anyone who reports a sighting leading to his capture will be well rewarded!" Sir Osbert turned to John Fields once more. "And reeve, we leave tomorrow, bailiff or no. Though I expect you'll make arrangements for our comfort should we decide to stay any longer," he said smugly.

Brayden wondered how John Fields could stomach the insulting tone. He turned to Bernard, wanting to ask him about Caelan, but Bernard put his index finger to his lips.

"Sir Osbert, we'll be happy to provide you and your men whatever comfort we can," John Fields responded, unfazed by the man's arrogance. "We wonder, my lord, what word have you of Lord Marshal?"

"Word?" Sir Osbert replied. "There is no word. Fear the worst, reeve."

John Fields and several others stood silently, letting the statement sink in. Sir Osbert turned his horse and continued on, slowly passing the villagers, his head carried high, as if he was proud of the uncertainty he had inflicted.

"My lord, can you spare some men?" John Fields asked, catching up to Sir Osbert and nodding at the column of men at arms.

Sir Osbert stopped and looked down, an expression of disbelief on his face. "Men? What on earth for?"

"We've had a fair harvest, but trade has stopped and we fear the forest from the banditry. We'd shelter and pay them. Any hand you can spare to protect our village, we'll take."

Sir Osbert smiled at him, then looked up and nudged his horse on. "Ridiculous. We're here to hunt a deserter and to make a delivery, nothing more, peasant. But, if we are treated properly I'll consider raising it with our fair and just steward upon our return."

"But what about us?" Brayden asked as he walked out from the crowd. Sir Osbert stopped and looked about for the small voice. His arrogant glance finally settled on Brayden. John Fields and the others stood in stunned silence.

"You call us thieves, though we're the ones who've been attacked. We are all in danger here, and need protection, not gifts for the bailiff," Brayden said.

John Fields and Bernard both grabbed him to push him back into the crowd, but Brayden resisted and surged forward again, standing defiantly before Sir Osbert.

"And who is this little whelp?" Sir Osbert hissed.

"I am Brayden Rider."

In an instant, Sir Osbert thrust his horse forward and with his right foot kicked Brayden squarely in the chest. Brayden gasped and fell, landing flat on his back, out of breath. Bernard covered him, shielding him from further blows. Brayden rolled on the ground, clutching his chest in pain.

"This little rat should be taught his manners. No cottar will address the captain of the guard like that again."

With his tally stick held high, the reeve stepped before Sir Osbert, forming a line of defense. "You'll not hit him again without reprisal, knight's captain or no." Bernard stood to face the knight, while two other villagers rushed over, flanking the reeve to either side.

The knight drew his sword at the challenge and aimed the point at the reeve's chest. Brayden watched from the ground, trying to rub the pain from his chest with his hand. Sir Osbert's face was twitching irritably, and Brayden noted the other knights had their hands on the hilts of their swords.

"Stay yourself, reeve," Sir Osbert threatened. His mighty warhorse snorted in agreement, its eyes staring warily at the crowd.

"Sir Osbert!" The knight with the clover on his chest was riding back toward the crowd. His frame was stout, and his surcoat clung to him snuggly. He had a wild thicket of red curly hair flowing in every direction and a long thick beard of the same color. His face was kind, in contrast to that of the other knights present. "Withdraw your sword from this man," he ordered forcefully, his own sword halfway drawn.

Sir Osbert redirected his angry stare at the approaching knight. "Mind your captain, Hugh Morgan, or spend Michaelmas in the presence of the county dregs in the castle dungeon."

"You may have Bellator's favor, Osbert, but you do not have mine," Sir Hugh said, his eyes not leaving Sir Osbert's. "We're not brutes. The penalty for harming these people is severe, and I'm happy to carry out sentence here and now."

Sir Osbert turned back to Brayden and the others. He considered them for a moment, and then leisurely slid his sword into its sheath as if nothing had happened. He smiled mockingly, and then directed his horse away from the boy's defenders to address the crowd. He looked down at John Fields once more.

"We understand the banditry here is severe, but no protection will we provide until that knight is found. As the regent of the steward, I command it."

He turned his horse and faced Sir Hugh.

"And as you seem so brave, it would appear Honeydown won't need *our* protection, now or ever. Enjoy your time with the lowliest, Hugh," Sir Osbert called over his shoulder as his horse trotted toward the manor home. "See to it you resist their bad habits and poor tastes. We depart this wretched manor village tomorrow, bailiff or no."

He waved in the direction of Hill's manor house. The remaining horsemen and men-at-arms took the cue and followed him up along the path.

The red-haired knight rode up to where Brayden was lying and dismounted. With a grunt, he waved off the protective stare of John Fields and knelt next to the boy.

"It always amazes me that a squire can somehow fit a swine into that fine suit of armor," he said, shaking his large head in the direction of Sir Osbert. The big knight's voice was strong, but calm and kind. "Here, lad, let me help you up." He placed a large hand under Brayden's arm. "Bad form to be introduced while one is lying in the muck."

"I am Brayden Rider of Honeydown," Brayden mumbled. It hurt to talk.

Sir Hugh leaned back, his hands on his hips. "Brayden Rider, is it? Any relation to Sir Ban of the same?"

"There is," Brayden blurted excitedly, without thinking. "He is my father. You know of him?" Brayden coughed. His chest was sore, and every breath seemed to hurt.

"I know of him, but only through the words of others. A fine man I understand him to be, but alas, I have no news for you good or bad." Brayden's excitement died immediately. "But," the knight continued, putting his hand on the boy's shoulder, "from what I've seen here today, you have your father's brave heart."

He turned to face John Fields, Bernard, and the others. "My name is Hugh," he said loudly, as if to ensure everyone could hear him. "Sir

Hugh Morgan of Fairborn." He looked in the direction of the forest. "Ah, here comes the rest of our party now."

Another cart was slowly making its way up the rutted road. As it approached, John Fields spoke briefly to Sir Hugh of the village's successful harvest, and they exchanged the usual concerns about the winter to come and further attacks on the villages. Hugh promised to address their concerns when he returned to the castle. Brayden tuned them out, and instead looked with interest at the approaching cart. It was flanked by a single rider wearing plain clothes. The horse was much smaller and thinner than those of the knights, and the rider wore a hood over his head. Behind the cart marched several more men-at-arms. The cart approached the group and stopped. Sir Hugh turned to the new arrivals.

Sir Hugh laughed loudly, his belly jiggling. "And now you finally show up, after missing all the fun. Say hello, Siegfried!"

A tall, wiry youth jumped off the horse and removed his hood. Long blond hair flowed out, and Siegfried bowed to Sir Hugh. He looked directly at Brayden, and his eyes widened immediately.

"Brayden!" he shouted. Before he could react, Brayden was lifted off the ground in a strong embrace. The pain in his chest made him wince as long hair tickled his nostrils. It was Siegfried indeed.

* * *

Siegfried had changed in the time since Brayden had last seen him. Always taller, the older boy now seemed to tower over him.

"When I heard they were delivering wine and gift rations to Honeydown, I asked permission of Sir Bellator to come. I'd not seen you in a year, and I doubt I'll see you again after this for many more." His voice was deep and strong, and his body muscular. His manner was confident, almost cocky. In the mid-afternoon sun, Siegfried seemed to cast a long shadow wherever he stood. He was a squire now, a boy no longer.

Brayden was still rubbing his chest, although the ache was slowly easing. Siegfried took note.

"Are you righted? I could see it from the edge of the wood. That Sir Osbert is such a folly maker. You should see him at the castle with the squires; you don't dare look at him. It's enough to make a man give up on knighthood and make his life on the farm. Still, best to address a man of his stature properly."

"Stature is not what it once was around here," Sir Hugh said. He faced John Fields. "We're off to deliver these casks, however undeserved, to this Handhafte fellow. However, if he's gone missing I doubt very much he would miss just one." He winked at Brayden, who smiled in return. Siegfried glanced at Sir Hugh, a slight look of disapproval on his face, but he apparently knew better than to disagree. Sir Hugh nodded to the men-at-arms, who proceeded to unload one of the casks. Several of the villagers stepped up to help.

"Thank you, Sir Hugh," John Fields said. "It will be good for the souls of these hardworking folk. Still, we need protection in Honeydown, not spirits."

"I'll do what I can for you, sir. Enjoy Michaelmas. We depart tomorrow," Sir Hugh said, looking directly at Siegfried who nodded quickly in acknowledgement. Sir Hugh put his big hands on Brayden's shoulders and looked down at him with eyes full of strength and understanding.

"Brayden Rider of Honeydown, until we meet again, au revoir."

He gave a short salute, mounted his horse, and rode off in the direction of the manor house. The men-at-arms and the cart followed slowly behind. The villagers began to disperse, several laughing as they rolled the cask in front of them toward the barn. John Fields patted Brayden on the shoulder as they started back to the village.

"Welcome back, Siegfried," Bernard said, coming forward and embracing the youth. "We have often spoken your name and thought of your adventures in the castle."

Siegfried smiled, shaking his head. "The adventures of a page and a squire are difficult and grueling. Sometimes I miss the simple life of the village."

Brayden considered how different their lives were. Siegfried had come with him, Bernard, and his mother from France those years ago, but had almost immediately moved into the castle as a page, as Brayden's aunt would have wished it. Brayden had stayed here in the village, learning lessons in between seasonal chores, chores that were the difference between a meager survival and starvation.

"Well, we are delighted to have you here again, even for so short a visit," Bernard said. "I'll insist you join us for supper later. Your aunt Alice would greatly enjoy seeing you once more."

* * *

Bernard pushed aside his bowl and grinned at the boys. "Alice, thank you as always for your hospitality. The sweet custard was especially delightful."

"It was indeed, Aunt Alice. Thank you for having me," Siegfried echoed.

"You're always welcome here, Siegfried," Alice said, blushing. She was not used to flattery, though Brayden suspected she secretly appreciated it. She stood up and began clearing the table. "So, we have you only until tomorrow?" she asked. "It is a shame. Where do you head to next?"

"I suspect we'll keep on tracking that errant knight, and I hope we do. No one should ever abandon their station. I only know him in passing, but they say Sir Caelan is sneaky as a fox. He fancies himself a regular treasure hunter, or so he brags, and will say and do whatever he has to find his mark."

Alice and Bernard exchanged glances. Brayden stiffened, ready to argue the point. Siegfried's words angered him. He had gotten to know Sir Caelan well over the intervening days, and even trusted him. What Siegfried said did not seem like the truth of it, but his cousin was a squire himself, and his own flesh and blood. Bernard sat forward quickly and cut Brayden off before he could speak.

"Uh, we'll be sure to report any errant knights, young squire. Won't we, Brayden?" He looked intently at Brayden, who was struggling to keep silent.

"Ah, right. Right we will," Brayden agreed awkwardly.

"Good, then thanks. We can't track outlaws alone, you know," Siegfried lectured. "The commoners must help. Besides, I'd very much like to make an impression on Sir Bellator by showing him my first quarry."

"I'm sure," Bernard said, raising his eyebrows and sitting back, his arms crossed. This was as close a signal as he would make to indicate his displeasure at where the conversation was going.

"I must say it is getting late," Bernard finally said, a hint of impatience in his voice. "Circumstances in Honeydown dictate I must make it back to the abbey before dark." He stood and whispered something to Alice, who was rinsing the plates with water from a bucket. He then turned to face the boys.

"Brayden, I'm sure Siegfried's party is wondering where he is. Why not escort him part of the way to Hill's manor home? I'm sure you'd both like to chat a bit more."

"Sure. And don't worry, Aunt Alice, I'll have him sent back well before his beddytime," Siegfried said half mockingly. Brayden just rolled his eyes at the older boy's barbs.

"Well, thank you for seeing to us," Alice said. She approached Siegfried and hugged him. "Your mother would be proud of you," she said softly, kissing him on the cheek.

"Indeed," Bernard said, putting a hand on his shoulder. "Mind your studies, but keep your eyes and ears open. Take good care now."

Bernard smiled at the boys, grabbed his staff, and headed out the door.

* * *

The boys walked up the main street and followed the road into the meadows. It was dusk now, the countryside darkening quickly and the shadows merging into one. A full, orange moon was rising overhead. Even from a distance, Brayden could see light and movement coming from the windows of Hill's manor home. They walked in silence, comfortable with not speaking for a while.

"So do you like living here?" Siegfried asked, looking back at the village at the base of the hill.

"My mother is here," Brayden responded quickly, taken off guard at the question. "And Bernard."

"You're not answering the question. It is not France, that is for sure. You don't live here like you would have there. Look at me. If not for my mother's request, I might well have been here with you too."

"I would have liked that," Brayden said, and he meant it, though Siegfried had changed. Gone was the boy he had known. He had a more arrogant air than Brayden remembered. Siegfried was obviously aware of his station in life and the potential he had as a squire and a knight.

"Thanks, but I'd yearn for the castle and a life there, no matter. Ever since I was younger than you I wanted to be a knight. I wanted to wear that armor and fight for my lord and lady. And very soon, under Sir Bellator, I'll have that chance."

Brayden cringed silently at the name of the steward, recalling some of the stories Caelan had told him. He wondered how Siegfried had become so attached to the man.

"One day I'd love to have that chance too," Brayden finally admitted. Siegfried slowed to a stop and looked at him.

"It is a hard life, harder than you may think, I wager. Sir Hugh mostly manages the pages, but Sir Osbert the squires, and he is not exactly kind-hearted, as you may have noticed." Siegfried glanced at Brayden's chest, and then started walking again. "Have you heard from your father?" he asked.

Brayden shook his head. "No, nothing. I know he's alive. I miss him, and I know my mother misses him terribly. She always seems sad to me now."

Siegfried stopped again, more abruptly this time. He faced Brayden a second time.

"Then farm boy or not, you staying here is the right choice to make. Not everyone is a knight, Brayden. We all have our place in the world. Taking care of her is yours."

Hill's manor home was very close now. They stopped at the rough stone wall that surrounded the property. In his ongoing desire to avoid the bailiff, Brayden had never been this close to it before. Grasses and weeds covered the property, and ivy the building. It looked ill kept, as if the bailiff cared not for its upkeep. The bailiff. How Brayden longed to speak to Siegfried about Sir Caelan, the men in the woods, and the attack on the village. But, he remained silent to protect his friend, watching the manor home. Light beamed out through the windows, and Brayden could hear laughter inside. Whatever was happening in there, it sounded like the visitors had made themselves right at home.

"Come in for a bit," Siegfried suggested. "I'm sure Sir Osbert is drunk with wine or ale already. He cannot hold it and will be asleep in no time."

Brayden looked down at the ground and considered the offer. He thought of being near Sir Osbert in the bailiff's home and how unwelcome he'd feel. He thought about his place in the world and where his father might be. He thought of Bernard walking home in the dark and of Caelan's ruined armor hanging on the scarecrow. But most of all he thought of his mother, she alone in their cottage and the rest of the village sleeping in fear, while these warriors stayed comfortably in the home of the corrupt bailiff.

"No, I don't think I should. I know my place tonight."

"Very well then," Siegfried said. "We'll be gone early in the morning, tracking that knight. I don't know when I'll be back again, but I hope it is not too long until we see each other." Siegfried patted Brayden's arm, then jumped the stone wall and ran toward the manor. "And I want you at my first tourney! No matter what chores you may be up to!" he shouted.

Siegfried opened the door, and for a moment the yard was illuminated. There was a moment of silence, then the laughter resumed, even louder than before. The door shut, and Brayden turned and walked back down the hill toward his home.

Chapter Twelve

Day of the Archangel

As was the custom on Michaelmas, many of the villagers had slept in, and those few who awoke early were cooking or preparing for Mass, the races, and the games. The village finally came alive mid-morning, the children eagerly waking the remaining adults who slept on.

The village had few horses, but those it did were raced at noontime, the villagers sharing one another's' animals for the day. While the horses were being fed, Brayden joined the other children playing hide and seek and tag. Meantime, the older children and some of the adults raced on stilts. Brayden paused to watch, laughing at their clumsiness, and convinced himself that next year he'd be ready to try.

Mass was held at the abbey, and the entire village joined in. The abbey was clean and comfortable, and sun filled the nave as the members of the village worshipped. Brayden was worried that Caelan or Sullivan would be discovered, and after services he looked carefully for any sign of them, but found nothing. Even the small room where Caelan had stayed was cleared out, as if he had never been there. Brayden's heart sank a bit, and he wondered where his new friend had gone. Despite the day of celebration, his mind kept going back to what he and Caelan had heard in the woods, about an attack while the village feasted. He didn't understand why there had to be so much secrecy. Better to have the truth out in the open so all the villagers knew. Returning to the village, he looked across the fields and toward the forest. Surely Caelan would not leave today, Brayden thought, not when he may be needed most.

As dinner approached, tables were set up in a semi-circle at the edge of the village overlooking the meadow. Each table was covered with food, and candles were lit as dusk approached. Even though it seemed they had been eating all day, Brayden's mouth watered as he looked over the platters of goose, plates of fruit, and stacks of blackberry pie. His favorite though was the bannock. The eldest daughters of the village had outdone themselves this year, he thought. The flat-bread pies had come out unbroken and moist. This was a good thing, as Bernard had reminded him, for getting the mixture wrong foretold bad luck in the upcoming year.

Brayden took his place between his mother and Bernard. John Fields and Dunstan sat opposite them. From where they sat, Brayden and the others could see the fields and the dark green of the forest. Daisies had sprouted everywhere, the pink, white, and purple flowers creating a beautiful mix of color across the lush green meadows. The sun was already low in the sky, and the air cool and crisp. He found it hard to believe, but in a few short weeks everything would be brown and gray, and many people would be confined to their homes for the long winter ahead. Never mind that now, he thought. For now, at this moment and despite everything, he felt happy, and safe.

Bernard stood, and the villagers bowed their heads for the blessing. The feast began immediately after. Brayden was careful to try everything at least once, so as not to insult anyone, as his mother had warned. Much talk focused on the success of the harvest and what had gone well. He could overhear some people discussing the visiting knights from the castle, and some debating over where they were now. One thing was certain, the bailiff had not returned. The old manor house, so busy with the visiting knights and men-at-arms just days before, now lay abandoned. No one, of course, from what Brayden could overhear, missed Corbat's presence.

After some time, Bernard leaned over to John Fields, who was busy finishing a goose leg. "John, you are the leader of this village. I believe a speech is in order," Bernard said, sitting down as John Fields stood up and put his food down on the table. All eyes focused on the reeve. Brayden and the others listened quietly.

"It was nice to see you all at Mass again in the abbey this morning. First, thank you, Bernard, for your tireless work on our beautiful church." John Fields lay a hand on Bernard's shoulder. The Holy man beamed.

"We celebrate another harvest with the end of one quarter year and the beginning of another. Despite much hardship, our harvest is strong this Michaelmas. While shorter, colder, darker days are ahead of us, I believe we've shouldered the darkest times together, and we celebrate the Feast of Saint Michael with prayers he will continue to look after us and protect our village."

John Fields stopped speaking. He seemed to have noticed that the villagers' attention was no longer on him or his words. He turned to look across the fields and at the tree line. There, against the knotted wych elm and the sessile oak trees was a line of armed men. At that moment, everything was silent. Time had stopped.

* * *

With a shattering, terrifying cry the line of men ran forward across the fields toward the village. The people of Honeydown stared in disbelief, unable to move, as they realized the men would be upon them in minutes. Brayden, too, could only watch as the screaming men came closer every second. It was just as Samain had promised that day in the forest, a surprise attack during the feast of Saint Michael. Brayden felt his world quickly closing.

"You know your places!" John Fields shouted. Brayden looked over in surprise. The reeve was holding his familiar tally stick aloft, waving it wildly in all directions.

Movement erupted around him all at once as the villagers shook themselves free of shock and scrambled to their places. Tables were quickly overturned onto their sides as food, drink, and plates fell and scattered on the ground. In seconds the people of Honeydown had formed an oblong barricade and collected themselves inside. Under the tables were piles of rough metal rods, each two inches in diameter—the same rods that the men had been taking from Dunstan's shop. The men and women of the village descended upon them. The armed men now crouched low against the tables, while the women gathered the children into the center of the barricade. Alice pulled Brayden close, a rough metal rod in her right hand.

"Stay by me, son. And keep your knife handy."

Brayden instinctively reached for his weapon. He held it close to his chest. It was the same dark red color as the rods Dunstan had been casting for the villagers. He stroked its cool metal in his hands, but it did nothing to quell the fear that gripped him. He was shaking. He realized now that Bernard and John Fields had prepared the villagers for this attack based on what he and Caelan had heard in the forest, but how well the villagers could protect themselves he did not know.

The roar was getting louder as the bandit army quickly approached. How many were there? He tried to look past the villagers and over the tables. The marauders were just cresting a hill, and he could see them clearly now. They were a mass of ragged clothes and animal furs, rough metal caps and swinging arms. While they were not trained warriors, and many of them held nothing more than wooden clubs or crude maces, they were a terrifying rabble nonetheless.

Many of the children were crying, and some of the men had fled, running away from the barricade to hide in their homes. Bernard turned and looked at Brayden, winked at him, and lifted his hand, motioning Brayden to stay put. In a sea of screams and panic, the bandits were upon them.

They crashed into the tables and attempted to climb over them. The men of the village struck back wildly, stabbing and swinging their metal rods at everything that moved. They repelled the first wave just as the second line of attackers pushed forward. To their left, a table had been lifted out of the way and the bandits were pushing past the remaining men trying to get to the women and children. Cecilia's sisters, as spirited as their deceased sister, broke off from the rest of the women, striking at the attackers and helping the village men hold the line. Bernard rushed to their aid, swinging his staff at anything that tried to get past. John Fields was near the center of the action, directing his forces to hold steady, but it was no use. One by one the men of the village fell or ran. The bandits were not as great in number as the villagers, but their weapons were too much for the defenders. Brayden watched as the defenders melted away, some running for their lives, others trying to reform the line toward the center of the barricade, toward Brayden and his mother.

Brayden looked at the meadow beyond the fighting, closed his eyes and prayed that his mother and he would somehow be saved. People were screaming all around him, and he covered his ears with his hands to block the sounds. He opened his eyes slowly, and saw something moving against the trees. It was gold and white and seemed to ride on the air. Focusing, he could see it was a man on horseback charging rapidly toward the rear of the bandit line. In seconds the man was upon them. The archangel had arrived.

* * *

Sir Caelan and Sullivan seemed to be everywhere at once. Caelan swung his sword wildly at the attackers, while Sullivan bounded back and forth, kicking and throwing his great weight against them. The bandit army scattered in every direction as they tried to escape the unexpected knight. Caelan shouted as he swung. Brayden couldn't make out the words, but he found the almost inhuman sounds coming from his friend terrifying. I would not want to be his opponent on this day, Brayden thought.

Suddenly Brayden saw the ragged man with the leather belts, the same man they had spotted in the woods near the abbey, the same man who had stabbed Caelan on his way to Honeydown. The man had his short sword drawn and was charging at them, a grotesque grin on his face.

"Brayden, behind me!" his mother screamed. Brayden could feel his legs go limp. He was frozen, watching the man approach them.

There was a thud of hooves as Caelan pulled Sullivan in front of the ragged man. Caelan jumped off the horse and with a single parry, he disarmed the ragged man, whose short sword flew away. People were jostling back and forth, and Brayden lost sight of the fighting for a moment. When he caught sight of Caelan again, the ragged man was slumping over. Then he fell flat to the ground, unmoving.

Caelan's arrival spurred the villagers on. They pounced, the feelings they had shared over so many months of living in fear turning to anger and retribution against these vile intruders. John Fields and Bernard led them forward, striking at the attackers as they attempted to flee Caelan's sword. It seemed everyone was charging forward at once.

It was over quickly, with the bandits in full retreat. Brayden looked around. Many of the attackers and some of the villagers lay on the ground, a few moving slowly, others not moving at all. The outlaw army was running back across the field to the safety of the woods. Cheers erupted as the realization of victory sank in among the people of Honeydown. Caelan was surrounded by everyone at once, all wanting to hug him or shake his hand. Bernard embraced John Fields, smiles on their faces. As the people of the village lifted the metal rods in celebration, the understanding sank in that their victory was not without cost. In moments yells of victory and the laughter ceased, as they turned to help the fallen villagers.

Brayden looked around at the remains of the battle and the feast they had enjoyed. His eyes went back to the fields. As he scanned the perimeter of the forest, just barely visible against the green stood a man in animal furs wearing a metal cap. The last of his vanquished forces disappearing among the trees, Samain turned and slunk into the forest, defeated.

Chapter Thirteen

Goodbyes

The wounded villagers were moved to the barn where they could be cared for together. Brayden helped by fetching clean water, dressings, and blankets. Old Robert helped too, happily serving the warm herbal remedies Bernard had prescribed.

Over the next several days John Fields and Caelan organized regular lookouts at the village perimeter to monitor the tree line for another attack. Days passed, however, and Samain's bandit army never came back.

Caelan remained in Honeydown every day now, meeting with the residents and providing advice on how best to defend the village against future attack. There was general agreement that a wooden fence surrounding Honeydown would be the best solution, though how and where it would be built remained a topic of debate. Word of the attack had been passed among the nearby villages, as had the story of the knight of Honeydown and his powerful warhorse.

Over the next few days Brayden learned that Bernard had revealed Samain's plans to John Fields, but had purposely neglected to mention Caelan's presence to anyone. Surprise had been complete. And while the metal rods Dunstan had fashioned for the villagers had helped, without

Caelan and his sword they would not have been able to repel the attack. Brayden watched the road every day, looking for Sir Osbert and his knights. It seemed to him only a matter of time until they learned of Caelan's whereabouts and came looking for him.

A week had passed since the attack, and Brayden watched happily as Caelan practiced swordplay with several of the village men. He would parry and thrust, then withdraw, giving the men a chance to copy him. He is *so* fast, Brayden thought to himself, wondering if he would ever be that quick with a weapon, or anything else.

"Ho there!" one of the lookouts shouted, waving from his vantage point at the northern corner of the village. Caelan, Bernard, and John Fields rushed over. "Look yonder. A single man comes to us on horseback."

Indeed, in the distance a lone rider was approaching. Brayden ran over to join the men, and instantly recognized the wearer of the bright green tunic and orange pants. The bailiff. He came into the center of town and dismounted among the gathering residents.

Corbat looked the assembled villagers up and down, as if sizing them up. He scowled, his face horrid as always, but his clothes still neat and clean. His gaze stopped at Caelan.

"S-s-o, you are Sir Caelan de S-s-pero, I assume. I take it you wish to reside here now." He walked around Caelan as he spoke, inspecting him. Caelan stood silently, eyes forward, his sword sheathed.

"We've no n-n-need of an errant knight here in Honeydown. I expect you t-t-to accompany me to the authorities in short order."

"He'll do no such thing, Corbat," John Fields said, stepping forward. "He saved the village. You owe him your gratitude, as we all do."

Corbat met him head on, his face inches from the reeve's.

"Bah!" he spat. "He is a c-criminal and w-wanted by the law. He will b-b-be turned in and fetch a fair b-bounty."

"A fair bounty you no doubt will keep for yourself," Bernard suggested.

"S-s-silence your preaching, old friar. Even a holy man c-can be r-replaced."

"As can a bailiff," Caelan said. The bailiff spun to face the knight. "You're a d-drifter, and by my authority y-y-you will be taken into c-custody."

Corbat motioned to two of the village men. They looked at each other and then walked slowly, reluctantly, to either side of Caelan.

"But it is you who helped the bandits!" Brayden shouted, thinking of the attack and what Samain had said in the woods.

The bailiff turned again, his ugly scowl now transformed into a face filled with rage.

"We heard them," Brayden continued. He just could not contain it anymore. "We heard Samain and the bandits talking of you. Of you, working with someone they called the 'little man.' The little man who attacked our home."

Corbat dove at him, enraged. Bernard pushed Brayden behind him as John Fields grabbed Corbat and threw him to the ground. The bailiff reached for a dagger at his side, and then hesitated, seeing Caelan's hand on the hilt of his sword.

"Is this true?" one of the men next to Caelan asked.

"Indeed, it is true," Caelan responded. "Brayden and I came across the bandit leader Samain and the man who attacked me weeks ago. They spoke of the bailiff Corbat and the attack on Michaelmas." He paused. "That is how we knew they were coming."

"The word of a knight outweighs the word of a commoner. Even a bailiff," Bernard said.

"You f-fools. You think f-fighting a ragged band of outlaws means you can now dictate terms to m-me? You do not understand w-what forces are at p-p-play. Lord Marshal himself…"

"Lord Marshal is not here," Bernard responded quickly. "And if he were, rest assured you'd no longer be bailiff of Honeydown. How much did they pay you to sell out your own manor village? Who are you in league with?"

"Bah!" the bailiff roared.

"Get out of our village," John Fields demanded. "We're settled on debts now. The harvest is in. Get out and do not come back."

Corbat Handhafte stood and brushed the dirt off his clothing, then mounted his horse, and spoke one last time.

"Mark me, f-fools. This is not the last you've heard from m-me. Honeydown's w-will shall be b-broken. Great things are at play." A nasty smile broke across his mouth, and he eyed Brayden, who turned his head away from the evil man.

Bernard ran up and swatted the rear of the bailiff's horse with his staff. The horse whinnied loudly and Corbat almost fell off as his mount jerked and took off quickly in the direction they had come from. The assembled townspeople chuckled amongst themselves hearing the bailiff urge the horse to slow down as it rambled down the hill to the road.

* * *

The next day Brayden sat outside the barn where Sullivan was feeding while Caelan brushed debris from the horse's long mane. The horse ate constantly, Brayden noticed. It seemed to always have its snout in a bucket, near the grass, or in a bush. Sullivan lifted his head and swayed. Caelan whistled to Old Robert, who was sitting nearby. The old man ran over and took the empty bucket from the horse, returning moments later with it filled once more. Sullivan began to eat again.

"He's stocking up, that one," Old Robert said. "He'll be ready for whatever journey you set out on."

Brayden shot a glance at Caelan. The knight smiled at him and quickly looked away, as if trying to stay focused on his horse. Bernard had left hours before, saying he was going to fetch some things from the abbey. Brayden's mother had instructed him to stay at the barn and wait for her while she met with John Fields. She hadn't returned. He felt as if something was about to happen, though as usual no one was talking to him about it.

Caelan looked over at him, as if reading his mind. "Come on, help me groom this horse."

Brayden walked over and took the brush from Caelan, who grabbed a stool and hoisted the boy onto it. Sullivan snorted approvingly.

"Are you leaving?" he asked without looking at Caelan.

Caelan bowed his head. "I cannot stay here, Brayden. Sir Osbert and the others will be back looking for me. We don't want them around Honeydown. They are not a particularly nice bunch." He paused, placing his hand on Brayden's to slow down the boy's strokes. "I cannot hide here," he continued.

"You can stay and protect us, like you said you would," Brayden erupted, trying to fight back his own emotion.

"Brayden, we gave those bandits a good walloping. They'll think twice before coming back here. And besides, John Fields has the people ready now. I must go back. My place is at the castle."

"Exactly!" shouted a familiar voice. It was Bernard. "And where else will we get to the bottom of these mysteries?" Bernard had a thin brown horse in tow, saddled and loaded with several thick leather sacks. It was packed for a journey.

Brayden dropped the brush, jumped off the stool, and ran to the friar, hugging him hard.

"Caelan's leaving," Brayden said, looking up and holding back tears.

"I know, Brayden. We both are. And so are you."

Before he could respond his mother rounded the side of the barn. Brayden ran over and embraced her. His mind was spinning.

"Mother, what is happening? Where are we going?"

She knelt, her eyes even with his. She spoke softly. "They go to Castle Strand, and I want you to go with them." He was stunned, and had to force himself to concentrate on what she was saying. "The three of us have spoken on this at length. You'll be safer with them at the castle, away from here, and under Sir Caelan's protection. And they'll—you'll—find out who is behind the attacks on our home. Perhaps even fetch some help."

His eyes welled with tears. The castle. He was at once embarrassed, saddened, and excited. He had not left Honeydown since their arrival here. He looked at his mother. She was steady, unwavering. Her decision was final.

"You can come too," he responded, almost sobbing, the thought of being away from her overshadowed everything else.

"I'll join you one day. But first you go. I'll stay behind and protect the village for us. You'll finally see the castle. Ask many questions. Find out what you can, and come back for me." She kissed his forehead. "Be brave, my son," she whispered.

She pulled him tight to her and hugged him firmly. Then she took his hand in hers and walked over to Bernard, who took his other hand. She let go and stepped back.

"Please listen to Bernard and mind your studies. They don't stop when you leave here." She turned to Sir Caelan. "Protect my son, sir knight."

He bowed. "I will, my lady. I will."

Brayden looked at his mother, wiping away tears. He looked up at Bernard and then at Sir Caelan. He would never forget this moment, he thought. Never.

Chapter Fourteen

Lady Josslyn

Castle Strand lay due north, or so Bernard and Caelan both suggested. Caelan later confided that while the direction they were travelling was correct, he could not make an accurate guess at the distance or how long it would take them to get there. Bernard himself had journeyed to the castle on only the rarest occasions since arriving from France, and he admitted his last journey back to the village from the castle was spent in the rear of an ox cart recuperating from an illness.

As much as he respected the men, Brayden thought it comical that neither of them possessed a strong sense of direction. Only two days from Honeydown and they had already been lost three times. He could not get his mind off of what he was leaving behind, and while the men tried to cheer his spirits, no amount of humor, no matter how well intended, would let him forget his mother and the danger she still faced because of him.

Every evening at dusk they would wait while Caelan explored the surrounding area. He would emerge from the forest some time later with a suggested resting place, typically one close to the road but defensible, if it came to that. They had seen few others on the road so far. A band of travelling minstrels had greeted them the first day, followed hours later by two gruff, tired looking men atop a cart filled with wool.

The main road they travelled was curious, not rutted dirt like the ones he was familiar with back in Honeydown. This road was of grayish white cobblestone, and very straight. It had what Bernard explained was a rain gully that ran down the middle of it. Grass and other plants had taken a hold at the edges, but its width would let two carts pass one another without pause.

"Who built this road?" Brayden asked.

"The Romans. A people who conquered these lands long ago," Bernard replied, "and are now long gone. Only some of their constructions, like these roads, remain."

"They must have been talented builders," Brayden suggested.

"Indeed. Their roads and monuments are all over the continent and beyond."

Dusk was approaching again, every day more quickly. Caelan as always careened off the road and disappeared into the brush. Bernard dismounted, leaving Brayden alone atop the palfrey.

"I'm not a young man anymore." Bernard arched his back and stretched. "Riding astride a horse all day makes a man stiff."

"How much longer, Bernard? Truthfully this time."

Bernard shook his head and smiled. "Truthfully, this time, I do not know. I suspect at least four more days at this rate, perhaps longer. Are you worried about bandits?"

Brayden nodded.

"Well, don't worry. We stay on the road all day and find good places to hide at night. They'll keep to themselves. Very likely word of the whipping we gave them on Michaelmas has spread by now among their cowardly ranks."

Brayden smiled. He prayed that was indeed the case. "Bernard, where do they come from?"

"Ah. Many are men for whom there is little hope of survival but by robbery and thievery. Some have perhaps returned from a crusade or a quest with no land and no servitude to a lord. Samain and his men, they found a master." Bernard sighed. "Times across this island are not favorable. Our king, alas, is not strong, and the lords and barons, good or bad, rule. The once illustrious knightly orders—their time is now past." He turned as a rider bounded out of the brush. "Ah, Sir Caelan has returned."

Caelan led them into the woods. In a few minutes they came to a small clearing, surrounded on two sides by a ten-foot-high rock wall. A brook cut across another side, providing a moat, as well as fresh water for the horses.

"The water is fresh," Caelan said, leading Sullivan to the brook. Brayden followed with the palfrey while Bernard began to unload the packs.

After starting the fire, they ate hard bread with butter and fruit. Bernard had been careful to pack ample supplies, not knowing how long it would actually take them to reach the castle or how many detours they'd have to take to avoid danger.

The sky was darkening fast, but Brayden could still hear and feel the forest life teeming all around them. He put the stale bread down. "Why don't we hunt?" he asked.

Bernard and Caelan looked at one another.

"A fine idea, if it were not illegal," Caelan shrugged.

"Illegal?"

"By order of the king. The forests are his domain, and royal licenses are given only to nobles."

"That doesn't seem fair," Brayden protested.

"Fairness has nothing to do with it," Bernard chimed in. "The hunt is turning into a sport, not a necessity. The privilege of a lucky few, despite the abundance the wood could provide."

Caelan stood up and stretched. "I've hunted only once," he said. "A fun adventure to be sure. Hart and wild boar. Bow, arrow, wolfhound, and spear."

Brayden sat up. He was excited by the image of the hunt, the chase, and the camaraderie it represented. He had only heard stories like this from Bernard, and never, except perhaps for his own father, met a true hunter. One aspect of hunting interested him more than any other. "I've heard there is a Grand Falconer in France who is almost equal to the monarch in stature. He has hundreds of falcons. Did you ever hunt with those?"

Caelan clapped his hands and laughed. "No, no, I'm afraid not, my friend. Falconry is a skill I can only dream about." His smile disappeared and grew into a mischievous look. He put his hand to his chin, as if in deep thought.

"Listen, Lord Marshal has a royal hunting license, and I'm still his loyal servant. In fact, all three of us are. How about some fresh meat to fill our bellies instead of this hard, dark bread? What do you say, Bernard? Up for the chase?"

Bernard wasted no time throwing a hard piece of bread at Caelan. The knight ducked, dodging it. He laughed heartily.

"Get out there and hunt for some more firewood, Sir Knight," Bernard said mockingly.

Caelan made a face, and then crouched back down next to Brayden and the fire. They sat silently for a few minutes watching the flames.

"Bernard?" Brayden finally said. There was something he had wanted to ask all day, and now by the fire seemed as good a time as any. "The Orders. You mentioned them earlier. I thought there was only one."

Bernard and Caelan looked at each other.

"You know of one, the Knights of the Temple, as your father *is* one. There are several others, though, each with their own peculiar customs and traditions."

Brayden turned to Caelan. "What about you? To what order do you belong?"

"Order? Me? I'm an independent contractor," Caelan said, laughing with Bernard. Brayden remained serious, not understanding the joke.

"Sir Caelan has been knighted, but not all knights belong to orders," Bernard said, trying to clear the misunderstanding.

"Very well," Brayden said. "Then, after the Knights Templar, what are some of the others?"

"The Knights Hospitaler are perhaps equally famous, and their order was founded around the same time as the Templars. In fact, they fought side by side in the wars to secure the Holy Land. Sometimes enemies, usually friends, and always competitors, if the Templars focus was bringing the Word to the land of the Saracen, the Hospitalers offered pilgrims protection and a place to heal. For this, they were famous and appreciated."

"Where are they now? Are they also being arrested?"

Bernard shook his head. "No, they remain free of the wrath of any petty king. After the fall of Acre they escaped to the island of Cyprus in the Levant. They are now headquartered on Rhodes, if I recall. They prefer a stronghold, and still fight the Saracen pirates, though by sea, not by land."

"There are also the Teutonic Knights, though of them specifically I know little," Caelan offered.

"Quite right. The Teutonic Knights are of German origin only. They wear a long white robe with a large black cross, and are imposing on the battlefield. They too have moved, to the east, I believe, to the Castle Marienburg."

"Those are the main ones, anyway," Caelan said, trying to move the conversation to a different topic. Brayden knew Caelan had grown to like and respect Bernard very much, but his stories, as interesting as they were, often became lectures. Bernard ignored his attempt and continued.

"But wait. There are more," Bernard continued, while raising an index finger. "The Order of Saint Lazarus is another, founded to protect our Christian faith and look out for the welfare of the leper. Where and what they are now I do not know. And, we should not forget the interesting Orders of the Iberian lands, such as Aviz and, of course, Calatrava. These and others fight to spread the Word and expel the Moor from our world."

Caelan rolled his eyes, making Brayden smile. Bernard went on for several more long minutes until, at last, he stopped and took a breath.

Brayden seized the opportunity, anxious to ask a question of the knight. "Sir Caelan, why are you going back to the castle? Won't Sir Osbert arrest you on sight?"

Caelan smiled. "Brayden, you cannot outrun trouble. You have to face it. Besides, someone has to show the steward he can't just ignore Lord Marshal's people."

"Brayden," Bernard interrupted, "Sir Caelan will be just fine. Rest now, my boy. We'll have a day full of more talk tomorrow."

Brayden lay down and looked at the darkness above. Over the crackling fire he thought he heard movement nearby, but as he closed his eyes it drifted away into the night.

* * *

Brayden noticed it first. It took him a few minutes to focus his eyes as he awoke to the bright light of morning, but there it was. In the center of their camp, just next to the smoldering fire, was an arrow stuck in the ground.

Caelan and Bernard had both risen and were staring at it too. Caelan pulled it out of the ground and inspected it. He handed it to Bernard, who scanned it for markings of ownership. Finding nothing, he in turn handed it to Brayden. Brayden turned it over and over. He admitted to himself that he didn't know what he was looking for. The arrow was unremarkable, with a small metal tip and ragged white feathers at the far end of the shaft.

Caelan stood and walked the perimeter of the camp, inspecting the ground for any sign of footprints. "I don't see anything," he said at last from where he stood.

"Based on the angle," Bernard added, "I'd say it was fired from well behind the stream, in your vicinity."

They spread out and searched, but found nothing else. In time, Bernard urged them to disregard the event and move on. It could, in fact, have been an errant shot. An errant shot each of them knew full well could have gravely injured one of them as he slept.

They walked on. Unlike on previous days there was less chatting, each of them silently searching the tree line for any sign of being followed. That night they found a small clearing by a shallow cave. It provided them defense against possible attack, but was cold and damp. As Caelan tended to the horses, Bernard gave Brayden an extra blanket and urged him to sleep as best he could. Brayden rolled to one side and then another, unable to relax at first as he lay on the hard ground. He listened carefully to the sound of the forest, but heard nothing other than the cool autumn wind winding through the trees. He finally fell into a deep sleep, and dreamt of fairies visiting him in the woods.

Morning's light came too early, and Bernard and Brayden awoke to Caelan urging them over to the edge of the clearing. Brayden rubbed his eyes and yawned. He slowly got up and followed Bernard over to where the knight stood. Numerous footprints were in the soft earth by Caelan's feet. Someone, or some ones, had been close to where they slept.

"At first I thought we had been visited by elves," Caelan said. "The prints are small, and I cannot tell how many individuals."

Brayden looked down. Indeed, the footprints were not much larger than his.

"They came right up to where we slept, but took no action," Bernard said. "Brayden, do you remember walking this way? Could these be your prints?"

A shiver when up Brayden's spine and he bit his lip. Bernard already knew the answer.

"I checked the horses and the saddlebags. All were undisturbed," Caelan noted.

"Can we go now?" Brayden asked quietly. He was tired, cold, and now scared. Whoever was out here was daring enough to sneak right up to where they slept. Brayden shuddered. Who knew what they would do next time they stopped for the night.

"We could ride all night," Caelan suggested, "and not stop. I just wish I had not slept."

Bernard considered this last statement for a moment. "It's not your fault, sir. I should have shared watch with you. We all need to sleep. I fear though that the roads have their own dangers at night, and it would seem we have become the hunted." He paused, letting that last statement sink in. He walked in the direction of the horses. "Come. I have an idea that may help us catch our friend. One thing is certain; we won't get to the castle by staying here."

* * *

The road was darkening when they finally came to a small clearing not twenty yards into the wood. Unlike their previous stops, this one was indefensible, flat and exposed. Trees surrounded them several yards away but there was no stream, cave, or rock wall nearby to offer protection. Brayden was uncomfortable here, and his feelings were made worse by having watched Bernard's odd behavior all day. The friar had been muttering to himself, and paused to dart into the woods on several occasions, only to come back with a handful of fragrant plants. Caelan had said little either, and Brayden thought it strange that this warrior put up no argument when Bernard proposed using this open site as their camp for the night.

Bernard instructed Brayden to gather firewood and, upon striking the fire, Bernard pulled out a small metal cup. He filled it to the top with water, dumped the fragrant plants inside, placed the cup on a bed of twigs, and watched the cup and its contents cook in silence.

"What is in it? It smells terrible," Brayden said, wiping his nose.

"An assortment of wormwood, lavender, fennel, and a bit of rosemary, for taste."

Caelan joined them and offered them bread. After several silent minutes spent eating, Bernard pulled the cup from the fire and let it cool. A few minutes later he passed the cup around.

"Drink."

Caelan took the cup and downed several deep gulps. He cringed a bit, as if he disagreed with the taste. He passed the cup back to Bernard, who took a few swallows in turn. Bernard handed the cup to Brayden.

"Drink," he said, motioning toward his mouth with his hands. Brayden did as he was told. The liquid was tepid and earthy. He almost gagged on the contents, but finished his turn and passed the cup back.

"The horses are tied up," Caelan said. "The food in the saddle bags."

"Good," Bernard said. "I suggest we retire. We should be at our destination in less than two days time, and I want us to be plenty refreshed." He stood up and prepared a place by the fire. Caelan followed suit, both of the men quickly getting comfortable and falling fast asleep. Brayden took a quick look around. The shadows were long and danced eerily from their fire. He moved his blanket closer to Bernard, afraid to close his eyes.

But he did sleep, only briefly. He was suddenly wide awake, though it was the middle of the night. He tossed, turned, and turned again. No matter what he thought of, or didn't think of, he could not sleep. Why was he not tired? He rubbed his eyes and tried to get comfortable again. It was cool, but no cooler than last night, and he was closer to the fire. Caelan and Bernard were nearby, each moving occasionally. Neither of them was snoring, so Brayden wondered if they, too, were awake. He remembered the broth Bernard had insisted everyone drink. Perhaps it had upset his eyes.

The horses whinnied quietly nearby. Maybe they were unable to sleep as well. Brayden looked up at them. He froze, his stomach churning suddenly. To his shock before the saddle bag that hung off of Sullivan's side was a small figure wrestling with the bag. The elf had arrived.

* * *

Before Brayden could shout, Caelan was bounding across the clearing. He was upon the small intruder almost instantly, grabbing him and dragging him over to where Bernard and Brayden now stood. Caelan released his grip and roughly threw the person down at their feet. He tossed a bow and quiver of arrows to the ground nearby, then drew a small dagger and knelt down.

"Are you alone?" he asked, waving the weapon in the air menacingly.

"Yes," the intruder answered boyishly. Brayden had a good look at him. He was not much bigger than himself, perhaps just two or three inches taller. He wore a long brown and green tunic with a thick rope tied tight around his waist. His pants were a grayish brown and, like the tunic, tightly worn. While dirty, the clothes looked tailored, almost new. The boots were black leather and, although muddied, in generally fine condition.

He was wearing a hood, and reddish blond hair poked out from within its confines. His face was handsome, almost pretty. Even in the dim light Brayden could make out striking blue eyes and freckles.

Bernard leaned close. "This is a child," he stated, putting his hand on Caelan's shoulder. Caelan looked at Bernard, who nodded slowly, then holstered his weapon.

"I am no child!" the intruder retorted. He straightened up and dusted the leaves off his tunic. "How dare you drag me over here, commoner!"

All three of them were speechless. Whoever this child was, Brayden thought, he was certainly not afraid of them.

"What is your name, boy, and what is your purpose with us, other than common thievery?" Bernard asked calmly.

"My name is Alwyn. I'm a scout for the castle guard and a protector of the lord's forests from hunters. You three are in violation of the king's license, and must depart these lands or face arrest."

"What?" Caelan retorted. "I'm a knight of the…"

Bernard again put his hand on the knight's shoulder. Caelan settled down, taking the hint to let the friar do the talking. Brayden recalled what Bernard had told him of forest law. While enforcement did not uniformly take place, those caught in violation faced a variety of penalties from the royal sheriffs, from fines to execution, based on the size and frequency of the offense. Evidence was often optional in deciding a case. Lord Marshal had historically been forgiving with those caught, preferring to dole out warnings and small fines. Since his disappearance, however, the new steward had driven a much harder line, and there were rumors of far harsher punishments. Of course, he would also be sending out armed men to enforce the law, not children like this one.

"We're in violation of no such thing," Bernard answered calmly. "In fact, we're on our way to the lord's castle now. Our business, however, is none of your affair."

"Nor am I interested in it. Who are you then? And yes, I have been following you for some days. You spoke of hunting some nights ago, which aroused my suspicions, and it is my duty to investigate and to issue warnings." The boy stood up and faced them directly. "And I take it you found mine."

Brayden recalled the arrow from the other night. Since then, and aware of the dangers that lurked in the woods, they had been fearful. Knowing that the cause of this fear was simply a boy pretending to be the forest law authority was at once a relief, and a cause of resentment. Brayden was sure his companions felt the same way.

"I am Bernard, friar of Honeydown. This is Sir Caelan de Spero, our protector. And this young man is Brayden Rider, resident of Honeydown. I take it your search of our saddlebags turned up no evidence?" Brayden could tell Bernard was enjoying the charade.

"Nothing. Nothing, so far. In fact, I am pleased by this, as I can let you off with a warning."

"Hm. Very gracious of you."

The boy nodded and looked them over one last time. If he sensed the tables were turning, he did not show it.

"Indeed. Now, consider yourselves warned. I will take my bow and leave you to your affairs."

"Not so fast," Bernard said. Alwyn stopped cold, his eyes flicking to Caelan's hand on his blade. The friar moved over to the boy, grabbed his hood, and pulled it down. Long strawberry blond locks fell over the intruder's shoulders and back.

Brayden looked at the young person before him, a person not much older than himself. With the hood off and the long hair, it was plain as day. "I think you're a girl!" Brayden blurted, trying to suppress a giggle.

Bernard stepped back. "Indeed. No lord, not even an absent one, would send a young girl to enforce forest law, even one so adept with a bow, as you've proven to be. Now, who are you really?"

"I know not of your business, and I will not tell you any of mine, commoner. This knight knows me. He will explain."

"She is Lady Josslyn Marshal," Caelan said. "Only child of Lord Marshal and his wife, the Lady Elaine. Your hood kept your disguise, my lady, but I recognize you now." Despite his obvious irritation at the girl's behavior, the knight bowed respectfully. Brayden and Bernard stood, thunderstruck.

"Now, why truly are you out here in these woods, my lady?" Bernard asked, still calm despite the revelation. "And, how have you survived all this time out in the woods away from home?"

"I brought supplies, and my father's taught me what can be eaten, and what cannot," Josslyn retorted. "Now, I have said enough." She put her hands on her hips and turned away, obviously flustered by her capture and discovery and determined, at least for the moment, to remain silent.

"Well, you're brave, or foolish, or both," Bernard said. "As we've discovered first hand, there are very real dangers in these forests. You'll accompany us to the castle."

This got Josslyn's attention. "I will not!"

"Indeed you will. You're a very valuable commodity to us, Lady Josslyn, and while our affairs are our own, we'll need as many of those commodities as we can bring."

Lady Josslyn crossed her arms and turned away in disgust. Brayden watched her, anxious to learn more about this noble new member of their party.

Chapter Fifteen

Arrival

The next two days of travel were uneventful, and the nights passed without incident. Lady Josslyn kept to herself, though she let it be known she would ride only with Caelan, the knight being closest to her class, as Bernard had explained her logic to Brayden. She had threatened to escape, but when Bernard described the events at Honeydown on Michealmas, she thought better of it.

They knew they were close to the castle, as the roads were becoming more crowded. Men and women in carts, on horseback, and on foot passed them frequently. Most of the strangers were quite friendly, and the party stopped to speak with many of them. Bernard and Caelan alerted fellow travellers about the bandit activity in the south. The strangers reciprocated with news of the other villages, harvests, and weather predictions. From what Brayden could understand, attacks on other villages and travelers had lessened since Michaelmas. Perhaps what we did at Honeydown that day has saved many other villages, Brayden thought proudly.

Brayden grew more and more excited with every step. A dream of his since arriving in Britain had been to see a castle, to be inside it. Now, he would not only see one, but would possibly *live* in one for a time. The worry of the dangers they had faced seemed to recede at every step, replaced by the excitement of the sights and sounds soon to come.

He glanced at Lady Josslyn, who was sitting impassively on Sullivan's back behind Caelan. She had barely said a word to him the entire trip. Of course, she had barely said a word to Sir Caelan or Bernard either. Oddly, the closer they got to her home, the more withdrawn she became.

As they crested a hill a small group of travelers came into view. One of the travelers was lying still on the ground, as the others milled about, tending to him. They waved to Brayden and his companions to slow down. Caelan and Bernard dismounted and walked over to investigate, leaving the children alone on the horses, Josslyn on Sullivan, Brayden on the palfrey. This had irked Brayden. He had, after all, befriended Sullivan first.

Bernard and Caelan spent several minutes speaking with the peasants. At length Bernard came over to the children.

"One of their party has a stomach ailment that I've seen before. I'm going to prepare a potion that may ease his discomfort. We won't be long." He pulled several small sacks out of a saddlebag and walked back to the others. Brayden and Josslyn sat on the horses, watching silently.

A gentle breeze was blowing, and it lifted Josslyn's long hair as Brayden looked over at her once more, unsure why she interested him so. Josslyn pushed her hair out of her face once, and then twice, using her legs to balance carefully on Sullivan. He stomped the dirt uneasily, protesting her movement while eyeing Brayden, and Brayden took it the horse would prefer him to her.

"I'm ten years," Brayden volunteered after Josslyn has steadied herself.

She rolled her eyes and didn't answer.

"He is a fine horse," Brayden said, watching her annoyance, half amused. "Sir Caelan and I rode him together when I stayed at the abbey." Josslyn looked straight on, as if pretending not to hear. Brayden tried again. "Do you have a horse?"

She ignored him.

"Do you have a horse?" he tried again, louder. For a noble girl she is certainly rude, he thought.

"What? Yes, of course, village boy. My family owns fifty of them," she replied curtly, not bothering to look at him and still struggling to keep the hair out of her face. Sullivan was moving around, again forcing her to concentrate on not falling off. By her tone it was obvious she wanted to end the conversation, but he tried again anyway.

"Well, do you have a favorite?"

Lady Josslyn turned to him, a disgusted look on her face. She held on to the horse with hand, and pulled on her hair with the other.

"First, you'll address me as Lady Josslyn, or 'my lady' or some such title until told otherwise. And for your information, I am twelve—two years your elder. And yes, of course I have a favorite, cottage boy. Her name is Lucy."

Brayden noted this was the most she had said in hours.

"Do you ride often?" he asked, ignoring her demands and the latest insult to his status.

"Only with friends," she replied, turning her head in the direction of Bernard, Caelan and the travelers.

Just then Sullivan reared back, and Josslyn gasped, almost falling over. Brayden reached over quickly and patted Sullivan's mane. The horse eyed Brayden, and settled down immediately, leaving Josslyn sitting atop him in stunned silence. Brayden gripped the palfrey's reins tightly and clenched his teeth. Enough was enough, he thought. The palfrey was a good head shorter than the enormous Sullivan, and his own legs just long enough to give it a kick. He rode forward in the direction of the group of travelers.

"As do I," he called back angrily as he trotted quickly to his friends, who were hovering over the ailing traveler, leaving her all alone.

* * *

"Will the sick traveler heal?" Brayden asked. He now sat atop Sullivan, Sir Caelan behind him on the saddle. As if sensing the tension between the children, Sir Caelan had suggested they switch horses for a short time. Bernard was walking next to the palfrey, guiding her and Josslyn forward up another hill. Bernard said he wanted to walk for a time, to stretch his legs, until they came out of the woods at least. Brayden looked toward Josslyn. When she saw him staring, she turned her eyes away as if pretending not to notice. Caelan patted Brayden gently on the shoulder, as if reminding him to keep his eyes forward.

"Oh, I think he'll recover," Bernard replied. "Not a disease thankfully, but something he ate. Of all the things you can learn, learn to master the art of healing. It will save you, and make you friends wherever you go."

Brayden admitted to himself that he knew nothing whatsoever of the art of healing, despite having watched Bernard come up with potions and remedies on numerous occasions. Bernard had told him that much of his own experience had come from living in the Outremer. This knowledge and its techniques had come not from other Christians, but from their Saracen enemies.

They reached the top of the hill. Below them the forest ended abruptly against a greenish brown meadow that stretched in all directions. The road curved up through the meadow and crested another large hill before them.

"We should be in sight of the castle once we reach that hilltop up ahead," Caelan said.

Brayden could barely sit still as they trudged up the hill, plodding one step at a time. He almost wanted to jump off the horse and run.

At last they reached the top. The meadow continued before them, a thick carpet covering innumerable hills and reaching to the horizon, where immense blue mountains, shrouded in cloud, lay in the distance. The road before them weaved through the hills and shrank to a point on the horizon. At the road's end, high upon an outcrop of rock, was the Castle Strand.

Chapter Sixteen

The Castle

Even from this distance the castle dominated the countryside. White-gray in color, its enormous guard towers jutted out from its rocky walls, casting long shadows against the surrounding fields. The massive keep near the rear center of the castle loomed over the fortress. Multi-colored flags fluttered from every tower, and there seemed to be a constant stream of activity at the foot of its walls.

"Come, let's move on. We'll want to make it well before dusk," Bernard suggested after a time. To his disgruntlement, Brayden took his customary place on the palfrey with Bernard, while Caelan helped Josslyn on to Sullivan. The men urged the animals on.

"I've seen many a castle, both here and abroad, but your father's still takes the breath away, Lady Josslyn," Bernard called back to her.

"It is cold and dark inside without him," she replied sullenly. "You'll see."

The castle grew more imposing with every step they took. The way ahead was getting busier as well, and Brayden could see that a town had sprouted up along the road leading to the castle itself. People and animals walked about in all directions under the shadow of the great structure, trading, selling, and socializing.

"The castle has been in the Marshal family for fifty years," Bernard observed, "given by grant under King Henry III, though I understand it was the site of one fortress or another for many, many years before that, going back to the ancients, like this road. The castle was built up mightily in the last thirty years or so to its current state. Our king's father devoted much time and treasure to building similar castles across this land to deter the Welsh princes from rising again. To his credit, they have not."

They were passing through the castle town. The cottages here were quite different from those in Honeydown. They were substantial, and most had two levels, with a second-floor overhang covering workshops and stores on the first. In these spaces, various merchants chatted about recent events and conducted their trade. Business appeared to be brisk as a steady stream of dwellers and travelers walked to and fro between the buildings.

Brayden looked up. Against the clear blue sky and beyond the town buildings he could clearly see the top of the castle walls themselves. Each wall was lined with battlements, and atop the walls he caught fleeting glimpses of occasional castle guards looking down, the glint of sunlight off a spear tip or helmet indicating their presence. One was staring down at their party now.

"Look," Brayden said, pointing. "I see the guards up there!"

Caelan and Bernard both looked up.

"Hello, up there!" Caelan called. He began to wave excitedly.

The castle guard did not wave back, but instead disappeared behind the battlements once more. Brayden and Bernard shared a smile, while Josslyn turned away, uninterested.

As they rode, Brayden saw leather workers selling shoes, iron workers selling pots and pans, and various carts and shops selling meat, pies, poultry, root vegetables, and fruit. Brayden could smell the food, and his stomach reminded him they had had little to eat other than salted meat and stale bread for days. He thought of his own village, and of how different this was, how plentiful everything seemed.

Brayden looked in vain for anyone he might know from Honeydown amidst the crowd. Squeezed in among the carts and buildings were tents. He turned as a commotion rose from a bright yellow tent nearby. Inside,

Brayden could see half a dozen men gathered around a circle drawn in the dirt. They were shooting dice. Bernard took notice of his interest in the sport.

"Castle grounds are always busy places, populated with activities both good and evil. I hope some of the more honest business will find its way into the surrounding villages. Honeydown certainly could use it."

It was slow moving through the crowd. If anything, the number of people conducting business had grown the closer they got to the castle. Many were chatting leisurely in the middle of the narrow road, despite Bernard's attempts to shoo them out of the way. On more than one occasion townspeople paused and stared at Josslyn. Apparently her face was known to more than just Brayden and his party.

At long last they rounded a tall smokehouse and found themselves at the base of the castle gatehouse. Brayden looked up in amazement. Two imposing multi-story towers stood at either side of the main gate. The thick wooden gate itself was open, and suspended above it hung an imposing metal-banded door. Sharp spikes lined its base. The portcullis, Brayden recalled, remembering Bernard's description of castles once long ago. A long corridor led into the castle itself, and Brayden could see another heavy wooden door open at the far end. He suspected it would be closed as well, if the gate and the portcullis should fail. Small cross-shaped windows were the only openings visible on the towers.

Brayden let his eyes flow up and down the massive stone walls. A breeze blew in, a fresh, clean smell unlike the odor of the town. He turned in its direction and inhaled deeply. The mountains, deep blue in color and white capped, seemed only slightly closer now. Something else in the distance caught his eye. He squinted. It was a hazy gray and seemed to go on forever.

"The sea," Bernard said, as if reading Brayden's thoughts. "The cold sea rests in the distance there. You cannot see it from here, but there are a number of ruined towers and fortresses along that coast, if I remember, Taunton Tower being one of the biggest and most complete."

"Who built them?" Brayden asked.

"The Romans, I suspect. The same people who built the road. Later, other towers were built over their ruins to protect against the Norsemen."

"Norsemen?"

"Another time. Perhaps we'll visit the coast one day. Come." Bernard motioned to Caelan, who steered Sullivan next to them. "Let's announce ourselves."

* * *

They walked slowly through the main entranceway and into the gate tunnel. The sound of the busy street outside disappeared almost immediately. The tunnel itself was unlit, except by daylight, and thick wooden doors lined the walls of the passage. Several guards stood nearby, and Bernard and Caelan nodded in acknowledgement as the guards watched them pass. The men wore an assortment of clothing of varying colors and protection, and none looked particularly friendly. Most had leather vests and metal helmets over roughly tailored tunics. One guard was leaning on a spear while another held his crossbow tightly against his chest. These men-at-arms were not knights, and none were of noble birth, Caelan had explained. Unlike the knights of the castle, whose duty was to Lord Marshal and the king, these men were mercenaries, and their allegiance could be easily turned by coin. As the men analyzed them silently, Brayden thought how happy he was that Sir Caelan was with them.

At last they exited the tunnel and were inside the castle, where they stepped into the outer ward. Brayden gasped at the scale of the building. Massive walls, forty feet high, towered over them on every side, hiding even the distant mountains. Wood gangplanks, ladders, and platforms crisscrossed the interior of the walls, and men-at-arms seemed to be everywhere, making modifications to the various structures or watching the countryside.

The inside of the castle was alive with activity. Merchants had set up shop here as well, selling many of the same goods as those outside. There were men hawking shoes, clothes, food, and weapons and offering games of chance. Various short swords, axes, and maces hung from the walls of several shops. The busiest shop was that of a butcher. The owner was offering small pieces of meat to the passing men-at-arms, trying to get them to buy more.

The floor of the castle was beaten earth and grass. No trees grew, although some of the grounds were cordoned off by brownish hedges. There were numerous small stone buildings built up along the castle walls. Brayden suspected they were armories for the men-at-arms and space for storing food. Armed men milled about everywhere.

The most impressive structure of all was several dozen yards before them. Beyond a smaller gatehouse and interior wall towered the keep. It was a small castle in itself, square in shape with circular watchtowers guarding each corner. Framed windows of glass gleamed from several parts of the structure, and the purple crest of Lord Marshal fluttered atop flagpoles on each tower.

Bernard stopped in front of the gatehouse. "Our test begins, my friends. Stay close, and let's mind our tongues." Bernard dismounted quickly, and Caelan followed suit. They led Brayden and Lady Josslyn on toward the gatehouse that guarded the castle keep.

***

There were no merchant stalls near the keep's gatehouse, and the guards were more numerous. In this part of the castle the guards wore finer clothing, though it was still plain in color and lacked the finery expected of a knight's.

Bernard leaned down and whispered in Brayden's ear. "These men are not knights, Brayden, or mercenaries like so many of the others. They are a class of soldiers in between—the keep guard. Loyal to the Marshals, one hopes."

"Ho there!" shouted one of the keep guards as soon as Bernard and the party were within twenty paces of the inner gatehouse. He was a burly man with a scruffy beard and an enormous belly, and a metal cap bounced precariously on his large, bald head as he walked over to them. Obviously in charge, he was weaponless save for a simple mace attached to a thin leather belt and two of the thickest arms Brayden had ever seem. Three other guards flanked him. Hearing other voices, Brayden looked up. Several other guards, many with crossbows, were watching them closely from the wall above.

"I am Caddaric, captain of the keep guards. What is your business here?" The big man stopped before them, hands on hips, looking at Bernard and Brayden curiously.

Brayden looked back. Caelan and Josslyn had stopped several feet behind them.

Bernard bowed his head slightly. "Captain, we come on an important errand. We travel from Honeydown, where I am friar. Our village has been, as have many other villages of Lord Marshal's barony, the target of attack by the local banditry. We have come to appeal to Lord Marshal for protection."

Bernard was lying, Brayden noted. He knew full well that Lord Marshal had disappeared and was not here. Josslyn shot Bernard a look.

"Alas, friar, Lord Marshal is long gone from his lands." Caddaric bowed his head. "When, or if, he'll return, I know not."

Bernard bowed his head respectfully. "That is indeed sad news. May we have a word then with his honorable steward?"

Caddaric waved his hands. "I am afraid not. The steward has given strict orders. None may pass."

Bernard nodded. "I see. Perhaps you can help us on another matter. During our travels, we came across this young girl."

Bernard pointed behind him as Caelan walked Sullivan forward, displaying Josslyn. The captain's jaws dropped.

"Lady Josslyn Marshal?" Caddaric asked, a look of happy amazement on his face. The assembled guards bowed at the mention of her name. Josslyn sat still, staring forward past the inner gatehouse. She looked pale, Brayden thought, a mix of anger and fear on her face. She was not happy to be home.

"She has been gone many days," the captain said. "We feared the worst."

"So you understand our delight at finding her during our travels. We'd like very much to return her to her mother, Lord Marshal's wife," Bernard suggested. "Will you take us to her? My name is Bernard. I will be familiar to her."

The captain gazed at them for a few moments, as if assessing the situation and unsure of what to do next. He was tough, Brayden suspected, but had a thoughtful, honest face. He did not seem threatening, but instead concerned for the Marshal family's well being.

"Surely you will do us the honor of seeing them reunited?" Bernard suggested.

Caddaric nodded. "Come. Stay dismounted and walk with me. Keep your weapons exposed as well, please. The steward's policy."

They dismounted as instructed, and Bernard and Caelan led the horses as the party followed the captain through the inner gatehouse. It was smaller than the gatehouse they had entered at the front of the castle, but built in much the same fashion. Caddaric's men lined the corridor, and open doors along the interior revealed storerooms lined with weapons. Two massive wooden doors were swung open at either end.

In moments they entered the inner ward. The keep sat at the far side of a large courtyard lined with a number of stone buildings. The inner ward was considerably better manicured than the area outside, with thick green grass carpeting the ground in all directions. Trimmed bushes lined the stone buildings and walls. A small flower garden grew nearby; a large herbal garden was just beyond. Bernard tapped Brayden on the shoulder. He looked to where Bernard was pointing. Along one side of the high wall was a stable. Dozens of horses stood in pens of various sizes. Even from this distance Brayden could tell that many were the size of Sullivan.

The keep itself was a massive stone tower, brightly whitewashed, with glass windows covering its exterior. A massive wooden door stood at its base. Here, Brayden thought, was the lord's residence, the home of the lord and his family, servants, closest advisors, and guests.

Caddaric led them across the courtyard on an even stone walkway.

"I'll take you in. The steward does not take kindly to unannounced guests, but Lady Marshal will be happy to see that one." He turned, smiling at Lady Josslyn, who smiled weakly in return.

"There are few about today," Bernard said.

Brayden noticed it too. Unlike the outer ward that was busy with activity, other than an occasional guard atop the walls, there were no people anywhere.

"Ah, Sir Hugh and Sir Rogers have been leading parties," Caddaric explained, "including the squires, out into the wood searching for Lady Josslyn. They'll be happy to see her safely back."

Brayden recognized the name of Sir Hugh, the kind knight he had met in Honeydown. He admitted he was curious to find out why Josslyn had run away when it was obvious so many people wanted her home and feared for her safety.

There was a shout nearby. At the foot of the tower they stopped as several armed men burst out of one of the nearby buildings. They approached quickly, swords drawn. Their colorful tunics indicated their status: knights.

Caelan had his hand on his sword instantly, and then glanced at Bernard, who motioned a cautionary signal with his hand. The weapon remained sheathed, and Caelan raised his arms. Brayden recognized the lead knight immediately. The cruel Sir Osbert de Clair stood before them.

"Captain! What is the meaning of this?" Sir Osbert yelled. "I told you and your useless men to alert me of any visitors, especially this one." He pushed Caddaric out of the way. The captain stood down, obviously knowing his rank and all too aware of the cold steal blades. Sir Osbert stood inches from Caelan.

"We hunt for you all over those putrid villages and yet here you are, back among us. I'll enjoy watching you rot in the dungeon," he sneered, and turned to the others.

"And the little boy and the wizard too. How nice. Captain, you'll escort these peasants out of the castle and away from the town. Let them brave the cold woods tonight. They'll find no solace here. And Sir Caelan is under arrest." Sir Osbert said, as a satisfied smile crept across his mouth. He held his sword towards Caelan's chest, his small eyes glaring at him. If Caelan was afraid, he did not show it.

"There will be no action taken until they've had an audience with the steward and my mother," Lady Josslyn said forcefully, speaking for the first time since they'd entered the castle. "That is a house rule of my father, which you are sworn to obey."

Sir Osbert stood silent, thunderstruck. His sword drooped, and his men looked at one another, shaking their heads silently. "You'll obey it, sir knight. The old friar and the boy will not go anywhere until they are granted an audience." Her voice was stern.

Sir Osbert fumed and paced, his face a bright red. "Very well!" he finally shouted. "Stable the horses and take them in!"

Two keep guards moved to take the horses, then paused when Sullivan stomped his front hooves and snorted angrily. Caelan stroked his mane several times, calming the horse.

"Shh, now. We won't be long," Caelan said quietly as he passed the reins to one of the keep guards.

They began to climb a short staircase to the keep door. Brayden noticed Bernard let a small smile creep across his face. They had used Josslyn to get inside, but her stand on a point of order had saved them from certain expulsion, and had saved Caelan from imprisonment, at least for now.

"But first," Sir Osbert said, stopping in front of the keep door. "Your weapons. *My* house rule."

Bernard and Caelan exchanged glances.

"You'll disarm now. Or shall we draw blood here before the audience you seek?" Sir Osbert and the others held their weapons aloft. Brayden trembled nervously. He knew Caelan and Bernard could usually take care of themselves, but even they would likely be no match for these warriors.

Bernard nodded at Caelan, and the knight loosened his buckle and handed over his belt and sword to one of Sir Osbert's knights.

Sir Osbert pointed, and another of the knights yanked open the massive keep door. Led by the captain of the keep guard and accompanied by Sir Osbert and his men, Brayden and his friends entered the keep for an audience with the steward of Strand.

Chapter Seventeen

The Steward

The party entered a dimly lit, square room lined with thick wood columns. Torches adorned the walls, their light flickering quietly. There were two wide doorways on either side, each leading to a long, poorly lit hallway. Sir Osbert pushed his way to the front of the group. A long staircase stood at the far end of the room.

"This way," he muttered, motioning them towards the stairs. They followed him silently. As they climbed, the light grew brighter, and they entered the main hall.

Brayden looked up and around him. It was the largest room he had ever seen. The ceiling rose high above his head, its belly lined with heavy wooden beams. The stone walls were painted in bright white, purple and red. Embedded in the center of each wall was an enormous fireplace in which embers burned brightly. Stained glass windows illuminated the chamber, and doorways leading to other parts of the castle seemed to be everywhere.

Finely woven tapestries, spun in every color imaginable and depicting religious events, knights, battles, and foreign lands, hung from the walls. One in particular caught Brayden's eye.

It was a picture of a city by the sea. The city was on fire and was filled with knights bearing crosses. Outside its walls were masses of what looked to be Saracen warriors attacking the city.

"Acre," he whispered to himself. His concentration broke as he felt a gentle hand on his shoulder. He looked up. It was Bernard, who nodded and silently led him forward.

The floor of the main hall was dark wood, but covered with fresh straw and various other dried plants for warmth and cushioning. From the odor the straw must be fresh, Brayden observed, and he could smell the lavender herbs mixed in. Long wooden tables and benches were everywhere, lined in uneven rows. The far end of the room was elevated, and he could see two large chairs in the center of the platform. Two more large doors opened behind the chairs, dim light glowing from beyond. Keep guards stood motionless at each end of the far wall. But Brayden's attention, indeed all of the group's attention, was focused on the large, darkly dressed man near the center of the room.

Sir Osbert led them forward as the large man walked up the steps and turned.

"Sir Bellator?" Brayden asked Bernard in a soft voice.

"Quiet boy!" Sir Osbert spat. "You'll speak when spoken to." Caelan bristled, but seemed to relax when Bernard glanced back at him reassuringly. Josslyn shrank behind Bernard; she had her hood on, hiding her hair and face.

Brayden and the others stood before the steward. He was tall, a full head taller than Caelan, and was his friend's senior by ten years or more, Brayden guessed. His complexion was dark, and his beard neatly trimmed to a sharp point. Dark, curly hair flowed down to his shoulders, and he was dressed in a long black tunic with purple accents and tall, shiny black boots. He wore a thick black belt with a large silver buckle, from which hung nothing save a short dagger with a brown handle. Though swordless, Brayden imagined him to be a formidable opponent.

Sir Osbert bowed slightly before the steward and took his place to the right of his master. The other knights spread out, keeping Brayden and his friends surrounded.

"We've unannounced guests," Sir Bellator said stoically. His voice was deep, crisp, and stern.

"Yes, my lord," Sir Osbert replied quickly. "The captain let them in without alerting us."

Bellator smiled. "I'm sure, as I'm sure the captain will be punished for his inability to keep his guards in line."

Caddaric bowed his head and stepped back into the shadows. Sir Bellator stepped down and inspected Brayden and his friends briefly before focusing in on Bernard.

"Who are you, and what is your business?" the steward asked Bernard directly. "Are you here simply to return our errant knight?" Sir Bellator shot a glance at Caelan, who stood impassively among the other knights.

"I am Bernard, Friar of Honeydown. This is Brayden Rider, also of Honeydown and son of Sir Ban Rider du Bayonne."

"Ah, I recognize the name. You settled here under the protection of Lord Marshal some years ago. And who is this other little one?" He pointed to Josslyn.

Bernard nudged Josslyn forward gently, and she removed her hood. If the steward was surprised at her appearance, he didn't show it.

"Captain, fetch Lady Marshal," he ordered. "I'm sure she'll want to know her wayward daughter has returned."

The captain nodded and quickly exited the main hall down one of the corridors.

"We thank you for returning Lady Josslyn to our castle," the steward continued. "She was missed by us all. You didn't come here just for that, though, did you? Other than entrance here, I suspect you ask a favor in return, friar."

Bernard stepped forward and held out his hands. "The villages have been under attack. We need protection from your forces."

"You've no bailiff?" the steward asked smugly.

"Your man, so we've observed, has proved to be ill equipped."

Brayden bit his tongue. Sir Bellator stiffened.

"Bands of outlaws roam the forests," Bernard continued before the steward could comment. "The bailiff is ill equipped, that is, without armed men at his side."

"Sir Osbert, did you and your men encounter any outlaws on your travels?"

Sir Osbert crossed his arms over his chest and smiled arrogantly. "Nothing, my lord. Though these peasants could use some humility."

The steward ignored him. "I'll have Sir Osbert look into the matter," he responded, his tone indicating that he was uninterested in discussing it further. "Anything else, or are we done?"

"We're interested in staying as guests for a time," Bernard said. "The boy here has a cousin who's a squire; he'd very much like to visit. Not long, of course, perhaps just until after Sir Osbert has finished his, uh, investigation, after which I'm sure the roads will be much safer." Brayden looked at Bernard, surprised at the bluntness of the request. Sir Osbert' s face was red, and he shifted his feet in apparent anger.

"Of course. Siegfried, I assume. He is a talented squire and growing into a fine young warrior." Sir Bellator looked Brayden up and down, as if trying to see any resemblance. "But as for your request, we have a tournament approaching in just a few days and we're hosting many guests from the surrounding lands. I'm afraid staying here for any length of time is out of the question."

Captain Caddaric came back into the main hall. A step behind him was a tall, well dressed woman. She was pretty, with long, dark blond hair tied neatly around her head. She had a gentle face, and wore a long blue and white dress. Numerous heads bowed, and though Brayden had never seen her, he recognized her immediately as Lady Marshal, wife of the lord. Josslyn broke free of Bernard's gentle hand and ran to her mother. They embraced, Lady Marshal holding her daughter tightly.

"Lady Marshal," Sir Bellator stated, "this friar recovered your daughter on his travels. In return, I have offered them assistance in securing their little village from the bandit raids that threaten our common folk."

Bernard and Caelan both tensed at the steward's lie. Lady Marshal looked at them, though, smiled, and bowed slowly. "Thank you," she said quietly, still hugging Josslyn.

Sir Bellator wasted no time and turned his attention to Caelan. "So, Sir Caelan, finally back among us. You know the punishment for deserters." He turned to Sir Osbert. "Take him to the dungeon. He can spend the next quarter thinking over his crime. We'll discuss fines later."

Two of the knights moved forward, each grabbing one of Caelan's arms. He attempted to wrench free, but stopped when a third knight drew his sword. The steward walked back up the stairs and stood near one of the large chairs in the center of the platform.

"Wait!" Bernard shouted. Everyone looked at him. "What crime is this man accused of?" he asked.

"Didn't you hear old man? Desertion of his post," Sir Osbert replied angrily. "He is bound to his lord and his lord's steward when the lord is absent."

"This man, this fair young knight, came to protect our village by his own free will. His actions almost singlehandedly defeated the rabble of outlaws that has been harassing Honeydown and other villages of this land. No other protection has been offered by this castle or its guard. We appealed even to Sir Osbert at Michaelmas, to no avail. Sir Caelan defended us on his own and at great risk to his own life."

Brayden let himself smile slightly as Sir Osbert's face turned from red to bright purple. He noted that Bernard made no mention of the letter Caelan had brought with him to Honeydown.

"This land has many troubles, friar," Sir Bellator began. "Not all of which can be remedied by my forces."

"Fair enough, but the people of the villages work in the service of the lord, and under him expect protection from banditry and hardship. Surely you agree to that."

Sir Bellator waved off this response. "Escort Sir Caelan out, and then show Bernard and the boy to the main gate. If they wish to stay, they can find an inn."

Sir Osbert and the other knights took their cue and again began to carry Caelan away.

"He also guaranteed Lady Josslyn's safe passage back to the castle." Bernard said, unperturbed. He looked expectantly at Lady Marshal who stood upright at the mention of her daughter's name. She looked at him hopefully, and then at Caelan.

Ignoring his pleas, the knights continued to drag Caelan off in the direction of one of the darker passages.

"I pardon this man!" Bernard shouted. Quickly, he produced a small gold cross. Brayden had seen it before. It was the cross of Friar Hobin, the abbey's previous builder, long-time friar of the manor, and friend of Lord Marshal. Brayden could tell by his expression that the steward recognized it immediately. Sir Osbert and the knights stopped and looked at one another in confusion.

Now it was the steward's turn to turn red with anger. He clenched his fists as he looked at Sir Osbert, and then glared at the friar. Brayden grabbed Bernard's cloak, fearful of what the steward might do.

Bernard continued, unfazed. "I pardon him on the authority of the church, and as friar of Honeydown, where he proved his true heart in defense of our village."

"Your jurisdiction here is weak, priest," Sir Bellator said, "no matter what old symbols or titles you invoke."

"I second the pardon!" Lady Marshal called out excitedly. Everyone turned to her in surprise. "I will see knight the redeemed as thanks for returning my and Lord Marshal's only child."

Sir Bellator turned his fury toward Lady Marshal, and Brayden suspected he had overplayed his hand. Inside he must have known that even if he could ignore the ruling of the church, he could not break both an edict of the church and a request from the Lady of the Manor, especially while Lord Marshal might still be alive. In moments the steward collected himself, and sat down slowly in the lord's chair. He stared forward, as if calculating his next move.

"Sir Osbert," the steward said after a long pause, "keep Sir Caelan under close watch with the castle guards. He is to remain weaponless, and will fulfill his time here in menial duty. He is not to leave this castle, and if he does so will face banishment, or worse.

Sir Bellator looked at Bernard. "The rumors are true; you are a clever old wizard, Bernard. Perhaps that is why Lord Marshal bid you welcome from France years ago." He turned to Caddaric.

"Captain, you may escort the friar and the boy out of the castle. Our previous arrangements will be honored."

"Wait," said a soft voice. It was Lady Marshal again. "My daughter tells me these persons asked for safety behind these walls and were refused. Why?"

Sir Bellator turned in her direction. "My lady, with the tournament approaching I simply thought they'd be more comfortable, elsewhere."

"Some guests of yours will have to bring their own tents, my fine steward. We'll find space for these people. It is what my husband would will, and I am still lady of this castle and these rights fall to me."

The steward sat back and simply nodded in response. His right hand was squeezing the handle of the chair, and Brayden thought the steward may tear it off and throw it at them if they did not leave the main hall then and there.

Brayden looked at Bernard. His friend bowed in thanks, and then grabbed Brayden's arm and began walking him over to where Lady Marshal and Josslyn stood waiting.

"Hold," Sir Bellator called forcefully. They both turned.

"You and the boy are guests here, but only until the tournament is over. In that time etiquette will be followed. Lady Marshal, please arrange for comfort befitting a man of God. The Rider child will spend his time with the pages. I'll not have a boy of his age running around wild inside these castle walls, not while I'm your husband's steward. He'll be put to work there, as is custom. It looks as if he could learn the finer graces, and he'll get a better understanding of castle life."

"My lord," Bernard started to protest.

The steward waved him to silence. "These are the orders of my office. You'll obey them, or be turned out now."

Bernard gave a slight bow to the steward, and then looked at Brayden reassuringly. "Go there for a time. I'll be down to fetch you soon enough."

Sir Osbert took Caelan out of the main hall, while Caddaric beckoned Brayden to join him. He followed, looking back nervously as Bernard, Lady Marshal, and Josslyn watched him leave.

Chapter Eighteen

The Pages

Caddaric led Brayden up several flights of curved stairs. Torches lit their way, and as they passed the occasional arrow slit or narrow window, Brayden would look out at the surrounding countryside below. Dusk had settled, bathing the land in deep purples and gray. Despite his curiosity, he found that more than once he had to pull himself away from the openings in fear. He had never been this high above the ground before.

While he was relieved that Sir Caelan had escaped the dungeon, the realization had sunk in that this would be the first time he would be truly alone, far from the village and his mother, and separated from his friends. The wonderment he felt upon seeing and being inside the castle was replaced by fear of the steward and his knights, and the sinking feeling that this was indeed a very dangerous place.

At least the captain was not unfriendly, and seemed to sense his feelings of loneliness. "Don't worry about your friends, lad. I promise you this. With the pages you'll see and experience more of the castle than you will following that old friar about."

"What will happen to Sir Caelan?" Brayden asked. He felt comfortable around this man, unlike the knights and guards he had met so far.

"Your old friend and Lady Marshal spared him the misery of the dungeon, that's for sure. He may never have made it out of there alive. Few do. Even the steward cannot strip him of his knighthood. They'll make him work, to be sure, perhaps managing the stores or the horses. But rest assured, if they need a hand in a fight he'll rightly get his sword back in no time."

"What about you?" Brayden asked, anxious to keep talking, and recalling what Sir Bellator had said about punishing the captain.

"Ah, Sir Osbert likes to mete out punishment, but he doesn't like to manage. I suspect I'll get a few days as a gong farmer and then be back at running the keep guards. Things would fall apart without me in charge," the captain responded, a noticeable hint of pride in his voice.

They rounded another staircase and came to a short door.

The captain wiped his brow with his hand. "Here we are," the captain stated. "Climbing these tower stairs gets no easier over the years." He took out a key, unlocked the door, and pushed it open.

They found themselves in a good-sized room lined with small straw beds. As everywhere, straw covered the dark wood floor, and colorful tapestries hung from the walls. The only light came from a bank of windows on the far side of the room. Clothes, boots, and equipment were strewn everywhere. Inside one wall was a small fireplace, and a pile of wood and sticks lay nearby.

Brayden walked over to the windows and looked out, careful to hold on tightly to the cold castle wall. Below, he could see the castle courtyard, a large, well manicured green field lined with small buildings and supplies. He took a couple of steps back, again nervous about how high they were.

"Ah, no one here," the captain said, inspecting the room. "I suspect Sir Hugh will have the boys back shortly. Let's tend to the fire until they return." Caddaric proceeded to light several torches which sat firmly in sconces set unevenly along the walls, and then began arranging the wood in the fireplace.

"Sir Hugh Morgan?" Brayden asked hopefully.

"The same. You know of him?"

Brayden shrugged. "He visited our village around Michaelmas."

"He is a good man. Strict, but good. Boys your age need strictness. Come, give me a hand."

Brayden handed fresh logs to the captain, who placed them carefully in the fireplace.

The captain held the torch low, and sparks flew everywhere. He had the fire going well in moments. "It is getting colder," he said. "Drafts blow through, up, down and around these walls. The tapestries help a bit, but best we have a strong fire tonight. You don't want to catch the cough."

Brayden stayed close to the fire, warming himself, and suddenly realizing his fingers had indeed grown cold. He focused on the red and orange flames, wondering where Sir Caelan and Bernard were, and how his mother was faring.

A few moments later he was jolted to alertness by a cacophony of approaching voices. The door flew open, and Sir Hugh Morgan entered, followed by a dozen boys, all Brayden's age or slightly older. The boys' boots were muddy, and many of them had leaves and burs stuck to their hair and clothing.

"All right, lads," Sir Hugh thundered, "get those filthy boots off, get those clean boots on. Mind the fire if you're chilled. Leave your things by your beds. Hurry up now. Nice neat piles. A light supper and then to bed!"

The large knight approached the captain. "Thank you for the fire, sir. And who do we have here?" he said.

"Sir Hugh, Brayden Rider of Honeydown village will be staying with us here in the castle, per order of the steward and Lady Marshal." Brayden stepped forward away from the fireplace and bowed slightly.

"The steward and Lady Marshal? How did anyone get them to agree on anything? Of course. Welcome to our castle." A look of recognition crossed his face. "We have met, have we not? Yes, I remember it well, in Honeydown at Michaelmas." He put his big hand on Brayden's shoulder. Brayden grunted, almost falling over. "Captain, this boy showed his bravery that day. He stood up to Sir Osbert, thereby protecting his village. And, Sir Osbert was ahorse!"

"Really?" the captain said, suddenly impressed. "He is here with his friend, the holy man Bernard. Sir Caelan is back as well, and they brought Lady Josslyn with them too."

"Lady Josslyn too? Well," Sir Hugh said. "Welcome, indeed. Some hero we have here."

The discussion had caught the attention of the other pages, one of whom, a tall, unfriendly looking boy with thick dark hair, stepped forward to get a better look at the new arrival. He stared at Brayden, as if sizing him up. Brayden stared back at first, and then looked away.

"Boys!" Sir Hugh called. "Give me your attention. I want to introduce to you Brayden Rider of Honeydown."

Sir Hugh proceeded to tell the pages about what had happened at Michaelmas, with Sir Osbert, and the rest, significantly embellishing the story. The tall boy, and everyone else, was staring at him. Brayden cringed, embarrassed to be the center of attention.

Sir Hugh turned at length. "Brayden, we're honored to have you."

Excited chatter ensued as several of the boys walked up to him and introduced themselves, asking questions about Lady Josslyn, his journey from Honeydown, and his encounter with Sir Osbert. Brayden was still embarrassed, but after the earlier feelings of dread and loneliness, the attention felt good. The taller boy who had been staring at him earlier kept his distance, busily getting a clean pair of boots on.

"Captain, thank you for your help," Sir Hugh said. The captain leaned over to Brayden on his way out. "Good luck," he said, "and welcome." He left the room.

"Boys, let's get moving!" Sir Hugh said sternly, obviously irritated over how long things were taking. The man thundered about the room, ordering the boys this way and that, cracking jokes and calling names. Brayden started to understand what the captain had said about Sir Hugh being strict, but good-natured. The boys finally lined up at the door behind the knight. Brayden stood silently in the middle of the room until two of the other boys pulled him into line, smiling in a friendly way.

"Quietly now," Sir Hugh warned. "Recall your manners in public halls. Some are retiring early. Some are in prayer. Be thankful we'll have a nice, warm room to return to. Now, off to dinner!" Sir Hugh marched forward, the column of pages traipsing after him.

* * *

Sir Hugh took the pages down several spiral staircases and through a long hallway. They passed the doorway leading to the scullery and entered a small room off the kitchen. A large rectangular wooden table sat in the middle of the room, surrounded by benches topped with cushions. The room was well lit by torches on the walls and oil lamps on the table and, as in so many of the other rooms, a small fireplace was built into one of the walls. Wood and metal shields decorated the walls near the ceiling, each brightly painted with various animals, shapes, and symbols. The walls were covered in dark wood paneling, a stark contrast to the cold stone walls of the rest of the castle. Next to the door was a small bucket of water.

"This is the shield room," one of the boys whispered to Brayden. "It is said these shields are gifts from the allies of Sir Allard."

"Sir Allard?" Brayden asked. He recalled the name, but not much more.

"Lord Marshal's champion," the boy replied quietly. "Disappeared with the lord."

They were not permitted to eat in the main hall. In fact, Brayden learned later that evening that no one was. It was reserved for the steward, the Marshals, and their guests only. Otherwise, it sounded as if much of the castle was fair game. Many of the boys were speaking quietly about their chores for the upcoming week in the various parts of the castle itself, and Brayden got the feeling he was going to see more of Castle Strand than he'd bargained for.

"Boys, rinse your hands and take your places. Brayden, you will sit next to Patch this evening," Sir Hugh commanded, pointing to the boy who had spoken of Sir Allard earlier, one of the boys who had pulled him into line in the page room.

Each in turn rinsed his hands in the bucket of water. To Brayden's surprise, the water was quite warm. He walked to the bench where Patch was already sitting.

"My name's Patch," the boy said proudly and without prompting. "Pleased to meet you." He bowed slightly. He had scruffy brown hair and was thin as a reed. Freckles covered his face, and his huge ears seemed to barely fit his head.

"It is nice to meet you too," Brayden responded as he took his seat to the boy's left. The bench shook as another boy sat down on the other side of Brayden. He was large with bright red hair, and he seemed to need more space than the others. He wedged his way in between the table and the bench and turned to Brayden, who was discretely trying to inch toward the thinner Patch.

"Daniel. Daniel Morgan," the large boy said, introducing himself as he tried to get comfortable.

"Daniel Morgan? Any relation to Sir Hugh Morgan of Fairborn over there?" Brayden asked half seriously.

"Sir Hugh is his father," Patch replied, not waiting for Daniel to respond. "And he won't let you forget it."

Daniel's only response was to stick his tongue out at Patch.

"Daniel!" Sir Hugh roared. "Manners, boy. Manners at the table. Do that again and I'll put a horsefly on your plate." Sir Hugh stood at the door. "Now, Lady Marshal will not be joining us tonight. She is spending time with her daughter, whom Brayden here was lucky enough to find."

Brayden blushed as the chatter began anew. Sir Hugh meant no harm, but being this well known this fast was not something he had expected. More than one of the other boys glared at him. One in particular, the tall boy who had stared at him in the page quarters, made him feel very uncomfortable.

"So, Lady Wymarda will be by to deliver supper and your manners training."

There was a collective groan, and several of the boys put their hands to their faces and shook their heads.

"Who is Lady Wymarda?" Brayden asked Patch quietly.

Patch gritted his teeth as if the discussion pained him. "She is the kitchen maiden, big and mean. You may have to work for her one day in the kitchen or scullery. She is horrible."

"Ah," Sir Hugh continued, "and here she comes."

The big man was almost knocked over as a large, squat woman burst through the doorway with a tray of pies. She immediately spotted Brayden.

"And who might you be?" she blurted, wasting no time in handing out pies to the other boys.

"This is Brayden Rider," Sir Hugh began. "The hero of Honeydown. He singlehandedly…"

Lady Wymarda cut him off with a wave of a thick, meaty hand. "Can he not answer for himself, sir? Is he without tongue, shy, dumb, or all of those things together?"

"None of those, my lady," Brayden croaked as he got to his feet. Everyone at the table was watching him. "I am Brayden Rider of Honeydown, son of Sir Ban Rider du Bayonne. I am here for a time, but I don't know for how long." He bowed deeply, trying his best to remember the lessons his mother and Bernard had taught him of proper behavior.

Lady Wymarda and Sir Hugh looked him over. A smile crept across Sir Hugh's face.

"All right then, nothing wrong with this voice." Lady Wymarda beamed. "And nothing wrong with his manners either. You lot could do worse than to follow Mr. Rider's lead." She pointed to the bench. "Sit back down there, Lord Rider. I'll fetch you a pie, as Sir Hugh never warns me when we have guests. And as you're new, you'll join us in the scullery after dinner. Guest or no, we work hard here. Now sit!"

Brayden sat down in silence. The tall boy across the table was glaring at him again. Brayden tried to ignore him and looked away.

"She likes you already," Patch teased. "A date in the scullery. How nice for you."

Lady Wymarda left, taking the bucket with her. A few short minutes later she returned with another pie. She placed it in front of Brayden. He noticed that Daniel was picking at his pie, nibbling at the crumbs. The kitchen maiden quickly swatted his hand away, and Daniel withdrew without protest.

"You know better than that, Sir Hugh," she scolded. "Be useful, and lead the boys in prayer."

Everyone bowed their heads as Sir Hugh said the dinner's blessings. As he did so, Lady Wymarda scanned the room, looking for anyone who was not repeating the words or not focused on their meaning. With an, "amen," in unison the boys raised their heads.

"Good. Now, before our dinner gets cold, who can tell me who is to sit first at a feast?" Lady Wymarda asked, looking for a volunteer.

"The lord," one of the boys sitting across from Brayden answered plainly. Lady Wymarda looked at him, disgusted.

"The lady," said the tall boy who had been eyeing Brayden since he'd arrived. He looked bored, Brayden thought, as if he knew all the answers and was ready for something new.

"Very good, Edwin," she responded. "Now, what is the first item we set at the lord's table?" She watched eagerly for a response. Brayden recorded the taller boy's name.

"Salt?" Patch blurted. He leaned over to Brayden. "Edwin over there serves the high table more than anyone, but no reason he should have all the right answers too." The boy named Edwin shot an angry glance at Patch.

"Right. Now, everyone sit up straight! Eyes forward. Good!" The boys sat bolt upright in unison. Brayden followed, not sure what to expect next. "Please eat," she ordered, opening her arms. "We'll continue after supper."

Brayden, Daniel, and Patch dug in as everyone around the table began talking amongst themselves. The pies were a medley of soft lamb, egg, autumn pears and strong cheese cooked in pastry. As he ate, Brayden looked up at the tall boy.

"Who is he?" Brayden asked Patch quietly, trying not to point.

"That's Edwin Stapleton. He's the son of Lord Stapleton, who is a vassal of Lord Marshal. I've never seen his father near, though I hear he's one of Lord Marshal's fiercest rivals."

"He is a pet of Sir Osbert," Daniel grunted between mouthfuls. "Are you done with that?" he asked, pointing at Brayden's half-eaten pie.

"Sure, take it if you like." The excitement of his new surroundings and the anticipation of what was to come next had robbed him of his appetite.

Daniel grabbed the leftovers eagerly and began digging in with both hands.

"Is your father a vassal of Lord Marshal, Patch?" Brayden asked.

Daniel and Patch exchanged glances. Daniel nodded, and gave his friend a wan smile.

"My father was Sir Armond de Mills," Patch replied. "He is gone."

"Oh, I'm sorry," Brayden replied, "I didn't know."

"It's okay. It's been many years. I'm taken in by Sir Allard now." Brayden recalled sadly that Sir Allard, too, was missing. "I hear your father is still in France," Patch said, redirecting the focus of the conversation.

"Yes, we don't know where, but I pray…I know…he is still alive." Brayden paused. "How did you know about that?"

Patch shrugged. "We all know he is a Templar."

Brayden looked across the table. Edwin Stapleton was staring at him again.

* * *

After supper, and following a long barrage of questions on manners and etiquette, the pages were dismissed, all except Brayden. He followed Lady Wymarda to the scullery and assisted two of the scullion maids with washing the plates and knives. The three of them stood around a large bucket filled with warm water and soap in which they scrubbed the castle dishes, wiped, and scrubbed again. Lady Wymarda darted in and out, giving bits of advice as she prepared the evening meal for Sir Bellator and his retinue of knights.

The maids themselves said little. To them, Brayden knew, he was just another new page. The work itself was hard, and the soap stung his hands. Lady Wymarda entered one final time.

"All is well then," she said. "If you've come all the way from Honeydown you must be plum tired now. Head to bed, Sir Rider. You and the others will be collected in the morning for early chores. I don't know about village life, but there is no end to work here."

He was indeed exhausted, and could barely walk. Brayden bowed and started off, then paused. He realized he had no idea where to go. Lady Wymarda seemed to recognize his confusion.

"Down the hall, up the curved stair, around to the right, door on the left. I'll have breadcrumbs tomorrow if you like," she said sarcastically. "Now get to bed!"

* * *

He followed Lady Wymarda's directions and entered the room. Other than the small, smoldering fire deep in the fireplace, the room itself was pitch black. He stumbled around the side of the room, looking for an empty bed, trying not to trip on the assorted shoes and clothes that covered the floor in all directions. It was silent, other than the straw crunching quietly under his feet. He found an empty bed, sat down, and began to take off his shoes. Someone kicked him suddenly in the back, so hard it knocked him to the floor. He rolled over in pain. He could just make out the silhouette of one of the boys staring at him from the bed. Brayden knew instantly who it was.

"You'll not come near me again, Rider," Edwin Stapleton whispered. "There are no empty beds. You'll sleep on the floor with the rats and the mice tonight." Edwin lay down and turned over.

Brayden, too tired to fight, found an empty space in a corner. He huddled close to the wall, covering himself with all the straw he could gather and any stray clothes the boys had left lying about. It *was* cold, and his back ached from where Stapleton had kicked him. The good feelings he had shared with some of the boys tonight dissipated, replaced again with a horrible, empty loneliness. Tears came to his eyes, and he cried softly to himself, not wanting any of the other boys to hear. Shivering alone on the floor, he closed his eyes and forced himself to sleep.

Chapter Nineteen

The Lady

"I trust your accommodations are comfortable?" Lady Elaine asked as she joined Bernard in the guest chambers. The rooms were large and well furnished with decorative carvings etched in the otherwise smooth stone walls. Tapestries hung from every side, and the hardwood floors were sprinkled with sweet smelling herbs instead of straw. Oil lamps hung from the walls and candles burnt brightly in tall metal sconces, providing more than enough light to read by. Bernard had no fireplace in his room, but the wooden bed was enormous and covered in heavy blankets. Necessary, he knew, to protect one from drafts. Bernard chuckled to himself when he first saw it, wondering how he'd ever climb in.

Josslyn darted in, carrying a water basin. She set it down near a thick wooden table atop which sat row after row of enormous brightly burning candles. She bowed in Bernard's direction and departed as quick as she had come. The girl looked completely transformed, apparently easing back into her household as if she had never left. She had bathed, her hair was tied neatly behind her head and she wore a long, light blue gown. Adaptable, he thought, and when clean and dressed she looked more like her mother than Bernard had noticed before.

"Yes, yes, this is very nice. Thank you for your graciousness," he replied. He had met Lady Elaine only once, many years before, shortly after arriving in Britain. It had been a brief visit, the Marshals departing soon after with their retinue on a six-month-long journey touring their lands and visiting some of the nearby baronies.

While she was rumored to be a firm, diligent manager of the Marshal house and its affairs, Bernard imagined the disappearance of her husband had taken its toll. She had not spoken of him since leaving the main hall, nor throughout their dinner. Though Bernard was curious about what she knew of her husband's whereabouts and the matter of his disappearance, he vowed to himself to avoid the topic out of respect for her feelings.

"Thank you again, kind friar, for returning my daughter. She means more to me than this estate and all our possessions combined."

Bernard waved his hand. "No, my lady. Thank you but there are others who deserve your gratitude far more. We have been fortunate to have had Sir Caelan's company." He paused. "I hope they spend the night in comfort. I admit a bit of guilt," he said, looking around the guest chamber. In truth, he was concerned about Brayden's safety, and was anxious to see him in the morning.

Lady Elaine looked at him as if reading his thoughts. "I'll be down in the morning to fetch the pages. Please try not to worry. Brayden and the other boys are in the care of Sir Hugh Morgan and Lady Wymarda tonight, and rest in the safest part of the castle. As for Sir Caelan, I suspect he can take care of himself, though I will ensure he is not mistreated."

Bernard smiled; of Sir Caelan's security he had no doubt. "You are too kind, my lady. Brayden and Sir Caelan are both brave, good-hearted people."

Lady Josslyn entered the room once more, this time with various linens and blankets. She placed them on a heavy wooden chest at the foot of the bed.

"This Brayden Rider," Lady Elaine said. "He is Sir Ban's son then, of the crusades, and cousin of Siegfried." It was less a question than a statement of fact.

"That is true," Bernard said.

Lady Elaine turned to her daughter, who was now lingering by the candles that were slowly oozing wax all over the table. "Josslyn, blow out the candles and then that will be all. Off to your chambers."

"Yes, mother," the girl responded. Josslyn took a deep breath and after several tries the candles were extinguished, briefly filling the chamber with a smoky haze. Bernard and Lady Elaine both turned away, coughing.

"What of his mother?" Lady Elaine continued as she cleared her throat, waving the smoke away from her face.

"Alice Rider remains in Honeydown," Bernard began. "After the attacks on the village and on her home, we suspected more than just banditry. We suspect foul play of a more insidious kind. We felt the boy would be safer here, under the protection of your house."

"Whatever resources I can offer, I shall. I know all too well the want of a mother to protect her own."

"Thank you, my lady. And thankfully Sir Caelan came to us like an avenging angel. Who, if I may inquire, was the origin of the letter he carried?" Bernard took a deep breath. He knew he was taking a chance by revealing the letter and his knowledge of it.

Lady Elaine looked stunned. She gazed at the candles for a moment, and then took a deep breath. "I came across it," she said calmly. "I knew not who the intended recipient was, nor its author, but I could not stand by and let a boy be kidnapped, and certainly not a noble boy whose father is a friend of this house. As you did, I felt Brayden would be safer here, hidden among the pages, under the protection of Sir Caelan and Sir Hugh. That is all I will say about it."

Lady Elaine turned away from Bernard, hiding her face while she wiped her eyes.

"My lady?" Bernard said, extending a hand. While he still did not know the letter's origin, he found himself now wanting to help her and her house even more.

She waved him off. "I am fine. With my husband gone it has been difficult, for me and for the people of these lands. My only regret upon seeing the boy is not bringing Alice here as well. I fear whoever seeks Brayden will not rest. There is something they want, and will stop at nothing to get." Lady Elaine stepped closer to Bernard and lowered her voice. "These are dark times here, Bernard. The steward is a cruel, selfish soul. He cares not for the welfare of the people, nor for the affairs of the barony. Though I have no proof, I fear he is scheming against my husband, for what purpose and in whose employ I do not know. He takes little counsel, other than perhaps from the man named Regin."

"Regin?" Bernard inquired.

"I know him only from a distance, but he appears small in stature and brutal in manner. He arrived soon after Sir Bellator took over as steward, though he seems to frequent the castle only occasionally. I know little of him, though it is rumored among the knights he is a metal worker of some renown. I don't know from what toad stool he sprouted, but I do not trust him. He never appears with the steward in public, hiding in the shadows when they speak."

"Have you asked the local baronies and your husband's vassals for help in securing your interests?" he asked. Bernard knew the Marshal name held respect across Britain, and while the Crown may not come to her aid, perhaps Lord Marshal's peers could be persuaded.

"I've written letters, but to no avail. There has as yet been no response from my husband's allies. I feel we are isolated here."

Bernard shook his head. "The villages are not much better off, I'm afraid. The outlaws attack without hesitation. At least the harvest has been strong. If we can secure the grain, the villages will not suffer this winter through want of food."

Lady Elaine smiled. "Well, we'll take whatever blessings we can find these days." She walked toward the door. "The steward has agreed to host my husband's yearly tournament. There, I hope to engage our allies for help. Please, stay at least until then."

Bernard stepped forward, his hands outstretched. "I cannot keep the boy from his mother forever, but I am reticent to go back until whoever penned that letter is revealed. What more, my lady, may we do to help you?"

"Only keep a watchful eye on the steward, and protect Josslyn as you'd protect Brayden." She paused. "I hear too that you are a man of accounts?"

Bernard nodded. How she knew of his long ago past he did not know, and did not consider questioning at this juncture. "I have dabbled, my lady, but more so Sir Ban than myself, of course. He has the talent with numbers and counting, among so many other things."

"I still have access to the castle accounts and records," she continued. "I suspect he views me as he does any other ignorant, feckless woman, but I am not, sir. Any clues you can discern about the steward's management, or mismanagement, of our affairs would be of great help in gaining support among the other baronies."

He bowed. "I'll shed what light I can, my lady."

"Thank you, Bernard. I'll leave you be now." She stepped into the doorway and stopped. "Rumor has it that Brayden faced down Sir Osbert around Michaelmas. Is this true?"

"He did more than that, my lady. He fought off the outlaws who attacked our village; evil men who attacked his home and mother."

She smiled. "Then it is true. There is indeed a lot of his father in him."

"That there is," Bernard replied, proud of the boy and confident of his decision to come to Castle Strand, at least for now.

Lady Elaine turned and walked out of the guest room, while Bernard walked over to the table and began picking at the congealed candle wax. The sliver of light blue material poking out from under the table was unmistakable.

"You've not the first child to be caught sneaking around a castle. It may amaze you, but I did some of that in my day." He backed up several feet and crossed his arms. "Show yourself, Lady Josslyn."

The girl crawled slowly out from beneath the table and stood before him. Her face was red and she worked quickly to brush off the stems and leaves from her gown. Bernard decided not to prolong the girl's embarrassment at getting caught, though he wondered how she would have escaped the guest chamber undetected after he had closed and locked the door.

"Now, I'm not sure how your mother would take to finding you outside your bed chambers at this late hour, let alone eavesdropping. Let's not find out, hmm?"

"Thank you, Bernard," Josslyn mumbled. She curtsied quickly, and almost tripped over her gown as she ran out the door.

Chapter Twenty

Inspection Day

Lady Wymarda burst through the door banging two metal plates together. "Up! Get up!" she yelled. "Down to the chapel!"

Brayden awoke with a jerk. He had slept, somehow, and was covered in straw from head to toe. He brushed off as best he could, picking filth from his hair and face. The room was bright with morning sunlight. He looked up. Edwin Stapleton was standing over him, hands on his hips.

"Look at him, boys!" Stapleton shouted. "Lying on the floor like a rat. Sir Osbert will love to hear about this!" Several of the boys laughed and pointed at Brayden. He sank back against the wall, embarrassed and angry at once. Lady Wymarda walked over, waving the plates to distract the boys from Brayden and to get them moving.

"So help me, Edwin, you'll not make us late to Mass again. Get your boots on and out the door!"

The boys began shuffling out of the room. She looked down at Brayden, who was still picking straw from his hair and clothes. "You're a right mess. Up you get. You can clean up later. God doesn't judge us on how we look." She reached down and propped him up by the arm. "We'll need to get you a proper bed before nightfall though. No page here sleeps on the floor. There is no surer way to fall ill. I'll speak with Sir Hugh on that account. Now go!"

Brayden jumped as she swatted at him with one of the plates. He headed out the door quickly, and though he was the last one out, he was surprised and happy to see Patch and Daniel waiting for him.

"Never mind that Edwin," Patch said. "He treats everyone like that. Chapel time is short, and then we're off to breakfast and the inspection."

"Inspection?" Brayden asked absently as Patch and Daniel ran down the hall ahead of him.

* * *

They were down in the shield room again after Morning Prayer, having a breakfast of bread and pears. Edwin hadn't confronted him again since they'd left the page quarters, and Brayden hoped he could avoid the larger boy as much as possible.

Lady Wymarda entered the shield room, followed by Lady Elaine.

"Up boys, honor the lady of the manor!" Lady Wymarda announced.

They all stood, faced Lady Elaine, and bowed, Daniel still with a mouthful of bread. She looked beautiful, Brayden thought, as if transformed from the night before. Her hair was tightly bound to her head, and her skin was powdered. As she walked around the perimeter of the room she filled it with the smell of perfume, and her blue and pink robes seemed to hover above the floor. She looked, Brayden thought, like an angel, a sharp contrast to the scruffy pages and Lady Wymarda's plainer working clothes. The pages followed Lady Elaine with their eyes as Brayden did, admiring her appearance as much as her station.

"Good morning, boys," she began, her voice sweet and smooth. "Today is a special day. Today we inspect the castle grounds, from the kitchen to the stables. Some of you helped me with this over the summer months, some of you are new." She paused, looking directly at Brayden. "We want the castle to be ready for winter, but this time is a special time." There was a murmur among the pages as several of the boys exchanged excited looks. "The steward has agreed to host this year's tournament for the new knights, and the surrounding baronies will be coming here. I expect the very best etiquette from each of you."

The murmur exploded into chatter, as the boys reacted to the news. It *was* exciting, Brayden thought. Last night's loneliness and his run-in with Edwin Stapleton were quickly fading into memory. First a visit to the castle, now an actual tournament!

"Well, finish your breakfast," she continued. "We meet in the kitchen, and then on to the main hall and the courtyard."

* * *

In the morning light the kitchen looked enormous. To Brayden it seemed almost as big as Honeydown's barn. Empty spits hung over several large fire pits. Built into the walls were three large stone sinks, and as many thick wooden tables. Razor sharp knives, enormous spoons and heavy black pots were stacked everywhere or hung from hooks in the ceiling. Herbs and root vegetables adorned every wall, giving the space a pleasant, sophisticated aroma. The only activity this morning was that of one of the scullery maids. Breakfast over, she was busily bringing in dishes and laying them by the sinks.

"Rider knows that line of work well," Edwin snickered quietly to one of the other boys, who began to giggle. Brayden knew he was referring to his work the night before, and focused on ignoring him as Lady Elaine stepped to the front of the troop.

"Our kitchen is one of the largest in Britain," she boasted. "For those who are new, we are also one of the few castles with actual running water, piped from a cistern above us." The boys looked up, amazed at the modernity of it all.

Brayden was standing near a small window, and looked out below. He could see people in the courtyard standing in groups of two or three. Several began running at once, as if in a race. He wondered if they could be the squires, and thought of Siegfried and what he had told him about the near constant exercise. Brayden admitted to himself his disappointment at not yet seeing his cousin, and hoped for the opportunity once their tour ended at the castle gardens in the courtyard.

Lady Elaine was walking around the kitchen, stopping at various points along the way. "Several of you may find yourselves in here at the feast. It is important that you listen carefully to Lady Wymarda and her attendants at all times." At that moment, Lady Wymarda conveniently walked in with an armful of pots. She dropped them with a clatter to the floor.

"Aye," Lady Wymarda agreed. "One page some years ago decided not to listen and fell into a cauldron. We feasted well that night. He made a fine stew!" She rubbed her stomach to indicate her enjoyment of the meal. Several of the boys stuck out their tongues and Brayden and Patch rolled their eyes at one another. Lady Elaine pretended to ignore them and walked on.

"You'll be asked to fetch food and drink, and you will come and go through this door." Lady Elaine led them through a short hallway and into the main hall itself. At her command, they lined up single file on the dais overlooking the entire hall. Unlike the night before, the tables were lined up neatly and covered with heavy gray cloth that draped all the way to the floor of the hall. Lady Elaine stood before them and began to explain the procedures for who passed to whom, who served what, and who was served first, second, and last. Brayden listened to her instructions, although his eyes wandered over the tapestries and colorful walls of the hall. The day's light gave him the chance to see the hall in its full splendor. This was where the business of the lord took place, where justice was done, and where celebrations were held. His eyes stopped abruptly on the far end of the room. In the shadows behind one of the larger tapestries he could see the outline of a person. He was startled, and grabbed Patch's hand.

"What?" Patch asked in an irritated tone. "I was daydreaming."

"Look there," Brayden whispered. "Someone in the shadows." They both looked, but the figure was gone. "Ah, you're seeing things," Patch said. "Shh. Listen."

"Boys?" Lady Elaine said, hands on her hips. "Are we paying attention?" Brayden and Patch turned to face her.

"Y-yes, mum," Brayden and Patch blurted at the same time.

"Good, so who is served meat first?"

They looked at each other and shrugged. "The lady of the house?" Patch finally said.

"Hmm. I should say not. Please pay attention. You'll both be in the kitchen at the feast, so I expect you to listen and learn. Even with the lord absent, our house has a reputation to uphold."

They followed her out and down the hall. As she walked, she called out the names of the boys who would be working in the main hall during the days of the tournament. Brayden understood the selection process for the jobs had to do with exemplary behavior, the kitchen and the scullery work falling low on the honor scale. Of course, Edwin's name was the first to be called. He would be serving the high table, and he let everyone know it. Brayden turned back toward the tapestries as they walked out. Whoever, or whatever, had been lurking there was no more.

* * *

They walked through the main doors of the keep and into the courtyard. It was alive with activity, and across the field Brayden could see the squires.

"Over here, please," Lady Elaine called to Brayden and the other boys who had become distracted. They gathered around a large plot of dirt surrounded by a short stone wall. Inside was row upon row of green plants of various sizes. Brayden recognized mint, parsley, and sage from his mother's own garden in Honeydown. As Lady Elaine was pointing out the varieties of onions, Brayden's mind drifted again to the squires playing across the field. Several were fencing with swords and small shields. Two others were fighting with quarterstaffs, and a few stood attentively while an older man who Brayden assumed to be a knight spoke to them. Others were holding bows, taking aim at targets hung from the castle wall.

"Brayden Rider!" Lady Elaine said. "Please pay attention. As a kitchen steward you'll be in and out fetching herbs and plants of various sorts throughout the feast."

Brayden focused his attention on the plants and their names as Lady Elaine continued. Then she pointed out several small stalls off to the side of the keep wall. It was here, she explained, the animals meant for the feast would be kept.

They walked around the garden, around the base of the massive stone walls, and back to the main stone path that cut through the courtyard. Brayden and the others watched the squires as they walked, and several of the pages chatted about the activities the older boys were participating in.

Brayden stopped. There, finally, was Siegfried. He had on loose-fitting garments and was playing swords with another boy. He held a small metal shield no larger than a dinner plate in one hand and a long wooden sword in another. Siegfried looked over at the pages and recognized Brayden instantly. Showing off, he swooped in on his opponent, almost knocking down the other squire with several swings of his sword, then threw down his weapon and shield and ran over.

"Brayden!" he called. Siegfried wrapped his arms around him and lifted him up. "I saw Bernard earlier this morning. He mentioned you were here too. You're getting taller, I think, just in the last few days!"

He put Brayden down and waved over a couple of the other squires, who joined them. Lady Elaine had walked off to speak with Sir Hugh, who had met them in the courtyard to see how the inspection was progressing.

"This is my cousin, Brayden Rider," Siegfried said. "Brayden, meet squires Gilbert Beauchamps and Herman Balk. They have been here since before I arrived, and I train with them every day. They'll be knights any day now." The new arrivals nodded quietly. Gilbert had bright red hair, and Herman was a foot taller than the next tallest boy. He had been one of the squires practicing with the quarterstaffs. Siegfried looked around at the other young boys, and then at Lady Elaine and Sir Hugh. "Brayden, are you paging? Does your mother know?"

Brayden considered what his mother would want him to say, and how ultimately she would not approve of him living the life Siegfried had been given. Still, she is not here, he thought, and he did feel proud to be among the other boys. Brayden inhaled deeply and pushed out his chest. "I am," he said, "at least for a time."

"Great!" Siegfried replied. "A better life here than in that old village. You may actually see some adventure, if you can ever get away from the kitchen. C'mon, Gilly!" Siegfried turned and put up his fists. He and Gilbert started to throw friendly punches at one another. Herman stood by with his staff, shaking his head. Numerous other squires had put down their gear and were mingling with the pages. Siegfried pushed his friend away and turned back to Brayden.

"You've heard about the tournament?" he asked.

"Yes, I hear they are having it this year even though Lord Marshal is still missing."

"Ah. Time goes on. Sir Bellator will make this the best one yet. I'll be in his tent that day. Perhaps I can have you invited."

Before Brayden could answer he saw Sir Osbert pushing through the crowd. The man looked, as always, infuriated.

"What is going on here? Who told you lot to stop practice?" He looked down at Brayden. "You, Rider. Everywhere I see you there is trouble."

"Sir Osbert," Siegfried began, "he is my cousin. We hadn't—"

"Quiet, squire! Pick up your sword and buckler and get back at it."

Siegfried waved goodbye and walked off with the other squires.

Sir Osbert wasted no time and stepped in front of Brayden, his nostrils flaring as he looked down at him. "I can make life more miserable for you than it already is, peasant boy. I have your friend Sir Caelan cleaning animal stalls with his fingers. I can make you join him."

"No page, or noble guest, will do any such thing, Sir Osbert," Lady Elaine said, storming over. "Back to your place with the squires. Leave these boys be."

"Lady." Sir Osbert bowed, and then looked angrily at Brayden once more. He spun and walked off, his nose held high.

Patch came up to him next. "He likes you," Patch said, giggling. The comment put Brayden at ease, if only slightly.

Lady Elaine watched Sir Osbert and turned to her charges. "Now, to the guest chambers. Some of you will be assisting with our tournament visitors, and I need you to be familiar with this part of the castle."

As the pages walked back toward the keep, Brayden looked up, squinting in the sun at the massive structure. He wondered absently by whose hand such an impressive building had been constructed, and how long it had taken. As his eyes followed the windows he stopped, sure he had seen someone looking out upon the courtyard. He covered his eyes with his hand, momentarily blocking out the sun. Staring back at him from inside the castle was Sir Bellator himself. Brayden felt his heart stop for a moment, and then ran to catch up with the other boys.

* * *

The guest chambers covered several floors, all connected by spiral staircases. Each chamber door had its own lock, and some could be locked from the outside as well as the inside. The nicest rooms had stained glass windows. Almost all had large wooden beds or plush mattresses. Lady Elaine walked the pages up and down the stairs and halls, instructing them on where they could go, and where they could not. Brayden learned the top floors consisted of the solar, where the noble family slept, and that no one was allowed entrance without Lady Elaine's leave.

"I bet Lady Josslyn is up there now," Patch said. "Maybe we'll see her at the tournament."

"Maybe," Brayden shrugged.

They continued walking along the hall. Suddenly one of the doors opened and out stepped Bernard. He was as surprised as the pages. He scanned the group and saw Brayden instantly.

"Ah, boys, good to see you up here. How is the tour going, my lady?"

"Very well, sir," Lady Elaine replied. "I trust we're not disturbing you."

Bernard smiled. "Not at all. I am in fact expecting a guest. I wonder, my lady, if I may borrow the Rider boy for a bit."

Brayden felt every eye fall upon him.

"I suppose so. We are done with our inspection for now, though I expect everyone will be ready to answer questions about their assignments with Lady Wymarda." Some of the boys shuffled their feet impatiently, as if they would rather be back doing dishes instead. Lady Elaine continued, unperturbed. "I expected as much. Please return him with haste to the shield room, Bernard. We have much to do."

* * *

Bernard sat Brayden down on a stool and shut the door. He remained standing, listening for voices outside for a few moments, and then sat down next to him.

"How are things with the pages?" Bernard asked.

"They're fine," Brayden said, happy to be reunited with his friend at least for a time. He looked around the room. It was large, cleaner, and vastly more comfortable than the page's quarters, with real furniture. Seeing the space, he wondered why he was not here in the guest chambers with his friend. While he had made some new friends, and certainly enjoyed visiting the different parts of the castle, he wondered why, if their visit was to be a short one, he was not staying here. He was angry at himself for being jealous, but didn't understand why the steward had separated him from his friends, and why no one had stopped him.

"Just fine?" Bernard asked. "Hmm. Are you enjoying the castle so far?"

Brayden shrugged. He didn't want to talk about Edwin Stapleton or the other boys, or how miserable a first night he had had. He didn't want to talk about the strange figure in the main hall either, or his feelings of being watched. There was a muffled knock at the door. He turned his head, relieved their conversation had been interrupted.

"Ah, our guest is here. I think you'll be pleased." Bernard got up and opened the door. Caelan was standing at the entrance.

The young knight took Bernard's hand and shook it, then spotted Brayden.

"Sir Caelan!" Brayden couldn't help but smile as Caelan came over and put a hand on his shoulder, though he was shocked by his friend's appearance. Gone were the knight's tunic and armor. Caelan wore baggy pants and a dark brown shirt, both covered in mud. His hair was filthy and wild. The smell of him was almost overpowering, and Brayden recoiled at the odor. He couldn't stop staring at what a mess his friend had become.

Caelan threw his head back and laughed. "I am a sight, aren't I? It seems a fitting punishment for my transgression is cleaning out the horses' stalls twice a day. A messy job, but at least it isn't the pigs. Besides, I get to spend a lot of time near Sullivan. I can't ride him, but I like having him close." Caelan looked around, hands on his hips. "Well, nice of the Marshals to place you in such plush quarters. Last night I slept in not much more than a ditch!"

"I admit to being pleased with the guest arrangements," Bernard. "Old age has its benefits, I suppose."

"Of course, for me it could well have been the dungeon. I owe you a mighty favor, Bernard. Thank you."

"Nonsense," Bernard said. "Thank Lady Elaine when you see her next."

"I will, but I have to ask. A pardon as friar of Honeydown? Is that really lawful?"

Bernard shrugged, smiling. "I was running out of ideas." He turned to Brayden. "The boy here is in with the pages."

"Really?" Caelan asked. "How do you like it? I remember paging. What I remember most are all the rules. How to bow. How to speak. How to eat. What not to do. What to do. Listen to them all, is my advice. Lady Wymarda runs a tight house, and you don't want to be on her bad side."

Brayden nodded automatically. He had figured that out on his own.

"How is morale among the knights?" Bernard asked.

Caelan shrugged. "I'm not allowed back in their ranks yet, but I understand the knights speak openly of desertion."

"Pay and plunder lacking?"

"Some of that, but there is more. The steward has been sending them on long quests of questionable value, supposedly to find Lord Marshal, but they return after days and weeks, having found nothing." Caelan paused and rubbed his chin. "I don't know."

"What is it?"

"It is as if he is trying to keep them away from something."

"I too noticed there are few knights about for a castle of this size," Bernard agreed.

"That, and many have been replaced outright by mercenaries of dubious value. I'm afraid if Lord Marshal does return he'll have no knights left to defend the barony, or will even have open rebellion on his hands." Caelan paused. "Still no word on him?"

Bernard shook his head in disappointment. "There has been no word of the lord's whereabouts or information on the circumstances of his disappearance. I fear for Lady Elaine. With Lord Marshal gone, she senses forces are closing in around her, and she doesn't mask her dislike of the steward. When asked, however, she did not deny supplying you that letter."

"Well, thankfully that worked out," Caelan said. "Did she say how she came across it, who it was meant for or who it was from?"

"No, and I believe her at her word. Though when we spoke last night, she did mention a man who has had some mysterious contact with the steward. She called him Regin."

Brayden's spine tingled unexpectedly. For some reason, he remembered the feeling of being watched he'd had earlier that morning.

Caelan shrugged. "I don't recognize the name, but I'll ask around."

"There is a tournament approaching," Brayden said hopefully, trying to lighten the mood and move to another topic.

"That there is." Caelan smiled. "You'll enjoy the tourney, Brayden. I'd love to have you in my tent, but I'll likely not be allowed to do much more than feed the horses. Perhaps we can get you into Sir Hugh's tent. The squires always need help, and it may get you a seat in the stands. It beats standing and pushing about in the crowd all day."

"Siegfried suggested I be in Sir Bellator's tent," he replied. He couldn't help but notice Bernard and Caelan looking at one another disapprovingly.

"Perhaps not a bad place to be," Bernard suggested at last. "You'd be sure to see something interesting, and I know Siegfried would like to have your help."

Brayden thought Caelan looked ready to say something, but the knight looked at Bernard and seemed to reconsider.

"Well," Caelan started again after a pause, "it will keep the remaining knights happy for a bit. Spirits will be lifted, albeit briefly. More rumors—I've heard the steward has an announcement to make at the tournament."

"Hmm. I wonder in what regard?" Bernard asked, rubbing his chin slowly.

There was a knock at the door, interrupting the conversation. Caelan froze, and then dove to the floor on the far side of the bed. He popped his head up, then back down. Bernard walked to the door and opened it. Josslyn stood outside.

"Lady Josslyn, what a pleasant surprise. Do come in," Bernard invited.

Josslyn stood her ground, unmoving. "Lady Wymarda begged me to tell you to escort Brayden down to the shield room. He is missing manners lessons," she said sternly.

Brayden put his hand to his forehead. "More manners lessons? I don't even live here. Bernard, can I not be excused?"

"You certainly could use them," Josslyn retorted.

"Now, now," Bernard scolded gently. "Tell the good lady we will be down in a few moments. Brayden, we're guests, and we'll abide by the rules." Bernard bowed. "Thank you, Lady Josslyn."

She nodded and walked off. Bernard shut the door behind her as Caelan got to his feet.

"I best be getting back anyway," Caelan said. "If I'm missed I'll be cleaning Sir Osbert's boots next."

"Agreed. Let's plan on meeting again soon," Bernard suggested. "I hope things will begin to become clear."

Caelan ruffed Brayden's hair and went to the door, looking both ways as if being careful not to be spotted.

"Sir Caelan, they'll smell you long before they see you," Bernard suggested.

Caelan smiled, winked at both of them, and then darted out the door.

Bernard turned again to Brayden. "And you, my friend, let's get you back to Lady Wymarda for those lessons. I'm sure you know most of the answers already, hmm?" But it wasn't Lady Wymarda's questions Brayden wanted answers too. He shuffled his feet nervously, wanting to tell Bernard about the figure in the main hall and the steward watching from the window. No, I'll be brave, he thought. He was being watched, he was sure of it, and nothing Bernard or anyone else could say would make him forget it. He promised himself then and there to find out why.

Chapter Twenty-One

The Library

Over the next few days Brayden tried to adjust to castle life. Daily, sometimes more than daily, manners lessons continued, as did lessons in Latin and French. He found he appreciated the language lessons Bernard and his mother had given him back in Honeydown, finding he was at least as proficient as the other boys his age. This was not lost on the pages, who couldn't understand how a boy who had never lived in a castle could possibly be their equal at reading and speaking the two most important languages in the world.

Each page was assigned daily chores around the castle. Some days these were the same, some days they were different. The pages had little choice regarding manners lessons, but they did have some choice in the work they performed since they were allowed to trade chores with each other in hopes of sticking with the work they liked the most. Of course, in reality some chores were more desirable than others.

To Brayden, it seemed that Edwin Stapleton and his bully friends were typically out helping the knights and squires, while he, Patch, and Daniel found themselves washing dishes or sweeping the floor of the main hall. Patch told him it had something to do with "seniority," whatever that meant. Brayden thought it had more to do with how much bigger Edwin and his friends were than most of the other boys their age. While Brayden would prefer to be out with Siegfried and the other squires, he was happy keeping busy. It gave him less time to think about how much he missed his mother and about the very real dangers he was starting to believe lurked within these walls.

The three of them had drawn lots on who would finish kitchen duty. Brayden had drawn the short stick, and Parch and Daniel eagerly returned to the page room to play cross and pile with the other boys. With a continuous, noisy clatter, Brayden dried and stacked pots and dishes. *These dishes really seem to pile up during the day,* he thought, wondering idly how they'd keep up with them during the tournament and the endless feasting that was to take place.

Finished at last, he hung the last pot and wiped his hands clean. They were wrinkled and sore, and he marveled at how the scullery maids could do this day after day. He walked toward the door and stopped. He heard something. Somewhere nearby a cat was meowing mournfully. Cats were common all over the castle, just as they were in the village, helping control rats and other vermin. He listened in silence and soon realized it was not a cat at all, but a person crying. But, where?

He tried to follow the sound. It seemed to be coming from behind the walls, but as soon as he thought he was getting closer, the sound would move away from him. He walked along the perimeter of the kitchen and came to one of the kitchen doors. He stepped outside into another chamber and then through another door to the courtyard. It was dark now, and stars twinkled overhead. The air felt cool to Brayden after being in the warm kitchen for so long. Torches flickered at various points along the castle wall, but other than the occasional patrolling guard along the castle wall and the muffled crying, the darkness seemed to conceal all movement and sound. He walked along the side of the keep and rounded the corner. There, crouching with her back against the wall sat Lady Josslyn.

* * *

Brayden stood over her, not sure what to do. Lady Josslyn looked up with tears streaming down her face. He waved hello silently, and she turned away from him and sniffled.

"What do you want?" she asked, obviously trying to stop sobbing. She wiped her nose and took a deep breath.

"I thought you were a cat," Brayden replied. "Why are you crying?"

"Never mind, farmer. I'd rather not say."

He ignored the insult, just as he had since meeting her in the forest days before. "It is getting cold. If you're going to cry, why not do it inside?"

"Do you not hear what I said, or are you deaf?" She let out one more sob and then got control of herself. "Leave me be!"

"I only said to get out of the cold air!" he shouted back before storming off.

"Wait, please wait," she called.

Bernard and his mother impressed upon him to be friendly, to be patient. But she was simply rude. Brayden clenched his fists and stopped, and then took a deep breath and turned around.

She wiped her cheeks dry. "I ran away before because of rumors I had heard. Now, I fear those rumors are true." Her tone had changed. In the brief time they had known each other he had gotten used to her sounding defiant, and a bit arrogant. Now, she sounded defeated.

"When you found me, I had run from this place, and hoped never to return. I'm going to go away again. Don't try to stop me," she warned.

"But this is your father's home," Brayden responded, not knowing what else to say. While he had lived in the castle only a short time, and found parts of it lonely and mysterious, he knew that for the residents it was the safest place in the world. Josslyn and her mother were surrounded by soldiers and thick walls no invader, bandit army, or any other threat could ever breach. He couldn't imagine any person, especially one of noble lineage, wanting to leave to live a short, hard, danger-filled life anywhere else.

"My father is gone, and I don't think he'll ever return. He would never allow this."

"Allow what?" Brayden asked. He was a bit confused, and growing anxious about being caught outside. The rules forbidding pages to walk about the castle grounds after dark were quite clear.

"Allow me to marry that wretched steward. What do you think I'm talking about?!" Josslyn said, clearly holding back more tears.

Of course! Brayden recalled what Caelan had said about the steward making an announcement at the tournament. He knew little about marriage, but was old enough to understand the advantage it played in social standing. Bellator would own her father's lands, castle, everything, despite being at least thirty years her senior.

"And he will announce this at the tournament, I suppose."

"How do you know that?" she asked.

He shrugged. "Just a guess. The steward is a knight too, and Bernard says knights are honorable."

"Just because Bernard says so doesn't make it true, Brayden." She stood up and straightened her clothes. She was in loose green leggings and a brown tunic, much like the outfit she had been wearing when they found her in the forest. "It will not do. I will not marry him. I will not marry anyone! He is a repugnant old man! I will run away again. I will escape and never return. I don't expect you to understand."

"I know something about running away," Brayden responded. He thought about their escape from France after his father's capture and how he missed him even now. "We ran away from France when my father was arrested. He's been gone years now. Some think he's dead, but I know he lives, and when I am old enough, I will find him."

"Sir Ban?" she asked.

Brayden nodded. "This castle is yours. I don't think I'd give it up, or give your father up. Can your mother not stop this?"

Josslyn pulled on her hair, a habit Brayden had noticed whenever something disturbed her. "She is a woman, Brayden. Despite being the lady of this castle, in this age she is a woman, nothing more."

They heard barking from several approaching dogs. During his time in the castle, Brayden had caught occasional glimpses of the castle dogs around the courtyard. They were enormous, fearsome, ugly hounds with long necks and even longer jaws. Used for hunting by day and for sentry duty by night, Brayden had heard about their ferocity from some of the other boys who had been caught out past curfew. The guards were only too happy to terrorize anyone they caught, and the pages hadn't snuck out since. The barking was close. To Brayden's horror it sounded as if it was just around the corner.

"Come, curfew is here, and the dogs are not kind to children out at night!" Josslyn took his hand and they ran back the way Brayden had come, only they passed the door to the kitchen and ran to a second, more concealed entrance. It took him a moment to recognize it. This door was behind a thick, thorny bush, and it was small; they had to get down on their hands and knees to access it. Josslyn went first and pushed open the door, and Brayden dove in behind her. She slammed the door shut and bolted it closed. They sat for a moment in almost complete darkness.

"This is how I slip out when I don't want to be seen," Josslyn whispered. "There are passages all over this castle, and I know them all. Follow me. We'll hide for now in my father's library."

Josslyn grabbed an oil lamp hidden nearby, lit it with a reed, and started on. They were in a narrow passage that gradually expanded as they walked. They turned several corners and darted past several dark, empty chambers. The floor sloped up, and the ceiling was low. Brayden imagined an adult would have a difficult time standing upright.

"They use this area for extra storage during sieges," Josslyn said.

"Sieges?"

He followed her until they came to a winding staircase with a wooden door at the top.

"It looks locked," Brayden suggested.

Without responding, Josslyn led him up the stairs. She twisted and turned the metal latch several times, this way and that. Finally there was a click, and she pushed open the door.

"The steward keeps the door locked," she said, "but if you know how to twist it just so..."

They entered a small chamber. Even with the lamp he could barely see, and Josslyn quickly lit several candles that were scattered about the room.

Brayden looked around. Along the walls were shelves containing row upon row of books, their spines in various shades of brown and black.

There was a heavy wooden table in the center of the room, with a single large chair at one end. Stacks of letters and books of all sizes covered the table. Above the chair in the wall beyond was a cross-shaped glass window. Though faint stars shone through the window, Brayden imagined that during the day it provided ample light to read by.

"I've never seen so many books in one place," he said, amazed at the number and selection.

"My father would spend much time here alone," Josslyn said. "He'd read these texts over and over, and not only the Gospels. Since he's been gone, I think I'm the only one who comes up here, or knows what is up here, other than the steward. That awful man has banned everyone from entering this room but himself, and he has his guards on the loose, always on the lookout for trespassers. I don't see why, he can barely read letters or numbers. I hear he can barely understand the castle's accounts." She waved Brayden over to one of the shelves. "Here, let's look around."

Balancing carefully, she pulled a large, heavy tome down from one of the shelves and dropped it to the table with a thud. She began to leaf through it. The book itself was dusty, as if it had been sitting for a long time. The pages were crisp and covered in detailed drawings of what looked like construction projects: cross sections of walls, roads, and large stone towers. Brayden looked at the text, all of which was in Latin, with some notes in French. Two words seemed to repeat, "Vallum Aelium."

"Do you know what these words mean?" he asked.

"I think Vallum is 'wall,' but I don't know for sure. A text on construction. There are a bunch of them."

Brayden went to the shelves. He was awestruck by the variety of literature. He recognized some books from Bernard's small abbey collection, including *The Song of Roland,* and many books he did not by authors he did not know. Some of the names, such as Bede, were barely familiar, but most not at all. His eyes fell on a thick greenish-black book. He pulled it out, looked at the cover, and began flipping through it.

"I know this. This is Chrétien de Troyes. Bernard would read these poems to me. They are about Lancelot and Yvain, the Knight of the Lion."

"Who?" Josslyn asked, flipping through a book of her own.

"Knights. You live here in this castle and you don't read about them?"

She shrugged. "They have a role to play, like anyone." She handed him the book she had been skimming. "Here, this is more to your immediate need."

He looked at the title, the *Book of the Civilized Man*, by Danielis Becclesiensis. "Very funny," he said. He opened to a page in the text and read slowly, struggling to translate the Latin to English and back again.

With attentive ears, hear the worthy words of your father as he teaches you. Listen to what he teaches you and writes for you my son. Let your father's teaching be grafted on your mind.

He sighed, as he recalled his father's, mother's, Bernard's, and now Lady Wymarda's lessons in manners. Bernard liked to speak about how learned Brayden's father was, and he wished his father could see this room now. He put the book down carefully and pulled out another from the shelf. As he did so, a ragged, thinner book that had been stuffed up against the wall fell to the floor. He picked up the book and inspected it. Its sides and cover were badly frayed, and its only identifier was a small golden letter "M" in the top right corner of the cover.

He put it down gently and began to carefully leaf through it, one page at a time. It was covered in scribbles and notes, not like a finished book at all, but more like someone's personal journal. There were details of buildings and drawings of mountains and the countryside. He stopped at one of the pages. The drawings here were maps, maps of what looked like a castle. It was hard to see detail in the flickering lamp light. He traced the lines with his finger. Yes! Here was the main hall, the towers, and the courtyard. Lines seemed to emanate from various points in the castle, some running off the page, others ending near a large, irregular shape surrounding a drawing of a fish.

"Look at this," he called. Josslyn put down a small text and walked over. "It's a map of some kind. It reminds me of our castle here."

"Our castle?" She looked over his shoulder, intrigued.

There was a shuffling at the bottom of the stairwell. They froze and looked at each other in the dim light. The guard!

Josslyn ran around the room and blew out the candles, then whispered, "This way." She dropped to her hands and knees and squeezed herself below one of the shelves, disappearing into the wall.

Brayden looked down, astonished. Hidden underneath the shelf at the base of the wall was a hole, large enough for a child, but not quite wide enough for an adult. He tossed the map book into the pile with the others and dove in after her. Josslyn led the way with the lamp, and as soon as he was safely in, she blew out the light. They were in a small alcove attached to a dark, narrow tunnel. The guard's light, which they could see through the entrance to the alcove, grew stronger, until at last he was in the library with them. He rounded the table, slowly scanning the room for any disturbance.

"He must have seen the candlelight from the bottom of the stairwell!" Brayden complained in a whisper.

"Shh! Quiet!" she whispered back.

The guard's feet came around to the base of the hole He was wearing dilapidated black shoes, the same as those worn by the castle guards. He stood there for a moment, and then walked to the other side of the room.

A cool breeze blew in Brayden's face from the dark tunnel. He felt trapped. "Where on earth does that go?" he asked nervously, pointing in the direction of the tunnel.

"Shh. It leads to the various chambers of the castle, including the steward's."

"What?"

"Quiet! Look."

Another guard had emerged from the stairwell. He stood in silence next to the first guard, and walked around the table like the first one had. His torch was casting off ash, which dropped to the floor in clumps. Brayden watched the ash fall, hoping the guards were smart enough to keep their torches away from the books. A fleck of ash blew into the alcove and flew into his nose. He sneezed furiously.

"Here!" the second guard shouted. Josslyn yanked at Brayden's arm as he sneezed again. The guard was on his hands and knees, peering through the hole and reaching in. They scurried down the tunnel, around a tight corner and out of sight. Brayden lost track of how far they had gone, but was tired from crawling and relieved when Josslyn finally stopped. In a few moments she had the lamp lit once more.

"Where are we going?" Brayden panted.

Josslyn stopped and looked at him angrily. "You bumbling page. They almost grabbed you!"

"Sorry," he said. "I couldn't help it. Where does this let out?"

"Just follow along. It makes me mad. My father would never have let those ignorant guards into the library," she complained. "I would wager they cannot even read their own names!"

"So, where are the chambers?" he asked after finally catching his breath.

Josslyn put her index finger to her lips, and then leaned over. She slowly, quietly, began pulling stones from the wall, creating a small opening. She urged him over, and Brayden peered into the opening. They were looking down upon someone's room. A small candle must have been burning somewhere in the chamber, as he could barely make out a table and bed in the darkness. He looked back at Josslyn.

"Sir Bellator's," she whispered, and began to quickly replace the stones. "This castle is full of loose walls like this. Some I found, some I made."

They moved on. The width of the tunnel expanded, and while still uncomfortably tight for an adult, it was perfectly maneuverable for someone their size. They rounded another corner. Josslyn finally stopped as the tunnel broke off into two directions.

"These tunnels lead all over the castle," Josslyn said. "That one on the left will take you to the main hall. Even I've not explored them all. They're good for spying on people. That is how I heard about, well, what forced my composure away from me earlier."

A cool, putrid breeze came from the tunnel on the right. Brayden looked into it, but could see nothing. The tunnel fell away almost immediately into pitch dark. Brayden shivered. "W-what's down there?" he asked, stepping away.

"I think it may lead to the dungeon, but I don't know, and I've never cared to find out." She turned her attention to the wall before them. "Never mind that now. Help me with these stones. And be careful."

Starting high and working their way down, they quickly created a hole in the wall large enough to crawl through. Josslyn poked her head out and, comfortable no one was nearby, carefully squeezed her body through. Brayden followed her and looked around.

"I bet we're in one of the towers," Brayden concluded out loud. Josslyn nodded.

They had entered onto a floor of one of the keep's four towers. There was a round staircase in front of them, going up, and another that would take them down. Weapons, barrels, and various supplies lined the walls. Straw was everywhere. Arrow slits were placed at regular intervals in each wall.

"How did you know there'd be no one here?" he asked.

"I didn't," she replied. "I just suspected the guards might be out looking for us, or asleep. Come on. Let's put the wall back and then I want to show you something."

He followed her closely up several spiral staircases. She moved slowly, quietly, looking around for more guards as they rounded each turn. They entered the top level of the tower. It too was unoccupied, though like the floors below filled with weapons and supplies. There was a single door, and a ladder that led up to a small opening in the ceiling. Brayden walked over and looked up.

"What is up there?" he asked.

"Shh. It's the mews."

"The what?"

"Sorry, I sometimes forget your lack of worldliness. The falcons are kept up there."

"Falcons," Brayden said to himself. He longed to see one close up, but Josslyn was suddenly pulling on his arm.

She led him through the door and out onto the tower balcony. Brayden almost gasped. From here, they could see the entire castle and the countryside beyond, bathed in blacks and purples. The stars twinkled brilliantly up above, and the land cascaded into darkness in all directions, save for lanterns and torches that lit portions of the castle walls or windows. It was one thing to see it from the ground looking up, another entirely from the top of the vast structure looking down. From here, even at night, the castle looked impenetrable.

"It is amazing," he said quietly.

"My father greatly expanded upon what was here. He was in the crusades too, you know. A bowman. He has told me of his adventures in the Outremer. He built much of this from what he observed there. This is his kingdom."

"This is your kingdom too. You can never leave it," Brayden said, still staring into the darkness. He knew out there, somewhere, was Honeydown and his mother. He longed to bring her to this safest of places. "Your father wouldn't let you, and neither will I."

Josslyn turned to him and smiled. It struck him that it was the first time she had ever smiled at him.

The quiet was broken by the sound of the curfew bell. It was well past the time either of them was allowed to be out of their chambers.

"We'd better go," Josslyn said. "The steward keeps a tight watch. The guards are instructed to take anyone caught past curfew directly to him." They headed back toward the door just as a guard rounded the corner, his hand to his mouth in mid-yawn. Josslyn and Brayden froze as the man stumbled back, his eyes wide with surprise.

Brayden grabbed Josslyn's arm, and they sprang through the door, ran across the tower, and bounded down the stairs. They heard footsteps behind them.

"Stop!" the guard yelled.

"C'mon! We can outrun him!" Brayden shouted.

They dashed down staircase after staircase. On one of the other floors they passed two guards playing dice. The men looked up, and a second later Josslyn and Brayden were gone.

"Hold!" one of the guards behind them shouted. "Stop!" shouted another.

The children could hear dogs barking outside, and imagined the guards they had escaped earlier were also hunting for them.

"Keep going! Not much further now!" Josslyn yelled, though she, like Brayden, was giggling wildly.

They bolted through a large door that opened into the main keep. Josslyn slammed it shut behind them and lowered the cross bolt. They ran on, and moments later could hear the guards pounding on the door.

They bounded up a set of stairs, and then another, passing the chapel, the kitchen, and then the shield room. The page quarters were now just up ahead. Josslyn stopped and leaned against a wall, breathing heavily. Brayden had his hands on his knees.

"We're almost back where we started," she said, slowly catching her breath.

They looked at each other and began laughing again. Brayden clapped his hands silently. It had been the most fun he'd had since arriving in the castle.

"I'm heading back to my chambers," Josslyn said. "I hope I won't be seen. I trust you know where to go from here."

He nodded, still breathing heavily, but happy, the happiest he had felt in days.

Josslyn ran off, and then stopped and turned. "Thanks for thinking I was a cat," she said, and darted out of sight.

Chapter Twenty-Two

Edwin

Brayden tried to pull the door to the page quarters open, but it was locked from the inside. He knew he was very late. Lady Wymarda had warned the boys about timeliness and punctuality, how important these qualities were to a proper nobleman, reminding them diligently about the need to mind the bells, and quizzing them periodically on the sundial in the courtyard and the cycles of the year from a large calendar she would produce from a thick book. He looked into the dim of the hallway in either direction. There was no sign of the guards, though he could still hear the dogs barking outside.

He put his ear to the door, wondering if he should knock. To his surprise, he heard muffled voices. The boys were up, and if an adult was with them inside, he couldn't tell. He decided to chance it. He knocked lightly on the door. Nothing. He tried it again, harder this time, and listened.

"Who is it?" said a voice.

Brayden pulled back in surprise. "It is Brayden."

"Brayden who?" the voice said.

"Rider, Brayden Rider."

"Rider? As in horseback rider?"

"No, it is me, the page! Or, well, actually I'm a guest, not a page."

"No pages here, only knights. When you get dubbed, come back, we'll let you in."

Brayden slumped back. He was concerned he'd be spending the night in the hallway.

The door opened suddenly. Patch peered out, smiling at him. "You may enter. And where have you been?"

Brayden pushed into the room and closed the door behind him. The boys were all awake. They were bunched into four groups, each group playing dice or jacks, and all were excitedly whispering and hopping up and down. In the middle of each group was a small lamp to illuminate the games.

"You're up late," Brayden said.

"You're one to talk," Patch replied. "And you didn't answer my question."

"I've been to the library, upstairs. Lady Josslyn showed it to me. Lord Marshal has the most amazing book collection," he said.

"The library, with Lady Josslyn?"

Brayden nodded. "Then we climbed to one of the keep towers. You could see the entire castle and the countryside from there. We also surprised some of the guards, who chased us, but we locked them in the tower."

"What?" Patch stared at him in disbelief.

Brayden thought the look on Patch's face was priceless.

The group nearest Brayden and Patch had halted their game of dice to listen intently. Out of the corner of his eye Brayden could see that Edwin Stapleton too was staring at him from his own group. The boy had a mean look about him, but then again he always did.

"And there are tunnels," Brayden continued, suddenly proud of the attention and relishing the opportunity to brag in front of Edwin, who he imagined was grinding his teeth right about now. "Tunnels throughout the castle. We were only in one area, but you can spy on anyone, including the steward."

"Incredible," was all Patch could say, shaking his head in amazement. "You've got to show us."

Before he could answer, Daniel yelled from the nearest group. "Brayden, come and play here! Tell us more!"

Brayden and Patch sat down with the other boys. Daniel handed him the dice, and they began to play raffle. Daniel won the first two rounds, getting two twos and two sixes. Brayden recovered quickly, however, and scored two ones, a high six and three fives.

Patch slapped Brayden on the back, laughing at his other friend's loss.

"You cheat!" Daniel called, shaking his head. The boys broke out in laughter and catcalls.

"He doesn't cheat," said a voice nearby. "His kind isn't smart enough to cheat."

The laughter stopped as Edwin stood over them. Pushing into the group, he kicked the dice across the floor. They slid erratically, coming to a stop several feet away.

"Stop that," Daniel said.

"Quiet, rat," Edwin responded. Two of Edwin's friends came up behind him, glaring down at Brayden and his friends. "Your father may be a rented guard, but he is *my* father's vassal." He smirked.

Edwin had the look, Brayden thought, of someone used to getting his way all of his life. He also seemed taller and bigger than ever.

Brayden took a deep breath, stood up, and walked over to pick up the dice. As he returned to the group, Edwin grabbed his hand, took the dice, and threw them against the wall.

"You do as you please in France? You do as you please in that hovel of a village?" he taunted. "I bet you follow the cows around with a shovel."

Brayden could feel the blood rush to his face. Anger welled up within him, but he didn't want to fight. Edwin was bigger and stronger, but more than that, the words his mother had told him about avoiding fights came to him. Fights solve little but cost much, she had said.

"Leave him be, you snotty-faced swine!" yelled Patch.

One of Edwin's friends, a squat, chubby boy named Montfort, came forward and pushed Patch down. Patch got up and charged, but Montfort grabbed him and put him in a bear hug. Patch tried mightily to break free, but his exertion was pointless.

Daniel started to get up, but Edwin's other friend, a lanky, homely boy named Torn, shoved him down. Torn quickly had his foot on Daniel's chest, pinning him down.

"Let them go," Brayden warned, still restraining his emotions.

Edwin laughed and cocked his head back, his hands on his hips.

"Or what?" he asked. "We know who you are, Rider. Listen, boys!" Edwin turned around and looked at the others. "This French peasant boy just gave me an order. We don't like your kind here, Rider. Your father was a heretic, and I bet you are too."

"I'm English," Brayden steamed, "and my father is a Templar knight."

"Your father is a thief who worships the devil. Or should I say, *was*."

He could take no more. Brayden lunged at Edwin, knocking the larger boy back against one of the cots. The entire room erupted in shouts and pushing as everyone pressed forward to see. Edwin recovered quickly and threw Brayden to the floor. Brayden got up and swung, but missed. Edwin hit him with a right cross, knocking him down once more. Brayden squinted and put his hand to his eye, but Edwin was on him again, punching and shoving, with Brayden doing the same.

The door swung open, and Lady Wymarda rushed in, Hugh Morgan at her side. They spared no time pulling the boys apart, both still swinging.

"Enough, enough!" Lady Wymarda shouted.

The pages silenced immediately. Montfort released Patch with a push, and Daniel shoved Torn's foot away. Sir Hugh grabbed Edwin, holding him back by the arms.

"Sit down," Lady Wymarda said forcefully to Brayden. He looked around in a daze and sat down on the nearest cot, trying to catch his breath. His head was spinning and his eye ached. Everything seemed to stop, and he realized he was not just out of breath, he was sobbing.

"The guards outside said someone has been sneaking around, so I came to see if everyone was here. I didn't expect to find this though," she said, her voice harsh as she inspected them, looking first at Brayden, then at Edwin. She focused finally on Brayden. He returned her glance, tears in his eyes.

"Sir Hugh, take Mr. Stapleton to the squires' residence. He will sleep there tonight. I expect better behavior from the offspring of a noble family such as yours. Now out of my sight! We'll speak in the morning."

"Yes, mum," Edwin grunted, bowing his head. He smirked again in Brayden's direction as Sir Hugh took him out the door.

Brayden knew this was no punishment at all. Every page in the castle yearned to spend time with the older boys. As he watched Edwin leave, Lady Wymarda turned her attention to him.

"And you, sir, what of it? You're here as our guest, not to cause trouble. It looks like you'll have a nice black eye. I'll fetch you some parsley and meat for that, but another fight, and I'll have you and your priestly friend escorted out of the castle." She turned to the assembled group. "And I don't know who was wandering this night, but I'll not have anyone out past the curfew bell again. The steward's rules. And no more games! Hand them over."

She held out her hand. The pages slowly placed the dice in her palm. She looked around one last time. There was absolute silence.

"Lights out!" she commanded as she stormed out of the room.

Everyone was in their cots moments later, whispering about what had just happened, what Edwin had said, and what Lady Wymarda might do. She came back minutes later and applied the parsley and a thin slice of cool meat to Brayden's swollen eye. It was still painful, but the remedy helped. She knelt by his cot.

"Sleep now," she whispered, delicately brushing the hair out of Brayden's face. "That Edwin can be a difficulty sort, and I know all about being new. I'll tell you about it sometime."

She stood and walked to the door, then paused, apparently hearing someone snicker in the dark.

"Silence!" she screamed. "Or by the love of the Holy Roman Emperor, you thorns in my flesh will not leave this room for a week!" She walked out and slammed the door behind her.

Brayden lay back in the cot and wiped his face clear of tears. He took a deep gulp of air, and thought about this night. Some things had become clear. Despite his trouble with Edwin, Patch, Daniel, and many of the other boys had accepted him. Though he feared the steward, he had befriended Josslyn and knew that while he lived here he was in the care of not only Bernard, but Sir Hugh and a strong, caring woman. He closed his eyes, and thought of his mother, hoping she was as safe as he felt right at this very moment. In moments he was asleep, sleeping as soundly as he had since arriving at the castle.

Chapter Twenty-Three

Happy News

The tournament was two days away, and every corner of the castle and the surrounding countryside was buzzing with activity. This was to be the last tournament of the year, and word had gone out to manor villages near and far. Visitors from across the countryside were arriving in droves. Cooler air had swept in as well. The season was getting late, and the days shorter. The trees had erupted in color, and leaves were quickly falling. Winter would be here very soon, and no one wanted to miss this last festival before the snow and ice came.

The population of the small town at the base of the castle had exploded, with innumerable new shops and stalls opening up to serve the tournament guests. There was a constant hubbub as people celebrated, shopped, traded, and socialized everywhere. Along with the tents and camps now dotting the surrounding hills, the road leading to the castle was choked with carts and makeshift stalls.

Brayden looked out from across the courtyard to the distant castle gate. He saw Caddaric dart through the gatehouse tunnel and disappear outside, followed by a squad of scruffy keep guards. The steward had released him from his confinement early. As Caddaric had predicted, Sir Osbert quickly found the crowds unmanageable, and upon his reprieve the captain was charged with keeping order at the castle gates and in the local area. The captain had told Brayden that there had already been numerous petty crimes, recalling at least two fights and various other unruly behaviors stemming from drunkenness. He was levying fines every day, he claimed, and joked that the treasury would not go wanting for funds this year.

The tournament itself would be held just outside the castle walls, and this morning Sir Hugh was giving Brayden and the other boys a tour of the progress. For many, this was their first tournament, and they were amazed at the work that had been done. The steward had arranged for laborers to come from across the barony to assemble the grandstand and set up the arena's fencing. The arena itself was a long oval, separated down the middle by a four-foot-tall wooden fence. This, Sir Hugh explained, was the tilt, and separated the two combatants. The earth inside the arena had been ground fine. Grandstands lined every side, and Sir Hugh estimated that when they were finished, hundreds would be able to watch the tourney from the ground, from the grandstands, and from the castle walls themselves. The knight rarely hid dislike for the steward, but applauded Sir Bellator for throwing one of the largest tournaments of the year.

Multi-pointed pavilion tents in every shade and hue were being set up around the arena and across the fields. Sir Hugh intimated that the preferred lodgings were in the town itself, though by now these were long gone and newcomers would be spending chilly nights outside. As they walked, Brayden and the other boys noticed that the competition had begun to arrive. Inside some of the tents, Brayden spotted carefully arranged armor and weapons, with squires and young boys, not much older than himself, quickly darting in and out. Nearby, ramshackle stalls were set up for visiting horses.

"How many knights will be coming, Sir Hugh?" Patch asked.

Sir Hugh looked around. "The steward sent out many heralds three weeks ago. I say we'll have a good turnout. Perhaps one or two hundred knights, in addition to those of Castle Strand."

Two hundred! Brayden could feel his eyes go wide in disbelief. He was as excited as the others at the spectacle about to unfold, and stole glimpses of every knight he could spot. Some were practicing swordplay, while others were adjusting armor with the help of their squires.

In the middle of the commotion, a man standing alone amid the pavilions caught his eye. The man was dressed in a dark gray tunic that fell to his feet, and was quietly, carefully, pulling various bowls and sharp metal instruments out of a trunk and placing them on a sturdy wooden table. Driven into the ground nearby was a white painted pole wrapped in blue and red cloth. A small brass bowl sat precariously atop the pole.

"Sir Hugh, who is that?" Brayden asked, pointing to the man.

"The surgeon," he responded evenly. "He'll be plenty busy in two days time. Come."

* * *

Like the visiting warriors, for the knights of the castle the days leading up to the tournament were filled with practice and drills. Sir Hugh had left Brayden and the other boys to sit along the garden wall to observe.

Brayden and the pages watched in awe as one knight after another came out of their residences, some wearing various pieces of armor, others simple tunics. A dozen or so practiced with swords or axes, taking turns hitting the small bucklers of their opponents or one of several thick wooden poles that had been set up around the courtyard. Another handful of knights took turns on horseback lunging at a straw dummy tied to a pole. The dummy, or as Sir Hugh had called it, the quintain, had a large metal shield tied to its side. Holding lances, the knights repeatedly charged, hitting the quintain on the shield, trying to jar it loose. With each hit the pages broke out in cheers.

A steady parade of guests came and went down the courtyard path and into the keep. Many stopped to watch the knights practice, some calling out to the warriors as they went about their exercises. Patch wondered aloud if the knights were practicing so close to the front of the keep on purpose, showing off to the arriving guests, many of whom were competitors themselves. Brayden suspected he was right, for the mock combat of the knights was an imposing sight.

Out of the corner of his eye Brayden saw a single rider charge out of the gatehouse and through the courtyard at full speed. Several passersby cursed and hollered as the rider nearly knocked them down on his way in. The rider stopped abruptly at the front of the keep, his mount snorting in protest. He was out of breath and dismounted quickly, almost tripping before landing safely on the ground. On his tunic was the purple and black falcon, the symbol of Lord Marshal's house. He disappeared into the keep. Brayden and the pages were not the only ones to notice the mysterious rider. Several of the knights and squires stopped what they were doing to see who it was.

After a few moments the knights were back at it. Brayden recognized many of the participants, either by face or by their colors. Sir Hugh and Sir Osbert were on horseback, and on the field with swords were Sir Rogers du Burgh, Sir Richard Grey, and Sir Pan Cornwall. Several squires were out as well, though Siegfried had been spending much of his time at the steward's side and was not on the field. Brayden also recognized Gilbert Beauchamps and Herman Balk, two of Siegfried's friends he had met before. They were running around picking up dropped shields and swords, and fetching water for the practicing knights. To Brayden's disappointment, Caelan was nowhere to be seen.

As he sat watching, Siegfried himself emerged from the keep and ran over to the knights, his face determined and serious. Brayden called his name as he went by, but Siegfried didn't hear. Something must have happened, Brayden thought. Siegfried addressed Sir Osbert and Sir Hugh first, and as he spoke the others stopped what they were doing and walked over, encircling him. Whatever it was, Siegfried had news.

Before he could guess what was happening, Lady Wymarda rounded the corner. She was wearing an enormous, yellow-toothed grin on her face and walking lightly, almost skipping. In his time in the castle, she had never looked happier. She stopped and stood in front of the line of boys, silently inspecting them.

"Enough gawking, boys," she said. "You'll see the real thing in just a couple of days. Now, I have exceptionally happy news! Sir Allard lives, and he is freed! He is on his way here now. And Lord Marshal will not be long in following!"

That was the news Siegfried bore. The pages started talking excitedly among themselves. Most had only heard stories of Sir Allard. He was rumored to be the greatest warrior in the barony, perhaps even in all of Britain. Caelan had spoken of him often, and had been his squire many years before. Brayden smiled, watching as Patch jumped up and down with joy. It was, indeed, happy news. He thought too of Josslyn, and how much the news of her father must mean to her.

"Now, all of you will follow me to eat," Lady Wymarda continued. She stopped and looked at Brayden. "All but you, Sir Rider. You're dining in your friend Bernard's chambers. How nice. Eat quickly and join us promptly soon after. Now off!" With a wave of her hand, Brayden and the other boys scattered, everyone still chatting about the return of the champion and the lord.

* * *

Brayden was welcomed to Bernard's chambers with a hug from his friend.

"I decided it would be nice to eat here for a bit," Bernard began. "The main hall is crowded now with the guests, and peace and quiet will be scarce while the tourney is going on."

Bernard had had a table and three chairs brought to his room. Every candle was lit, and the sun was just starting to go down, making the room feel cozy and warm. In the center of the table were two plates filled with an assortment of fruit, a small cooked bird, and a loaf of bread. Brayden's mouth watered at the sight, until his concentration was interrupted by a knock at the door.

"Ah, excuse me. There are three of us for dinner tonight."

Bernard opened the door, and as before, Sir Caelan stood in the entranceway. The last time Brayden had seen his friend he was covered in filth. Though not at all clean, he no longer smelled of the stable and he wore a light green tunic free of dirt.

"Good evening, sirs. Well, Sir Allard returns, and soon Lord Marshal too. Many prayers have been answered it seems," Caelan said.

"Yes, yes, indeed happy news," Bernard replied. He motioned for Brayden and Caelan to sit down. They did as they were instructed. Bernard said a short blessing, and they began to eat.

"I did have a chance to speak with Lady Elaine after the messenger brought the news," Bernard said. "She is, as you can imagine, ecstatic. The circumstances of their capture and escape are not yet known, but things should become clear soon." Bernard raised an eyebrow, and bowed his head. "Bless them Lord that they both live," he said quietly.

"They were held by more than country footpads, I suspect," Caelan suggested. "And this is not entirely good news for the steward."

Bernard raised an eyebrow and reached for the fruit.

"Will you be in the tournament?" Brayden asked, anxious to hear what Caelan had planned now that his freedom from Sir Osbert would soon be granted.

The young knight laughed. "Ah, with my hard labor I'm in good shape, but a bit out of practice weapon-wise. With Sir Allard's return on the morn, I suspect I will be freed. We'll see." Caelan finished off his bread and stretched, then pulled off a piece of the bird. "I've none of my own weapons, but Sir Martin left me his sword and dagger before he passed. I'll have those at least."

"Sir Martin?" Bernard asked. "The same Sir Martin you mentioned was killed at a tourney?"

Caelan nodded his head as he nibbled on a small bone. "The same. Sir Martin was a good man, and I believe I mentioned once a close friend of Sir Bellator. They met one another many years before in the king's army and joined Lord Marshal here in the king's fight to subdue the Welsh and outlaw princes. Sir Martin knew these lands well, and was a mapmaker for the king before retiring here. He spoke and wrote more languages than I have fingers on one hand."

"An odd place to end up," Bernard said. "Surely with such an educated background he could have remained in service to His Majesty. Talented mapmakers provide a decisive advantage in wartime."

Caelan nodded. "True. He drew extensive maps of the surrounding countryside and this castle itself, keeping his notes in a small book that he kept very close. Some said he had involvement with the Mappamundi of Hereford as well, but one cannot be sure."

"What is that?" Brayden asked. He was enjoying the conversation, his friends' company, and especially the cooked bird. He took another piece and chewed happily.

"A map of the known world," Bernard responded. "Hereford's is especially impressive, I hear, though I've not myself seen it. What, again, were the circumstances surrounding Sir Martin's demise?"

"Things became strange about him," Caelan continued. "He would disappear for long stretches—without his horse—and suddenly reappear, as if he had not gone anywhere. He said to me once he was looking for something. What, I am not sure. He became withdrawn as the end drew near, as if he were afraid of something, or someone. He was certainly an old man, being a couple of years over forty. Perhaps age played a role in his behavior."

Bernard caught the comment full on and raised an eyebrow in irritation. Brayden knew full well his holy friend was a good deal older than that.

"He was killed at tourney, true?" Bernard asked. "His armor shattered."

Caelan nodded. "Killed, in a joust, by the steward's lance."

The three of them exchanged glances.

Brayden's mind raced back to that day at the abbey and what Bernard had done to Caelan's armor. He then thought back to the night in the library with Josslyn, and to the maps in the small book he had found. Could they be Sir Martin's? He opened his mouth to speak, and then stopped himself. He wanted to help his friends, but did not wish to reveal his or Josslyn's whereabouts the other night, let alone lead any of them into danger.

"The maps, what are they like?" Brayden asked innocently, deciding not to volunteer any information yet.

"Drawings of the castle and the surrounding countryside. Caves and tunnels underground he had found and been exploring, or at least so much as I understood it. It was a peculiar talent, but the maps and all of his work were well hidden, and to my knowledge were never found after his death."

"Do you know something, Brayden?" Bernard asked, a hint of curiosity on his face.

"No, no," he avoided their eyes. "Just interested, that's all."

"There is one more thing," Caelan continued, leaning close and lowering his voice. "Sir Martin was not just drawing maps. He was *looking* for something. There *is* rumor of treasure in this land. Roman mines filled with gold. As much or more than that of the Templars."

Bernard's face filled with disbelief. "Mines? Hmm. Rumors are just that, my friend. Ancient pagan stories. Besides, while the Romans built some amazing machines, even massive wooden wheels to carry out water from deep underground, those mines would have flooded or collapsed long ago. No one could recover whatever is down there." He stopped and looked about the room slowly, as if reconsidering. "But, you suspect Sir Martin believed it to be true? You suspect Sir Martin was after it?" he asked.

"I do. And, I suspect whoever else is after that treasure would kill for it," Caelan responded coldly.

A chill went up Brayden's spine. He stood up and walked around the room, rubbing his arms with his hands. Treasure, and close by. Despite the danger, he could only imagine the things he could do if *he* found Sir Martin's treasure for himself, and for his family. His mother would never want for protection, and perhaps he could even find his father.

"Brayden," Bernard said, breaking Brayden's concentration and drawing him back to the table. "I want you to stay close to Sir Caelan during the tournament. Keep your eyes open for anything out of the ordinary, and let him know right away."

Brayden nodded. He felt better being counted in and given a job, no matter the role.

"I'm going to stay close to Lady Elaine and Lady Josslyn," Bernard said.

"You suspect they are in danger, even with Sir Allard returning?" Caelan asked.

"I suspect they're in greater danger now than ever," Bernard replied. He took the last piece of bread and began to eat it. Caelan and Brayden remained silent, letting Bernard's statement hang in the air.

Chapter Twenty-Four

The Champion

Early the next morning, Sir Hugh and Lady Wymarda rushed Brayden and the pages out to the courtyard. The morning air was crisp and cool, and Brayden shivered as he stood with the other boys, many still in their bare feet. A ghostly fog hung about the base of the castle walls, and the sky was a dark gray. Caelan and several of the knights had emerged from their quarters and joined the pages and squires by the entrance of the great keep. Guards lined the castle walls overhead, looking on. Bernard, Lady Elaine, and Lady Josslyn emerged from the keep and stood nearby. Brayden looked around, but saw no sign of Siegfried or Sir Osbert.

One of the gatehouse guards shouted, and seconds later a large man on horseback stormed in. He covered the length of the courtyard quickly, yanked his horse to a stop before them and jumped off in one smooth motion in front of the assembled crowd.

After his own father, Sir Allard was the most impressive man Brayden had ever seen. He was older than many of the other knights, but was enormously strong and powerful in appearance. His eyes were a piercing blue, and his grayish brown hair hung down to his shoulders. His beard was long and full and covered a thick, strong jaw. He wore a coat of chainmail over a heavy leather garment. A long black and purple cape hung from his shoulders, fastened with a silver chain. He adjusted the long broadsword that hung at his side, and approached Lady Elaine.

"My lady," he said in a deep voice, bowing.

"Welcome home, Sir Allard. Welcome home." She smiled, cupping her hands. "We have prayed for this day."

"My lady, it is good to be home, and sweeter still, your husband, our lord, is not far behind."

"Thank you," she replied, her eyes tearful.

"Lady Josslyn," he said, bowing before Lord Marshal's daughter. "You've sprouted up like a strong rose." Josslyn blushed, and bowed in return.

He looked at Bernard, recognition crossing his face as his mouth opened into a broad smile.

"Bernard? Bernard of Honeydown? How long has it been? We welcome you as a resident here finally?"

Bernard smiled and bowed his head. "Years, steward. Years. But no, I'm merely an honored guest of the House of Marshal."

Sir Allard looked at Sir Hugh and Lady Wymarda, standing amidst the pages. He took Sir Hugh's hand and shook it firmly. "Sir Hugh. It is good to see you, to see all of you, and thank you boys for the welcome." He scanned the pages. "Some new faces, I see." Sir Allard looked directly at Brayden, his hands resting on his hips. "And who is this?" he asked.

"Sir Allard," Bernard said, "this is Brayden Rider. You will remember him as the only son of Sir Ban Rider du Bayonne."

Sir Allard bowed his head slightly, and Brayden admired the powerful man, embarrassed and unable to speak.

"Ah, I do remember, and turning into a fine young man. I know of your father, Brayden. A noble man he is. Welcome, Brayden, to our castle."

He said *is*, Brayden thought.

Sir Allard looked around at the assembled crowd. Before he could say another word Sir Caelan and the other knights embraced him. They shook hands, laughed, and patted the lord's champion on the back.

At length Sir Allard broke off and walked into the keep. They all followed him inside and climbed the steps to the main hall. Sir Allard strode confidently across the room, looking straight ahead as if the space and everything within it belonged to him. He paused briefly when he recognized Caddaric, and shook the captain's hand. Then he made his way to the center of the hall.

Sir Bellator and Sir Osbert were standing on the platform at the far end of the room. Siegfried was nearby, standing alone by a table. While Sir Osbert looked at the steward, then at Sir Allard, and then back at the steward repeatedly, Sir Bellator's face was expressionless. Numerous noble guests and friends of the Marshal family milled about nearby.

Sir Allard stopped at the platform edge.

"Welcome home, Sir Allard," Sir Bellator said quickly. He bowed slightly, never once taking his eyes off Lord Marshal's champion. He opened his hands. "We prayed for your safe return."

"Your prayers have been answered. And Lord Marshal's too, I hope," Sir Allard replied.

"Of course," Sir Bellator agreed. "How is our lord?"

"Lord Marshal returns in three days time, in time for the tourney. He hopes to bring with him our prey."

Sir Bellator's face went blank. "Your prey?" he asked quietly.

Sir Allard turned to face the people who had followed him in. "Our capture and detainment was no random incident, but an orchestrated event, by whom, we do not yet know. But we have uncovered evidence implicating a man of these parts. We hope soon to have him and his accomplices in our hands when we will find out how deep this treachery goes."

"Very good," Sir Bellator muttered.

"Sir Osbert?" Sir Allard said, facing the steward and his man once more.

The knight straightened up. He looked nervous and uncomfortable, like a boy whose father had just caught him stealing.

"En route I heard many accounts of villages being ransacked by unchecked banditry. I am sad to say these accounts are true, and I'm disappointed in your effort, if indeed there ever was one. You are relieved of the title of protector of these lands. You will be allowed to compete in the tourney, but henceforth are confined to this castle until Lord Marshal decides otherwise."

Sir Osbert looked plaintively at Sir Bellator, who ignored his gaze, as if indifferent. Brayden and Caelan smiled at one another. Brayden looked over at the pages. Edwin, who had come in with several of the squires, stood nearby, fuming.

"Perhaps these reports are exaggerated," Sir Bellator finally suggested. His face was red, as if anger was boiling under that mask of calmness. "We sent out parties to search for you and Lord Marshal. Finding you both has been our priority these many months."

"You were no aid to our escape, and the village death rolls do not lie," Sir Allard responded sternly, apparently uninterested in Sir Bellator's excuse, "and things will be placed in their rightful order now. You've conducted your last duties as steward of this barony." He again turned to the audience of knights, pages, squires, guests, and nobility gathered in the main hall. "Friends and guests, tonight we feast in celebration of a strong harvest and the return of our gracious lord. Let it be known that our barony is safe once more, and all will be put to right, in this castle and in the villages beyond."

Everyone erupted in cheers and laughter as Sir Allard stepped back into the crowd and began speaking with the various people assembled. It seemed everyone at once wanted to speak with him about their ordeal and Lord Marshal himself.

In the midst of the celebration, Brayden noticed that Sir Bellator and Sir Osbert had shrunk into the shadows. Brayden wanted very much to speak with Siegfried, but his cousin was nowhere to be seen.

* * *

Brayden caught up with Josslyn as she was exiting the hall.

"Listen," he started, "I'd like to go back to the library tonight."

"What did you say?"

"The library. I think there is a treasure map there left by one of the knights. I think the steward, er, Sir Bellator now, is after it."

"What makes you think that? Please make some sense, farmer," she said, apparently amused but at the same time, if Brayden was reading her reaction correctly, intrigued.

"Yes, please make sense," Patch interjected. Unbeknownst to Brayden, he and Daniel had been standing nearby. "What about this treasure? You say you have a map? Whose treasure is it?"

Brayden put his hand to his head, exasperated. "The Romans, I think, and I don't need any more help, from either of you."

"Romans?" Patch and Daniel said together. They looked at one another in confusion, and then at Josslyn. It was then Brayden noticed his two friends looked hurt. He knew his friends could be trusted, but he didn't want them endangered. He also knew that he *did* need them, more than he wanted to admit.

"Fine," Brayden stammered, "but it could get us in trouble."

"What are we? Children?" Patch replied instantly.

"And last you told me, this is still *my* castle," Josslyn reminded him. "We'll escort you to the library. No arguments, cattle herder."

"What is a Roman?" Daniel asked.

They broke out in laughter. "All right," Brayden said quietly, leaning forward so they could hear. "We'll meet after tonight's feast by the shield room, as soon as everyone is asleep. I've not been to a tourney before, but I wager after a day of contests, drinking, and celebration, everyone will be good and tired soon after curfew."

"Deal!" Patch and Daniel said simultaneously.

His friends began chatting excitedly among themselves about the upcoming day of festivities and games and the adventure ahead. Brayden thought only of Sir Martin's book, and what Sir Caelan had said about what one would be willing to do for it. He prayed that if that was indeed what Sir Bellator was looking for, the former steward had not yet found it.

Chapter Twenty-Five

The Tournament

The horns blew at exactly noon. Brayden and the other boys stopped what they were doing and looked at each other. They all knew what the signal meant: the tournament had begun. All morning they had been busily preparing the kitchen and main hall for tonight's feast in celebration of the season and the tournament, and now, the return of Sir Allard, and soon, Lord Marshal. Everything they had been preparing for was about to begin.

They had readied the tables in the main hall by covering them with long thick cloths, and the lord's table on the platform of the hall they covered in silk. While Patch and Daniel carefully placed candlesticks across every table, Brayden had the honor of carrying out the saltcellar. The silver dish was heavy, and he moved slowly so as not to trip, finally placing the receptacle in the center of the middle table on the platform, exactly in front of where Sir Allard, Lady Elaine, and soon, they hoped, Lord Marshal would sit. Other boys brought out large wooden vessels shaped like boats, placing them on the ends of the long tables. These nefs would hold every spice the castle could provide for the guests' enjoyment.

Lady Wymarda told the pages they could depart for the tournament as soon as the horn blew, and Brayden and the other boys wasted no time running out of the keep, and darting across the courtyard and out the main gate. They rounded the castle wall and scrambled through the field of tents, finally coming to the arena.

Brayden looked around. The grandstands were already packed with onlookers, and there were crowds of bystanders everywhere. People lined the road that led through the village, and Brayden could hear the cheering growing louder in the distance. Colorful banners fluttered overhead, and he noticed for the first time that a crowd had even gathered atop the castle wall. Struggling to see past the adults, he wished he had thought of that himself.

The procession rounded the corner of the last house and started toward the arena. The crowd turned and cheered in unison, clearing a path for the knights and their retinue. The knights looked magnificent, Brayden thought. They were dressed in full regalia, each wearing armor and colorful surcoats and carrying a lance with his banner flying upon it. Many of the men wore colorful crests of one symbol or another on their helmets, and upon their backs were slung their shields, each adorned with a coat of arms or other symbols of their families or lands.

Alongside the knights walked their squires, their aids, and several judges who had arrived from various counties. Brayden spotted many of the knights of the castle as they strode by: Sir Hugh, Sir Osbert, and even Sir Caelan were mixed in with all of the visiting knights. Caelan's outfit was a bit more ragged than his peers'; as predicted he had been freed of his duties shortly after Sir Allard arrived and allowed to participate, but he'd had little time to prepare for the tournament itself.

Sir Bellator followed several moments later. He looked superb, Brayden thought, despite his personal dislike of the man. He wore a dark surcoat, with a shield slung upon his back emblazoned with golden battleaxes. Siegfried walked next to him on his far side. Brayden yelled, and Siegfried looked around, saw Brayden, and waved excitedly.

The herald began his announcements as soon as the knights had entered the arena. They circled once in turn, and then stopped, lances lifted and facing the gathered crowd. Brayden and his friends struggled to hear over the cheering and shouting. There was to be, he gathered, a principals' tournament, in which the squires would be competing against one another and in front of their knights. There were to be two days of jousting, starting early in the morning and going until dusk. The herald noted several other events, including sword duels and archery contests, which would take place over the next two days during breaks in the action. The herald then thanked the Marshal family for hosting, informed the crowd of Lord Marshal's impending return, and began to introduce noble guests and the contestants themselves. Brayden could just make out Lady Elaine and Josslyn sitting under a colorful tent in the center of the grandstand.

The introductions went on for over an hour, with each knight's name, family name, and history being announced. The herald stopped speaking only to take an occasional sip from a nearby mug.

"Very interesting, but will he ever stop?" Patch asked at length. Brayden knew the herald was one of the busiest persons at the tournament. It was he and his peers who had travelled across England and Wales to announce the tournament. It was he who had arranged the rules with the approval of the various competing nobles. It was he who had been responsible for arranging the schedule of events and he who would be the announcer throughout the tournament. It must be an exciting, if taxing, job, Brayden thought.

"I hear he does this all again tomorrow, starting early in the morning," Daniel stated.

By the time the herald was finished, many in the audience were sitting on the ground, more than a few were yawning, and an older man nearby was fast asleep, snoring gently while lying sideways in the dirt. At long last, the herald took one last sip from his mug, and announced the beginning of the tournament. Another cheer erupted as the horns blew again, and the crowds and the knights dispersed. There would be time for games, and then the principals' tournament would begin.

* * *

Brayden, Patch, and Daniel spent the afternoon running from one game or event to another. To their delight, Lady Wymarda had allowed the pages free time until they were needed in the kitchen that evening, and the boys took advantage of it.

They had been fortunate enough to bump into Bernard, who upon hearing that they had not eaten all day, happily gave them each enough silver coin to purchase almond fruit patties. As they ate, they walked by various booths and tents. It seemed as if every vendor in the country was here, selling everything from shoes to wool, toys to pots and pans. Brayden enjoyed listening to the surrounding conversations as they walked, and it struck him that there were so many things he did not know. They passed a heated argument between several Englishmen and a foreign merchant over a tax on wool the king had recently imposed. The merchant, who Brayden gathered was from Florence, was complaining loudly in a heavy accent about the tax and its effect on his business in Britain. He repeatedly threatened never to return.

The boys walked on and came across a crowd gathered around a colorfully dressed woman. A painted sign nearby indicated she was a fortune teller. Brayden stopped to listen as Patch and Daniel continued on.

"Famine, I predict. Famine and poor harvest. Never ending cold and rain," she kept warning.

"How do you know that?" asked one of the onlookers.

"Never mind that! When? When will this happen?" inquired another.

"Our sins will be punished, just a few short years from now!" she cried, raising her hands to the sky, then dropping them and pointing to a small metal dish with a few coins inside.

Patch grabbed Brayden's arm. "C'mon, that is nothing but superstitious silliness. How could there be a famine? This is the strongest harvest we've had in years. Let's go see the Butts."

* * *

The Butts was the archery range. Here, a long, flat field separated several lines of archers from the target mounds, which were large piles of dirt with various colorful rings painted on them. Brayden had never used a bow before, though he understood archery was the only sport allowed in many parts of the country, and by law every man was to own a bow.

The archers took aim and fired one after the other. At the far end of the range a man yelled, "Nock, mark, draw, and loose!" over and over. Some of the archers followed his signal; others ignored it and fired at their own pace. Brayden could hear the arrows whiz through the air, most of them missing their targets entirely.

"Look, over there," Patch pointed. Josslyn herself was at the front of one of the rows, preparing to fire. They walked up to her. A neat row of arrows was sticking out of the ground at her feet.

"Funny to see a girl here," Patch commented.

Josslyn ignored him, concentrating intently on her aim.

"Say," Patch continued, "I always wondered, what kind of name is Josslyn? French?"

"English. And my friends call me Joss," she responded, her eyes fixated straight ahead.

"Joss?"

"You're not my friend."

Patch subdued, Daniel decided it was a good time to show off. "My father has already showed me how to mark and shoot. I bet you won't make it halfway to the target," Daniel commented.

Josslyn lowered her bow and looked at them in disgust. "Very well," she said, "take aim." She offered Daniel the bow.

Daniel took it and positioned himself. Josslyn was the tallest of the four, and while Daniel was easily the strongest, the bow was longer than he was tall. He took one arrow after another, aiming carefully. Each one in turn whizzed far overhead or wide of the target.

Josslyn grabbed the bow back from him, shaking her head. "Perhaps you should go back to your father for more practice," she cracked. She pulled an arrow out of the ground and calmly took aim. The arrow launched, spun through the air, and hit the white circle on the mound with a light thud. She hadn't hit a bull's eye, but she'd come far closer than Daniel and many of the other archers nearby.

"Wow," Brayden and Patch said simultaneously.

Josslyn shrugged. "I still prefer the sling myself—you can hide one easily enough, and I take one wherever I go. But, my father was once an archer in the king's army, and he insists I practice with the bow."

A horn blew. Everyone around them stopped what they were doing and looked in the direction of the arena. The principals' tourney was about to begin. The boys said goodbye to Josslyn and made their way quickly back to the joust.

* * *

The lists were crowded with onlookers, though the people had dispersed a bit since the morning, enjoying other activities. Brayden, Patch, and Daniel had little trouble making their way near the front, maneuvering under and around various bystanders.

On the far side of the arena Brayden could see the squires hastily putting on armor while trying to control their horses. They were to a man smaller and much less impressive figures than the nearby knights, who stood by wishing them well while laughing at their clumsiness.

Brayden knew this was an important event for the squires. Here, and for many for the first time, they could practice their new skills at horsemanship, jousting, and dueling against others their own age from other parts of the country. All were likely nervous, Brayden thought, though proud and eager to show off too.

Brayden spotted Siegfried at last. He was leading his horse by the reins out onto the field. He looked crisp and ready, prepared, unlike so many of the other squires straining under armor that was too heavy for them or struggling with weapons they could barely lift. At Siegfried's side walked Sir Bellator. They stopped near the end of the tilt. Sir Bellator inspected him, whispered something in Siegfried's ear, and walked off in the direction of the grandstand. Brayden wondered what he'd said.

In minutes, Siegfried was atop his horse, a light brown palfrey. He held his shield up high and his lance straight up, and awaited the judge's signal. Brayden watched as his cousin barely flinched despite the heavy equipment he bore. In contrast, Siegfried's opponent on the far side of the arena was struggling to keep his horse steady, much less his lance; on more than one occasion the boy almost dropped his shield

At long last the horn sounded, and the squires charged. In moments they were riding at full speed, their horse's thundering toward one another. Brayden blinked as they crashed, and he could hear the crowd all around him express their delight at the spectacle. Siegfried seemed to easily parry the blow of his opponent, whose lance bounced harmlessly off his shield. Siegfried's lance hit as well, almost knocking his opponent over before the boy was able to steady himself and remain ahorse.

The contestants wheeled their horses around and prepared to charge again. Once more they bounded down the field, lances pointing straight ahead. Again, the lance of Siegfried's opponent was deflected, but this time Siegfried did not miss. Aiming high, he hit the opposing squire just under his chin. The boy's helm popped off, as the head of the hapless youth snapped back and forward violently. He tumbled off his horse and landed with a thud upon the dirt below, unmoving.

"Brayden, your cousin is good with that lance," Patch said excitedly, "and I bet that poor fellow will be less a few teeth."

Brayden nodded, while he and the rest of the crowd sat, watching quietly as the downed squire's knight and another man ran out to tend to him. They emptied a bucket of water on the boy's head, helped him get up and slowly walked him off the field.

There was a smattering of applause as Siegfried lifted his lance and shield in triumph. Brayden began to get up to run across the arena and congratulate his cousin but stopped himself when Sir Bellator appeared next to Siegfried's horse. The former steward took his squire's lance and shield, and then shook Siegfried's hand, finally raising it up above Siegfried's head. Both of them were laughing.

"Shall we go see your cousin?" Patch asked, apparently anxious to run over to the area where the squires and knights were before another round of jousting began.

Brayden looked at Sir Bellator and Siegfried together, and then glanced over at the boy who had been knocked off of his horse. He was lying outside a tent by himself, his face covered in blood. His knight walked out from inside the tent, yelled something indiscernible at him and then threw a dark brown rag at his face. "No," Brayden said, shaking his head. "You can if you like, but I think it best if I head back to the kitchen. I suspect Lady Wymarda is looking for us by now."

Patch and Daniel looked at each other and shrugged. "We'll go back with you," Patch said. "Two more days of this anyhow, and tomorrow with real knights, not these amateurs."

They got up and ran across the busy field toward the castle gatehouse.

Chapter Twenty-Six

The Feast

The kitchen was a madhouse. The kitchen staff expected at least one hundred guests every night of the tournament, not including the various musicians, jugglers, and other entertainers, and by Brayden's count there were at least twice that many. The music in the main hall was loud, filling the air with sound that Brayden and the others could hear inside the kitchen despite the commotion.

To serve all the guests, there were ten cooks on hand and at least as many sculleries and servers, of which Brayden was one. Patch and Daniel were both on dish detail, with the occasional opportunity to go into the main hall to deliver spices or other small items. Every room seemed crowded, and people were coming and going in every direction. Brayden wiped his forehead. Normally as cool as the rest of the castle, the kitchen on this night was sweltering.

There were five main courses, with as many smaller side dishes and desserts. Each main course was a different meat dish, served on enormous platters to each table. The first courses were the roast lamb and roast pig, both of which had been cooking slowly on massive rotating spits in the center of the kitchen. Dozens of venison pies were sitting out to cool, and rows of salted, baked cod lay nearby. Various meat and potato puddings sat steaming in heavy black cauldrons, and a large pot of chicken and nut bokenade made Brayden's stomach growl uncontrollably. Despite the copious amount of food, he and the other boys had been offered nothing more than stale bread and fruit.

Desserts were still being arranged, with various pastries, candied fruits, and cream pies under construction in different parts of the room. To Brayden and most of those present, the most impressive dish by far was the wild boar. It sat, cooling, on a massive platter that would be carried out to the hall by four men when ready to serve. Surrounding it, and indeed, as Brayden understood, inside of it, were dozens of cooked and stuffed birds of every color and variation. An enormous red apple was jammed into the creature's mouth. This was the night's masterpiece, the creation of Lady Wymarda and the other cooks.

Brayden had already been back and forth between the kitchen and main hall dozens of times. His feet ached, and he was hot. He thought of the feast at Michaelmas back in Honeydown, and how different this experience was. There, the villagers were purely thankful to still be alive another year. In the castle, these noble people wanted for nothing, but more food and drink, half of which seemed to end up on the floor. Brayden took a deep breath. Despite how tired he was, and how much he wanted to get away from these people, he was determined to be patient, to get through the evening and then escape to the library as planned.

Sir Allard, Lady Elaine, and Josslyn sat at the high table atop the platform. As each new course was presented, Siegfried and several of the other squires carefully served them first and remained on hand to cut up and serve the remaining dishes as they arrived. Brayden darted in between the tables and guests, many of whom seemed more interested in the wine than the food, bringing platters of steaming meats and long loaves of hollowed out bread. Each guest served themselves with whatever knives they had on hand, while throwing scraps to the abundant number of dogs that multiplied in number as the evening wore on. Looking around, Brayden saw Bernard sitting at one of the tables near the high table speaking with another guest. Caelan was sitting further down, conversing with several other knights Brayden didn't recognize.

He listened while he served. The guests' conversation seemed to be a never-ending babble of silly gossip and deal making. He heard one agreement to wed a daughter of some standing to a young boy she had never met. Another table was having a rousing discussion on the safety of living near the coast where there were fears of a rebirth of Norse marauders. When he overheard at least one man speak of the drop in banditry since the events in Honeydown, Brayden suddenly felt proud. He paused, anxious to ask a question, but was immediately pulled back to duty by a nearby guest demanding more mead.

Brayden passed Siegfried on the way back to the kitchen. His cousin pulled him aside and leaned over.

"Brayden, did you see my joust this afternoon?" he beamed.

Brayden nodded. "I did. You really knocked him off his horse."

Siegfried smiled proudly. "I did indeed. Sir Bellator was right. Aim for the head."

"Wasn't that against the herald's rules?" Brayden asked.

Siegfried brushed the comment aside. "Only if they don't call it," he answered. He winked at Brayden, and then looked around to see if he was needed at the table. Everyone around seemed to be laughing and enjoying conversation.

"Listen, I know Sir Bellator is no longer the steward, but he has many friends, in this barony and others. He may be leaving Strand when Lord Marshal arrives, and he's asked me to join him. I thought maybe I'd ask him if you could come."

Brayden's head spun. Leaving Honeydown, and his mother, for the castle with Bernard was one thing. Leaving with Siegfried in the service of a knight he distrusted was another altogether.

His surprise registered with Siegfried, who put his hand on Brayden's shoulder. "I know it's a lot to think on. If it's about Aunt Alice, I understand it is hard to be away. But you're barely a child anymore, and you have to think about where you will be if, well, if your father is gone."

Brayden was taken aback. "What do you mean? He is only imprisoned," he answered defensively. His face grew hot, and he had an uncomfortable feeling in the pit of his stomach.

"I know you believe that, and that is good. But what if he is not? What then? You'll have nothing, other than what you can win, like me."

The music stopped as four men entered, carrying the boar on a thick platter. The crowd hushed, and then erupted in applause and shouts as Sir Allard stood and began to clap.

"We'll speak on this later," Siegfried said as he and the other squires rushed over to clear the high table. The fabulous dish was placed carefully in the center, and arranged so that all assembled could gaze upon it, apple and all. Despite how he felt about what Siegfried had said, Brayden could not stop staring at the spectacle.

Sir Allard stopped clapping and remained standing, motioning for everyone to sit and waiting for the guests and musicians to silence themselves.

"On behalf of Lady Elaine, wife of Lord Marshal, we welcome you all, our friends, to Castle Strand, the barony of Lord Marshal in the realm of our King Edward." He turned to Lady Wymarda, who had emerged from the kitchen with several of the other cooks. He bowed in her direction. "And we thank you, Lady Wymarda, for this wonderful feast. Lady Wymarda has served many feasts in this hall, and this one will be remembered just as fondly. I was a young squire, if I recall, at my first one. She has again outdone herself."

The assembled guests clapped and hollered in appreciation. Lady Wymarda blushed and quickly curtsied.

"We await Lord Marshal's return," Sir Allard continued. "I know that gives boundless joy to his wife and daughter, and it should to us as well. For too long have the people suffered from unchecked banditry and fear. This tournament shall mark a turning of the corner, as we begin to set things right."

Brayden watched as the assembled crowd clapped once more. The applause died down, replaced with murmurs among the guests as Sir Bellator slowly stood. Despite his demotion the former steward was dressed as fine as any noble, wearing a well-cut black and purple tunic trimmed with velvet. Like many others at the feast, he had removed the chaperon from his head, and his thick dark hair hung loosely about his face.

"You're forgetting, brother Allard, the hard work we put in to manage this estate while your lieges were off fighting the king's wars."

Brayden looked over to the main table. Sir Allard was standing still, coolly smiling at this challenge.

Sir Bellator continued. "Our champion here must recall the depletion in our coffers and in our men from the wars against the Scots. How much plunder did the people see? I ask, in all that time, only, where could it be?"

"Y-you speak like a snake, Sir Bellator!" It was Hugh Morgan, shouting from across the room. A large mug of dark liquid was still in his hand, its contents sloshing out onto the floor.

Sir Bellator only smiled, keeping his focus on Sir Allard. "As I was saying, my lord, we've men fine enough to train squires and little pages, but good for little else. Drink to yourself, Hugh."

Sir Morgan roared, and slammed his mug to the ground, the ale splattering against the table and one of the tapestries. He began to move forward in challenge, but Sir Allard raised a hand and Sir Morgan stopped, fuming. Sir Allard and Sir Bellator stood motionless, staring at one another. It was then that Brayden noticed how close Sir Bellator's hand was to his dagger.

The great hall was silent as a tomb. Brayden finally let his eyes scan the room. He could see his friends, Patch and Daniel, at one of the halls' entrances, their mouths open wide. Lady Wymarda was by the kitchen entrance, nervously chewing on a thick pink knuckle, while the rest of the kitchen staff had stopped what they were doing and joined her. Lady Elaine and Josslyn looked up at Sir Allard, while Siegfried stood nearby the main table silently waiting, like everyone else, on the champion's next move.

"Out of respect for our guests, brother, perhaps we could settle this argument on the field tomorrow?" Sir Allard suggested. Lady Elaine turned to face the room, a blank look upon her face.

Bellator leaned back and smiled, his hands on his hips. "So be it, brother Allard. We'll engage after the morning rounds, at high noon. Sleep well tonight. I trust this time you won't be late."

The two men stood silently for several more moments, as if waiting for the other to sit first. Bellator took a deep breath, and took his place at the table. Sir Allard followed suit, giving the signal for the music to resume. In moments, the assembled guests were speaking loudly once more, and Brayden watched as supporters and the curious suddenly surrounded both men. All around him he could already hear bets being made on tomorrow's match.

Siegfried made his way over to Brayden. "They've never liked one another, and my silver is on Sir Bellator."

***

The feast went on for another several hours, though the guests became noticeably less raucous as the night wore on. The large quantities of food had taken their effect, and by the end many of the desserts remained untouched. Cups, platters, and uneaten food were everywhere. Even the dogs were lounging around, their bellies as full as their human hosts'. Sir Allard gave the servants permission to take what they could for themselves and donate any excess to the less fortunate who, as custom held, had gathered outside the castle walls. Many of the servants paced the hall waiting for the guests to leave, anxious to get their hands on as many leftovers as they could carry.

Several large buckets had been placed at the ends of the tables for the guests to wash their hands, and people were slowly dunking their hands in and wiping them dry on their own clothes.

Two French knights walked up to Brayden as he was bringing in another bucket. Their smocks were decorated with gold fleur-de-lis. As they dipped their hands into the murky water, he focused in on their discussion.

The first knight snorted loudly. "The Templars. Rumors persist that they are heretics, and worse. Their leader de Molay is the worst of the lot."

"Yes, King Philip will leave none alive," the second one added. "Burned at the stake or left to rot is the best for the lot of them." He looked down. "What do you stare at, servant boy?"

Brayden realized his hands were shaking. Just as he was about to let go of the handle, someone darted into his field of vision. Caelan grabbed the bucket from Brayden, and nodded respectfully to the knights as he held it up for them.

"Uh, bonjour. Sir Caelan de Spero, at your service. We welcome our guests from France," Caelan said, bowing awkwardly.

The French knights, their hands cleaned to their satisfaction, grunted in return and walked off, mumbling to themselves in French. Caelan put the bucket down. "Here." He picked up a ginger cookie from a plate and handed it to Brayden. "Let's get some air."

Moments later they were outside. The air was cool, and they were not alone. Groups of people huddled together, continuing their mealtime discussions and deal making. Many were speaking openly about the tournament tomorrow, and the excitement of seeing Sir Allard and the former steward battle the next day.

"Don't listen to those French knights," Caelan suggested. "They know nothing about it."

Brayden stared at the ground as they walked. Other than Edwin's goading, he had heard little mention of the Templars over the past several weeks. The conversation of the French knights, and the one he'd shared with Siegfried earlier, had brought his emotional connection with his father and the Order back all at once.

"What if it were true?" Brayden asked at last.

"Listen, I don't know your father, but if he's anything like you, he is a tough one, and a cunning, brave man. He'll do fine. Just ask Bernard when you see him again." He smiled, and messed Brayden's hair as he changed the subject.

"For tomorrow, I could really use all the help I can get. I've no squire other than what Sir Hugh will lend me to help with my things. I've borrowed some armor, and Sullivan and I would be honored to have you in our corner."

"You're going to joust?" Brayden asked excitedly. While Caelan had been in the opening procession, Brayden wasn't sure how serious he was about the competition.

Caelan shrugged. "It is what a knight does. Look, I'll likely be knocked off in the first round, but I'd like your help until then. After that, we can take a break."

"May I bring a couple of friends?" Brayden asked, thinking of Patch and Daniel.

"Sure, if Sir Hugh hasn't claimed them first. He can't hit a stuck pig with a lance, but he loves a following."

They stopped, listening as Lady Wymarda started calling for her help to return. Caelan and Brayden smiled at each other.

"I spent many a long night as a page in the kitchen," Caelan said. "You'll miss it one day, I promise. Life only gets more complicated. Now, get going. I'm off for some rest before tomorrow. Find me in the morn by the arena!"

"And Sir Caelan," Brayden called after him. "Bonjour means 'good day' in French."

"Oh, right. Then what should I have said?"

"Bonne nuit."

"Very well then, my friend. A bonne nuit to you and our French guests!"

Caelan bowed and walked off. Brayden's mind drifted only briefly to the work still ahead of him in the kitchen. Though tired, he was already focused on the rendezvous he and his friends had planned for later that night.

Chapter Twenty-Seven

Capture

A mess of food, spilled drink, and sleeping people covered the tables and floors of the main hall. Lady Wymarda had put the boys to work cleaning the hall and the kitchen, but recognizing the futility of the task, retired in exhaustion soon after midnight, bidding the boys to find their own way back to their quarters. Moments after she disappeared from sight, the boys crept to the shield room. They waited anxiously for several minutes, but Josslyn was nowhere in sight.

"Just like a woman. Late," Daniel grumped.

"Shh!" Patch insisted.

"Shh, what?" Daniel said. "Nothing can be heard over all that snoring out there."

"Quiet," Brayden ordered. "I hear something else."

"Of course you do," a voice said behind them.

The three boys jumped in surprise, Daniel almost darting out the door. Josslyn emerged from behind a wall, holding a small oil lamp.

"And who was saying I'd be late?" she asked, straightening out her clothes.

Brayden and Patch reflexively looked at Daniel, and then up at the ceiling.

"Where did you come from?" Patch asked.

"Where we're going." Josslyn pointed to a small hole at the base of one of the walls. "As I've said on more than one occasion, my castle is full of secret passages. Now, come on, let's get to the library quickly and get that treasure map."

The boys stood about the hole in the wall, dumbfounded. For all the times they had been in this room, they had never noticed it before. Josslyn explained the loose stones, and showed them how to properly rebuild the wall when they were through. They followed her in, one at a time. Daniel, the largest, had the hardest time squeezing through the opening in the wall and maneuvering the tighter passages. They went right, and then left, following the dim light from Josslyn's lamp as Patch demanded to know how much further with every step. Brayden paused when he recognized they were at the place in the wall that overlooked Sir Bellator's chambers. He caught himself reaching up, ready to pull a stone from the wall to see inside.

"Brayden!" he heard Josslyn call from the front. He quickly caught up with his friends and crawled through the hole and into the library.

Josslyn quickly lit several of the large candles with her lamp, and the room glowed with light.

"Look at all these books!" Patch said. He and Daniel immediately started leafing through the first books they could get their hands on.

"I cannot read more than every fourth word, but Lord Marshal must be truly learned," Daniel said.

"Be careful with those," Josslyn warned. "Mind your filthy hands." She looked over at Brayden. "Hurry, remember the last time we were in here."

"What are we looking for again?" Daniel asked.

"It's a small, thin book with the letter "M" on the front," Brayden replied. "It belonged to a talented knight named, Sir Martin."

While Patch, Daniel, and Josslyn inspected the various texts, Brayden searched for Sir Martin's book on the shelves. It was not where he remembered leaving it. He looked on every shelf and under every book scattered on the table, but found nothing. The others helped him search the stacks as well, but they couldn't find it either.

"Someone else has been to the library," Brayden said at last. "Sir Martin's map book has been taken." His heart sank as he considered what could have been.

He was shaken out of his discouragement by voices nearby. He couldn't tell if they were guards or not, but as before there was movement at the base of the stairs. Josslyn motioned the boys into the tunnel, blew out the candles, and then dove in after them. Brayden followed right behind.

They waited several minutes, but no one else entered the library.

"Where do these tunnels go?" Patch asked at length.

"All over the castle. Some lead outside," Josslyn said. "I think they are for drainage, but I've never found water in them."

"You could spy on anyone from these," Patch suggested.

Josslyn ignored him and turned to Brayden, who sat quietly, thinking about Sir Martin's book. "I'm sorry, Brayden. Perhaps whoever else was searching for it finally did find it. Let's head back."

On their return they took the same route. As his friends continued, Brayden paused once more at the point in the wall that overlooked Sir Bellator's room. Curious, he pulled one stone out of the wall, and then another. He looked in. Unlike before, it was now well lit. He could plainly see a large bed, a chest, and a wood table adorned with several thick candles burning brightly. In the center of the table was an open book. Brayden squinted, studying it closely; it was the book of maps.

"Wait!" he cried. His friends stopped, and tried as well as they could to turn around in the small passage.

"What are you doing?" Josslyn asked crossly.

"What is it?" Patch asked, pushing past Brayden to look through the hole.

"Sir Martin's book. It's in the steward's, er, Sir Bellator's chambers. Look there." He pointed.

"Well, you can't go in there," Patch said dismissively. Daniel was nodding in agreement, a worried look on his face.

"Say if I wanted to. How would I?" Brayden asked.

Patch shrugged. "Clear the rest of the stones, climb down the wall, and pray no one is about," he answered simply.

Josslyn looked in. "I don't think this is a very good idea," she said.

His friends looked at him anxiously. Brayden knew they would not follow, and he didn't want them to. But he wanted that map more than anything he had wanted in a long time. He listened for a few moments and heard nothing. He cleared more of the stones, stacking them carefully on the floor of the tunnel. He went in feet first and slid down the wall, scratching his back on the rock as he wiggled through the small opening. He hung momentarily by his hands then dropped with a thump to the cold wood floor. Wasting no time, Brayden bounded over to the table and stood over the book. It was opened to the same map page he had seen in the library before. He carefully tore out several pages and tucked them under his belt, and then turned to the wall. The faces of his friends, staring back at him from the opening in the wall, had turned white with fear. He followed their eyes. The door to Sir Bellator's chamber was slowly swinging open.

* * *

His heart almost exploded in terror. His eyes darted around the room in every direction. The bed! He dove under it just as the door opened wide. A man in heavy boots walked in. He was followed shortly thereafter by another man, this one wearing ragged brown shoes covered in what looked like black soot. His filthy shoes left tracks on the floor. Brayden stretched out from under the bed as far as he dared, but could see nothing but their feet.

"So, your man has everything set for tomorrow?"

Instantly, Brayden recognized the first voice as Sir Bellator's. The man's feet were pacing the length of the room, back and forth. Brayden stole a glance at the opening in the wall from under the bed, praying neither of the men would notice it.

"Aye," the other man said. "They are ready."

"Good. And pray for their skins they are. I'm still outraged by the failed attack on the village, and we do not have much time."

"The knight's appearance in Honeydown was unfortunate, but Samain knows what to do. His men will catch Lord Marshal in the **Nifylog** Pass. The lord will never make it here. The other responsible party has been, well, dealt with."

Brayden shuddered. Samain. The name hit him like lightning. The bandit leader they had seen in the clearing, the man who had led the attack on his village.

He tried to focus, and though familiar, he could not place the second man's voice. It was scratchy, almost chilling. He thought back to something Bernard had said about a mysterious associate of the steward. Regin was his name, he recalled. He wanted to look out from under the bed, but forced himself to remain absolutely still and breathe quietly. Now he knew these men had been responsible in some way for Lord Marshal's capture, and intended to intercept and likely kill him on his return home.

"You baited Sir Allard well at the feast, my lord," the second man said.

"Yes. For a moment I thought he'd let that buffoon Morgan challenge me, and the game would be up."

"Hmm. Not likely. Lord Marshal's champion is a man who fights his own battles."

Sir Bellator's pacing stopped suddenly. "What are you implying?" he asked. Brayden could sense the tension in the man's voice.

The second man seemed to ignore him and continued. "Only hit him in the chest with the tip of your lance."

"His armor is arranged then?"

"He will fall at noon, if your aim is true. Remember Sir Martin."

Sir Martin and the shattered armor! Brayden's mind spun. He recalled the stories Bernard and Caelan had shared about the fallen knight.

"I told you never to speak of it!" Sir Bellator roared.

Brayden could see the second man's feet take several steps back, away from Sir Bellator's fury. But he continued to speak, as if unfazed. "My apologies, my lord. And the lady?" he asked quietly. "What of her?"

"We'll be rid of Allard and Marshal in one day's time," Bellator responded curtly. "Leave her be for now. We'll keep her and her daughter close to us, just in case."

"As you say." The second man chuckled. "With the map, you have everything you want."

Brayden forced himself to collect his thoughts. He knew he had to escape and warn Sir Allard, Caelan, and Bernard. But how? He could not get to the wall without being caught. He'd have to wait for Sir Bellator to retire and then try to sneak out.

"Almost everything. Indeed, my master will be pleased," Sir Bellator said. "Go now, we meet at the tower in two days time."

The man with the ragged brown shoes went out and shut the door behind him. Sir Bellator walked to the table and sat down, shuffling papers. He became quiet, and Brayden guessed he was reading. He prayed Sir Bellator would not miss the pages he had torn out. Brayden remained still. He was afraid, but anger burned within him as well. A part of him wanted to jump out from under the bed and challenge the former steward himself.

There was a knock at the door. Sir Bellator grunted, got up, and opened it. Brayden peered out from under the bed. While he couldn't see faces, he recognized the voices immediately.

"Excuse us, sir," Patch began. Brayden noticed his friend's voice was quaking. "We, uh, we found the page quarters locked and wondered if you would be so kind as to open the door for us."

Brayden peered up at the hole in the wall and then in the direction of the door, ready to jump out if Sir Bellator tried to hurt his friends.

"What?" Sir Bellator snapped back.

"Sir," Daniel chimed in. "The page quarters are—"

"I heard him the first time!" Sir Bellator yelled, cutting him off.

Brayden could see Patch and Daniel step back fearfully, and then Sir Bellator appeared to push them both out into the hall.

"Guards!" Sir Bellator shouted. "Guards!"

Brayden couldn't see his friends anymore, but wasted no time scrambling out from under the bed and across the floor.

"My liege?" One of the guards responded to Sir Bellator moments later.

"Take these whelps to the squires' quarters," Bellator bellowed. "Tie them to a bed if you have to. Gag them, guard them, and ensure they miss the opening ceremonies of the tourney tomorrow. If you find them out again, see them to the dogs."

Brayden grasped at the wall, trying to climb up the stones toward the hole, but he couldn't get his footing. He jumped, stretching himself to reach the opening, but it was just inches from his fingers. Suddenly, just as he was about to run back under the bed, two arms reached out. It was Josslyn. He grabbed her and she tugged him up. She pulled and he pushed himself up with all the strength he had. They wasted no time rearranging the stones in the wall, and then stopped as they heard Sir Bellator reenter the room.

"Did you hear?" Brayden whispered, panting as he tried to catch his breath. "Did you hear what they plan?"

"Not so loud, and I-I did, or most of it. Who w-was that awful man with Sir Bellator?" she stuttered. Her hands were shaking.

"I didn't see him, or, well, at least not his face. Did you?"

"O-only partially, I didn't want to be seen. He was frightening. He was short, and had scars up and down his hands and arms."

"Scars?"

Josslyn nodded, her face fearful, yet determined. "Come," Josslyn urged. "We have to find Sir Allard. We have to save my father. Wait here. I'll see if the library is clear. Here, take this."

She handed him the lamp with jittery hands and shuffled down the tunnel toward the library, disappearing quickly into the darkness.

There was a crash, then a thump, and finally silence. Brayden strained to hear, but there was nothing.

"Joss!" he called quietly, still mindful of his proximity to Sir Bellator's chambers. He looked through the cracks in the wall at the room below, but it was now empty. The man had disappeared. "Joss! Are you there?"

There was no response. A breeze blew from behind him, as if a door had opened. The flame in the lamp fluttered uneasily. He felt alone, cold. Then he heard it. A chilling exhale only feet from where he sat.

"Joss?" he called fearfully, this time in a whisper. He looked about wildly, waving the lamp, but seeing and hearing nothing else.

Brayden backtracked, moving in the direction of the breeze and away from whoever, or whatever, lurked beyond. He moved quickly, not thinking. Instead of using the tunnel to the main hall, he turned right, following the breeze. Could this be a faster way out? He only hoped. The tunnel grew wider here, and after several minutes it began sloping downward. He put a hand to the floor, feeling its dampness. It was colder here too; the air was dank, and a sweet, rotten stench seemed to suddenly surround him.

He stopped and held the oil lamp aloft as the tunnel ended, realizing he was in a small room with a large metal door on the far side. Alcoves were cut into the walls, and rusted cages big enough for a man were set in each. He gulped. Decaying straw and filth were everywhere. He held the lamp to the first alcove, then the second, settling in on the third. He recoiled in horror. There, his face mangled and frozen in fear, was the body of Corbat Handhafte, the bailiff of Honeydown.

Brayden dropped the lamp, plunging the room into absolute darkness. He fell back, screaming, almost tripping over in shock. Someone grabbed him from behind, and he lurched forward in a panic trying to jerk free. His every limb twitched wildly, but his opponent was too strong. His attacker pulled him close and covered his mouth and nose with a moist rag. The strong smell of mandrake filled Brayden's nostrils. He could feel his eyes roll back as his body went limp. No more struggle, his mind demanded, as a deep, peaceful darkness overcame him.

Chapter Twenty-Eight

Rhiannon

Brayden awoke in a cool, darkly lit chamber. His head ached, and his hands and feet were bound in tight leather straps. He tried to swallow, but his mouth was gagged. He blinked several times, trying to clear his vision.

His eyes finally focused, and he looked around. The surrounding walls were made of rough stone, with narrow windows looking outside. Lit torches sat in sconces on the walls, and there was a heavy wooden door opposite him. Numerous weapons littered the walls and floor. He looked up. Several strong timbers supported the ceiling, each several feet apart, and he could see a ladder leading to a large opening above. Then it suddenly struck him. He was back in the topmost level of the tower he and Josslyn had snuck into several nights before, the night they had been to the library for the first time. The opening in the ceiling led to the rookery, and the door in the wall led outside to the top of the tower. He heard a groan nearby and looked around.

Leaning up against one of the walls was Josslyn. Her eyes were open, though her hands and feet were bound like his. When she saw he was awake, she began mumbling and awkwardly pointing with her chin. He rolled away from her and froze. Across the room, near the spiral staircase, a thin, ugly man with a dark complexion was sitting on a wooden stool. His pants were dirty and he wore a leather coat and a light brown cap. One of Sir Bellator's men, Brayden suspected. As the man stared back at them, he twirled a long, sharp dagger. He smiled at Brayden, revealing a mouth devoid of teeth.

"Awake so soon? Let's rest a bit more, boy," he suggested. "Your time is coming." The man walked over to him, and as Brayden struggled, he produced a plain glass jar. Brayden could smell the mandrake from where he lay. Brayden squirmed uselessly. Not again, he thought. The man poured the foul smelling mandrake onto a rag and shoved it under Brayden's nose. Brayden gagged, trying to shake loose, but his head grew heavy, dizzy. Unable to fight, he succumbed to sleep once more.

* * *

Sun lit the chamber as Brayden opened his eyes, squinting. He wanted to cough, but his mouth was still bound as tightly as his hands. The sickening smell of the anesthesia permeated the room, and he felt nauseous. He looked in the direction of the staircase. The stool was there, but the toothless man was gone. The torches had burned out, and judging by the light, it had to be midmorning. He closed his eyes and listened. Yes, he could hear the faint sound of cheers and shouting. The tournament was taking place somewhere outside. He struggled to get free, but stopped after several pointless moments of trying.

"Make no sound," Josslyn said. He had forgotten she was there. He looked over in amazement as she casually sat up. His eyes grew wide when he saw that her hands were free.

"I've been rubbing the leather binds against that battleaxe all night," she said. "The captain scolds his men to stow their weapons. Lucky for us they rarely listen."

Against the wall, partially covered in straw behind where she had lain, was a small silver battleaxe with a thick wooden handle. She winced in pain as she rubbed her hands together. Brayden noticed that her wrists were bleeding and bruised. She had been lying on top of the axe, keeping it out of the guard's sight while she cut through her binds.

She worked quickly, leaning over and loosening the gag that covered his mouth. Brayden coughed, finally getting the hideous taste out of his mouth. Ignoring the straps that still tied her own legs, she got up and hopped over to the ladder. She looked up toward the opening and began calling quietly.

"Rhiannon. Rhiannon."

"What are you doing?" he asked, annoyed that she had left him bound.

"Shh!" she scolded him. "Rhiannon!"

"Cut me loose and we can get out of here," he cried desperately. "The tournament has started. We have to warn Sir Allard!"

"Quiet, please!" She leaned over him. "I'll tighten that gag again. The guard could be back at any second, and besides, we are in the tower and have nowhere to run from up here. Rhiannon!"

He took a deep breath, telling himself to trust her. They had been up here before, of course, and if the guard was watching the staircase below them he knew they truly had no way out. He lay his head back, looking at the ceiling once more, feeling totally helpless.

Suddenly, there was a loud flutter of wings. To Brayden's amazement, an enormous falcon swooped down from the rookery and landed peacefully on Josslyn's arm. Falcons were relatively common in the skies over the forests, but he had never before seen one of the majestic birds so close. Its sharp beak was a bright yellow and its dark brown wings complemented a thick white chest. It stood upright, its head surveying the room gracefully, as if awaiting instruction.

Using a bit of ash from one of the torches and the tip of her finger, Josslyn scribbled something on one of the leather straps that had tied her hands. Then, she proceeded to tie the strap to one of the falcon's feet. If the bird's sharp claws bothered her, she didn't show it.

Satisfied with the knot, she repeatedly whispered into the falcon's ear something Brayden could not hear. Then, with a swing of her arm, the bird launched back up to the rookery and out of sight. She shut the door and took her place on the floor next to Brayden.

"Where did you send your falcon?" he asked.

"I never said it was *my* falcon," she responded curtly.

Brayden rolled his eyes. "Fine, then what did you whisper to it?"

"Mother," she responded quietly.

Brayden watched her in puzzlement as she grabbed the gag and quickly tied it back over his face, silencing him. He worked his jaw to soreness but could not get the gag out of his mouth. She put a finger to her lips, gesturing him to be quiet.

Then she lay down next to him and arranged the leather straps around her wrists so it looked as though she had never broken free of them.

* * *

The guard returned moments later. He sat down and produced a large, rock-like chunk of grayish brown bread. Since the man had no teeth and could not bite, Brayden and Josslyn were forced to watch the man suck on the bread grotesquely.

"Let us go, villain," Josslyn demanded forcefully. The guard smiled his toothless smile in return, unmoved by her demands.

"My family can reward you well," she added. "Horses. Gold. Welsh land, perhaps?"

The guard stopped sucking, as if thinking for a moment. Brayden was struck by the repulsiveness of the man. At once he felt himself angry with the guard, angry with Josslyn, and frightened by the situation they found themselves in.

"My master warned me to keep a gag on you," the guard finally replied.

"Name your price," she pressed. "My father will pay it."

"Soon your father will be no more, my little lady. And Sir Bellator will have enough money to buy an army. My reward is coming." He began to gnaw again at the rotten bread.

Brayden looked over at Josslyn. She looked back at him despondently, as if she had given up hope.

The man stood up and walked over to them. Brayden wiggled wildly, trying to distract the man but the guard ignored him as if he were a butterfly trapped in its cocoon. "I can silence you, girl, like him, with the syrup," he said. "No more talking, or…" He reached down to grab Josslyn.

"Rulf!" Someone called from the base of the spiral staircase. The man froze. He dropped the bread to the floor near his seat and proceeded down the staircase.

"They are awake?" the voice asked. While he had to strain to hear, Brayden recognized it instantly. It was the man he had heard the night before in Sir Bellator's chambers. Brayden felt a chill thinking about him. He looked at Josslyn, who nodded fearfully. She had recognized the voice as well.

"Why do you speak with them? I told you to keep them gagged!"

"The peasant boy, yes, but the girl is nobility."

"Not for long," the little man replied sharply. There was a pause. "Kill them both," he said.

Brayden froze, his stomach churning.

"But Sir Bellator says to keep them up here until the end of the tourney."

"I pay you. Do as I say," the man hissed. "We have no use for them anymore. Your reward will come. Now, make it look like an accident. Put away the dagger. Throw them off the tower."

There was a pause, as if Rulf were thinking again.

"Now!" Rulf's master shouted.

Josslyn lurched upward, desperately untying the binds to her feet. Seconds later, she'd removed the gag from Brayden's mouth and was working on the binds around his hands.

"Hurry!" he demanded desperately.

"I'm trying!" she replied, still straining to release him. They both knew that in the tower they had nowhere to go, but at least they could try to give the guard a good chase.

Brayden's hands were free, but it was too late. Rulf emerged from the staircase, dagger in hand. Josslyn stood over Brayden, as if protecting him. If Rulf was surprised that Josslyn had escaped her binds, he did not show it.

"Whatever your reward, we will pay you double. Triple," Josslyn pleaded once more.

Rulf scratched his head and smiled his rotten toothless smile again. He stepped closer, slowly, again twirling the weapon. Perhaps Josslyn could evade Rulf long enough for him to untie his binds, Brayden thought. But then what? His mind raced, but every alternative came to the same conclusion: there was no escape for either of them.

There was a sudden crash, and a shadow burst up the staircase behind Rulf. Brayden watched as Sir Caelan rounded the corner, followed by Bernard, Caddaric, and Lady Elaine. The knight had Rulf disarmed immediately, and in a flash the man lay facedown, unconscious, on the floor. Sir Caelan picked up the dagger, rushed over to Brayden and cut through his binds. Lady Elaine hurried to Josslyn and embraced her daughter.

"Your friends, Patch and Daniel, were detained in the squires' quarters but managed to escape when their drunken guard finally fell asleep. They didn't know where you were," Bernard said. "We started looking. Then Lady Elaine came to us with this."

It was the leather strap Josslyn had attached to Rhiannon's leg. On it were scrawled the words:

Help, in eastern tower.

Joss

Brayden heard the flutter of wings. He looked over to one of the arrow slits. Rhiannon stood there, silently watching. The falcon's eyes blinked, then with a flash she flapped her powerful wings, swooped above them, and joined the other falcons in the rookery.

"Are you two all right?" Caddaric asked. Both Brayden and Josslyn nodded.

"There was another one," Josslyn said. "We didn't see him. He stayed at the base of the stairs."

"Another one?" Caelan asked. Without hesitation he signaled to Caddaric, who bounded down the stairs to search the area.

"What time is it?" Brayden asked. He walked over and peered out one of the narrow windows in the direction of the cheering. He just could see some of the tents outside the castle wall, but not much else.

Caelan shrugged. "I never could tell time." He looked at Lady Elaine and Bernard, as if hoping for an answer.

"Midmorning," Lady Elaine replied. "Around ten o'clock."

Brayden looked at Josslyn. They shared a look of relief. "Good," he said. His face was serious, and the others took note. "Sir Allard's armor is the same kind Bernard shredded at Honeydown. They've swapped his real armor with it. They want to kill him during today's joust, at noon. Luckily we still have time to stop the match."

"Who swapped the armor?" Caelan asked.

Josslyn and Brayden exchanged glances. "Sir Bellator and the little man he's been working with," Brayden replied.

"How do you know this?" Bernard asked.

"We overheard their plans last night," Josslyn replied in support. "Brayden snuck into Sir Bellator's chambers."

"What?" Bernard and Caelan both said at once.

"They also plan to attack Lord Marshal on his way home," Brayden added.

"Lord Marshal?" Lady Elaine cried. "Are you sure, my love?"

Josslyn nodded. "Mother, it is true. We have to save him!"

Bernard's eyes lit up. "If these things are true, we have less time than we thought on both counts. They've moved the match to midmorning *from* noon."

Just then, Caddaric emerged from the stairs.

"Anything?" Caelan asked.

The captain shook his head in silence. "Nothing. No sign of anyone else."

"Well, c'mon then, we gain nothing by waiting here. We've got to stop that match!" The knight bounded out of the room and down the staircase, the rest of the party following close behind.

* * *

The party ran through the castle and out the main gate. The castle grounds were empty, save for the occasional guard who watched curiously as the lady of the manor, a knight, an old friar, the captain of the keep guard, and two children ran by. Brayden could hear near-constant cheering as the herald shouted, rousing the crowd for the next match, the match they had to stop.

They crossed the field and approached the arena, the entire way Brayden explaining between gasps for air what he had heard and seen since being trapped under the bed in Sir Bellator's chambers. They broke into the crowd and began to fight their way through the mass of people, slowly making their way to the jousting area.

"This way! Move!" Caelan yelled, trying to push his way forward. With shouts of anger and annoyance, the assembled onlookers slowly parted, allowing them to pass. Brayden held tightly to Bernard's hand so as not to fall behind.

They came to the wall surrounding the contestants. Sir Allard and Sir Bellator were already mounted, facing each other from opposite sides of the arena. Before Caelan and the others could react, the herald waved the red flag, and the two knights charged at one another.

Caelan wasted no time. He bounded over the wall and ran toward the center of the field, waving his arms wildly. Brayden stood helplessly as the rest of the crowd watched in disbelief, many already cursing angrily in disapproval of the interference. Both charging knights wore heavy feathered helmets with narrow slits for their eyes. For them to see him, Brayden knew, Caelan would have to get right in front of them. Everyone in the audience understood the danger he was in as hundreds of pounds of armor, weapons, man, and horse barreled at one another at full speed.

Sir Bellator's horse saw Caelan first and pulled left just as the knight's lance was upon Sir Allard. There was a gigantic crash of smashing wood and metal as Sir Bellator's lance shattered against Sir Allard's shield, knocking the lord's champion off his horse and to the ground.

Sir Bellator wheeled his horse around, and threw down the ruined lance. He dropped from his mount, tore off his helmet, drew his sword in one fluid motion, and walked briskly toward Sir Allard's motionless body. Caelan ran to engage him, drawing his sword and standing over Sir Allard. Caddaric, Bernard, Brayden, and Sir Hugh had dashed into the arena and were near the fallen knight. Sir Hugh motioned for the surgeon, who raced over moments later and began to attend to Sir Allard. Sir Osbert had come out to the field as well, and stood to the side of Sir Bellator. The crowd, which had been shouting and cheering wildly, became silent.

"What is the meaning of this?" Sir Bellator demanded.

Caelan stood before him, sword aloft, panting heavily. Caddaric was behind him, his hand resting on the hilt of his mace.

"We've reason to believe Sir Allard's armor has been tampered with," Bernard said. "Replaced with armor that offers no protection at all from sword or lance."

"Replaced by whom?" Sir Bellator demanded, his face red with anger. He too held his sword high, ready to strike.

"We had hoped you'd reveal that yourself, my lord. Or, perhaps the man named Regin has the answer."

"Outrageous," Sir Bellator said haughtily. "State your proof for these accusations, or I'll make sure you never speak again."

Sir Caelan and Sir Hugh bristled, ready to defend Bernard. Brayden emerged from the group, Bernard gently pulling him forward. Bernard looked down at him, smiling encouragingly.

"It is true," Brayden started. "I was in the steward's chambers as he planned this with another man I could not see. I was then captured and imprisoned in the tower."

There was a collective gasp among the assembled people nearby, followed by murmurs of anger and disbelief.

"The village boy lies!" Sir Bellator shouted. He stepped threateningly close to Brayden. Sir Caelan and Sir Hugh closed around the boy.

"No!" Josslyn stepped forward. "It is true. I was there. I heard this as well, and they plotted also to trap my father, our Lord Marshal, at **Nifylog** Pass."

"This is an insult!" Sir Osbert cried as he pushed his way forward. "You accuse a knight of these ills, but what would he gain?"

"Perhaps to install himself as baron," Bernard suggested. "The king is weak and far away; there would be no argument against it. Perhaps a convenient union would solidify his rule." He looked directly at Josslyn, who shrank back against her mother.

"My lord," Sir Osbert said, turning to Sir Bellator. "Let me silence these swine." Osbert's eyes fixated on Sir Caelan who had positioned himself in front of his friends.

Sir Bellator nodded silently and stepped back into the crowd, sheathing his own sword.

Sir Osbert drew his weapon and approached Caelan as spectators formed a rough circle around the combatants. Brayden saw Patch, Daniel and several other pages nearby. He waved to them just as Bernard pushed him back forcefully.

"Bernard?" Brayden looked up. "I don't understand."

"Sir Osbert is taking Sir Bellator's place as his champion, much as Sir Allard would do for Lord Marshal. Sir Osbert will not fight me, or children, so Caelan is doing the same for you, Josslyn and me. I fear though that if Caelan loses, Bellator is free, no matter his crime."

Brayden looked over at the former steward. His face was calm and impassive, as if he had no stake in the outcome. Why Sir Bellator had not challenged Caelan directly was something Brayden couldn't fathom. He bowed his head and whispered a silent prayer for his friend.

Sir Caelan and Sir Osbert circled one another slowly, as if measuring each other for weakness. Impatient, Sir Osbert attacked first. Their swords erupted with a loud twang as steel connected with steel. Sir Osbert swung again, and again, knocking Caelan back several feet with each blow. Caelan finally responded, each thrust blocked easily by his opponent.

Sir Osbert drove forward, thrusting and stabbing once more. He spun and caught Caelan on the arm. Brayden gasped as red blood flowed from the gash, staining Caelan's tunic. Caelan tried to protect his injured arm as Sir Osbert continued the offensive, again knocking Caelan back. His friend was losing, Brayden realized, and there was nothing they could do. Caelan backed up toward the tilt, Sir Osbert coming at him with renewed fury.

Sir Osbert yelled and swung. Caelan ducked under the tilt just as his opponent's blade connected with it, immediately getting stuck in the soft wood. At that moment Caelan thrust, striking Sir Osbert in the gut. The man yelled in agony and let go of his weapon. He fell back, writhing on the ground.

Caelan stepped over to Sir Osbert and pointed his sword at the man's chest. The onlookers murmured in approval as Caelan raised his sword, and then brought it down harmlessly to the dirt.

"Our fight is with Sir Bellator and his accomplice," Caelan said. "Let Lord Marshal decide this one's fate, not I."

Sir Bellator! Brayden and the others looked around, but the steward was nowhere in sight. It was as if he had melted into the crowd.

"Sir Hugh," Bernard said, "gather your men. Lord Marshal is still in danger. You must ride to meet him at Nifylog Pass before the bandit leader Samain and his warriors do." Sir Hugh nodded silently and hurried to round up the knights. Bernard turned to Caddaric. "Captain, arrange search parties. We must find Sir Bellator and his associate. Start with the steward's chambers. We'll rendezvous in the main hall."

"Right," Caddaric replied as he moved off.

The crowd dispersed in irritable conversation and debate. The herald quickly assembled musicians who began to play happy music, trying his best to lighten the mood. Brayden watched as the surgeon and two aides tended to Sir Allard and Sir Osbert, preparing to carry them off the field. Both men were conscious, and the surgeon shuttled back and forth, fetching clean dressings for them both.

Caelan walked over to where Lady Elaine and Josslyn stood with Brayden.

"Thank you, Sir Caelan, for being our champion," Josslyn said.

"It was an honor. Every now and then Sir Osbert needs to be kept in check." Caelan raised his arm, and then winced in pain. They watched him with concern. "I'm fine," he added. "I've had worse."

Brayden remembered how Bernard had found his friend, lying unconscious face down in the mud near the abbey. Caelan couldn't walk and almost didn't survive the night.

"The surgeon is there for a reason sir," Lady Elaine lectured. "Join us in the main hall when you've been attended to, and not sooner."

Caelan bowed appreciatively, turned, and walked quickly after the surgeon.

Chapter Twenty-Nine

Decisions

Bernard, Brayden, Sir Caelan, and Sir Hugh had gathered in the main hall, situating themselves around the lord's table. Caelan wore a heavy bandage around his arm, and though he was in obvious pain, he was adamant he'd have it off by the end of the day. The large room had been cleaned up considerably since the feast the night before, and the tables were already set for another celebration that night. Despite the day's events, Lady Elaine had ordered the castle staff to go forward with another elaborate dinner. As Brayden understood it, to do anything else would result in rumors that the Marshals had lost control during the very time in which Lord Marshal was to return home. To that end the games continued outside, though none of those assembled were interested in joining them.

Sir Allard was resting in the guest quarters. His head was bruised and his chest cut, but with treatment and rest the surgeon expected him to be up and about in a day or two. Caddaric had two guards posted outside of his room, despite Allard's insistence that they were unnecessary.

Sir Hugh had dispatched Sir Grey, Sir Cornwall, and several other knights to catch Lord Marshal before his party reached the Nifylog Pass. The knights would then lead them through another, albeit longer, route, delaying their arrival until at least the following day. Lady Elaine and the others did not care so much when they arrived as long as they arrived unscathed. Brayden understood that Sir Grey was one of the oldest, most experienced knights in the castle. If anyone could find Lord Marshal's party and lead them back to safety, this man could. Several other castle knights had been sent on a hunt for Sir Bellator across the surrounding countryside. So far, not a trace of him had been found.

It was the matter of where Sir Bellator had disappeared to that occupied Bernard and the other adults completely. Lookouts had been posted along the castle walls, at the main gate, and in the town itself, and the keep guards continued their search throughout the castle. As for Regin, no one recalled encountering him, and other than rumors of his short stature, no one even knew what he looked like. Brayden had decided to stay in view of Bernard and the other men at all times. While he hoped Sir Bellator would be found, knowing Regin remained on the loose terrified him.

Caddaric and two of his keep guards entered the main hall and approached Brayden and the others. The captain looked hot, tired, and disheveled, and walked awkwardly as if he had been on his feet for hours. He was carrying a heavy leather sack.

Caelan saw him coming, picked up a pewter flagon and poured a thick, dark red liquid into a round metal cup. He put one hand on the captain's shoulder and handed him the cup. "How go things, captain?"

Caddaric put the sack down on the floor, took the cup, and rested his other hand on his hip. He inhaled the wine and slammed the cup down on the table. "The steward's, I mean, Sir Bellator's, chambers were untouched. Wherever he went, he went in a hurry." The captain wiped his face with a thick forearm. Caelan poured him another cupful.

"Did you find the book?" Bernard asked.

"We searched everywhere, but found no sign of Sir Martin's book of maps." The captain took a long swig of the liquid and grimaced. "This here wine is thicker than oxen blood."

"Sorry," Caelan replied. "We've nothing but our own English wine left. If we're ever in France, I'll pour you a cup of the real stuff."

"What of the castle blacksmith's shop?" Sir Hugh asked.

Caddaric took another sip of the wine, and then winced, as if trying to prevent the horrid drink from coming back up. "We found Sir Allard's armor, or parts of it, the accouterments of a smithery, some scraps of paper, nothing more. All of it is in this sack."

Lady Elaine and Josslyn entered the room with two guards close behind. They were back to inspect the main hall, the kitchen, and the staff before the night's dinner. The assembled men acknowledged them with a bow, and Josslyn and her mother joined them at the table on the platform.

"Any sign of Sir Bellator or that creature Regin?" Lady Elaine asked.

"I am afraid not yet, my lady. Led by the good captain, we've searched everywhere we know of to search," Bernard responded.

Brayden looked over at Josslyn. She glanced up at him quickly, and then looked down at the floor. She was as disappointed as the rest of them, he thought, and consumed with worry about her father.

"We'll all sleep more soundly when they're caught," Josslyn said quietly.

"Amen, my lady," Sir Hugh acknowledged.

Brayden noticed that Lady Elaine looked exhausted. Her cheeks were pale and her hair loose. The concern for her daughter's safety and that of her husband's appeared to be weighing on her heavily.

"We must find those men," Caelan said, frustration evident in his voice as well.

"What about the tunnels?" Josslyn asked. "Perhaps that is where they went."

"The tunnels?" Bernard asked.

The tunnels. Of course! Brayden reached inside his pants, felt the papers and pulled them out. "I have Sir Martin's maps of the castle and beyond," he said. Everyone looked at him in stunned silence. "Or, at least of the castle and the tunnels within. The treasure maps of Sir Martin."

"My dear boy, you are full of surprises." Bernard took the pages and spread them flat on the table so everyone could see. He brought over another candle to improve the light. "How did you come by these?"

"Last night in Sir Bellator's room. I tore them out of Sir Martin's book. I only wish I had taken the entire book itself." He put a hand to his face, angry at himself for his haste.

Caelan stood over him. "No matter, Brayden," he said. "If you had taken the entire book that night you may not have lived to tell about it. Who knows what they would have done to you in that tower."

"There is the gatehouse," Sir Hugh said as he inspected the papers.

"Yes, yes," Bernard agreed. "And notice how these lines, the tunnels, branch off, away from the main structures? The gatehouse, the keep, the towers."

"Follow this one," Sir Hugh suggested. He pointed at a faint line that disappeared in the midst of the residential chambers. "There is where we, well…"

"Yes, here is where we found Corbat's body, as Brayden had told us we would earlier today," Bernard said. "This drawing is a bit smudged, but through this connected passage one finds the dungeon." Brayden shivered at the mention of the place. Bernard noticed, and laid a gentle, reassuring hand on his shoulder.

"Is there truly treasure?" Caddaric asked excitedly. "Whose is it?"

"Sir Martin thought, perhaps, it was the Romans, and possibly our former steward as well," Bernard responded. "Whatever the case, I suspect that Sir Bellator wanted not only the barony for himself, but Sir Martin's treasure as well. The former steward's desire to protect the existence of the treasure and his plotting against Lord Marshal finally led to Corbat's demise." He paused and looked around. Everyone in the room was listening intently, waiting for him to continue. "We know now that Corbat was using Samain's bandit gangs to ransack village traders and merchants, robbing his own people to enrich himself. When Sir Bellator, and I suspect, Regin, found out, not only did they not stop it, they took payment and employed the bandits for kidnapping and other crimes."

"How do you know of this?" Sir Hugh asked.

"The castle records show that Sir Bellator and his minions were poor accountants. With a little numerical knowledge, which is about all I still possess, one can trace the record of payments. Thank you to Lady Elaine for extending the privilege." He nodded in Lady Elaine's direction, and she returned a slight smile.

"So why did they kill him?" Caddaric asked.

"Ah. The record of payments was the first link, this is the second." Bernard pulled out a small piece of parchment paper and placed it on the table. The others leaned forward, straining to read the words scrawled on it. "Our keep guards found this when they searched the bailiff's body. It is a letter to Sir Allard. Corbat sensed the tide was turning and he was going to implicate Sir Bellator in the lord's confinement. My assumption is Corbat got greedy and was threatening them. For this, they killed him."

"No honor among thieves. A cretin among cretins he was," Caelan said in disgust, shaking his head.

The collected men murmured in agreement.

"We need to find those mines," Caelan pressed. "I agree with the Lady Josslyn. It is a good bet that is where they went."

"The mines?" asked several of the party together.

Bernard nodded, and quickly explained the stories of Sir Martin and his search for Roman treasure buried somewhere in the countryside. "I have to agree with my knightly friend. I suspect if we find the mines, we'll find Sir Bellator and Regin, or at least a clue as to where they may be."

They examined the pages for several long minutes, trying to make sense of the jumble of lines and scribbled drawings on the worn-out documents. The fading made it nearly impossible to determine exactly where most of the tunnels could be accessed, let alone which among the dozens of routes Sir Bellator and Regin may have taken.

"Look." Josslyn said at last. "This line leads far from the castle and branches in different directions." Her finger tracked the line to the edge of the page. "Where do you think it goes?"

Everyone leaned in to get a better view. Bernard took the other sheets and arranged them, first one way, and then another.

"There!" Caelan said excitedly.

Indeed, it was clear. The separate pages connected like a puzzle, displaying the various parts of the castle, but also, more interestingly, the numerous tunnels and caves that seemed to crisscross the countryside. The one Josslyn had been following branched off in many directions, thickening in some areas and finally ending near a large dark swath of ink.

"What is that?" Brayden asked, pointing to the dark spot.

Bernard put his hand to his chin. "Remember the day we arrived at Castle Strand? You asked about it. I suspect it is the sea."

"These tunnels run right across the country, under mountains and villages," Sir Hugh added.

"That they do," Bernard agreed, "and I doubt if by nature's hand alone they were made."

"They could be used to compromise the castle during a siege," Caddaric suggested.

"Indeed, my dear captain, or to escape from it."

The members of the group exchanged curious looks. Bernard focused on the section of the map where Corbat had been found.

"Do you see where this branches off?" he asked the group.

The others looked at where he was pointing.

"We know this chamber leads into the dungeon by way of this passage," he continued. "But this tunnel, it seems to come right out of the side of the wall, perhaps leading deep underground."

"Another secret passage." Caelan leaned back. "The castle and the surrounding country are riddled with them. It would take months to search them all. Incredible."

"True," Bernard responded, "and where it and the others lead and what is to be found along the way is anyone's guess." He turned to the captain, who was still staring at the maps. "Captain, these maps show the castle's every weakness. They must be protected until Lord Marshal returns and can be apprised of their value."

Sir Hugh scratched his head. "Imagine what else is in the papers of Sir Martin's book? Just imagine."

There were murmurs of agreement as they each considered the possibilities. Sir Brayden recalled what he had heard of Sir Martin's long career as a knight and a mapmaker, across the island and overseas. The value of his book was indeed hard to imagine.

"Papers?" Bernard said suddenly, as if something had just jogged his memory. "Captain, where are those scraps of paper you mentioned—the ones from the blacksmith's shop? Perhaps they offer a clue."

"Right you are," Caddaric answered. "Here." He lifted the bag and set it on the table with a heavy thud. The captain reached in and felt around the parts of Sir Allard's armor they had found. He removed assorted instruments of the blacksmith's trade from the bag, and after a minute he pulled out several scraps of linen paper.

"We looked at each piece, but none of us could read a word," the captain said. "That is fine Italian paper, though. I thought I'd keep it, if no one wants it, that is."

Bernard took several of the pieces and began examining them individually. "Of course, of course," he agreed absently, reading one sheet after the other. "Very wise of you. Very w—."

Blood seemed to rush from his face as he stared silently at the paper. He handed the sheet to Caelan, whose reaction was the same.

"What is it?" Brayden asked, tugging on his friend's robe.

"Sir Hugh," Bernard said, urgently waving the warrior over to him. "I pray you have more men available. You must go now to Honeydown. And go with haste. Alice Rider is in great danger."

Chapter Thirty

An Enemy

Brayden was lying on a cot placed near the fire pit, inside which warm flames crackled. Lady Elaine had insisted they retreat to her chambers, the safest place in the castle. Bernard and Caelan stood nearby, watching him silently. Outside the door was another of Caddaric's trusted keep guards. Brayden had been despondent and unable to move since they'd read him the letter. He kept seeing the words in his mind, playing them over and over, and shuddering in fright and helplessness each time.

Bring me the Rider woman, preferably alive.

T

After they'd arrived in Lady Elaine's chambers, Bernard had described to him the contents of the letter she had supplied to Caelan. He and Caelan again spoke of why they had come to the castle, why they thought it would be the safest place to be. They had instead, he thought angrily, separated him from the only home he knew and the person who loved him the most. The journey and the castle had proven anything but safe, and the entire endeavor almost foolish. Brayden wiped a tear from his eye. I could not even protect her.

Bernard sat next to him, gently brushing the hair from Brayden's forehead.

"What of my father, then?" Brayden suddenly wondered aloud. "What part of this has to do with him?"

"I suspect whoever is behind this hopes to take you and now your mother as hostages," Bernard said. "There is something important Sir Ban knows and his captors want, and they'd use you and Alice to get it. Your father lives, Brayden, of that I'm sure. And your father *will* live for as long as his secret does, and he is not one who reveals secrets easily. Where he is, we do not know. But you have my word we will never stop until we find him."

Brayden buried his head in his hands as more tears welled in his eyes. Bernard noticed, and wiped his eyes gently. His thoughts went back to his mother and where she could be. It made no sense. Why would anyone want us? If me first, why now her?

"What secret could father possibly possess?" he cried.

"Remember the stories I've told you about the Templars? Your father is not just a Knight of the Temple, he was their treasure keeper. He knows, or they believe he knows, where the Treasures of the Temple are, truly one of the greatest stores of wealth in the world."

"Sir Hugh is one of the fastest riders in the barony," Caelan added, trying to comfort Brayden. "He'll arrive in plenty of time to get her back to us here."

"And what if he doesn't? What then!?" Brayden asked loudly, sputtering.

"Then we'll search this entire island for her," Bernard replied, again wiping the boy's face with the cloth. "Above the ground, and below, until she is found."

There was a knock at the door. Caelan walked over, peered outside, and opened it. One of the kitchen maids entered and placed a small steaming mug of liquid on the table. She curtsied and left the room. The sweet smell of apples filled the air.

"I was out of this one," Bernard said, "but Lady Wymarda's collection of remedies is most impressive. Here, my boy, sit up."

Bernard helped Brayden lean forward, then reached for the mug and put it to his lips. The liquid was hot but smooth, almost soothing. Before he knew it, he had finished the entire mug.

"Chamomile," Bernard said. "I may have a cup myself tonight."

"Save me some, friend," Caelan agreed.

Brayden lay back. His mind was still racing, but more slowly than before. He tried to think of the happy times he had had here at the castle with Patch, Josslyn, and Daniel. He thought of his little home in Honeydown and pictured his mother's comforting face, and thought of his father and those distant memories of their manor in France. He barely heard Bernard and Caelan speaking as he drifted off to sleep.

* * *

"He's not rested a bit in two days, poor boy, until now," Caelan said. He and Bernard stood in the chamber next to where Brayden slept, close enough to watch him, but far enough from earshot.

"Indeed. These last days and nights have been worrisome for him and for us. Bless us these next few will deliver better tidings."

Caelan pulled Bernard aside. "Tell me, friend, who truly is stalking the boy?" he asked quietly. "The single letter 'T'. I see that same signature on the letter here and on the one I carried to your village. Who now are we dealing with?"

Bernard bowed his head and took a deep breath. "His name is Turpin."

"An acquaintance?"

Bernard shook his head. "An enemy, an enemy to all of us. He was once an honored knight and cleric, though what diabolical god he now worships I do not know. For his greed Turpin was cast out of the Templars, he and his followers, and though I cannot be certain it is he, there are the letters, and the dagger."

"The dagger?"

"Found by John Fields after the attack on Honeydown. Turpin had them made for the fell men in his employ. Each constructed with a serpent handle." Bernard looked through the chamber opening at Brayden who was at last sleeping peacefully. "The boy does not need to know these facts. Not yet."

Caelan nodded in agreement. "The steward and Regin are in this man's employ," Caelan said simply. "How do we find him?"

"Knowing Turpin, if indeed it is him, he will find us first."

Chapter Thirty-One

Hostage

Brayden awoke to birds singing outside. It was light, and though he could not tell how long he had been asleep, he suspected it had been straight through the night and into the morning.

He got out of bed and stretched. The events of the last few days hung over him, but he felt stronger, refreshed. He put on his clothes and opened the door. The keep guard looked down at him.

"I'd like to see Bernard," he said.

The guard nodded and led him through the guest chambers and several hallways, and into the main hall. At the end of the hall, Bernard was sitting at the head table with Lady Elaine and Josslyn, a platter of bread, fruit, and nuts in front of them. They waved him over. Caelan stood nearby, leaning quietly against a wall.

"Good morning to you, Brayden," Lady Elaine said. "Here, have something." She pointed to the platter. "You have been asleep for a night and a good part of the day."

Brayden couldn't even remember dreaming. Still drowsy, he grabbed the table to steady himself. Bernard rushed over and helped him to a chair.

"Easy, my boy," he cautioned gently. "What Lady Elaine says is true, and you're the better for it."

"Bernard, my lady, has there been any word about my mother?"

Bernard put a hand on his shoulder. "No word yet, but we'll find her and bring her here. Now, please eat. You help her best by staying strong."

He did have more than a flutter of hunger in his belly, and quickly took some bread and an apple. He scanned the hall as he ate. It was a mess, though less so than the first night of the tournament. He listened as Lady Elaine explained that many of the guests, particularly those who had had poor luck at the joust, had finally departed. The food served since then was simpler and consisted of fewer courses, encouraging people to retire earlier.

Lady Wymarda suddenly burst into the hall, and hurried up to the main table.

"My lords, Sir Hugh has returned," she said, out of breath.

"What?" Bernard said, rising from the table. "How can that be? So soon?"

"I know Sir Hugh's face as well as my own," Lady Wymarda scolded. "Come, he wants to speak with you all."

Everyone followed her out of the keep and into the courtyard. Sir Hugh was dismounting from his enormous stallion. Nearby were two other men, mounted on thin palfreys and dressed in long ragged cloaks. Their faces were hidden under hoods. Brayden noticed immediately his mother was not among them. The men took the knight's signal, and both dismounted simultaneously and approached Bernard. The men removed their hoods, and Brayden was shocked to see John Fields and Dunstan Smith standing before them.

"It has been some time, gentlemen," Bernard said. "Welcome to Castle Strand. I only wish the circumstances were better"

"Hello, boy," Dunstan said, winking.

"Good to see you, lad." John Fields patted Brayden's shoulder.

"I present to you Lady Elaine, Lord Marshal's wife, and their daughter, Lady Josslyn."

Both men bowed respectfully. Lady Elaine nodded at them. "Welcome to our home," she said.

Bernard got right to business. "Forgive us. While be assured we are pleased for the visit, we are a bit shocked to see you here. Sir Hugh, did you make it to Honeydown?"

Sir Hugh stepped forward. "We did not. These men met us near halfway, and recognized me from our Michaelmas Eve visit to Honeydown. They were coming to the castle. Coming with news."

"News? What news? Did you get to Alice? Where is she?"

The men looked uncomfortably at Sir Hugh before John Fields finally turned to Brayden.

"I'm sorry, boy," he said. "Your mother was taken from Honeydown in the night."

Chapter Thirty-Two

Sir Caelan

The party reconvened in the main hall. The visitors had been offered food, but no one ate. Caelan had returned from speaking with Caddaric, requesting that he and his men start questioning travelers on Alice's whereabouts. Josslyn sat next to Brayden, looking at him hopefully, as if trying to comfort him but unsure of what to say.

"They came in the early morning," John Fields explained. "We had let many of the animals out, and most of the village was out in the fields when they snuck in. Alice usually joins us, but stayed back on this day. I came back to check on her with a couple of the hands, but she was gone. We searched everywhere, even the abbey, but there was not a sign of her.

"Who were they? Did you see them?" Caelan asked.

John Fields' gaze fell to the floor. "No. We supposed it could be the same rabble that attacked us on Michaelmas, but we've seen and heard nothing of them since then. We've had guards posted, as you instructed, Sir Caelan, but they saw nothing. Whoever came for her disturbed nothing, nor anyone else. It was as if they came just for her. I left immediately for here. Dunstan caught me on the road halfway to the castle and was kind enough to join me."

"We were too late!" Bernard shouted suddenly, slamming his fists to the table and standing up. "Fools we are! She should have come with us." He stormed around the table, waving his arms and muttering loudly to himself, as upset as Brayden had ever seen him.

Watching Bernard in this state of mind pained him, as he was sure it did the others. All his life Bernard had seemed the calming force, through his sermons, his stories, and his presence. On this morning, upon hearing the details of Alice's disappearance, he had finally snapped. Brayden had to look the other way, holding back his own tears. Josslyn touched his arm, and he jerked it away.

"What direction did they go?" Caelan asked, almost shouting at Dunstan and John Fields.

"They headed north, we think," Dunstan said. "Men in a caravan heading south said they passed several riders, one of which they thought was a woman, heading north from Honeydown. We hoped to find them along the same road, but we saw no one."

"You have to find her!" Brayden cried, unable to control his emotions and not even sure who he was talking to. Tears streamed down his cheeks. He felt ashamed for crying, but could not hold back any longer. He stood up and ran out of the hall.

Caelan glanced at Bernard, who was standing against a corner, his head low. The knight walked over and bowed to Dunstan and John Fields. "I am sorry for shouting. You are only here to help. Please see to Bernard." Caelan glanced at Lady Elaine, and then took off after Brayden.

* * *

Brayden was already in the stables when Caelan caught up to him. They walked past row upon row of stalls, slowly winding their way to the back of the structure. The air inside was musty, thick with the smell of manure and beaten hay. Late autumn flies buzzed about their heads and feet. Brayden noticed that most of the stalls were empty. The few horses and their masters who weren't out searching for Sir Bellator or escorting Lord Marshal home were still involved in tournament activities. They walked to the back of the stable and stopped at the last stall on their right. Something inside stirred, then Sullivan announced his presence with a loud snort.

"Sullivan!" Brayden cried.

"You haven't seen much of each other," Caelan said. "He's also not eaten much today. Would you like to feed him?"

Brayden nodded, and for a brief moment he could feel his spirits lift. Caelan walked around the corner and in a few moments returned with a bucket piled high with a foul-smelling mixture of hay, oats, and beans. He put the bucket down and let Brayden scoop the unappetizing mixture into Sullivan's trough. The horse whinnied appreciatively, and then buried its snout in the stuff.

As they watched Sullivan eat Caelan pulled out an apple he had taken from the morning's breakfast table. "For dessert," he said. "Here, take it and give it to him when he's done."

Brayden took the apple, and as soon as the trough was empty he fed it to Sullivan. The horse nodded happily as Brayden stroked his mane. They stood for several minutes, not saying anything, but enjoying the horse's company.

"Sullivan, I don't know what I'd do without you," Caelan mused. He turned to Brayden. "Listen, what Bernard has said is true. We meant only to protect you."

"I don't need protection," Brayden responded defensively.

"I think you do. I think we all do sometimes," Caelan said, "no matter how brave we are."

The horse dug its hooves into the straw and flicked its tail at the flies. Brayden thought back to their time in Honeydown, how much it had meant to ride this horse for the first time, and how desperately he wanted to ride him again, to let the cool wind wash over him and clear away his feelings of fear, hurt, and worry.

"We'll have to take him out again, as soon as I get back."

"Get back?" Brayden asked in surprise, looking at his friend quizzically. "From where?"

Caelan's face was serious. "I'm going to find Alice for you, Brayden. I'm going to bring her back."

Brayden put his head down. "I know," he said. "I trust you." He held back tears once more and took a deep breath. He knew in his heart Caelan would not rest until he found his mother and her captors, risking everything, including his own life, if he had to.

Caelan took down the bit and bridle from a nearby wall and handed them to Brayden. Then he pulled down a thick blanket and saddle and arranged both on Sullivan's back. He circled the horse, checking each buckle twice. He lifted Brayden up so his head was level with Sullivan's. Brayden struggled at first, but finally fit the bridle over the horse's huge head. Caelan took the bit and inserted it into Sullivan's mouth. The horse snorted excitedly and, anxious to be let out, put up little resistance.

"He is a fine charger. I hope to have a palfrey to ride one day, so Sullivan can be spared for martial service alone. Maybe in next year's tournaments I'll have better luck," Caelan sighed. He checked the contents of his saddlebags, then lifted his sword from his belt and attached the scabbard to the saddle, giving it several tugs to make sure it was secure. "Or, perhaps one day you and I can find some of that Roman treasure together, hmm?"

"Have you ever found any? Any treasure, that is?"

Caelan smiled and looked down at the ground. "No. So far I've not been much of a treasure hunter. But, I am still young. It is a big world out there, I hope to live long enough to see it."

"Take me with you," Brayden pleaded. "Please." He wanted to help, to do anything but be left here to wait and worry.

Caelan hesitated, as if thinking it over. "No. Stay here, my friend. You don't need to prove to anyone anymore how brave you are."

"It is not about proving anything!" Brayden shouted. He stomped around the stable then stopped. "I wish I were a knight," he mumbled.

Caelan knelt before him and looked him in the eyes.

"Brayden, being a knight, being an adult, is nothing to wish for. I know little, but I do know life is short. Rush nothing. Take your time, and one day you'll know what you are meant to be."

"I don't understand," he replied, not hiding his disappointment and frustration.

"No, I know you don't, but I know one day you will." Caelan stood and put one hand on the saddle and one foot in a stirrup. "Stay here and watch over Lady Elaine and Josslyn for us. They are not out of danger yet. We'll find Alice, and then, one day, your father."

"You promise?"

Caelan scuffed his head, winked, and mounted Sullivan. The horse grunted with the extra weight and stamped around the stall, growing more eager to get outside.

"I'll be back with her, Brayden." Caelan pulled on the horse's reins and steered him toward the stall door. He trotted out quietly, and then, with a sudden kick, Sullivan was off, galloping across the courtyard and out the castle gate.

Brayden walked across the courtyard and up to the keep. The image of the maps, the tunnels, and the room by the dungeon flashed into his mind. He smiled, and it was the first true smile he had had in days. A plan had begun to form.

Chapter Thirty-Three

A Little Distraction

As soon as he returned to the keep, Brayden learned he had been assigned a guard, and the man was his constant companion the rest of the day. By the time late afternoon arrived, the first guard had been joined by another. The pair of them followed him everywhere: into the kitchen, through the shield room, out to the courtyard, and back to the kitchen once again.

"Can't you two leave me be?" he finally exclaimed.

The two men stared expectantly at one another, deliberated briefly, and finally shook their heads. "Captain's orders," they both said at once. They supplied no further details.

Exasperated, Brayden walked to the pages' quarters, to look for his friends.

Just as Brayden and his escorts got to the door, Edwin Stapleton walked out with his little crony, Montfort.

"Well, Brayden Rider is here," Edwin said. "We hear you almost got yourself killed, and then blamed the steward."

"That is not what happened, Edwin."

Edwin looked him over, that nasty smirk permanently painted on his face. "Well, you sure have everyone at your service, peasant boy. I assure you, it makes no difference to me. Say, we never finished our business from the other night. How about now?"

Before Brayden could speak, Edwin's hands became fists and he started coming at him. Brayden tensed, preparing to be struck, knocked down, or both.

He waited. Nothing happened.

Brayden felt pressure behind him. The two guards leaned to either side of him, pushing him behind them. They stood ominously over the other boys, and Brayden noticed their hands were menacingly close to their weapons. Neither guard said anything, nor did they have to.

Edwin gulped and backed off. "W-whatever you've done now, Rider, I d-don't want any part of it." He and Montfort ran off, never looking back.

Perhaps these guards had their uses after all, Brayden thought. He entered the pages' quarters. Patch, Daniel, and several of the other boys were situated in different parts of the room. Some were practicing French or Latin with one another; others were playing games on the floor. Brayden walked up to his friends, the guards standing on either side of him.

"Who are these two dolts?" Patch asked. He wore a mocking smile and inspected the guards closely, as if he was assessing their fitness as protectors. "Don't you know, boys only in here!" Patch called at last.

The guards grunted, but otherwise did not react.

"They are my constant companions, per Bernard and the captain, for who knows how long."

"Lucky you!" Daniel cried. Several of the other boys were looking on admiringly.

Brayden shrugged. With everything that had happened, he now found he didn't mind the attention from the other boys, or, he admitted to himself, the guards. He knew, of course, that he could not accomplish what he sought to do with these men following him everywhere.

He leaned over close to Patch and Daniel. "Listen," he whispered. "Join me in Lady Elaine's chambers in one quarter of an hour. If I know my time, Lady Elaine, Bernard, and most of the adults will be in services, and I'm allowed up there, as they say it is the safest place in the castle. It's the only place they'll give me peace." He motioned in the direction of the guards, who had backed away several feet and were distracted watching a group of boys play queek. One after another the boys would toss a stone, trying to hit the designated square on the cloth board. There was an eruption of applause and laughter whenever someone made a good shot.

Patch and Daniel looked at each other and then looked back at him, their faces serious. Without either saying a word, Brayden knew he could count on seeing them shortly.

* * *

Brayden hadn't been in Lady Elaine's chambers more than a few minutes when he heard shouting out in the hallway.

"Hands off us, you shrews!"

Brayden recognized Patch's voice. He ran to the entrance and peered out. Patch and Daniel were outside, each being held by one of the guards and struggling mightily to get free.

"Arnald, Odo, leave them be," Brayden said, waving his hands. "I invited them here."

The guards, as always, looked at one another before responding. As if they shared a brain, they let go of Patch and Daniel simultaneously and each took a step back. Brayden pulled his friends inside and pushed at the door, leaving it open a crack so as to assuage the guards' suspicions.

"You know the names of those mulemen?" Daniel asked, straightening his clothing. "I'd have had them shackled by now, if we didn't have more important matters to discuss, that is."

Brayden shrugged. "I figure I'd ask them for their names. Truthfully I don't know how long they'll be attached to me. It could be a while, at least until Regin and Bellator are found."

"Any sign of those cowards?" Patch asked.

Brayden looked down at the floor, avoiding his friend's eyes. Despite what he was planning, he hadn't thought of what he'd do if he did find them first, and he didn't particularly want to think about it now.

"You're going after them, aren't you?" Patch said excitedly, as if reading Brayden's face. "You're going to locate the entrance to the Roman mines and find out where they are hiding!"

"Shh!" Brayden hushed him quiet, hoping the guards didn't hear. "How did you know about that?"

"The mines? Everyone's talking about it. We all wish we had the maps. Is that where you think those devils are?" Patch asked.

"No, I'm not going after them. I'm going after *her*," Brayden said sternly, and truthfully.

Patch and Daniel exchanged glances, apparently knowing he was referring to his mother. By now, the entire castle had heard not only about the mines, but also about Brayden's escape from the tower, the steward's treachery, and Alice's disappearance. Already bounties were being posted for Bellator, and Brayden knew, to his disgust, that bets on when, and if, his mother would be found alive were also being made about the castle.

"Good for you!" Daniel said at length. "I hope you find her *and* those rotten souls and bring them back here for Sir Caelan and my father to practice lance drills upon."

"Yeah, so what do you need us for? Can we come too?" Patch asked, always ready for an adventure and apparently anxious to get to business.

"Look, I'll never get down there with the guards about me all the time. I have to get away from them long enough to make an escape."

"You mean *we'll* never get down there," Patch said. "There you go having all the fun. You're safer with us there at your side. No deal unless we can come."

Patch and Daniel looked at him, as if eagerly waiting for an answer. He knew what he wanted, and knew that he needed, their help.

"All right," Brayden said.

"Good. It's settled." Patch stroked his chin, as if thinking deeply. "Now what we need is a little distraction."

"A distraction?" Daniel asked.

"Yes, you dumb oaf. A way to keep the guards occupied so our man here can get to where he wants to go." Patch said.

"Do either of you have any ideas?" Brayden asked.

"I have one," Daniel said. "We can set fire to the castle, perhaps the main hall."

"Are you daft?" Patch retorted. "We need a distraction, not a crime. We'd surely be executed for that!"

"Sorry."

"No worries. Imaginative thinking is what we need." Patch paused, again rubbing his chin. "Ah. I have one. How about we go out there and pretend we're sick. We can both throw up on their feet. Old Arnald and Odo out there will be so sick themselves, you'd be sure to get away from them."

Brayden rubbed his forehead. "I don't know. Is either of you ill?"

Patch and Daniel looked at each other and shrugged.

"I feel fine," Daniel said.

"Besides," Brayden continued, "I don't think the guards would be fooled by that, at least not long enough."

"How about the animals?" Daniel tried again.

"Huh?" Patch and Brayden both said.

"They've been brought in by now, the horses of course, but the cows, sheep and chickens too. They're back inside the castle walls. There are too many people still from the tourney milling about, and nobody wants to risk someone making off with their property."

"Get to the point. What are you talking about?" Patch prodded impatiently.

"We can let the animals loose and scare them into running about the yard. We'd have to get the two guards outside in the middle of it, but maybe it would work." Daniel shrugged.

Patch and Brayden looked at each other. Patch was smiling. Brayden admitted to himself he had no better ideas, and while the animals running around the courtyard would keep everyone busy for a while, the extent of the damage would be nothing but nibbled hedges and a denuded garden or two.

"We'd have the whole castle staff chasing them," Patch said. "I love it! C'mon. Brayden's mother is waiting."

* * *

The boys stepped out of Lady Elaine's chambers and were immediately blocked by the guards.

"We're going outside to, uh, play," Brayden said.

The two men looked at one another and made way, then followed the boys as they progressed through the keep and out into the courtyard. Once outside and a few paces away from the guards, the three huddled to plan their next steps.

"Listen," Patch said quietly, looking over his shoulder at Arnald and Odo, who were both looking around in all directions as if enjoying the fresh air and the feeling of being outside. "I'll head to the chicken coup and pigsty and set them loose. Daniel, you get to the stalls and let out any horses you can find. We'll meet at the cow pen and finish the job. Once we have everyone chasing the animals all about, it won't be long before those two dolts are running around the yard like everyone else. We'll meet at the shield room, inside. Ready?"

"Wait. What do I do?" Brayden asked. They were doing this for him, but he felt left out nonetheless.

"You wait here with them, of course! Just be ready to run when the time is right."

He nodded. Even his friends were telling him to wait.

Patch and Daniel trotted off. The guards watched them go, and then they went back to observing the various activities happening in the courtyard.

Evening was fast approaching and before long the people of the castle would be asleep. Nearby, a chambermaid was washing clothes in a large basin. She was in good spirits, humming a happy tune to herself as she worked. Another chambermaid was hanging the wet clothes from a clothesline slung between wooden poles. Brayden could smell bread being baked somewhere nearby, and it made him suddenly hungry. Far across the yard, several archers were firing at targets at close range. One archer was much shorter than the others, and Brayden soon recognized it as Josslyn. She was wearing a plain white tunic and dark pants, dressed down significantly from the past few days at the tourney. A gray leather quiver of arrows was slung across her back. She saw him as well, lowered her bow, and waved. Please don't come over here, he thought. He did not want to drag yet another friend into this latest adventure, and hoped for her sake she'd stay where she was and not interfere. She began to walk in his direction, but was stopped by one of the other archers in midstride. Brayden exhaled in relief.

Patch and Daniel were long out of sight. Near the center of the courtyard, on the stone pathway, were two well-dressed young men sitting at a small table, on which held what looked like a checkerboard, and on top of the checkerboard were brown and white figurines of various sizes and designs. One man would move a figure, then, after moments, the other man would move. Bernard and Sir Hugh had told him about many of the games people played while living in the castle, but with everything going on he'd had very little chance to learn any. Looking about the courtyard, he also thought of how much he *had* learned in so short a time. This place, this castle, could be a home, if only his mother were safe.

There was a wild squawk as several dozen chickens came into view, running aimlessly about the courtyard. Moments later some pigs dashed past, heading straight for the herb garden. Brayden caught himself laughing at the sight. Two horses darted out of the stalls, followed by another, and then another. It had worked! As predicted, Arnald and Odo were transfixed on the animals, as were the rest of the adults. As chickens flew between their legs and a piglet strolled by, the guards seemed to become anxious, staring at the animals as if wondering what to do.

The commotion all around was comical. People were now running in all directions chasing after the animals. Men-at-arms ran after chickens, knights tried to corral the horses, and chambermaids were swatted at the pigs in the garden.

"Don't just stand there, you twits!" Sir Rogers yelled at Brayden's guards as he tried to corner one of the piglets. "Help us with this blasted rabble!"

Once ordered by the knight, Arnald and Odo sprang into action immediately, completely forgetting about Brayden as they chased any animal they could find. It had indeed worked. Brayden looked once more around the courtyard. The two young men were on their hands and knees, trying to pick up the figurines that had fallen to the ground when one of the first cows had come barreling out of its pen in their direction.

Patch and Daniel were finished, their work masterful. They ran across the courtyard towards the keep, where Brayden now stood waiting for them by the main door, watching Arnald and Odo carefully.

His friends were not twenty feet from him when Sir Rogers burst into view, grabbed both of them by their shirts and pulled them towards him. Patch and Daniel were caught, but Sir Rogers and the two guards had not yet seen Brayden. While Sir Rogers scolded, dragging the boys away from the keep and toward the knights' chambers, Patch turned his head and looked at Brayden. He could not hear Patch's words, but knew instantly what he was trying to say: "Go."

* * *

Brayden darted into the keep and instead of to the shield room, ran as fast as he could to the pages' quarters. The door was wide open and to his relief, the room was empty. He looked out the window at the scene below. People, the pages included, were slowly collecting the animals. Patch and Daniel were no longer visible, and he hoped his friends would not receive too much punishment on his account.

He rushed over to the cot in which he had been sleeping and reached under the rough straw mattress. His knife was there, the one that his friend Dunstan had made for him. He looked it over and slipped it into his pants. He ran out of the room, passed the kitchen, and stopped at the entrance to the main hall, looking inside. There was no one near. He ran along the wall, trying his best to be quiet, and darted down one of the hallways finally coming into the base of the tower. Pausing occasionally to listen for approaching guards, he pushed and pulled at the stones, until he finally had an opening in the wall he could squeeze through. He took a deep breath before going in. I've made it, he thought.

He recounted the plan in his head. He'd sneak first into Bernard's chambers and find Sir Martin's maps. Bernard was keeping the maps locked inside, but judging by what Brayden had learned from Josslyn, he could sneak into his friend's chambers through a loose portion of wall behind the bed. He just had to figure out where, in the innumerable walls and tunnels, his friend's room was, and the precise location of the loose stone. It suddenly sounded daunting, but nevertheless, it was the path he would take. He had one foot in the hole when he heard someone behind him.

"I know where you're going, Brayden Rider," a voice said.

His spine stiffened as he realized he'd been caught. He stepped back and turned around. Josslyn Marshal stood over him. She held her bow in one hand, and a quiver of arrows was still strapped to her back. In her other hand she held an oil lamp, its flame burning softly.

"Leave me alone," Brayden said, turning back to the hole and preparing to enter.

"No. This is my castle, not yours, what is above ground and what is below. Isn't that what you told me once? Say, was that your doing out there, with the animals?"

"I-I don't know what you're talking about."

"Whatever. Your distraction worked, but I suspect you'll still need help what with Patch and Daniel caught."

"I will not," he protested. He was angry and a bit embarrassed at having been discovered, though relieved it was by her and not someone else.

"It will be dark as night down there. Do you even have a light?" Josslyn asked.

He didn't, and hadn't even thought about it until now. "I'll come across a torch along the way, I'm sure," he responded, suddenly worried about how he'd find his way once inside. He stared longingly at the oil lamp she held in her right hand.

"Quite a plan you have. And how, I wonder, will you get anywhere without this?"

Josslyn produced several scraps of Sir Martin's map, holding them just far enough away so that he couldn't grab them from her.

"How did you get that?" Brayden asked.

She smiled, and stuffed the maps back into a pocket. "The same way you did that night in Sir Bellator's chambers. Let's just say your old friend Bernard should do a better job of locking up his possessions. People around here leave entirely too much out in the open, even with a keep guard at the door."

He had been outdone, and he knew it. He was glad she was here, even if he would never admit it to her directly.

"Very well," Brayden said, trying and failing to appear stubborn and in charge. "You may come, but stay behind me."

"Yes, my lord," Josslyn snapped back, pretending to curtsy. They looked around one more time for anyone near, and slipped into the tunnels of the Castle Strand.

Chapter Thirty-Four

The Mines

Brayden and Josslyn followed the tunnel into the darkness. It sloped downward and widened, finally entering the alcove room where Corbat's body had been found. Brayden took a deep breath as he stepped inside. The memory of that horrible night came rushing back—finding the bailiff's body, the sense of dread as he realized he wasn't alone, and the feeling of terror when he was grabbed from behind. He remembered the horrid, sweat smell of the mandrake. He shivered suddenly.

"What is it?" Josslyn asked.

"N-nothing," he lied. "I'm just cold, that's all."

"Here, let me go on ahead." Josslyn held the oil lamp above her head and walked slowly across the room, peering into each alcove. She stopped to listen at the door at the far side of the room before walking back toward him.

"The room is empty," she said. "Handhafte, or whoever he was, has been removed. The other alcoves are empty as well."

He took a deep breath, walked across the room, and looked around. To his relief, it was true. The cages were empty, and every sign of the body was gone. He ran his fingers along the wall. Every inch of the rock seemed moist, and the air smelled old and rotten. He crossed the rough stone floor and tried the door to the dungeon. It was locked tight. Recalling the stories he had overheard from some of the castle residents, he could only imagine what horrors lay waiting on the other side.

"Here, let's look at this," Josslyn called.

He walked back to where she was standing. She was holding one of the map pages under the light, one of the same pages they had studied in the main hall earlier. Brayden traced over the lines, trying to discern where on the drawings they might be.

"We're here, are we not?" he suggested.

Josslyn looked around. "No, that is too far over, and much too big a space. We're still under the keep, remember. Here, hold this. Let me get us another page."

Brayden took the page as instructed. Josslyn reached into her pocket and pulled out a second page, holding it up so they both could see.

"This line, here," he said, inspecting the map carefully.

"Yes, that looks familiar," Josslyn agreed. "I think this line, I mean tunnel, leads into the first map we just looked at. I remember this now. We're in here."

She pointed to a small rectangular space, the room they thought they were in. Judging by the drawing, one of the alcoves was more than what it seemed. A thin, faint line branched off from it. She looked around, trying to orient their location with the drawing on the paper.

"This way," she said. "It seems as if it stems from this part of the room."

They felt their way along the wall. It was incredibly dim, and while the lamp helped, Brayden found himself staring at the wall, not sure what he was looking for. Would it be a hidden door? Bernard and Sir Hugh had sent several parties out to look for entrances to the mines. If one of the parties had made it in here, they had left no clues as to what they had found. He patted the walls with his fingers, trying to discern anything out of the ordinary. They came to the far alcove, nearest to the dungeon door.

"Here, help me with this." Josslyn started pushing at the stones, looking for any sign of movement. They went around the room and back again, twice, into each alcove and out again. There was no movement in the rocks and no sign of any hinges. They went around again. We must have already touched each brick twice, he thought, becoming frustrated. Josslyn continued around once more on the opposite wall.

"This is a waste of time," he complained at last.

"Whose idea was this, anyway?" she fired back. "I could just as easily leave you here in the dark!"

In frustration Brayden kicked at a large stone that stuck out of the wall at an odd angle. The stone fell back, and in seconds several stones in the wall collapsed inward, revealing a hole almost large enough for them to crawl through.

Josslyn ran over and looked down at the hole. "You've found it! We must have been holding the map upside down."

They both went down on their hands and knees to remove as much rock and stone as they could. In minutes they had created a hole in the wall they could step through. Brayden leaned forward and peered inside, but could make out nothing in the absolute darkness beyond. Josslyn reached into her pocket and pulled out a rushlight. She lit it, and threw it into the hole. It illuminated the floor, but not much else, showing only what appeared to be roughly carved steps winding down from the hole and into the murky blackness before them.

"Well, here it goes," Josslyn said. She stepped gingerly over the remaining rocks and into the stairwell, carefully balancing the oil lamp so as not to drop it. Brayden followed her in, anxious, but relieved to finally leave the alcove room.

* * *

Brayden picked up the rushlight and walked closely behind Josslyn. The steps ended abruptly and the passage sloped down, straightened, and then sloped down again. While the floor was surprisingly smooth, they found themselves disoriented in the gloom, and had to resort to gripping the rocky sides of the tunnel to keep their balance. The tunnel turned several times, and then straightened out for what seemed like an eternity, while the floor grew progressively more rugged. They moved slowly, their eyes alternating between looking for uneven spaces in the ground and outgrowths of rock from the walls or ceilings. Brayden had explored caves in the forest near Honeydown, but had never been anywhere like this before, and knew a twisted ankle or sudden fall could spell disaster. The air had cooled considerably, but at least the moist, rotten smell of the alcove room was far behind them.

Brayden noticed that the rock had begun to take on an odd shape, as if it had been sculpted and covered with plaster. Some parts seemed smooth, almost polished. As they moved along the corridor, the dim illumination of the lamp and the rushlight cast eerie, menacing shadows against the stone. Then something odd caught his eye.

"Wait," he called.

Josslyn stopped and turned around as Brayden held the dim rushlight to the wall to examine it. What he saw made him jump back in terror. Josslyn stepped closer, shining the light from the oil lamp first at him and then at the wall. She screamed and almost dropped the lamp to the ground. Brayden yelled as he bumped into the wall behind him, dropping the rushlight, which promptly went out. He turned and shrunk back once more as he faced the same frightening sight. Both walls, along the entire length of the tunnel as far as they could see, were lined with human skulls.

Resisting the urge to run back the way they had come, they concentrated on one another's faces and took deep breaths to calm themselves. Once Brayden composed himself, he turned and examined the walls more closely. The skulls lay upon alternating stacks of bones, the rows of human remains reaching almost to the height of the ceiling.

"What is this place?" Brayden whispered. His voice was uneven, but a welcome sound inside the lifeless cave. "These bones go on forever."

Josslyn nodded. "A crypt of some kind? Whoever built these tunnels must have buried them here, or *been* buried here. Maybe these were slaves."

Brayden thought of Honeydown and recalled stories travelers from the continent had shared of ancient crypts and catacombs and the treasures buried within. While his mother didn't approve of him listening to these stories, they remained a popular topic of conversation long after the travelers had left the village. Still, he never imagined something like this so close to his home, let alone finding himself inside one.

They walked on. The alternating rows of bones and skulls continued as far as they could see. The height of the tunnel itself was dropping, and

Brayden suspected a tall adult would be forced to crawl if the tunnel narrowed much further.

"Look," Josslyn said, holding the oil lamp high. Above them, someone had carved letters into the rock. Brayden tried to read them.

NIHIL VERUM NISIL MORS

"What is it?" he asked. "It looks like Latin, but I can't read Latin well." Josslyn did not respond. She was staring at the letters as if reading them again and again in her mind. "Joss, what does it say?" he asked again, more forcefully this time, trying to get her to snap out of it.

She stood still, quietly mouthing the words over and over. He grabbed her arm and shook her. "What does it say?" Brayden insisted once more.

She didn't even look at him as she said, "Nothing is true, but death."

* * *

Brayden took the lamp from Josslyn with one hand and led her forward with the other. She remained silent, as if still thinking about what they had just seen in the crypt. Soon after they'd passed under the Latin carving, the rows of bones stopped, replaced once more by roughly chiseled rock. The tunnel twisted and turned again and again before straightening for a long stretch. It was becoming moist in areas, with water dripping down the walls and forming puddles on the floor. He watched the oil lamp as they walked. The oil was burning quickly, and he wondered how far they had gone, and how much further they could go.

They started up an incline, and then, without warning, Josslyn stopped suddenly. "Listen," she said quietly.

Brayden did as he was instructed. Other than the sound of their breathing, there was absolute silence. Then, he heard it—a shuffling, scratching sound.

"Do you hear it?" Josslyn asked, whispering.

He nodded his head and was suddenly scared once more, thinking of his kidnapping in the alcove room. He moved the lamp around slowly. The weak light flickered, and he had to focus hard to see anything in the dark. The sound seemed to come from every direction at once. Josslyn pointed. "Ah! There!" she shouted, moving away quickly. He whirled around.

Rats. Their dark, hairy bodies scurried along the walls and into hidden places. Their little eyes lit up as their noses twitched in protest at being disturbed. Brayden calmed himself, and even managed to crack a smile. Compared to what had happened to him in the alcove room, and after walking in a long, cold dark tunnel past a mountain of human bones, a few rats were the last thing they needed to fear.

"S-sorry. Rats d-don't usually bother me," Josslyn said nervously. "Still, it's a welcome sign, I hope."

"The rats? Why?" Brayden watched as the small furry animals disappeared from sight, one after another. Good to see rats? They were so common in the villages and the castle; he had never bothered to notice them before. Then it struck him that these were the first they had seen in a long, long time.

"Why do you think?" Josslyn asked. "We must be coming to the end. Where there are rats..."

"...there are people," Brayden finished for her.

* * *

Lord Marshal had expanded and lushly decorated the castle chapel prior to his detainment. The walls were painted gold and white, and bright tapestries hung on every side, splashing the room in color. Chairs and benches, each adorned with soft velvet pillows and blankets, lined the walls. The exquisitely carved altar was solid oak, its surface enhanced by a dark red tapestry trimmed in golden fringes. The floor, too, was wood, but swept clean daily unlike so much of the rest of the castle. Candles were lit around the perimeter of the room, but light also streamed in from the stained glass windows, giving the interior of the chapel a warm, soothing glow. The thick walls and heavy wooden door ensured a quiet, peaceful escape from the world during services and in times of contemplation.

Bernard knelt by the altar, his head bent, deep in prayer. He had lost track of time since entering the chapel, and though tired, he could not bring himself to leave. He looked up and through the stained glass windows. While he was sure God would forgive him for his foolishness, he himself never would. He cursed himself silently for what had happened to Alice and Brayden. How could he have left her behind, and worse, how could he have let Brayden out of his sight? He saw himself now as an arrogant, silly old man, at once unable to help his lord against the evil of Philip and his allies, and now cursed for losing his lord's family. Bernard bowed his head and wept.

"Bernard?" It was John Fields.

Bernard looked up, quickly wiping his eyes. "Yes, friend. Please join me."

John Fields walked up to the altar, crossed himself, and bowed. After a few moments he lifted his head and spoke.

"Are you all right, friend?"

"I am. I am fine, John. Merely praying for the family's safe return."

"I've prayed the same." John Fields placed a hand on Bernard's shoulder. "Bernard, I fear I must bid you goodbye. Dunstan and I will be leaving Castle Strand for Honeydown soon, and I wanted to thank you for all you've done for us. We're needed at the village I'm sure. I'm sorry about Alice and the boy, but every knight and man-at-arms in the barony is searching for them, and I have faith they will turn up unharmed."

"I pray you are right, friend."

"I'd thank Sir Caelan too, but he's left as well. Please give him our blessings upon his return."

"Of course," Bernard nodded.

"Very well then, as soon as I can find Dunstan, we'll be off." John Fields paused. "I can't seem to hold on to anything since Alice disappeared. Just today I lost that dagger I had found, and now him." John Fields walked back to the door, and then stopped. "Friar?"

"Yes, John?"

"Do say a prayer for Dunstan too. I'm afraid he's not been right since Cecilia's death."

"Not a surprise, I suppose."

"No, but he speaks with no one now, saying nary a word the whole way here. And then there was the incident at his shop."

"Oh?" Bernard bowed his head once more at the base of the altar, wishing John would leave him alone.

"Some days ago a few of the boys got into his shop and uncovered a new coat of mail, buried under the floor. They were playing with it, and he caught them. They had torn it to shreds. Gave them a real lashing he did. I have never seen him in such a rage."

Bernard opened his eyes and turned around. "What did you say?"

"Dunstan gave them a real lashing. He's always been such a friendly sort, with children, he—"

"No," Bernard interrupted. "Before that. The armor."

"It was new, just made. The boys were able to rip it apart with toy wooden swords and sticks. I've never seen anything like it." John Fields paused, looking at the holy man curiously.

"And the dagger, with the serpent. Missing you say?"

"That's the one. Gone. It was such an old thing. Who would steal a man's knife?"

"A monster." Bernard was on his feet and rushing toward the door. "Gather the good captain. I'll fetch Sir Hugh. We have perhaps found who we have been searching for. I just pray we are not too late."

Chapter Thirty-Five

Regin

The air was becoming warmer, and a slight breeze came from the direction the children were walking in. The tunnel had changed in complexion as well. Heavy timber beams lodged in various places held up the roof, and smaller tunnels broke off from the main one. Some of the smaller tunnels looked partially collapsed; others appeared to go deep underground, forever. The passage itself had become very narrow.

"Look," Josslyn said, pointing. "I think I see a faint light up ahead."

Brayden followed her finger, but could see absolutely nothing past the light of the oil lamp. They moved quickly, anxious to see what lay ahead. The floor was uneven and rough, forcing them to balance carefully against the walls of the tunnel and each other. They had no more rushlights, and each looked nervously at the oil lamp as they walked, knowing it was near its end.

Brayden coughed, wishing for the fresh air of the outside world and something, anything, to drink. He suddenly felt dizzy, and put a hand against the wall to steady himself. They must have been down here half the night or more, he thought morosely, and what if there is nothing up ahead? They would be trapped here in the pitch dark, breathing this stagnant air while his mother remained a hostage up there somewhere. No. He shook his head violently, trying to regain his senses. That will not happen.

Then, he spotted it too. There was indeed a faint trace of light up ahead.

"I see it!" he blurted out excitedly. He found his pace quickening, as if new energy had entered his body with the thought that they'd soon be free of the darkness.

They crossed a jagged corner and reached an opening with two timber beams on either side. Josslyn hesitated, looking inside cautiously. Brayden darted past her and stepped through.

They were inside a large, circular, carved-out room. The floor was pounded flat, and the walls were covered in carefully placed stones, many of which had fallen to the ground. The light they had seen came from two torches that burned brightly against the far wall.

He avoided saying what both of them were thinking: someone had lit those torches, and that someone might not be far off.

He looked around. Metal tools and bits of rock littered the floor, the rocks glistening strangely in the torchlight. Baskets of various sizes and chunks of pottery lay about everywhere, as did the heads of what looked like iron pickaxes, though all were missing their wooden handles. A small bowl and spoon sat on a small chair nearby, and Brayden wondered how long it had been since the bowl had held food. Brayden started to inspect one of the shiny rocks nearby, but paused when he saw the device at the far side of the chamber.

Against the wall lay a large wooden wheel set upon an axle. Small boxes lined the diameter of the wheel, and what looked like a trough hung suspended in the wall above the wheel, leading out to another chamber up above. Brayden walked closer and looked up, straining to see the details of the wheel in the dark. It was big, like the water wheel of a millhouse, perhaps five times his own height.

"What is that?" Josslyn asked, standing beside him and staring at the device in fascination.

Brayden inspected the wheel, touching the frame, and then pushing down on the boxes. The wheel creaked, turning slowly by a couple of inches. He stepped back.

"These are Roman mines, and I think this is a water wheel of some sort, like the grain miller's wheel in a village. Only I think this one removed water instead of turning a stone to grind grain. I bet these mines would flood, and that trough up there leads to a series of other wheels, each one carrying the water higher up until it's dumped outside."

"Outside?" Josslyn asked, suddenly transfixed.

Brayden shrugged. "I think we have to climb. I don't want to go back, and those other passages looked to lead nowhere but down." They both looked at the sputtering oil lamp, and Brayden walked over to the torches. "We'll take these," he said. "They'll last a while longer." He lifted the torches off the wall and handed one to Josslyn.

Brayden knew that while any passages above could lead out of the mine, it was equally likely they went nowhere. He suspected Josslyn thought the same thing, but neither of them volunteered that possibility.

"Let's hurry," he said. "Whoever lit these could be back at any minute."

Josslyn nodded. "I'm impressed you know what this is," she said, looking at the wheel.

"As am I," said a voice behind them.

Brayden jumped, and then turned around. He recognized the man instantly.

"Dunstan?"

The little man grinned hideously. "Regin," he rasped.

* * *

He had a terrifying, wild appearance. His dark hair seemed to jut out in every direction, and his eyes glowed an eerie yellow in the flickering torchlight. His body was covered by no more than a long, dirty leather tunic tied at the waist with a thick rope.

"It pleases me to see you again, boy," he said, stepping closer into the torchlight. "Do not fear me. You know me well."

It was then that Brayden saw the deep red gashes on the man's arms and hands, the same gashes Brayden had inflicted upon him the night Honeydown was attacked. Brayden recalled the terror he felt, and how helpless he was there trapped inside their home. He remembered his friend

Dunstan holding poor Cecilia. His mind raced to the figure lurking in the shadows of the main hall and of the plotting he'd overheard in Sir Bellator's chambers. He remembered the sickening smell of mandrake and the evil voice, as he lay trapped in the tower. He remembered Michaelmas.

"I…I do," Brayden responded, trying to be brave and stand his ground despite the fear that was consuming him. "Or, I thought I did. It was you who attacked our village."

Regin nodded, coming closer. "Hiding your knight friend was clever. He is the only thing that saved you and your little village. But, he is not here now, is he?"

Brayden thought of Sir Caelan, and how he wished he were here now. "A-and you kidnapped me, and tried to kill Sir Allard and Lord Marshal."

"When I saw you in the main hall with Lady Elaine that day, I was pleased you had come. Though it's twice you've escaped me. Not again," Regin said, coming even closer.

"And what of Cecilia?" Brayden cried, his voice wavering. "You killed her?"

"Unfortunate. She saw things she shouldn't have seen."

"You know where my mother is, don't you? Where is she?!" Brayden yelled, the fear in his heart replaced by passionate, all-consuming anger.

Regin smiled wickedly, ignoring the question. He stood before Brayden now, his grubby face leering at him like a demon's. The kind, caring image of his friend Dunstan had disappeared completely, replaced by this monstrous gargoyle of a man.

"There is something your family has that my master and I must possess. Don't try to run. From these mines, my mines, there is no escape. Flee, and you, or better yet, your little friend, will perish here."

"Your master, Bellator?" Brayden asked, unsure as to why. It made no difference. He glanced about the room. Josslyn was nowhere to be found. Perhaps she had escaped, he thought.

"No, not Bellator, though I admit he was always a bit more interested in keeping you both alive, than I."

Regin reached behind his back and produced a long, sharp dagger. Even in the dim light Brayden recognized it instantly. It was the serpent dagger John Fields had shown them at Dunstan's shop. Regin twirled it once, then twice, and then lunged.

Brayden dropped his torch and darted one-way, and then another, trying to escape. Regin grabbed Brayden's tunic. Brayden heard the sound of cloth tearing, and then Regin screamed suddenly and fell to the floor. Brayden wrenched free and looked over and up. Josslyn was kneeling and trying to maintain her balance atop the wheel, bow in hand. Regin was writhing in agony, an arrow locked in his side.

"C'mon!" Josslyn yelled. She picked up her torch and began waving to him, urging Brayden up upon the wheel.

"Where is she!" Brayden demanded of Regin.

"You'll not find her, boy; you'll not live long enough."

To Brayden's shock, Regin stood, dagger in hand. He looked down at this side and grabbed the arrow shaft. With an inhuman scream, he pulled it out of his body and threw it to the floor.

"Run!" Josslyn shouted.

Brayden wasted no time racing to the wheel. He scrambled up, box by box. The wheel creaked and groaned in protest, wobbling back and forth as its ancient age supported the weight of both of them. Brayden slipped, then found his footing and made it to the top, still clutching the torch.

"This way," Josslyn said. "I think you were right. I think we can follow this trough up and out!"

They climbed the trough, and emerged into another chamber, smaller, but with a similar wheel at the far side. They scrambled across the room and began to climb again.

Brayden looked back. Regin had picked up the other torch and was emerging into the chamber.

"Hurry!" Brayden said desperately from behind Josslyn. They made it to the top of the second wheel, across its trough, and into the next chamber, Regin right behind them.

Rocks and boulders were strewn everywhere, and the wheel in this chamber was off its axel, broken and cracked. They paused, unsure of what to do. The ground next to the wheel fell away into the dark, and Brayden surmised that the ceiling above and the floor below had caved in at some point.

They looked up. The trough to the next wheel chamber was intact above, but could they reach it? They heard Regin struggling behind them, and not thinking any further, they scrambled onto the wreckage of the wheel. Its boxes and wood frame fell away as they climbed.

Brayden was at the top when he heard Josslyn scream. She had fallen back to the rocks.

"Josslyn!" he yelled.

Her torch sputtering on the ground, she stood, pulled her bow from her shoulder, and tried to string an arrow, but was too late. Regin was upon her. He grabbed the bow and slammed it against a boulder, shattering it into pieces. Then he knocked Josslyn to the ground, where she lay motionless.

"Joss!"

Regin looked up at Brayden, smiling. He stepped on her torch, putting it out of its misery. From Brayden's position above, Regin looked like a grotesque troll.

"Every one of us toils for a lord," Regin said. "And mine wanted you brought before him, with your father."

"What of my father? What do you want from us?" Brayden demanded, watching helplessly as Regin approached.

"We want what your father won't tell us, Rider. But since we have your mother, perhaps we don't need you."

Regin tossed the torch to the floor, put the dagger between his teeth, and threw himself up against the wreckage, climbing with ease. It groaned and swayed violently, protesting the man's weight. Brayden looked down again at Josslyn, who was still not moving, and then looked up at the next trough. He could reach it, and fear of this creature climbing the wheel before him made him want to run, but he could not leave his friend behind. He stepped back, and suddenly remembered his knife. He pulled it out, the same blade he had used to repel this invader from his home those long weeks ago.

Regin was at the top, soon just inches from him. Brayden raised his knife, and Regin paused, his own eyes wide with surprise. But he didn't hesitate. Holding on to the wheel with one hand, he pulled the dagger from his mouth with the other, and raised it to stab at Brayden. The wheel swayed, and Regin swayed with it, backward. With all his strength

Brayden brought his knife down on Regin's hand, the one that was holding the wheel, and pulled the knife free again. Blood oozed forth as the little man screamed. He scrambled to balance himself on the wheel, letting go with the bleeding hand and trying to steady himself with the one that still held the knife. Brayden backed away. There was a loud crack, and with a hideous scream Regin fell backward. He bounced off a large rock and plummeted into the chasm below, disappearing from sight. Brayden jumped to the ground, landing with a thump next to Josslyn.

* * *

Brayden crawled over to where Josslyn lay. He turned her over and laid her flat on her back. Her forehead was bruised, but not cut. In one hand she still held the arrow she had intended to shoot at Regin.

"Josslyn?" He patted her hand. "Joss?"

Her hand squeezed his, her eyes fluttered open and she lifted her head. "Regin!" she cried, looking around in fear.

"He's gone, I think. I hope," Brayden said. He looked over at the chasm beside the wheel, unsure of how far down it went, and bracing himself to see Regin climb out of the pit at any second.

Josslyn followed his eyes to the hole.

"Are you all right?" Brayden asked.

She slowly propped herself up. "I'm okay, I think. I hit my head pretty hard, but I'm ready to go." She stood slowly, steadying herself against the rocky wall, and rubbed her head.

"Did you throw him down into that pit?" she asked, and then looked at his hand. He was still holding the small knife, unable to let go. "You defeated him with that?"

Brayden looked at the bloody knife. He had forgotten it was there. He quickly slipped it back into his pocket, thinking how silly it was that he was still embarrassed by its small size.

"C'mon," he said, leading her back to the wheel. "This one is much more fragile than the last, so be careful. Perhaps we can stack some of the wood and rocks to reach the next chamber. Let's see if we can find our way out of here."

They piled everything they could find against the remains of the wheel. Josslyn picked up the last torch and went first, and once she reached the trough she reached down and helped Brayden up. They followed the trough into the next chamber and at the next wheel they paused. Brayden noticed that the air seemed much cooler, and fresher.

"I pray we're getting close," Josslyn said. She and Brayden looked at the one torch they had left. If they were wrong, this would have to last them somehow, and it was almost out. Without light, there was no way they'd make it back down through the various chambers, let alone back through the tunnels to the castle. They would be alone in the pitch dark.

They climbed the last trough, and instead of entering another wheel chamber, they found themselves in a small, cramped tunnel that angled downward. The torch was barely a flicker, and they hastened forward, navigating the jagged, slippery rock as best they could. The tunnel came to an abrupt end, and then took a sharp turn. As they looped around, a strong gust of air hit them. Josslyn screamed, and Brayden desperately tried to shield the flame from further wind, but it was too late. The gust had extinguished the torch for good. They sat, disoriented, in total darkness.

"Oh, Heaven save us," Josslyn pleaded. Brayden too was shivering with panic. Not even in the castle had he experienced anything so hopelessly dark. He felt the floor, the walls, and the ceiling of the tunnel, but each angle felt the same. As he moved around, he wasn't sure if he was going back the way they had come, forward, or down an adjacent tunnel. He stopped, tired and terrified. Josslyn breathed heavily nearby. Then he felt it. The faintest of breezes.

"Joss," he said, almost breathlessly. "The wind. Follow the wind!"

They felt their way along, remaining silent, hands reaching in every direction as they tried to pick up and follow even the lightest stirrings of the air. Suddenly a stronger gust hit them, and Brayden sensed they were rounding another corner, still heading down slightly. "There!" he shouted.

Several yards ahead of them the rock was illuminated, if only slightly, in pale blue. They scrambled forward and rounded yet another corner. They stopped there, staring at the sight. The tunnel walls were lit with sunlight. Before them lay the exit to the outside world.

Chapter Thirty-Six

Discovery

Brayden and Josslyn emerged from the mine and onto a ledge overlooking a large rock-strewn plain. The sun was already rising, its faint hues casting eerie shadows as the first light hit the white stones of the jagged landscape. In the distance Brayden could make out a stone tower, and beyond that, the sea. They each took several deep breaths, silently enjoying the fresh morning air while trying to forget the dark, horrible place they had just left.

"Taunton Tower, I think," Brayden said, recalling Bernard's description of the place when they'd first arrived at Castle Strand. "There were once old Roman ruins here, and then someone built a tower over them to protect the shore from Norsemen marauders. I had hoped to see this one day. I just didn't expect it to be like this."

"Resourceful people, whoever they were," Josslyn responded. "Look!" She pointed at the horizon. In the distance, they could see the faintest outline of a ship approaching through the gray-blue mist.

"Yes, I see it," Brayden replied. "They must be heading to the tower. Could it be your father's men?"

"I doubt it. My father mentioned this place just once."

"Did he ever take you here?" Brayden asked, trying without luck to make out any markings on the ship.

Josslyn shook her head. "No, he forbids it. He ordered us to stay away."

At that, Brayden decided not to ask any more questions, and joined Josslyn in silently scanning the landscape further. Before the tower was a row of white tents on a bright green, grassy field, their canvases fluttering in the wind.

"There are people down there," Josslyn said.

Brayden leaned forward, but could see no movement from where they stood.

Just then, they heard footsteps behind them. Josslyn turned white, and Brayden's heart fell to his stomach. There was nowhere to run, and a jump from this high was out of the question. They turned around in terror, expecting Regin. Brayden almost lost his footing on the rocks before a strong hand quickly emerged from the darkness and grabbed his arm.

"Caelan!" they both shouted at once.

The young knight extinguished the head of his smoldering torch against the rock, and then smiled and embraced them both.

"How?" Brayden started at his friend, his mouth wide open in surprise as a feeling of relief coursed through his body.

Caelan looked them over. "You two are filthier than me. And do you have water? Here."

The knight pulled a small hide from his pack and the children drank deeply, passing the hide between them several times. To Brayden, after so many hours underground, it was the sweetest taste he could remember.

Caelan wiped the grime off of their faces and inspected them again. "It's interesting. Soon after Sullivan and I left the castle, we came upon some rabble attacking an oxen cart. We engaged them. For some reason, being held at sword point makes men talk. It turned out these were some of Samain's men. They had been en route to a cave, which upon investigation was not only a cave, but an entrance to a mine. This mine." Caelan pointed a gloved hand behind him. "I tied up Sullivan, went in and wandered around in the dark for a while before finding my way here. While I did get a lot of exploring done, I must have been in there half the night and for a time never thought I'd get out. It is quite an operation someone had down there. Those mines and caves crisscross the countryside, just as Sir Martin's maps tell us. I didn't find any treasure though. Oh well. I'm glad to see you both. By the way, what *are* you two doing up here?"

Josslyn and Brayden smiled at each other, happy to have made it this far, and happy to be reunited with their friend.

"We thought you were Regin," Brayden said.

"Regin? He's here?" Caelan's hand instinctively went to the hilt of his sword.

"Brayden fought him in the mines," Josslyn responded. "They fought, and Regin fell off one of the wheels and into a pit. We've not seen him since."

Caelan looked thunderstruck.

Brayden shrugged, a bit embarrassed. Josslyn winked at him, and then told the knight the story of how they had come upon the entrance to the mines and everything that had transpired since.

"Sir Caelan," Brayden said after Josslyn was finished, feeling sad with sharing the news. "Regin and Dunstan Smith. They're the same man."

"What? The blacksmith?" Caelan looked into his eyes, speechless for a few moments as the revelation sank in. "The faulty armor. Well, you truly are your father's son," he finally said. "You two are a good team. Wait until I tell Bernard and Sir Hugh. Perhaps I should hand you my sword and follow you both down there!"

Caelan nodded to the tower in the distance by the seashore. Brayden looked as well. While they were no bigger than insects at this distance, he could now clearly see several men moving about the base of the tower.

"I'd wager they're preparing to load whatever they've found in the mine onto that approaching vessel. I suspect, too, that Bellator is down there, awaiting his master."

"And who would that be?" Josslyn asked.

"I intend to find out." Caelan put down the pack he'd been carrying, got up from his crouched position, and began making his way down the ledge to the plain below. Pebbles slid from beneath his feet as he slowly descended to the base. He looked up. "You two stay here. You'll find rations in my sack. If I am not back by mid-morning, I want you to go back overland. Stay to the base of the mountain and you'll find the cave I entered. You'll hopefully find Sullivan too. From there, east, it is less than a day's journey to Castle Strand. Proceed there and tell Sir Allard what is transpiring. He'll know what to do."

"We can help!" Brayden cried.

Caelan shook his head. "No, stay there. If I find anything, I'll be back for you." He waved good-bye, and then began weaving his way around the largest rocks so as not to be seen. Within minutes, he had disappeared among the boulders.

Brayden sat back in frustration. He knew what Caelan meant by "anything." He knew if Sir Bellator was down there, his mother very likely would be as well.

"If it makes you feel any better, I don't want to sit here all morning either," Josslyn said. "I didn't come all this way to watch the sun rise across some scarred Welsh plain, and then go home."

Brayden desperately wanted to continue on, but he had faith in his friend. "He will be back. He always keeps his word."

They sat and ate, as Caelan had instructed. Brayden grimaced as he bit into the hard cheese, harder bread and salted meat. The light was strong now, and the shroud of mist was breaking. The ship was clearly visible, though still a long way from the shore. It cast a strange, uneven shape against the sky. More men scurried around the base of the tower. From their vantage point, they could make out nothing of what the men were doing, let alone where Caelan or Sir Bellator might be.

A high-pitched, terrified scream pierced the air. Brayden stood upright, cupping his hands over his eyes and staring in the direction of the tower. He had heard that scream before. Josslyn looked up at him, her face filled with concern.

"My mother," Brayden said quietly. He was chilled, scared, and angry all at once. His thoughts wandered back to that horrible night the village had been attacked, the night of the attack on their home.

"What? Are you sure?" Josslyn asked. She was standing too, trying to figure out where in the distance the scream had come from.

"As sure as I can be. I'm going to her." Brayden began to climb down, forgetting all about what Caelan had said moments before. He almost lost his footing more than once as he maneuvered quickly down the rock face.

Josslyn followed him. "So much for doing what our knight says," she said half jokingly.

Chapter Thirty-Seven

The Treasure

They landed on the rocky plain, Brayden leading the way toward the tower. Most of the rocks were taller than they were, and the landscape was so rough it was difficult to continue moving in any one direction. They finally wound their way through the maze and emerged onto a small field of grass. They climbed a low boulder and peered over it. The grass was part of a narrow road, carved through the boulders. It led directly to the tower, and back toward the mountain they had emerged from. The road was wide enough for several men, or even a mule cart or two, to pass through comfortably.

"That makes sense," Josslyn said, tracing the path of the road with her eyes. "It's an easier way to haul things to and from the mines than climbing over all of these rocks."

"Perhaps that's another old Roman road," Brayden replied. "Come on, it will be a faster way to get to the tower."

They hopped down and followed the road. The faint impression of wagon wheel tracks was visible in the grass. The going was easy, and they quickened their pace, listening carefully for signs of activity in front of and behind them.

They were getting close. The sound of the sea was just audible now, like distant thunder. The wind carried an occasional voice, though exactly what was being said by the men and exactly where the voices were coming from was difficult to make out. Brayden looked up. He could see the top of the tower over a rock wall. He turned to Josslyn.

"We're almost there, just a little further. I'm going to go around this last corner and see if I can get into one of the tents." He walked on.

"Brayden!" she hissed.

The largest man Brayden had ever seen was rounding the corner, heading right towards them. He wore a filthy whitish tunic over which was slung a bur-covered coat of dark brown animal fur. Covering his long blond hair was a large metal helmet with a single horn protruding from the front. In one hand he carried a thick wooden club with a metal hook at the end, in the other, an ax. Without thinking Brayden dove into a shallow alcove formed by two boulders, then peered slowly around the edge so he could see what was going on. Joss! He looked around, but she was nowhere in sight.

"Sker!" another man yelled, scurrying around the corner after the larger man.

Brayden recognized the name immediately. Sker was the same man the bandit leader Samain and his henchman had mentioned those many days ago in the forest near the abbey.

Sker grunted as he was joined by the smaller, though no less frightening, man.

"I don't want to go back to the mine!" the smaller man complained. He held a thick wooden club. A long rusty dagger was tied to the end of it with a rope.

"You don't ask, you just do," Sker replied curtly.

Brayden listened closely, trying to hear every word. While they spoke in English, their accent was thick, unfamiliar.

"You barely fit!" the smaller man complained. "And raiding villages is a world more fun."

"There'll be no more of that. You heard what happened at Nifylog Pass."

"I did."

"Then you know Lord Marshal and his knights will be here soon looking for the steward."

Brayden closed his eyes and said a silent prayer of thanks. The mission of Sir Grey, Sir Cornwall, and the other knights from the castle had been successful. Lord Marshal was alive. He hoped Josslyn had heard too, wherever she was hiding.

"That is all very well, but what about the gold?" the smaller man asked

Sker grunted once more. "I've thought of that. We'll take what we can before anything is loaded onto the boat. Let's walk on. We'll double back after a time. The steward will never know."

The men passed by and Brayden waited several minutes, listening carefully, until he was sure they were gone. These men were treacherous, and while they intended to cross Sir Bellator, Brayden was sure they'd waste no time dispatching Josslyn and him if they were caught.

He slowly emerged from the alcove. To his relief, Josslyn crawled out from behind a large boulder at the same time. She looked happy, despite the danger.

"You heard about Lord Marshal?" Brayden asked.

She nodded, smiling, knowing that her father was safe and would soon be here.

"Who were those men?" Josslyn asked nervously, looking around as if expecting them to return any minute.

"Norsemen, I suspect, at least they looked like it," Brayden replied. "They're in the employ of Sir Bellator, who I can only guess is up ahead somewhere too."

Brayden had heard many stories of the Norsemen and their barbarous ways. Bernard had told him tales of long-ago Viking raiding parties attacking up and down the coast of Britain. The tales had romanticized the Norsemen in his mind, as he dreamt of their dragon ships and horned helmets, and the dangers of long journeys at sea. Now that he had been up close to them, he found them frightening beyond anything he had imagined, and there were likely many more up ahead.

"Let's go find your mother," Josslyn insisted.

"You still want to go, despite everything?"

Josslyn nodded quickly. "Of course. You helped save my father. Let's go find her and bring her home."

"All right," Brayden said, trying to be brave. "Let's move as fast as we can and stay close to the rocks."

They continued on, peering around every corner and listening for anyone approaching. At last, they came into the plain before the tower. The sea air here was cool and fresh. Taunton Tower sat on a small hill several yards away. Around its base were numerous roughly built tents. The tower itself was surrounded by rubble and looked collapsed in places, as if it had been the scene of a long-ago battle. There was an opening at its base. No flags or other identification flew from the tower or any of the tents.

They scanned their surroundings. Other than the wind rippling against the tents, nothing stirred. The voices they had heard not long ago were gone. The dark ship they had seen earlier was much closer now, and would be docking shortly.

"That ship is almost here. Let's make this fast," Josslyn whispered. "Perhaps we can find something in these tents."

They sprinted across the plain to the first tent. Josslyn first listened for voices, and then peeked in through the flap. She waved Brayden over, and they both entered.

The tent was unoccupied, save for numerous empty barrels, various linens, and a few weapons stacked in a corner. Josslyn wasted no time and went on to the next tent moments later.

"Same thing here," she said quietly. "Here, you check the next one, and let's hurry."

Brayden didn't need her to remind him. His heart pounded at the thought of the Norsemen or Sir Bellator appearing any second out of one of the tents or from around the tower. He took a deep breath and looked into the next tent. He couldn't believe his eyes.

"Joss, come here!"

"Is someone inside?" she asked anxiously, as she looked in every direction for signs of movement.

He stepped in, and Josslyn darted in seconds later. This tent was also filled with crates and barrels, but unlike those in the first two tents, these were filled with rocks with veins running through them that gave off a yellowish sheen. They walked up to get a closer look, though both knew what was inside. Brayden touched one of the rocks.

"Gold," they both said at once.

"The Norsemen *are* in the employ of Bellator, and they're taking the gold from the mine," Josslyn said. "Right under my father's and Sir Allard's noses. There is a fortune here."

Brayden nodded. "And whoever is on that ship is going to leave with it." He gazed back at the rocks on the way out, feeling somewhat disappointed. Gold yes, but he had imaged the treasure itself would be a bit more spectacular than these rocks.

They ran to the next tent, and the next. Each was filled with barrels and crates of gold. In the last tent Brayden paused when he saw several short swords, gold-decorated armor breastplates, and bright yellow amulets stacked neatly in the center of the room. To his eyes, the objects seemed to glow. He walked in and looked carefully at one of the swords, admiring its beauty. The letters, "SPQR" were inscribed on the hilt.

"S-P-Q-R," he read out loud. "What does it mean?"He turned to Josslyn, and someone else was there.

"Senatus Populusque Romanus. Latin. The Senate and the People of Rome. That is what it means, though I don't really care why."

Brayden wheeled around and froze. There at the opening to the tent stood Sir Bellator. Over tight chain armor he was wearing a dark tunic and black cloak, and a long broadsword hung from his heavy, silver-accented leather belt. A smile of eerie satisfaction crept across his face.

Seconds later, two of the Norsemen joined the former steward on either side. One dragged Josslyn in by the arm, and then pushed her violently toward Brayden. She recovered quickly, straightening her clothes out and pushing the hair from her face, as if ready to face their captors.

"You're two inventive children," Sir Bellator said. "Regin had hinted he'd try to dispatch you both, but apparently he failed. Good. You'll both be of value to my master and me."

"This gold is being stolen," Josslyn protested. "This is Lord Marshal's land, and the King's!"

Sir Bellator walked up to Josslyn and clutched her chin in his hand, holding tight. "Quiet, little one. I'll not be lectured by a child. You see, since your father escaped our trap, I'll need you to keep him at bay. He and Sir Allard will not strike while you're in our possession. A pity. To think, we could have been wed." The Norsemen laughed quietly as Sir Bellator let Josslyn jerk her head away. He turned his attention to Brayden, the same satisfied smile on his lips. "And you, Rider boy, now that you've fallen into my lap, you'll accompany me to France after all. Your father will indeed be pleased to see you."

France. Brayden's mind raced. Was it possible his father was there waiting for him? No, it could not be that simple. This evil man and whomever he was working with would use him, just as Bernard had said they would, to get whatever they sought from Sir Ban and the Templars. As much as he desired to see his father again, he knew in his heart he could not let that happen. Just then he heard a quiet moan. It was coming from somewhere inside the tent.

Brayden looked around, trying to follow the sound. Ignoring Sir Bellator and his men, he walked behind a pile of sacks. There, bound, gagged and bruised, but alive, lay his mother.

Chapter Thirty-Eight

The Tower

Alice was covered in dirt and had obviously been struggling to get free. Their eyes locked. Brayden dropped to his knees, and forgetting all about Sir Bellator and his men, he worked quickly to remove the gag. Her cheeks, wrists, and ankles were red from the tight bindings.

"Brayden!" his mother said. "What are you doing here?"

He put his head to her chest, and listened to her heartbeat. He started to cry. He was embarrassed at first, but found he could not stop himself. He held her close and felt safe and happy, if only for a moment. At last he pulled away.

"How…how did you find me?" she asked.

"I heard you scream," he replied, wiping his eyes.

"All will be fine." Alice looked quickly at Josslyn. "And who is this?" she asked.

"Lady Josslyn Marshal," she responded, not waiting for anyone else to answer for her. Brayden thought she was trying to remain brave, despite the danger they were in.

"She came to help me, mother, but now we're all trapped."

Alice shot a glance at Sir Bellator, who was standing over both of them. "Brayden, they raided our village again, coming for me. I agreed to be taken, out of fear for the safety of the other townspeople. I was blindfolded, gagged, and bound, thrown upon a horse, and taken here. I was never sure of my surroundings, and when I screamed, they knocked me out. I know not what they want."

Brayden grew increasingly angry as he heard his mother's account. He clenched his fists, and his face grew hot. "They shouldn't have done those things to you," he sputtered, turning to Sir Bellator and then back to Alice.

"Shh," his mother said, smiling proudly, reassuringly. "I am fine, now that I have been rescued by my brave son."

"Our hearts are touched," Sir Bellator said. "If only that were the case. Now, I think we've heard enough." He gave a signal, and the Norsemen were upon the children.

Brayden and Josslyn tried to resist, but the awful men were too strong, too fast. In seconds they found themselves bound at the hands and feet, lying on the ground next to Alice.

"Relax, little page," Sir Bellator mocked as he checked Brayden's bindings and then stepped away.

"What do you want of us?!" Alice shouted. Brayden and Josslyn drew back from her anger.

"We want what is being hidden from us, and only your husband knows where it is," Sir Bellator sneered.

"Then what I heard is true," Alice said quietly. "He lives. Let them go, sir. You have me."

"Your son is a precious commodity. I tried to convince Regin your boy would provide far better leverage than you ever would, but my little friend was always a bit irrational. It appears you led Brayden right to us. Our boat, and my master, will be here soon, and your son will be coming with me. You and the girl, on the other hand, now belong to my Norsemen. Payment for their loyalty."

Bellator chuckled. The Norsemen grinned toothlessly.

"You coward!" Brayden shouted.

Sir Bellator's face turned red. He casually walked over, stood over Brayden once more, and kicked him in the side. Brayden yelled and winced in pain. Alice and Josslyn screamed. Sir Bellator looked down at them and smiled. He gave another signal to his men, and the Norsemen were upon them once more, gagging their mouths tightly so they could not speak.

"Enjoy your time left together on this Earth. The little page will be taken out with the gold as soon as my master's ship docks." Sir Bellator faced his men. "Mind the tent, fellows, and the tent only. No one touches either the girl or the woman until our ship is off." He turned and walked out, heading for the sea.

Brayden's side ached horribly, and he strained against his bindings to relieve the pain. Josslyn was straining too, but making no progress in loosening the ropes.

The Norseman spent a few moments watching them struggle; their eyes focused on his mother and Josslyn. The men shared a laugh and uttered several words in their native language that Brayden couldn't understand, and abruptly walked out of the tent and closed the flap, leaving the three of them alone.

* * *

Brayden tried to remove the gag from his mouth with his tongue, but it was tied so tightly it would not budge. He looked over at his mother. Her eyes remained strong, focused, as if telling him silently that everything would be all right.

He was angry at his own helplessness. Not only had he not saved his mother, he was a pawn being used to compromise his father. The rage grew inside him as he thought of the harm they could do his mother and Josslyn. He screamed against the gag, exerting all the strength he possessed against his bindings, but to no avail. He looked at Josslyn. Her eyes were fearful. She was his friend of only a short time, but one who had loyally stood by him. He had brought her here, into this, and he was responsible for what would happen to her.

He looked up at the ceiling of the tent, closed his eyes, and prayed silently. The wind was growing stronger, and the walls of the tent rippled wildly, creating a strange, scratching sound. He opened his eyes and looked back at Josslyn, who was now motionless, staring at something behind him. She moved about wildly and moaned, as if trying to get him to look away from her. The scratching grew louder, closer, as if it was coming toward him. He followed Josslyn's gaze and turned. He couldn't believe his eyes.

A blade was cutting through the tent wall, not a hands-length from his head. He rolled over and away as the blade continued to saw through the canvas inch by inch. Brayden stared in disbelief, wondering what could possibly happen next. When the knife finally reached the base of the tent, it retreated, and two hands appeared and pulled the fabric apart. Caelan stuck his head through and looked around. Their eyes locked.

"Well you didn't think I'd leave you three here with these brutes, did you? Let me cut those bindings and let's get out of here!"

* * *

Once the three of them were free, Brayden and Caelan poked their heads out of the hole in the rear of the tent. Nothing stirred. Against the rocks Brayden could barely make out the path over which he and Josslyn had come. In the distance loomed the mountains, shrouded in cloud. They pulled back into the tent. Josslyn and Alice were sitting by the sacks, rubbing their wrists. Caelan spent a few moments inspecting the armor and swords, and then turned to Brayden.

"Brayden, take Lady Josslyn and your mother back the way you came. I suspect Bellator and the Norsemen are busy with that ship. You'll be able to get back safely to the castle the way I instructed you. Find Sullivan. Tell whoever you encounter what has transpired here."

"And what of you?"

Caelan smiled. "Me? I'm going to see who and what is on that ship, perhaps get on board. Sir Bellator and his master are not getting away this easily."

Brayden faced his friend. "Sir Caelan, you could be killed."

Caelan put his hands on Brayden's shoulders. "Oh, if I could only live so long as to see you knighted. You're a brave, good-hearted lad, but your place is at your mother's side. Get her and Lady Josslyn safely back to Lord Marshal. I'll find out where your father is, and I'll be along as soon as I can be. Go now."

Brayden led his mother and Josslyn out of the tent and into the rocks. They crossed through the boulder field slowly and quietly, trying to avoid being seen or heard. They finally exited up the road.

"This is the way we came, I think," Brayden said. He looked at Josslyn. His friend's face was anxious, concerned.

Brayden started to walk along the road in the direction of the mountain. He stopped after several paces, thinking of Caelan and the danger he was in. He turned to face his mother and Josslyn. They hadn't moved.

"We should help him, shouldn't we?" he asked. Brayden looked deep into his mother's eyes, instantly reading her thoughts. As much as they wanted to run, as much danger as they were in, these men *knew* where his father was.

Alice nodded silently.

"Let's go back." Josslyn said.

Suddenly they heard shouting coming from the direction of the tower. They ran toward it without thinking and moments later emerged back on the plain. There, at the base of the tower, Caelan was fighting off the giant Sker and another large man wearing animal furs and a metal cap. At his friend's feet lay the thin Norseman with the wooden club Brayden had seen earlier, apparently felled by Caelan's sword.

They moved closer, and Brayden recognized the man in the metal cap: the bandit leader, Samain. He was swinging his axe with one hand and thrusting a dagger with the other. In seconds, the two had Caelan pinned against the tower wall and were shouting for help. Caelan was almost on his knees, parrying blow after blow with his sword, fighting for his life.

"We must help him!" Josslyn bounded forward without hesitation. As she ran, she reached into her tunic and pulled out a long leather band. Her sling! She paused for a moment to pick up some loose stones, and then loaded it quickly.

"Josslyn!" Brayden's mother shouted as they both ran after her. Sker turned in the direction of her voice.

Josslyn swung her sling in a wide loop and released the stones. Brayden could hear them whizzing through the air on their way to Sker. They missed left, bouncing uselessly off the tower wall behind the Norseman. Sker stalked toward Josslyn, enraged. She reloaded quickly, swung, and fired. Her second shot was true. Her stones hit the massive Sker directly in the left eye. He fell back, in obvious agony, dropping both his axe and his club to cover his missing eye. He roared in anger as he stumbled off toward the tents, blood pouring from his face. Caelan wasted no time in righting himself, and faced Samain head-on.

With a swing of his ax the bandit leader knocked a chunk of rock out of the tower wall. He struck again and missed as Caelan quickly ducked. On the third attack, Caelan was ready. He caught Samain's blow with his sword and at the same time kicked the bandit leader in the gut, knocking him back. Caelan slashed at the man repeatedly, and Brayden thought his friend's blade looked more like a lightning strike than a sword. With one final swing, Caelan cut across Samain's chest and throat. The bandit leader gurgled something Brayden couldn't hear, and then doubled over and fell to the ground. He was dead. Caelan wiped his brow with one hand and raised his sword in his opposite fist as he looked over at his friends and smiled. Brayden, Josslyn, and Alice ran up to the base of the tower.

Their victory was short-lived. "Look out!" Alice shouted.

Caelan and the others turned as Bellator and two more Norsemen rounded the corner of the tower.

"Kill them. All of them!" Sir Bellator screamed. They couldn't run. Sir Bellator and his men stood between them and the plain, and they were trapped against the tower. Caelan waved the three of them over to the tower entrance. For the first time Brayden noticed that his friend's arm was red with blood. Caelan pushed Brayden and Alice inside. "Inside. Up the stairs!" the knight shouted.

Josslyn paused at the tower door and fired her sling in Sir Bellator's direction. Her shot bounced off his chest, and in seconds he was upon her. He hit her across the face with his fist, knocking her to the ground. She lay motionless.

"Joss!" Brayden shouted.

"Get up to the top!" Caelan yelled behind him as Brayden and Alice climbed the steps. The interior of the tower was cool and unlit, though arrow slits provided some light. Rubble was everywhere, and they had to steady themselves against the walls with their hands to avoid tripping.

Brayden watched his friend. With a well-aimed thrust of his sword, Caelan brought down one of the Norsemen at the door. The man's pike fell to the ground as he collapsed with a grunt. The other entered the tower, swinging his mace wildly. Caelan lunged at him and brought his sword down on the man's shoulder. The Norseman collapsed with a scream of pain.

"Go!" Caelan shouted. "We have the higher ground!"

Brayden and his mother wove their way up the spiral stairway as instructed, Alice pulling on his arm constantly as he stopped every few paces to watch the fight. Caelan backed up the stairway behind them, facing the entranceway where Sir Bellator now stood, his eyes ablaze with fury.

Brayden and Alice reached the head of the staircase and quickly exited at the top of the tower. Through the battlements they had a clear view of the water, the coast, and the dock where the dark ship Brayden and Josslyn had seen earlier was now moored. The Norsemen and bandits were moving about the dock, loading the barrels and crates of gold from the tents. Brayden squinted. A slim, mysterious figure stood motionless at the bow of the ship, his dark cloak blowing in the wind, his face hidden behind a hood.

Shouting from the direction of the staircase gave him a jolt. Brayden and his mother turned as Caelan and Sir Bellator emerged, weapons flying in all directions. Caelan was thrusting with his sword, and Bellator had a sword in one hand and a pike in the other. Caelan fought bravely, though his wounded arm seemed to be slowing him greatly.

He lifted his sword and slashed, but Bellator dodged at the last second and Caelan's attack clanged harmlessly against the rock of the tower. In that moment Sir Bellator's eyes locked with Brayden's, and the man lunged at him. Brayden stood frozen as Caelan dove forward, blocking Bellator's blow.

Sir Bellator swore with fury, and swung at Caelan with the pike. Caelan dodged and recovered once more. He knocked the pike from Sir Bellator's hand with his sword, but lost his balance, if only for a moment. It was enough. As the pike fell to the floor and Caelan stumbled back, Sir

Bellator took advantage and thrust forward with his sword. Caelan let out a cry and fell back against the tower wall. His eyes looked up to the sky, and then fluttered to a close. Sir Bellator turned, a hideous grin on his face, and focused his rage on Brayden's mother.

"No!" Brayden screamed. He charged, swinging his fists wildly at the steward. Sir Bellator hit Brayden full across the face with the back of his hand and knocked him backwards across the floor, where he landed next to Caelan. Brayden's face ached, and he could taste salty blood in his mouth.

Dazed, Brayden shook his head and looked up. Sir Bellator was instantly standing over him with his sword raised, preparing to land a final blow.

"Damn what my master wants, I finish you now, Rider boy," the steward spat. Then he let out a horrid cry. His eyes opened wide and his head jerked forward unnaturally. The sword fell to the ground with a clang, and Brayden had to roll away to avoid it. The man's knees buckled, and Sir Bellator fell to the floor.

Alice was standing behind him, the pike in her hand, its point dripping in blood. The steward lay dead, his torso exposed through the cracked, shattered armor of Regin that had covered his body. Sir Martin's little book lay nearby, its pages fluttering quietly in the breeze.

Brayden and his mother gathered next to Caelan, who sat propped up against the tower wall. He looked dazed, his face pale. Blood covered his chest and arms.

"Sir Caelan?" Brayden said.

Caelan looked around as if searching for the voice. His eyes finally focused on Brayden's face.

"Ah, my young friend. Is it safe? Is the treasure safe?"

Brayden nodded, tears filling his eyes. "It is, sir. It is, sir knight," he lied.

Caelan smiled weakly. "Good, good. Sometimes finding it is not important, but keeping it safe for its proper owner is."

Josslyn stumbled through the head of the staircase and gasped when she saw Caelan. She walked over and knelt next to Alice.

"Shh. Rest," Alice said to Caelan, taking his hand in her own.

"You've a brave boy here, ma'am. A brave boy, like his father." Caelan coughed. His body stiffened as his breathing grew ever more forced. "Here," Caelan said, trying with his good arm to drag his sword closer. Brayden reached over, grabbed the pommel and pulled it to him. "Take my blade. It is not much, but I own little."

"I will," Brayden said, wiping tears from his cheeks.

"And Sullivan. Please find him and be good to my friend. I know you will be."

Brayden nodded, unable to respond. His mother stroked Caelan's forehead. The young knight seemed to lose focus once more, and then looked around wildly before locking in on Brayden again.

"Brayden, find your father. Promise me. And when you do, tell him about me, all right?"

"I will. Of course, I will. Please, please don't go."

Caelan lifted his hand and smiled once more. His chest heaved and he exhaled as his eyes closed for the final time.

Brayden slumped back, sobbing. His mother embraced him, holding him tight. At the base of the tower, against the sounds of the sea, they could hear the thunder of horses galloping and men shouting.

Chapter Thirty-Nine

The Lord

Brayden and Siegfried stood on the castle wall overlooking the innumerable pastures and fields beyond. Greens had long ago faded to browns, and the trees were barren now. Every day it seemed things were slowing down, quieting, as if life everywhere was shutting off, preparing for the cold winter ahead. Trade outside the castle's great walls had almost ceased, with merchants off to warmer markets and farmers awaiting the spring. Even inside the castle, talk focused on counting supplies and on protecting plants, animals, and skin from the frost. There would be the Christmas celebrations, of course, although, still weeks away, they were but a small oasis of joy in a long stretch of cold whites and grays.

Brayden considered his cousin as the boy gazed silently at the countryside. Siegfried's face was hard and grown-up, as if he had aged years in the short time Brayden had been gone. In the days since his return from Taunton Tower, they had barely spoken. In fact, it occurred to him that Siegfried had not smiled since Sir Bellator had disappeared. He felt, Bernard had explained to Brayden the night before, doubly betrayed; betrayed first by the cruel actions of this friend and mentor, and betrayed again by the death of the same at the hand of his own aunt. Siegfried's eyes remained fixated on something in the distance. Brayden followed his eyes, noticing for the first time a lone cart approaching from afar.

"I like this time of year," Siegfried finally said, taking a deep breath without looking at Brayden. "I like the cold."

"You don't have to go anywhere. Mother and I are returning to Honeydown. It can be your home too. Come with us and stay."

Siegfried bowed his head and smiled, as if the suggestion was not worth considering. He continued to stare in the direction of the cart, as though perceiving something out in the land beyond only he could see.

"Or Sir Allard," Brayden tried. "Stay on with him, as father and Bernard intended."

"Sir Allard paid no mind to me, Brayden. His vows were broken long ago in my eyes. No, I've made my arrangements to travel. My father had a brother he was close to, many years ago. He has lands in Burgundy. I don't know him, but I am grown now, and thought he could use a hand around the estate, perhaps a warrior to serve him one day." Siegfried finally looked at Brayden, surprising him. "Come with me instead."

Brayden was speechless, unable to hide his confusion.

Siegfried laughed and looked up to the sky. "You can no more leave this place now than I can stay, cousin."

"I don't want you to go," Brayden pleaded. His mind filled with images of that horrible day at the tower, seeing Caelan collapsed on the floor. That man, Siegfried's man, had killed his kind, brave young friend. Now he faced losing Siegfried, a boy he admired and wanted to be like, another physical link to his very own father.

"You have a mother, and Bernard, who is sworn to protect you. Not only that, but a lord who owes you his barony. Sir Bellator would have been my liege lord, and now I have none of those things." Siegfried looked out again. The cart was close now, and Siegfried was watching it intently. "Do you remember your father, Brayden?"

Brayden nodded. "I do. Of course I do."

"He loves you, you know. More than you can imagine. I know he thinks of you every day, as you do him, no matter where he is."

"How do you know this?" Brayden asked. Tears were welling in his eyes. He quickly wiped them away, hoping Siegfried hadn't noticed.

"Remember the stories Bernard told us of the glories of knighthood? Life is short and hard, but worth living for a cause. Your father never once looked upon me the way he did you. Seek him out. You cannot find that kind of love again."

The cart had pulled around the wall and was out of sight near the castle gatehouse.

"Perhaps, cousin, we'll meet one day again." Siegfried ruffled Brayden's hair a final time and was off, bounding down the wooden stairs along the castle wall and across the courtyard. Brayden watched him, tears streaming down his cheeks. He was unable to turn away as his only cousin disappeared into the gatehouse.

* * *

Brayden stood by the door to Sullivan's stall. The large horse stirred quietly, stomping his big feet and slowly swinging his large head back and forth. Brayden had visited Sullivan every day since Caelan's death. The horse had refused food or attention from anyone else, and Brayden was careful to follow Caelan's instructions in caring for him. It was quiet in the stables, much more so than when he had first arrived at the castle. The recent tourney had not been kind to the castle knights. Many horses had been lost in contest, and several of the knights themselves had deserted upon hearing of Sir Bellator's demise.

During each visit Brayden spoke to Sullivan about Caelan and what had happened. The horse seemed sullen, as if he knew from Brayden's words that his master would never return.

Brayden heard another visitor enter the stable through the main door. The person approached quietly from behind the wall of the stall. Sullivan lifted his head over the doorway to look out, as if expecting to see Caelan somehow returned to him. As the visitor neared, the horse reared back in his stable, disappointed yet again.

Brayden looked out to see who was there. He could feel his jaw drop as Lord Marshal stood before him.

Not much older than Bernard, Lord Marshal was stocky and strong, and looked much like an older version of Sir Allard. Brayden imagined he had been a formidable warrior in his youth. His hair was long and gray. His white beard had been neatly trimmed since his return to his castle. He wore a thick green robe accented with gold trim over a white tunic. His leather boots were high and finely made. A black leather belt with a gold buckle fit snugly around his waist, upon which hung a small dagger.

Lord Marshal had not spoken to him when they were introduced at Taunton Tower, though Brayden understood that the lord had felt great shock and sadness upon seeing Caelan. He and his men had gone toward the sea at Bernard's direction, the friar's memory of Dunstan's map of the coast and Sir Martin's drawings leading them to the tower. Though Lord Marshal and his knights had been too late to save Caelan or stop the ship from departing, they had finished off the Norsemen and secured some of the remaining Roman gold. Lord Marshal stepped closer, and Brayden bowed, not knowing what else to do. The lord raised his hand, urging Brayden to stand up tall.

"I'm not the king, Brayden Rider, and for all you've done for me, my daughter, and this barony, it is I who should bow to you." Lord Marshal looked at Sullivan affectionately. "And how are you, old friend?" The horse snorted softly as Lord Marshal reached out to pat him on the snout. "So, how is this fine warhorse doing? You're the only one he'll accept feedings from, I understand."

Brayden nodded, not sure how to address this wealthy, powerful man who ruled over a powerful barony in the heart of Wales. Above him was only the king, and below him every province and town as far as the eye could see, including his own faraway Honeydown.

"I take it you've ridden him?"

"Yes, yes, I have, my lord. When Sir Caelan stayed with us in Honeydown. We rode together."

Lord Marshal nodded and began to stroke Sullivan's mane. "I miss Sir Caelan as well, Brayden. But this steed will need another young man to ride him again someday. Come, let's walk for a bit."

Brayden scratched Sullivan on the neck and followed Lord Marshal past the other stalls, out the stable door, and into the courtyard. Once outside, Lord Marshal looked up at the darkening sky. He took a deep breath and stretched his arms over his head. There were no clouds, and the moon and stars were just becoming visible above them.

"Sir Caelan de Spero is one we will not soon forget," Lord Marshal stated. "He came to us from a cousin of mine in Northern England who found him as a boy abandoned in a manor home, orphaned when his parents had died of plague. With the threat of the Scottish wars—which I may add we are still fighting almost twenty years later—we agreed to host him as a page, much as we did with you. He was brave and loyal to our house since the day he arrived, and he took to knighthood easily. My, did he love to ride. I imagine him now in Heaven, atop a grand steed and casting out evil spirits with his lance."

"I'm imagining he's missing Sullivan," Brayden added.

Lord Marshal smiled down at him. "Indeed, and missing you as well, no doubt." They began a stroll around the inner perimeter of the castle, Brayden following him.

As they walked, Lord Marshal surveyed the castle's walls. The guards atop the walls bowed as he approached, and he waved respectfully at every one of them.

"I repay the loyalty of these men not only with money, but also with a home, our food, and companionship. I want them to be here, cared for, happier than they would be elsewhere. It is good for a soul to be content with what one has. It works for most, though not all."

Brayden thought of Sir Bellator and the greed that seemed to have overtaken him. He remembered seeing Siegfried for the last time, riding away on a cart across the countryside. He wondered what contentment his cousin sought out in the world beyond. He thought of all the other knights and ladies and others he had met since arriving at the castle.

"My lord, what became of Sir Osbert?" Brayden finally asked, curious about Sir Bellator's ally. He had not seen the knight since his fight with Caelan in the arena, though in conversations with Bernard and Caddaric, Brayden had learned that even Sir Osbert had not known of Sir Bellator's and Regin's evil plans.

Lord Marshal smiled. "I think bringing him down a notch or two was warranted, don't you think? He's repented for his mistakes, and he's renewed his vows of fealty. He'll continue to serve, but under Sir Allard's watchful eye. Lord Marshal looked him over. "You remind me of Sir Caelan when he was young," he said. "You have the same spirit, the same heart."

"I am not an orphan," Brayden replied quickly, perhaps too quickly, he thought, worried he may have unintentionally offended this powerful man.

But Lord Marshal only chuckled. "No, you are not. You are blessed more than you know. Your mother loves you dearly, and your father does as well." He paused, acknowledging another guard who was standing at the entrance to the corner tower.

"Welcome home, my lord," the man said, smiling broadly and bowing respectfully. Lord Marshal and Brayden turned and headed in the direction of the keep.

"I met your father in the Kingdom of Jerusalem, at the end of the Orders' time there."

Brayden was stunned. "You were a Knight of the Temple?" he asked.

Lord Marshal lifted a finger. "No, a Hospitaller. The Orders were in league for many years, until the fall of Acre. I fought in the crusades, until the capture of the Krak. I returned to Acre twenty years later with ships to supply the city and its garrison. It was there I met your father."

They were nearing the thick stone wall of the keep. Brayden looked up. One of the falcons was circling far overhead, its white underbelly just visible in the evening light. He wondered if it was Rhiannon, remembering how the bird had helped them escape. All along the wall and the towers, torches were going up, as if in reaction to the dark, cold night that was coming. There was something else. Singing. He could hear singing, though faintly, and wondered where it was coming from. It was beautiful.

"This is my favorite time of day," Lord Marshal said. "Night is not to be feared, but embraced." Brayden remained silent, hanging on every word and anxious for Lord Marshal to continue.

"Your father was one of the few remaining Templar knights in Acre, the last outpost of Christianity in the Holy Land. The city had been in Christian hands for one hundred years. The Saracen Prince Khalil laid siege to the city for a month, surrounding it with thousands of men."

"How did you come to be there, Lord Marshal?" Brayden asked.

"Acre was a magnificent port, surrounded by walls greater than these, and towers that housed all of the renowned knightly orders. We brought food and weapons for the defenders of the Holy Land. When we arrived in March of that year, war was in the air, but the city was intact and in Christian hands. When we returned in May, the city's defenses had collapsed. That is when I met your father. He approached me, asking for help in ferrying women, children, and the wounded out of the city. I agreed. He fought bravely, buying time for us to fill every inch of our vessels with the defenseless. I searched for him to thank him for his bravery and eventually found him there, hurt, unable to move. We brought him aboard our ship and escaped just as the Saracens overwhelmed the remaining defenders." Lord Marshal paused and looked around at his castle, surveying the torchlight that had erupted everywhere. "One by one the towers fell, until, as we sailed away, the city disappeared in a cloud of dust and smoke. We knew our crusades were at their end."

"You saved him."

Lord Marshal chuckled, his laugh deep and strong. "No, no. He saved me. He saved hundreds. I feared he'd harbor anger toward me for giving him escape while so many of our brothers and sisters died, but he never uttered an ill word, thanking me, instead, for giving him another chance to continue his good works and have a family of his own."

"He never spoke of this. Bernard and my mother never spoke of this," Brayden said, shaking his head. His thoughts drifted to the stained glass window in the abbey of Honeydown, and the brave knight who had saved the city.

"Well, it was a long time ago. Your father is a great man; let no one tell you differently. As long as I breathe this sweet British air, we will not rest until we find him."

Brayden wiped a tear from his eye, and then looked down at his chest; at the tunic his mother had sewn him, and the patch of the small shield she had stitched over his heart. He reached up with his right hand and grasped the flying golden griffin emblazoned across the shield. "Valor, perseverance, and the guardian of treasure," he whispered. His father's symbol was now his own.

Brayden thought of the letter that had brought Caelan to Honeydown, and the mysterious signature he had since learned belonged to the man named 'Turpin,' though Bernard would speak no more of it. Brayden had also learned it had been Josslyn Marshal who had found the letter whilst sneaking about the castle, her mother being the one who had supplied it to his friend in the hopes of protecting Sir Ban's only son.

"Where is Turpin?" Brayden asked, knowing now the answer would be one he could never let go.

Lord Marshal put his hand on Brayden's shoulder and his fear and sadness seemed to evaporate. Brayden at once felt safe and comforted, as if hope, and a purpose, had become clear. "A question, perhaps, for later," Lord Marshal said quietly.

They were in front of the massive doors leading into the keep. A guard stood at the doors, waiting for a signal from his lord.

"My wish is that you and Alice stay here with us. But you are free people. Wherever you go, I swear to protect you and your mother."

Brayden bowed his head. "Thank you, my lord. I'd like to stay very much."

Lord Marshal smiled down at him and waved at the guard. With a nod of his head, the guard opened the door, and Lord Marshal and Brayden stepped inside. They climbed the stairs and entered the great hall. Inside Sir Allard, Sir Hugh, and Caddaric stood up from a nearby table and bowed as Lord Marshal and Brayden approached the platform. Alice and Bernard came in from around a corner, and Brayden ran to embrace them. Lord Marshal joined Lady Elaine and Josslyn at the head table. Brayden looked around at his friends and family, as happy and as safe as he had ever felt.

THE END

Epilogue

Siegfried looked out across the desolate countryside that lay all around him. The castle had disappeared from sight long ago, and all along the rocky road nothing lived, and nothing stirred. He took a deep breath and held it, letting the cold evening air settle in his lungs. After all those years in the castle with its busy inhabitants and the near-constant lessons and training, he had almost forgotten how empty the land could be, especially as darkness approached.

He thought back to the life he was leaving behind, to the friends he had made, and to Brayden and Aunt Alice. Everyone he knew had urged him to stay, but this was for the best, he told himself. He would be on his own as his father had been, reliant only on his hard work, strength and prowess.

He bounced uncomfortably as the cart navigated noisily down the rutted road. He didn't want to speak to the cart driver, and so far the man had stayed silent, other than when quoting him a price for travel to the coast. Siegfried glanced over at him. The cart driver wore a rusty, threadbare robe that covered him completely. A cold gust of wind forced Siegfried to pull his own robe tight. He shivered slightly, and quickly covered his hands in his sleeves.

"Early cold this year, eh?" the cart driver suddenly asked. "It already smells of winter."

Siegfried jolted to attention, feeling as if a ghost had spoken. It was a long trip and he didn't want to talk. He remained silent and looked out across the shadows of the countryside, hoping the cart driver would take the hint.

"You go to France, then?" the cart driver inquired once more.

Siegfried rolled his eyes in frustration. The voice was eerily familiar, but from where he did not know. "I go to the coast," he said, finally relenting. "From there on, it is my affair only."

The man nodded, remaining silent for several moments before speaking again.

"Running from something?" he asked, almost mockingly.

"Excuse me?" Siegfried was surprised and angered by the man's intrusiveness, let alone the insinuation of cowardice. "I run from no man."

"Spirits then. Perhaps you run from spirits," the cart driver suggested. It was not a question.

"I am a squire," Siegfried said, "and you will address me as such. Now keep to your self."

The cart driver was unperturbed. "Squire, eh? Where then is your knight, squire?"

Siegfried looked into the distance, thinking of his friend Sir Bellator, once the steward, the one knight who had shown interest in him and sponsored his selection. The cart driver was silent for several moments, and then continued.

"We shared the same friend, squire, one that was and is no more. But, there are many other friends left to make."

Siegfried looked at the cart driver. The man had rolled up the long sleeves of his robe. It was then that Siegfried noticed the scars that ran up and down the man's arms.

"We've a long journey ahead, young squire. Let's talk about our friend, and about who else there is to meet in France."

The cart bounced up and down the road, casting a long shadow as the evening sun disappeared from the sky.

Short Glossary of Medieval Terms

Bailiff – A manor official typically charged with overseeing the operation, profit and expenses of one or more manors on behalf of a lord. Unlike peasants, the bailiff was a free man, giving him additional privileges within medieval society.

Battlement - Alternating openings along the walls of a castle. Also called crenellation and looking a bit like teeth, the battlements offered protection for the castle's defenders during wartime.

Bokenade – A thick, meaty stew often served with nuts and a healthy dose of herbs. Bokenade was typically used for dunking, and thereby softening, hard bread.

Butts – A practice field reserved for archery, typically with painted mounds of dirt at one end that are used as targets. In medieval England, all free men were required by law to learn archery, so the butts became very popular places indeed.

Chaperon – A highly customized hat popular in the medieval age. The chaperon was similar to a hood, used for both fashion and warmth, and later evolved long tails and decorations.

Cottar – One of the lowest social classes in medieval Europe. A cottar typically occupied a cottage in exchange for work on small parcels of land or menial jobs performed on behalf of the other villagers or the lord.

Fiefdom – The lands (or fiefs) and associated property owned by a medieval lord— the greater the fiefdom, the more powerful the lord.

Footpads – A group of common robbers who typically preyed on pedestrians and travelers.

Flagon – From Middle French, a serving vessel, typically made of pewter or some other metal, and often used for serving wine.

Gong Farmer – The unfortunate individual charged with cleaning medieval privies and transporting the contents to the fields to reuse as fertilizer. Typically (and thankfully to the inhabitants of a castle), this unappealing work was done at night when everyone else was asleep.

Hayward – The individual in a medieval manor village responsible for the management of a crucial raw material: hay. The hayward managed the hedges and fences of the manor village and often oversaw the sowing and reaping of the fields.

Leal – From Old French, "leal" means to be loyal, faithful, and true (as to a lord).

Liege-lord – An independent lord or master. In the feudal system, commoners would owe their allegiance to their liege-lord.

Lists – The arena in which a jousting tournament was held. Typically, this was an earthen field around which spectators watched either from the ground or the grandstands. Also, if one is "in the lists" that meant that person was competing in the tournament itself.

Manor – Medieval manors were portions of land owned and overseen by a lord. Manors typically employed peasants who worked the land, as a well a number of officials appointed to manage production of crops and livestock. A common manor held one or more villages, with the lord and his family living in a large, sturdy manor home. A lord held at least one manor, and great lords of the time controlled multiple manors.

Michaelmas – Also known as the feast of Saint Michael the Archangel, Michaelmas was traditionally celebrated on the 29th of September. One of the more important holidays on the medieval calendar, it was associated with the end of the year's harvest, the accounting of the year's production and the beginning of autumn.

Nave – The longest portion of an abbey or church. The nave typically had the main entrance at one end, with the high altar at the far end.

Nefs – A spectacular metal object, usually in the shape of a ship, used for serving spices and salt. These being expensive and rare in the medieval age, the presentation of the nef and its contents during a feast or other ceremony was a memorable event.

Outremer – From French, meaning "overseas," the term identifying the crusader states of the Near East (the modern day countries of Israel,

Lebanon, and portions of Syria and Turkey) including the Kingdom of Jerusalem and the lands of Edessa, Antioch and Tripoli.

Pannage – In the medieval age, during autumn it was common to let the pigs out into manor forests to feast on acorns, chestnuts and other wild nuts. The practice of pannage had two primary benefits: it removed nuts poisonous to cattle from the forest, and it fattened the pigs before slaughter.

Pinder – The village official responsible for animal management and control. Stray animals were often held in a holding pen called a "pin-hold," until their owners were able to claim them.

Portcullis – A heavy iron grated door that raised and dropped vertically. The portcullis was an effective means to prevent access to a castle during times of war.

Pottage – A thick gooey stew of root vegetables, herbs and when possible, meat. Easy to make with anything at hand, pottage was a staple of medieval village life and typically cooked in a thick pot.

Queek – Popular among medieval children, the game queek involved a checkered cloth spread out on the ground. The competitors would take turns tossing pebbles on the board, calling out in advance where the pebbles would land.

Quintain – An object, such as a shield, board or manikin, attached to a pole, which a mounted warrior would attempt to strike with a lance or sword as part of a training regime.

Raffle – A game where competitors would take turns throwing three dice, the object being to get all of the dice to roll the same numbers, or pair of numbers of the same numbers. Raffle was a popular betting game.

Reeve – The reeve was the official responsible for managing the peasants' work on the manor's land. Either appointed by the lord or voted in by the residents of the manor, the reeve ensured work was performed on time and kept careful records of the manor's production.

Reliquary – A container, often ornately decorated, for holding religious relics.

Rushlight – A small candle made by dipping the stem of a rush plan in fat. Plentiful and inexpensive, rushlights were a popular artificial light source for people of the medieval age.

Saltcellar – An ornate metal container for holding serving salt. Salt being rare in the medieval age, the saltceller typically had a lid to protect its valuable contents.

Saracen – A crusader-age, derogatory term for non-Christian residents of the Near East.

Tally Stick – The reeve, like many peasants, was unable to read, so accounts of manor production (e.g., number of animals year to year, bushels of grain stored, etc.) were recorded by cutting notches on a wooden stick.

Thresher – One responsible for separating the grain from the straw. Typically, the thresher used a long pole with a heavy chain attached to one end.

Tinker – A common surname of traveling menders of pots, pans, and other cooking instruments. The approach of a tinker was often noted by a "tinking" sound, due to the metal devices they carried.

Vassal – In the medieval feudal system, a vassal is one who has sworn allegiance to (another) lord or monarch. Typically, being a vassal implied the provision of some level of military aid when called upon.

Villain – The common people in the medieval feudal system. Villains are bound to the land and owned by the lord.

25938530R00201

Made in the USA
Charleston, SC
19 January 2014